Firefall

Other Books by Ed Ruggero

The Common Defense
38 North Yankee

Firefall

Ed Ruggero

POCKET BOOKS

New York   London   Toronto   Sydney   Tokyo   Singapore

This book is a work of fiction. Names, characters, places, and
incidents are either products of the author's imagination or are
used fictitiously. Any resemblance to actual events or locales or
persons, living or dead, is entirely coincidental.

POCKET BOOKS, a division of Simon & Schuster Inc.
1230 Avenue of the Americas, New York, NY 10020

Copyright © 1994 by Ed Ruggero
Map by GDS/Jeffrey L. Ward

Library of Congress Cataloging-in-Publication Data

Ruggero, Ed.
    Firefall / Ed Ruggero.
        p.   cm.
    ISBN 0-671-73010-X
    I. Title.
PS3568.U3638F57   1994
813'.54—dc20   93-39888
                                                                 CIP

First Pocket Books hardcover printing May 1994

10 9 8 7 6 5 4 3 2 1

To the United States Army.

Yesterday, Today, Tomorrow.

Acknowledgments

If the story is born in my imagination, its final shape is the result of the combined efforts of people who are generous with their talents and their time. I owe a great deal to John Stoner, who at the end of every response to my many questions asked, "What's next?" Thanks also to Sharan Daniel, who kept me out of trouble as we wandered about Europe, chasing the story. Thanks to Jim, who tossed me a computer lifeline.

Thanks to Paul McCarthy, an editor's editor.

And a special thanks to the staff of the Ranger Regiment and the men of the Third Battalion, Seventy-fifth Infantry (Ranger), who generously let me share a rainy drop zone and a long, chilly night with them. It was good to be reminded that while I—and the rest of the nation—sleep comfortably, dedicated men and women stand guard over all that we hold dear.

May you live in interesting times.

—*ancient Chinese curse*

Firefall

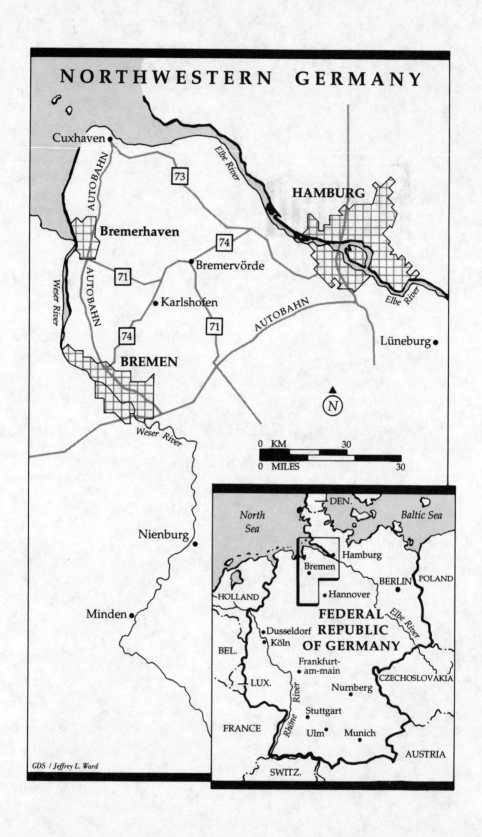

NORTHWESTERN GERMANY

Cuxhaven

AUTOBAHN

Elbe River

73

HAMBURG

Bremerhaven

74

AUTOBAHN

71

Bremervörde

Weser River

Karlshofen

71

AUTOBAHN

Elbe River

74

Lüneburg

BREMEN

Weser River

N

| 0 | KM | 30 |

| 0 | MILES | 30 |

North
Sea

DEN.

Baltic Sea

Hamburg

Bremen

BERLIN

POLAND

HOLLAND

Hannover

**FEDERAL
REPUBLIC
OF GERMANY**

Elbe River

BEL.

Dusseldorf
Köln

LUX.

Frankfurt-
am-main

CZECHOSLOVAKIA

Rhône River

Nurnberg

FRANCE

Stuttgart

Ulm

Munich

AUSTRIA

SWITZ.

Nienburg

Minden

GDS / Jeffrey L. Ward

Ultra-Right Threatens
German Stability

BERLIN. Some members of the German Parliament, speaking in the halls of the recently renovated Reichstag, today argued that Germany must acknowledge the serious threat the government faces from right-wing political factions.

"We do not need more laws enacted," said Hans Eisen, of the opposition party. "The Weimar Republic did not fall because it lacked laws on the books. It fell to tyranny because not enough people of conscience denounced the fascists."

The setting for today's angry denunciations was supremely ironic, as the very building in which the politicians voiced their dire warnings was burned by Nazi sympathizers to undercut formal opposition to Hitler. The shadow of Germany's painful history falls heavily on these discussions as the government struggles to handle an ever-increasing flood of legal and illegal immigrants without giving in to the xenophobic excesses of the most radical factions.

Prologue

Bremervörde, Germany

The winter wind blew off the North Sea steady and stone cold and un-broken by anything in the intervening fifty kilometers of gray landscape. It was as wet here as at the shore, and the moisture clung to the gray trees and gray buildings and everything else in sight in this dreary place.

Leutnant Manfred Elest shivered inside his great coat and pulled his shoulders up even higher in the vain attempt to cover his neck with the stiff collar. He knew that his neck would ache later from the strain of walking around all day with his shoulders shrugged, but at the moment all he cared about was being warm again. He picked his feet up one at a time, marching in place in small steps, but there was no feeling down there. He looked down at his boots and tried to move his toes, but for all the sensation of movement he got, the black boots might have belonged to someone else.

"Cold, Herr Leutnant?"

Elest looked up and managed a weak smile at Major Krafft, who stood, patient as an ox, a few feet away. There were crystals of ice on Krafft's mustache, and a line of snow lying neatly in a fold of his scarf along the back of his neck. Elest wondered why the man didn't brush off the wet-ness. Unbelievable.

"I was just thinking, sir, that I must be stupid for leaving my thermal underwear back in Berlin."

"Well," Krafft said, "we shouldn't be out here much longer."

That's what you said twenty minutes ago, ass, Elest thought.

The two Bundeswehr, or German Army, officers were standing outside the administration office of an equipment storage site near Bremervörde in northern Germany. They had been standing outside for some twenty minutes, whipped by the wind, waiting for the civilian functionary who was supposed to be helping them to come and open the door to the tiny office. Elest wondered at Krafft's patience.

Krafft thought nothing of dressing down a junior officer for some small or imagined infraction against his precious regulations, but for the past twenty-four hours he had all but kowtowed to the paper-pushing civil-ians who ran the storage site. Elest knew there was some concern in Berlin—the new seat of the federal government—over possible glitches in their mission, but it still seemed pretty straightforward to the young officer. They were to arrange for the removal of army equipment to bases in other parts of Germany—areas where the political showdown between the federal government and the ultra-right-wing German People's Union

· 3 ·

wasn't so volatile. Elest thought the GPU a collection of ignorant bigots who simplified complex economic problems into a pabulum for the masses—they blamed everything on foreigners. If it wasn't the Turkish workers or the Vietnamese refugees it was the damned Americans and their constant meddling and omnipresent military.

Still, the brass was taking it all seriously enough: the rumors about the paramilitary force the GPU was fielding, the even wilder rumors that the GPU planned to seize Bundeswehr war stocks to equip its own extralegal forces.

Elest didn't see it that way. He believed—before they left Berlin and even more so since they'd arrived—that the thing to do was to show a little spine. He'd have handled the civilians and their meddling quite differently from the way Krafft had. He'd have banged some heads together, made them jump a bit. Weren't they being paid by the federal government? Who the hell did these little shopkeepers think they were, to try to interfere with army business?

Elest stomped his feet harder. It didn't warm him up any but it made him feel better.

All that equipment, everything from small arms and ammunition to tanks, so much extra baggage now in the wake of the Cold War. The German Army had been cut nearly in half, and the deepening worldwide recession was forcing the government to cut spending even further as the downward spiral of the economy threatened unrest at home.

"Where are those bastards?" Elest said, stepping up to the door for the tenth time to peer into the darkened room.

"I would advise you, Leutnant, if you want to get out of this ice box in less than two weeks, to show a deferential attitude toward our civilian friends."

"Yes, sir," Elest said with perhaps a shade more enthusiasm than the moment warranted.

"May I ask you something, sir?" Elest ventured. Perhaps he was worn out by the cold, or perhaps he was just curious as to what—if anything—Krafft thought about the situation, but he was suddenly determined to find out what was going on.

Krafft turned his head slowly, and Elest could see that the ice on his mustache was thickening. He wondered if Krafft was going to wipe it off.

"Do you believe any of the rumors we've been hearing about . . . this equipment being in jeopardy?" Elest congratulated himself. The question was as politically inert as he could make it.

Krafft paused for a moment, settling his large head farther down into the collar of his coat. "It's fairly obvious that they don't want to turn the material over," Krafft answered.

Elest waited.

No kidding, he thought. *It took us a whole day to get an appointment to see this one glorified clerk.*

But there was more to it than that.

"I think there may be some truth to the rumor that the GPU has designs on this equipment," Krafft said.

"You know that many people think that they merely want to hold it in their territory up here in the northwest, as a bargaining chip."

"Yes, I've heard that," Krafft said.

As he watched the older man, Elest began to wonder if his initial impression—that Krafft was a slow-witted old fool—had been valid. Perhaps, Elest thought, he had simply run into a man who thought before he spoke. He watched as Krafft chewed on the icy mustache. For a moment Elest forgot how cold he was. Could Krafft be talking about a civil war?

But the major didn't answer. Instead the two men heard a strained wheeze, set against the uneven sound of someone shuffling uphill through the gravel and snow. They turned to see a round little man, wearing an army overcoat with the insignia of a captain, heaving himself up the short hill.

"Captain Sievers appears to be having some difficulty," Krafft commented.

Elest was prepared to be entertained. He did not like the captain, the third man in their party, and he'd be glad to have a laugh at the officer's expense. But when he turned, Krafft was not smiling, he had merely made an observation.

Sievers stopped before the two officers and rendered a theatrical salute—bringing his arm up in a wide arc from his belt—that threatened to knock him off balance and send him tumbling back down the incline he'd just negotiated. Then he lit one of his ubiquitous cigarettes.

"How do you like our weather, Herr Leutnant?" Sievers asked after a few labored puffs.

Always the comedian, Elest thought.

"Not at all, sir," Elest said.

Sievers's thick neck was wound tightly with scarves, so that when he turned to the major, he was obliged to pivot his whole body.

"Our friend should be here soon, sir," Sievers said. He lifted his eyebrows and, as if on cue, a man dressed warmly in civilian clothes came around the corner of the building that blocked the view of the parking lot. Sievers was always doing stuff like that, uncanny bits of timing and prediction. That was why Elest hated him.

But Major Krafft was paying no attention to Sievers; he was focused on the new arrival, the keeper of the keys. In a voice that was louder than what was called for, Krafft shouted, "Good morning."

"Good morning, Herr Major," the man said. "I am sorry you had to wait for me. I was held up."

Elest was surprised that no further explanation was offered—the man was almost thirty minutes late—but he was not surprised that Major Krafft let it pass again.

"No matter," Krafft said. "Our work here shouldn't take any more than a few hours, I would think."

Why doesn't he speak plainly? Elest thought. *"Look, you sonofabitch. You get your act together or I'm going to run your ass back to Berlin and yank this cushy little job right out from under you."* Elest had wanted to kick down the office door fifteen minutes ago.

"You are optimistic, Major," the civilian said. "Or perhaps you have been dealing with some agencies that do slipshod work. I can assure you that we will do things by the book here."

Elest didn't think his reaction—a low groan at the thought of spending the day in the tiny cramped office—was audible, but the civilian looked at him. Krafft shot him a stinging glance.

As Elest expected, the site manager took his time getting around to looking at the paperwork they presented, documents that would transfer control of some 150 vehicles and several tons of communication equipment to Major Krafft, who would then arrange for a convoy of regular army troops to come to Bremervörde to begin transferring the material from this motor park and a couple of nearby warehouses.

Captain Sievers took a seat immediately upon entering the room. Major Krafft, a model of courtesy, showed an unenthusiastic face for the captain's familiarity. Sievers stood and waited with Krafft some forty-five uncomfortable seconds until the civilian asked if they would like to sit down. There were only two chairs in front of the desk, so Elest—the junior officer—stood.

Elest studied the room for some clue that he was dealing with men who were deliberately trying to thwart the federal government. There were no GPU posters on the wall of the kind Elest had seen in several shops in the area; no tracts of racist diatribes against the modern invasions of Turks, Vietnamese, Arabs, Lebanese, and Kurds upon whom the GPU laid the blame for Germany's ills. The office had one gray metal desk with a chair behind and two in front. The only adornment was a photograph of two teenage children on the corner of the old man's desk.

When he finally did get around to it, the old civilian made a great show of reading the papers Krafft presented, even though the forms had been seen by half a dozen of his cronies at the installation.

After a few moments in which Elest had nothing better to do than track the course of the perspiration that was now running down his back—the tiny room became stuffy quickly, and the winter uniforms that were not heavy enough outdoors proved too heavy indoors—the old man looked up at the three soldiers and smiled.

"I'm afraid you've come a long way for nothing, gentlemen," he said. Captain Sievers snorted. Krafft sat up even straighter in his chair.

"What do you mean, Herr Walthers?" Krafft asked.

"Well, your inventory of goods here does not match ours, which makes me wonder if the federal government isn't losing control over the area of property accountability also."

He emphasized the *also* a little too much, Elest thought. *So he is a GPU man.*

"And you have nothing in here about the road clearances you'll need for the convoys."

Krafft paused a moment before answering, and Elest could see the major measuring his response.

"As for the inventory," Krafft said in measured tones, "the discrepancy may be in your records." Walthers recoiled a bit, but Krafft smiled at him. "Of course, it doesn't matter much who's at fault. In the case of discrepancies, only a full inventory can account for differences."

Shit, Elest thought. *He means to do a complete inventory of all these vehicles—and that means every spare tire, lug nut, every single tool in every single tool box, and in this weather.*

"And as for the road clearances," Krafft continued, "the transportation ministry provides those to the army."

"That was how it used to be, Herr Major. But we here in the north have decided that Berlin has no right to dictate policy for our highways, policies that do not comply with our own . . . safety requirements."

Elest thought for a moment that the two men were going to throw down the gauntlet. But they were back at the silly courtesy game again, each playing as if there was no animosity between them. Walthers had brought up the issue of safety. What army officer, what leader of any stripe, could be against safety?

"I see," said Krafft. "Well, we can proceed with the inventory while I send Captain Sievers to straighten out the problem of the road clearances."

Elest was incredulous. He stole a glance out the tiny window to the motor park, where a line of grayish green vehicles appeared and disappeared in the blowing snow.

He means that we're going outside to check serial numbers on all those vehicles, Elest whined to himself. What was supposed to have been a two-day trip to this miserable part of the country was turning into a standoff that might keep them here for a week or more.

The old man was caught off guard, that much was clear, but he recovered quickly. "That is impossible today, I am afraid," Walthers said. "I cannot work outside in this weather."

Elest found himself rooting for the old civilian. But the sight of Krafft standing there, unshakable in the face of such an obvious attempt to interfere with army business, made Elest feel guilty. Whose side was he on?

"Then I shall expect you to have someone here at six o'clock tomorrow morning, so that we can start then," Krafft said. "Leutnant Elest and I will be here with our inventory sheets."

Krafft looked at him, and Elest realized his mouth was hanging open. Wasn't there some way around this? He felt like rattling Walthers, grabbing the old clerk by the arms and just shaking some sense into him. Couldn't he see that Krafft was not going to be beaten by a few bureaucrats; nor was he going to run back to Berlin to complain to his superiors? How had grown men let some stupid political squabble degenerate to this point?

"Let's go, gentlemen." Krafft stood and turned on his heel without saying anything further to the old man.

Outside, Elest felt the sweat freeze on his back and under his arms. Tomorrow was going to be an impossible day. When the three men got in the government sedan, Elest was surprised to see that Sievers was smiling.

"You see something humorous in this, Captain?" Krafft said, his voice leaden.

Incredibly, Sievers continued to smile.

"I was just thinking, sir, about how ironic it is that one little old man can throw such a wrench into the workings of the federal government."

"We'll still get the job done," Elest piped up, surprising himself. He was not in favor of crawling around all day on the icy ground, looking for serial numbers on the engines of cold armored vehicles. But he wasn't going to let a paunchy little bureaucrat get in the way of his duty, either.

"I think he's a GPU man," Elest said.

The remark dropped heavily. The only sound in the car was the crunch of snow under the wheels and the tiny, muffled protests of the seat springs.

"The GPU makes a lot of sense," Sievers said, pausing slightly before adding, "to these people."

"They're simple-minded racists," Elest said.

Sievers glowered at him from under heavy eyebrows, but the lieutenant felt emboldened by Krafft's presence—Krafft had finally gotten angry. Captain or no, there was nothing Sievers could do, after all. They were merely discussing politics.

"The workers here have suffered enough because of Berlin's policies," Sievers intoned. "They are simply fed up and are using due political process to right the wrongs they see."

That phrase gave him away. *Due political process* was a pet phrase of the

GPU, chanted like a mantra in all party speeches, as if saying it could make respectable even the most outlandish claims and actions.

"Tell me, Captain," Krafft said, drawing out Sievers's title. "Do you think there is a danger of this equipment falling into the wrong hands? Being used by a GPU force?"

"I have no idea, sir," Sievers said, suddenly interested in something outside the car window. "I would have no way of knowing that. Of course, the equipment was bought to protect Germany, and one could argue, as I believe the GPU has, that the GPU would use it for that reason, to protect Germany from enemies within."

The three men rode in silence to the small hotel where they occupied separate rooms, Sievers and Krafft on the second floor, Elest in a smaller room on the third. When Elest went down for dinner with Krafft, he was surprised that Sievers wasn't there. He had assumed that the major would go over the plan for the next day while they ate. Krafft was clearly agitated as they made their way to the table and ordered drinks. After the waiter moved away, Krafft leaned over the table conspiratorially.

"Captain Sievers is gone," Krafft said.

Elest was surprised enough to forget his military courtesy. "Gone?"

"I sent him a message that I wanted to see him this afternoon, and the clerk told me he'd left the hotel shortly after we returned."

He's paranoid, Elest thought. *Another one who sees bogeymen behind every tree, who thinks the GPU dolts are the new Brownshirts.*

"Perhaps he had some personal business to attend to, sir," Elest offered.

"That is just what I am afraid of," Krafft said, sitting back in his chair. He placed his hands flat on the table, stretching the tablecloth as he moved them from a center point to the edge.

"I have a few things to tell you, Herr Leutnant," Krafft said.

By the time they left the hotel an hour later, Elest was convinced that one of two things was true. Either Krafft and his superiors were suffering paranoid delusions, or he and Krafft were in a lot more danger than he had anticipated. Whatever the case, it was clear that Krafft was now determined to act. He had allowed the civilians great latitude during the first twenty-four hours of their visit; but when the old man, Walthers, tried to turn them back, Kraft dug in for a fight.

When they stepped outside, Elest was shocked at how cold it had become. The wind blew steadily from the north, and the roads and pavements were coated with a thin sheet of ice that made walking and driving a treacherous affair. Elest drove the sedan back toward the warehouse and motor yard just north of the city limit.

"Turn off the lights," Krafft said as they approached.

Elest complied, saying a silent prayer as he did so that he wouldn't run into anything and get them stranded out here where they'd surely freeze to death. He pulled the blacked-out car into the same parking lot they'd left a few hours before. Elest was surprised to see lights on in the office.

"No, no," Krafft said, "park back there." He indicated the far edge of the lot, where the overhanging branches of some evergreens would hide the car. Elest did as he was told.

"Turn the motor off," Krafft ordered. "They'll see the exhaust."

Elest turned to see several shapes behind the frosty glass of the office where they'd met the civilian caretaker earlier in the day.

Elest was a bit more suspicious, though not quite ready to believe Krafft completely. "What are we looking for, sir?"

"I'm not sure," Krafft answered without taking his eyes off the office windows. The two men sat quietly, Krafft watching the door, Elest thinking about how quickly the temperature in the car was falling. After a few moments, two men came out of the office and went behind the building into the motor park. Krafft and Elest watched as they pulled a truck into one of the warehouses. Elest was about to ask why these men were down here at night when Krafft raised his hand. "Look."

Two more men had come out of the office. One of them, short and fat, lit a cigarette as soon as he was outside.

"Captain Sievers," Elest said. Krafft merely nodded.

"Do you think they're stealing stuff from the stores?" Elest pressed.

"No," Krafft said. He turned to the lieutenant. "I think it's more likely that they're putting it back."

Elest was still trying to digest this information when Krafft reached up and flipped the switch on the courtesy light, insuring that it would stay off when they opened the doors. When Sievers and the other men walked around to the warehouse, Krafft pulled at the door handle, then turned to Elest. "We must be careful here, Manfred."

It was the first time Krafft had ever used Elest's first name. For that matter, it was the first time Elest ever remembered the stiff major using the first name of any junior officer. There was no time to think about the significance; Krafft was already out of the car and walking to the office door. Elest got out quickly and followed, staying a few feet behind. At the door, Krafft held up his hand in the infantryman's silent signal for "halt." While Krafft looked inside, Elest peered around behind them. The lot was empty, their car well hidden under the tree branches. When he turned around again, the major was moving around the side of the building to where the truck had entered the warehouse. He stepped carefully in Sievers's tracks in the snow.

Before they could turn the corner, someone pulled open the big garage door, throwing yellow light out over the small yard between the office and the warehouse. Krafft and Elest flattened against the wall of the office building and listened to the men inside the warehouse.

A voice that Elest recognized as belonging to the old man, Walthers, said, "We can get the second truck in here, now that we have all that stuff up off the floor."

They heard the crunch of snow as one man walked to where another truck must be parked out of their view. At that moment, Elest's teeth started to chatter.

He clamped his hand to his jaw, but the chill spread and soon his whole body was shaking. Krafft turned to him, put his hand up to Elest's shoulder, steadying him. They were just like that when three armed men stepped out of the shadows.

1

THE BIG ALUMINUM AND STEEL DOORS SWUNG STEADILY IN-
ward on either side of the aircraft, carving black holes that caught the
frigid air outside and sprayed it through the troop compartment at a
hundred and ten knots. Major Mark Isen could see the soldiers on either
side of him tense, burrowing helmeted heads deeper into scarves and
parka collars. Isen shrugged his shoulders, wishing his own scarf up his
neck just a fraction of an inch farther. But it wasn't working, the parachute harness was too tight. He sat on its lumpy package, his legs pried
apart by thick straps like some medieval torture device. His seventy-
pound rucksack pressed against his shins, one sharp corner of the metal
frame digging at an instep. The ruck was just far enough off the floor of
the aircraft that whatever weight wasn't pushing on the top of his boot
was pulling at the juncture where the nylon bands held it to his parachute
harness, twisting wickedly at his groin.

Isen and the other soldiers on the plane, all of them U.S. Army Rangers,
had done in-flight rigging, a staff officer's euphemism for the hour-long
melee in the crowded, rocking belly of the airplane in which they struggled to get the harnesses on over the bulky cold-weather gear they were
wearing. In the course of that mayhem Isen had worked up a good sweat,
soaking his T-shirt. Now, with the doors open and the icy wind bearing
down on him from the tail of the aircraft like the breath of an especially
malevolent devil, he wondered if the shirt could freeze to his skin.

The only relief for all the discomfort lay outside the aircraft door, where he would soon step into the winter air some eleven hundred feet above the German countryside. There, at least, he'd no longer feel like a piece of tightly packed furniture, and the shock of the temperature change would take his mind off the various pains his equipment was causing him.

I'm too old for this stuff, Isen told himself for what seemed like the hundredth time since they'd left Fort Benning, Georgia, fifteen hours earlier. He was just at the edge of feeling a little bit sorry for himself when he remembered his late mother's even response whenever he mentioned that this or that training was too hard or uncomfortable.

"Just quit," she'd say.

And he'd smile at her, as if they were sharing an inside joke, as if he might ever consider quitting something he'd begun. And though she usually smiled in return, there was little joy there. As the wife of one career soldier and the mother of another—and both of the men combat veterans—she'd been a model stoic when it came to enduring hardship, separation, and sacrifice. Isen wondered, not for the first time, if his mother had hidden the kind of rebellious spirit that finally drove his— Mark's—wife away from the Army and her husband.

The women in his life would have been happier—his wife might even still be around—had he chosen another profession. But Isen could imagine no other life—everything about him was invested in his being a soldier.

He didn't look like the recruiting poster or the Ranger stereotype: he was of average height and build, neither handsome nor homely. He used to joke with his wife that he was somewhere in the great gray middle. But that was true only of his looks. He stood out when it came to imagination, tenacity, perseverance. At thirty-five he was wise enough to know that the same single-minded determination that made him a good soldier had been counterproductive in his personal life. He had the combat decorations and divorce papers to show for it.

Long ago and far away, he reminded himself.

The soldier across the tiny aisle began to stamp his feet on the aluminum deck. They were getting closer to their destination, and in their enthusiasm and optimism, the soldiers were sure that whatever was out that door was better than sitting crushed like a veal calf in a box. Soon, others picked up the slow tempo. *Thump, thump, thump.* Down the port side of the aircraft, where Isen sat on the long sling bench that ran along the centerline of the aircraft, holding two rows of paratroopers back to back. Other soldiers sat on the benches along the fuselage, so that there were two tiny aisles and four rows of troopers facing each other, less than six inches of space between opposing knees. *Thump, thump, thump.*

He could make out their faces in the dull glow from the few red cabin lights—red to preserve their night vision—left on for the final minutes. They looked like great bugs, all straps and bags and steel clips. Somewhere under the brim of each ungainly helmet there was a young face, painted with sticky camouflage paint and, most likely, grinning as they lost the foot-stomping rhythm and ended the display shouting and howling against the roar of the aircraft's engines. The long trip was coming to an end.

Isen watched as the jumpmaster—the man responsible for getting all the paratroopers out the door safely and on target—went through his check procedures undeterred by the gale force wind pressing him away from the open door. The NCO ran his gloved hand around the edge of the door frame, checking for anything that might snag a trooper on the way out. Then he leaned out of the door, checking the outside of the fuselage. The outside. Two or three thousand feet up and in the teeth of a hundred-and-twenty-knot slipstream that pressed the flesh on the man's face back to a grotesque parody of his normal looks.

Parachuting, Mark Isen knew, figured prominently in the glamorous ads favored by Army recruiters. The truth was that, in training exercises such as this, airborne operations consisted of sitting for hours in a parachute harness, first on the departure runway, then in an aircraft that was by turns stiflingly hot or cold enough to store meat. Then came the jump itself, with all the myriad things that could go wrong with the exit, with the parachute, and finally with the landing. Once Isen had jumped over a farmer's field in north Georgia and watched, all during his descent, a dozen cows run back and forth below him, trying to escape the terrifying noise of the helicopters. Luckily, he didn't find out what it was like to land on a cow.

A few feet away from Isen, the jumpmaster stood by the open door, ready for the next stage. Beside him, the U.S. Air Force loadmaster spoke over a headset to the pilot of the big C-141 Starlifter.

The loadmaster held up his hands, fingers splayed in the red light. Six minutes to drop time.

Isen looked to his right, down the webbed seating and the darkened tube of the crowded aircraft, and was reminded of one of the songs the troops sang when running in physical training formation.

> *C one-thirty rollin' down the strip*
> *Sixty-four Rangers on a one-way trip*
> *Mission unspoken, destination unknown*
> *Don't even know if they'll ever get home.*

Well, it wasn't quite that dramatic, Isen thought, but it was a pretty important mission. The operation they were about to begin was the first major field exercise for Isen as the operations officer, or S3, of the Third

Battalion of the U.S. Army's Seventy-fifth Infantry Regiment—"The Rangers."

"Get ready," the jumpmaster shouted, barely audible, at a range of a few feet, over the enormous bass of the engines and the tearing wind that filled the dark aluminum tunnel of the aircraft fuselage.

"Inboard personnel, stand up." The paratroopers responded to the commands and the accompanying hand signals in their practiced sequence. Like so many other things in the Army, the soldiers drilled this routine until they could do it in their sleep.

"Outboard personnel, stand up."

The jumpmaster raised his hands sharply from his waist, like an emphatic priest blessing his camouflaged flock.

Isen, standing now, shared the tiny aisle space with the men who'd been sitting across from him. They squeezed together, moving and adjusting so that each man had room. There were no privileges of rank—everyone was equally uncomfortable.

"Hook up."

Isen took the end of his static line, the webbed strap that would pull his parachute from its pack before it broke away, and hooked the metal clasp to the cable that ran overhead the length of the aircraft.

"Check static line."

He tugged at it twice, sharply, to make sure it was secure and would stay anchored to the plane.

Isen was the sixth man on the port side. He now faced the rear of the aircraft and could see the jumpmaster studying the first paratroopers in the line, or stick. The NCO looked at them with a deadly seriousness, as if he might be able to tell from a glance which of the troopers in front of him was wavering in his resolve to step out of the door.

"Check equipment. Sound off for equipment check."

Isen ran his hand along the brim of his helmet, as he'd been taught almost twelve years earlier at jump school. He knew he was looking for those same sharp edges he'd seen the jumpmaster hunt on the edges of the doors, but he wasn't sure what he would do if he found a problem—there was only one way out of this aircraft. He looked down at his chest, where the straps of the harness came together under a round metal disk, the release that would free him once he was on the ground. Isen checked the parachute rig of the man in front of him, just as the man behind him checked his, following the static line down from the cable to where it wound on the top of the packing. From the back of the stick he could hear men slapping each other with the signal.

"OK."

The man behind him hit him on the upper arm and shouted in his ear, "OK," and Isen did the same to the man in front of him. A few seconds later, the jumpmaster leaned outside again, so that the top half of his body seemed cut off by the door's edge. Then they were passing back the warning. An extended index finger.

One minute.

Isen looked at his watch and was amazed again that the air force could fly them across the whole ocean and drop them on a particular field in Germany at precisely the time that was called for in the order.

Thirty seconds.

The first paratrooper stepped closer to the whistling black hole of the door, sliding his static line along the overhead cable to the jumpmaster, who pulled it close. Then the red light died and the green light came on and the jumpmaster said "Go" and the soldier was gone.

"GO, GO, GO, GO." The NCO clicked them off smoothly, ushering the soldiers out into the darkness beyond the little green light. Finally it was Isen's turn. He looked the jumpmaster in the face as he handed over the static line, tucked both hands on the top of the small, reassuring bundle of the reserve parachute slung across his stomach, turned slightly to his right and stepped out into black space.

There was no sensation of falling; instead, he always felt as if he were being swept upward. Isen opened his eyes wide against the violent air and saw, some twenty-five feet above his head, the horizontal stabilizer of the aircraft's tail pass over him, a ghostly shadow darker than the surrounding night sky. He began to count, *one thousand, two thousand*, then lost it and had a half second to marvel at the image of himself tumbling above the earth when there was the sudden violent tug at his shoulders as the static line pulled open his chute, breaking away as the canopy filled and slowed him down. Isen gulped the cold air, then looked up to see the reassuring roundness of the canopy. That was one critical point passed.

Below him he could see the lights of the town that was just beyond the north edge of their drop zone. He looked around him where the other chutes, like so many mushroom tops, reflected the dull light of a winter moon partially covered by clouds. This was the best part, the half minute or so of floating where you watched the horizon and forgot that the earth was rising below you at eight feet per second.

Isen looked down again, trying to judge the distance to the ground. When he thought he was at one hundred feet he released the lowering line on the top of his rucksack, now swinging in front of his legs. The heavy ruck raced down until it dangled fifteen feet below him, the idea being that it would be near him when he hit the ground, but he wouldn't land on it.

Isen pressed his feet and knees together, even though it caused more pain where his harness already squeezed his testicles. But he had no desire to be hauled off the drop zone with a broken leg. He looked down past the toes of his boots just as the thin moon slipped behind a cloud, and suddenly the ground disappeared. In the darkness he lost his sense of whether he was moving forward or backward, which would mean the difference between a controlled landing and a crash. Now he might hit at anytime, and he braced himself for the impact.

Now. Now. Now.

A few yards away he heard a grunt as another Ranger hit, then suddenly there was the great dark plate of earth rushing up and slamming him on the soles of the feet. The parachute yanked him backward, so that instead of the graceful unfolding of a good parachute landing fall, he hit feet, buttocks, head. He grunted and rolled over on his side, working the release to free himself from the chute that was trying to drag him across the drop zone. He scrambled out of the harness and got to one knee, instinctively checking his holster for his weapon, then followed the lowering line along the ground until he found his rucksack. One leg was a bit wobbly and his head was ringing, and he remembered what one of the senior NCOs had told him after his first jump with the battalion: once you're over thirty, there're only two kinds of jumps—the ones that hurt, and the ones that hurt a lot.

There was just a trace of snow on the ground, but the field was frozen and covered with brittle stalks of last summer's grass that crunched under his feet as he secured his parachute. Another Ranger came down almost on top of him, a ghostly apparition of rustling nylon, but Isen ducked away.

All about him men ran heavily in thick winter clothes, strapping on rucksacks or rolling parachutes for recovery. Dark figures stumbled on risers—the lines that connect jumper harness to parachute—or worked to free equipment from the thin underbrush, cursing in tight, low tones. Now, on the ground, Isen could see the three or four chem lights that winked at the edge of the drop zone. The luminescent tubes, each just a little bigger than a fountain pen, glowed dully red, green, yellow, or blue, at various points around the perimeter of the drop zone, and Rangers were already making their way through the dark to the assembly areas marked in the colored code of lights.

This was the point of their greatest vulnerability, Isen knew. There were soldiers still in the air, coming around with the planes in their racetrack pattern for another pass. The soldiers on the ground were, as yet, separated from their leaders. And though they moved quietly and steadily in the blackness, there was some degree of disorder.

Isen found the confusion strangely comforting. During the flight he'd been a mere passenger, keenly aware that his fate was in the hands of the Air Force. He'd boarded a windowless airplane in Georgia and flown a quarter of the way across the globe, and he could only trust the air crew that when he jumped out, he'd be at the one spot on the whole continent of Europe where he was supposed to be. Now, the paradox: on the ground, in the dark, in an area he'd visited only on maps, he could begin to exert control.

Isen pulled his compass from its pouch at his belt, flipped open the cover and allowed the floating dial to settle. He turned due south, the azimuth that would—theoretically—take him to the edge of the drop zone where he was supposed to meet the other men in the headquarters element. He looked up at the horizon for a frame of reference, then began to jog across the frozen earth.

Once he linked up with the command group, he and the other leaders would begin forming order out of the chaos that surrounded him, where men who'd been scattered during the drop hurried to organize themselves into units. For a few brief moments, though, he was glad to be by himself, moving through the night alone, trying out his legs, which had survived another jump without injury.

Although he'd been with the Rangers only a short while, Isen had been involved with the planning of Operation Solid Steel since its inception nine weeks earlier. His five-hundred-man battalion, one of three in the Seventy-fifth Infantry, the Ranger Regiment based at Fort Benning, was the only American unit participating in the joint exercise with the Germans. Though he wasn't privy to all of the political considerations that went along with the agreement to train with their former NATO allies, Isen and the other officers had—as a matter of course—brushed up on current affairs in the host nation. They'd learned that the German military they'd be working with was far different from what it had been at the end of the Cold War.

The German armed forces, the Bundeswehr, had been hit by the same tremendous budget cuts that had drawn the United States Army down to half is Cold War size by the middle of the century's last decade. But the concurrent slowdown of western economies had hit Germany particularly hard. During those years of reduced growth, the Federal Republic had had to fight several fiscal battles.

First, there was the tremendous cost of absorbing the eastern sector, with its antiquated service and utility infrastructure and its badly polluted landscape. On top of that, Germany became, in the early nineties, the new promised land for hundreds of thousands of refugees from the political and economic maelstrom that engulfed eastern Europe and the wreck of the Soviet Union. The federal government, with generous social programs and a tradition of open borders, reeled from the cost of feeding and housing these people during the long process of sorting the bona fide refugees from the gold diggers. Finally, the sluggish economy put tens of thousands of Germans out of work, and these hungry voters provided the impetus for change in the social climate. Unfortunately, the heirs of the generation that had built Europe's strongest industrial nation from the ashes of World War II turned away from social reform and progress, embracing instead the reactionary legacy of Germany in the 1930s: xenophobia, bigotry, racism. German workers found an easy target for their anger and frustration in the highly visible armies of immigrants.

The German Ministry of Defense, the Bundesministerium der Verteidigung, faced with dwindling resources and unable to sustain the large armored formations that had stood guard on the eastern border for decades, moved much of that armored strength to the reserves. The active army began to concentrate its resources on small, well-trained units. So the ministry sought the advice of their American allies, whose elite formations were designed to answer a variety of needs. This call had brought the Rangers—and Mark Isen—to Germany as part of Operation Solid Steel.

Isen neared the dark shapes of the trees at the edge of the drop zone and heard voices murmuring there. A few feet more and he recognized the slow cadences of one of his radio operators, a steady Texan named Hatley. But the moon had been swallowed up by the fast moving clouds, and Isen still couldn't see a thing. He fumbled for the night vision goggles hung around his neck.

"Down here, sir."

That would be Sergeant Gamble, Isen's other radio operator. It was just like him to spot Isen first.

"Where?" Isen said. He still didn't have his goggles up.

"Down here." Gamble's voice came back, slightly amused.

At times it seemed to Isen that one of Sergeant Tommy Gamble's chief pursuits in life—and a source of unending joy to the younger man—was to be a step or two ahead of his boss at all times. He'd already been good at it when Isen arrived in the battalion, and he was getting better all the time.

When the moon played out again Isen could see two or three forms sitting in a concrete-lined drainage ditch at his feet. He sat down on the edge and slid in beside his men.

"We up?" Isen asked.

"So far," Gamble answered. "We're talking to everybody who's on the ground."

"Just made contact with Charlie Company," Hatley added, holding the handset of his radio away from his face. Above them, another flight of three aircraft thundered out of the darkness at the horizon. Isen could see the little figures spilling out into the moonlight, their parachutes trailing behind them like flimsy streamers. Then the great nylon chutes filled with air, blossoming like spots of black ink against the lighter palette of the sky, while the jumpers swung below them in circles.

Isen was still in awe at these night jumps. When he joined the unit his lack of experience as a paratrooper had been the topic of much speculation by the soldiers and NCOs. Isen had made less than twelve jumps—five in Airborne school to get his silver wings, the rest in Ranger school—before his surprise assignment to the Rangers. Most officers in the Regiment were part of what outsiders—straight-leg grunts like Isen—referred to as the Airborne Mafia. These men found their way into jump slots early in their careers and tried always to get back to these units.

It was highly unusual for Isen, who'd never been in an airborne unit before, to be assigned to one as a major. Most officers of his grade in the unit were on their second, some even on their third tour with the Rangers. He'd started out as an assistant to the operations officer, who was the battalion commander's right hand when it came to training and running the unit in the field. When the ops officer was hurt in a jump, Isen had been tapped to move up. He knew the choice had rattled a few cages around the Army, since he'd been selected for the prestigious assignment over men with more orthodox credentials.

Isen had been handpicked to come to the Rangers by the newly named commander of the Third Battalion, Lieutenant Colonel Ray Spano. The two men had worked together before, and Spano had learned to respect Isen's quiet persistence, his intelligence, and his compassion for soldiers. Mark Isen might have been a newcomer to the Rangers, but he was no stranger to the Army or to combat. He'd served as a staff officer in Desert Storm and as an advisor on a decidedly dangerous mission in the drug war.

But it was as a junior captain and the commander of a light infantry company that Mark Isen had learned what the profession of arms was really about. His experiences in combat had taught him several things: there was no substitute for good hard training when it came to keeping soldiers alive and accomplishing the mission, and there was nothing as insufferable as a man who glorified war. More than that—and this was important to Spano—Isen was a fighter.

As the Army drew down and officers were less and less sure that they would have a job when they showed up for work each day, conservatism gained sway in decision making. No one wanted to go out of his way to get himself noticed during those years when personnel boards studied officers' files for the tiniest reasons to put them out of the service. Mark Isen was meticulous in his planning and preparation, a fanatic about doing as much as possible to rule out chance. But when the time came to gamble, to stick his neck out, Isen was willing to do it. And he put his mission above concern for his own career—something that was becoming increasingly, dangerously rare.

"Bravo Company is in position, sir," Hatley said.

"Good." Isen checked his watch. They were actually a little ahead of schedule. When he looked back up to where the parachutes were deploying, there was a man standing a few feet away. Before Isen could say anything, Gamble spoke up.

"Halt."

The figure stopped, apparently unsure, in the unreliable moonlight, where the voice had come from.

"Seven," Gamble said, using the close-in challenge.

"Four," the dark figure answered. The total was as it was supposed to be during the first twelve hours of the operation.

"That you, Manny?" Gamble asked.

"Yeah." Specialist Manning, one of Colonel Spano's runners, crouched down by the side of the ditch. "I'm looking for Major Isen," he said.

"Right here."

"The colonel is down to your right about fifty meters," Manning said, motioning with his head.

Isen and his two radio operators picked up and followed Manning along the ditch. Around them they could hear soldiers moving to their unit rallying points. It would take the better part of an hour to account for everyone and be ready to move out.

"How does it look, Mark?" Spano asked before Isen could even see him.

"Charlie and Bravo are in position, sir. Once we get Alpha up, we'll have the wagons circled."

The first task was to get the rifle companies to form a loose perimeter around the drop zone, an enlarged oval that would give them a secure place to take care of any injured and would protect them if they got hit by opposing forces, which might take place at any time. The plan for Solid Steel called for the Rangers to move from the drop zone to seize a small airfield at nearby Karlshofen, a town about thirty miles from the North Sea port of Bremerhaven. Normally, when the plan called for an airfield seizure, the Rangers jumped directly onto the strip, as they did in the 1989 invasion of Panama. But the Germans, who had borrowed the field from the local flying club for a few days, were concerned about possible damage to the small civilian aircraft. They asked the Americans to offset the drop.

On the ground, the Rangers would face war-game opponents from the Bundeswehr, the German Field Army. Since the "enemy" in this scenario was mounted on Marders, tracked fighting vehicles that were roughly equivalent to the American Bradley Fighting Vehicle, speed was a critical part of the paratroopers' plan.

The scenario called for the Rangers to hold the airfield against mock attacks while real German and notional American and British reinforcements were brought in by aircraft. The Rangers were being used in one of their standard missions, the lead punch in an assault that would over-whelm the enemy with quickly deployed forces. Everything depended on swiftness.

"Who's the lead platoon for Charlie Company?" Spano asked.

"I think Hawk is taking us on this one, sir," Isen said.

Hawk was First Lieutenant Ken Hawkins, a twenty-five-year-old former Auburn University linebacker and runner-up for the Mister Ala-bama body-building title who was the most colorful junior officer in the battalion. Isen suspected that Hawkins, or "The Hawk Man," as the lieutenant sometimes referred to himself, was more appearance than sub-stance. Spano knew Isen's opinion.

"You arrange that?" Spano asked.

Isen thought his boss might be smiling, but it was impossible to tell in the gloom.

"No, sir," Isen said. "I'll be too busy trying to monitor my own screwups without trying to invent mistakes for other people."

A few hundred meters away along the bowed line of the quickly de-veloping defensive perimeter, the second platoon of Charlie Company lay behind a small rise that overlooked a dense evergreen woodline some fifty meters in front of them.

"Cold enough for you, Sergeant Bishop?" Lieutenant Ken Hawkins asked as he moved, stoop shouldered, to where his first squad leader had positioned himself in the center of his squad. Two or three men, barely visible in the shifting moonlight, manned hastily scratched fighting po-sitions near Bishop.

"Won't be so bad once we start moving," Bishop replied.

"Hey, sir," a soldier called in a stage whisper. "The hawk is out, huh?"

The "hawk," soldier slang for cold weather, gave some of the troops an excuse to use their platoon leader's nickname. Bishop was just about to chastise the trooper for unnecessary noise when Hawkins answered, "You know it, man."

Bishop couldn't see it in the darkness, but he was sure his lieutenant was flashing his trademark grin at the soldier in the next position. Staff Sergeant Bishop thought that young Lieutenant Hawkins was a little too lax with the troops, a little too buddy-buddy. Bishop, an eight-year vet-eran who'd spent most of his time in the Rangers, where strict military discipline was a point of pride, had mentioned the situation to the pla-toon sergeant, the ranking NCO in the platoon, on two different occa-sions. As far as he could see, nothing had changed.

Bishop shook his head. The Rangers recruited first lieutenants (as op-posed to newly commissioned second lieutenants), men who'd already been platoon leaders in other units, because they were looking for experience and maturity. In Sergeant Bishop's opinion, offered to no one but his peers, the criteria should be changed to maturity and maturity.

Most of the junior officers were sharp soldiers in spite of their relative inexperience, young men who were, like the soldiers they led, physically courageous, fast learners, serious about mastering their profession. The tricky part was just this: their professional education depended, to a great extent, on how much they were willing to listen to their more experienced subordinates, the noncommissioned officers who accomplished or supervised the thousand thousand tasks and details that kept the fighting machine moving.

"We should send a team out into that woodline, sir," Bishop offered, pointing to the thick growth in front of them. He already had two men out in a listening post, but he thought the platoon leader should strengthen the security.

Hawkins crawled forward on his elbows. "You're right. We should. But I want to be ready to move out as soon as we get the word. No slack."

Bishop and the rest of the NCOs in the platoon figured that Hawkins had been given this important mission, lead platoon for a battalion movement, as a test of his abilities. As professionals, they'd do everything in their power to accomplish the mission, but that same professionalism made them balk at cutting corners.

"This position isn't secure with all that thick growth right in front of us, sir," Bishop persisted. But that wasn't the point. Hawkins could see as clearly as anyone that an occupying force needed to control the woodline to prevent an enemy from using that cover to get to within fifty meters. The point was that Bishop wanted the soldiers to learn to do things—secure the area, in this case—correctly, and he believed that Hawkins was one step ahead of himself.

"Just stand by," Hawkins said. "When I say go, you're up in a flash and moving out toward the airfield. Right?"

Bishop paused a full beat. "Right, sir," he said.

Hawkins, who was lying beside the squad leader, suddenly raised himself into the front leaning rest, his own substantial body weight and that of his sixty- to seventy-pound rucksack resting on hands and toes, and began doing pushups on the cold ground.

"I'm friggin' psyched for this operation," he said. "Aren't you?"

"Always, sir," Bishop said flatly.

Hawkins stopped. "Where's my man Brennan?"

"He's over to the right, sir," Bishop answered. He was about to say that he'd keep an eye on Brennan, but he let it ride. Lieutenant Hawkins thought Brennan, a specialist from Boston, wasn't Ranger material. Brennan had never been in trouble, had never missed training or fallen out of a run. Staff Sergeant Bishop figured that the platoon leader didn't like

Brennan because the boy was small and soft spoken, with the bookish airs of an academic. All these qualities stood out in a unit that loved size and bluster and men like Hawkins.

"You keep your eye on that boy," Hawkins said.

"Wilco, sir."

When Hawkins melted back into the night, Bishop moved forward a few more feet, crawling on his hands and knees, silent, serious, playing the game.

"Hey," he called to the two men immediately in front of him in the listening post near the woodline. "Y'all keep your eyes on those goddamned trees, you hear?"

Hawkins found his radio operator, an Iowa farmer's son named Marty Keefer, a few meters behind Bishop's position. "Any word yet?"

"Nothing, sir."

"Wish they'd hurry up," he said, mostly to himself.

Hawkins wasn't good at waiting, and he was anxious to get started. Unlike his NCOs, Hawkins didn't see the mission as a test but as a reward for hard work, an acknowledgment by his company and battalion commanders that The Hawk was the best platoon leader in the battalion.

Hawkins had been in the Rangers for just seven months, and he expected to spend another four or five as platoon leader before he moved up to another job. Then he'd go back to Benning for the Infantry Officer Advanced Course, followed by a stint in some leg—that is, not parachute—outfit with time for company command. Then he'd get back to one of the Ranger battalions, or "batts," where he'd make a name for himself.

Hawkins loved the Ranger battalions because they got more training money than any other unit, traveling all over the world while other units made do with local maneuver areas. But he also saw the Rangers as a way of rising above his peers. In the shrinking army he had entered as a Distinguished Military Graduate from Auburn's ROTC program, he knew that it was difficult for a young man to get recognition, especially at the wide base of the personnel pyramid occupied by junior officers. But selection for service with the Rangers had already moved him ahead of his contemporaries. Unfortunately, there'd be little chance to distinguish himself in combat; the world was getting too peaceful. But, if it was going to happen at all, the Rangers would be there.

"This is Alpha two five romeo," Keefer said. The RTO had been walking with the set pressed to his ear, balancing his rifle in the crook of his other arm. "I copy *goalpost*, over."

This was it. Hawkins stepped off powerfully before Keefer had even signed off. The soldier hustled through the night to keep up with the big platoon leader, who'd warned him to stay within arm's reach at all times. The pair headed to Sergeant Bishop's position.

"Let's go, first squad," Hawkins said too loudly.

Bishop had his men up and moving in a tight wedge in less than two minutes. Keefer could see only their rough-edged outlines as the men stood, shouldered their rucksacks and took up their positions on the move.

"Good, good," Hawkins said out loud. "Keep it tight and keep up the pace."

Keefer could easily imagine Sergeant Bishop giving Hawkins his poker-faced glance. *No need to tell that man how to do his job.*

"Let's go, Keefer," Hawkins said.

"I'm right behind you, sir."

Keefer wondered what he might do if Hawkins made this much noise in combat, with deadly eyes peering out from the underbrush, looking for noisy Rangers to signal their position. He wondered how he'd fare, when the bullets started flying, always standing next to a man who seemed bent on attracting all the attention to himself.

But try as he might, he found it hard to imagine that they might wind up in a real shooting match, though he kept the observation to himself. Most of the men took things with a deadly seriousness, and Keefer felt sorry for the soldier who let on, especially in front of those NCOs who'd been through Grenada and Panama and Desert Storm, that this was a game. Keefer never stuffed his ammunition pouches with candy, but he still thought of the whole thing as some elaborate charade. And so even though the perspiration on his back and legs was beginning to chill him mightily in the night air, Keefer was amused at what they were doing. When Hawkins turned around to check on him, Keefer bent over quickly, mocking the stance of readiness they taught him in basic training, head up, eyes wide open, knees flexed, rifle balanced neatly in both hands, ready to spring to action.

"Hooah, sir."

Because he was a smart soldier, Marty Keefer was chosen by the platoon sergeant to carry the platoon leader's radio and help keep the lieutenant straight. And because he was smart, and observant, Keefer knew quite a bit more about his platoon leader than Hawkins would have guessed. Keefer guessed that the officer, in spite of his bravado, was insecure, nervous about letting his guard down. He had come on board with this image of the big, tough football player who got into brawls for fun, and he couldn't just let go of that. He lived it; he was his own image.

They all had roles to play, Keefer knew. Hawkins was the big tough guy; Keefer's was that of the sharp soldier, always prepared. They were comfortable in those poses.

Up in front of him, Hawkins suddenly looked around, as if he'd forgotten something.

"Keefer," Hawkins said without turning around.

"Already called in the first checkpoint, sir."

"Good. Good job."

2

PAUL GEDERN RAN FROM THE PARKING LOT, UP THE WOODEN steps that led to the back gate of the motor park, dragging his half-packed canvas bag of field gear and extra uniforms, and wondering all the while why he was running in the first place.

As he entered the circle of lights from the yard security system, he recognized a soldier from his squad. "Heidegger, what's going on?"

"Don't know," Heidegger managed. He was gasping for breath, dragging a surprisingly plump version of the same issue bag Gedern had with him, left over from their days on active duty service in the field army.

"Looks like you're planning a long stay," Gedern joked.

"Might be," Heidegger replied.

Gedern caught himself before he made another offhand remark. Corporal Heidegger might be a lump when it came to physical activity, but he always seemed to know what was happening around the station. Gedern wanted to stop and quiz him, but some NCO they didn't recognize was yelling at them to run, now, run, *run*, so Gedern dutifully swung his bag over his shoulder and began to trot through the cold and the yellow glare of the motor park lights to the line of hulking shadows that were the unit's Marders, the tracked infantry fighting vehicles that had only recently been transferred to reserve control from the regular forces, the Bundeswehr.

Gedern opened the back hatch and climbed in, dragging his bag behind him. It was cold as a tomb inside the steel box of the troop compartment.

He removed one of his gloves to retrieve his flashlight from a parka pocket, skinning his knuckles on the cold edge of the seat.

"Ver*dammt.*"

He pushed his hand down between his legs and held it there while looking out on the yellow-lit park framed through the personnel hatch. Men were still running by, coming and going singly and in small knots, but some sense of order seemed to be bubbling up. Here and there soldiers teamed up to move the heavy tool boxes and spare track pads that were to be mounted on the Marders, others passed cases of rations from the back of a trailer, fire brigade style, stacking the boxes behind the line of vehicles. Gedern squeezed his hand between his thighs.

This is stupid, Gedern thought. *Running around like the barbarians are at the gates.*

"I wish I knew what in the hell is going on," he said out loud, his voice tinny in the cold vehicle.

At first, in spite of the cold, the alert had been fun. There was the call in the night and the code words for a rollout of vehicles, just like the old days in the Bundeswehr. The roads were empty as he drove the twenty kilometers from his home to this motor park north of Bremervörde, and he relished the fact that he wasn't afraid; there was no worry anymore that the Soviets were pouring across the border in their hundreds of thousands. Gedern was no longer a Cold Warrior, but merely a Territorial Forces soldier, a reservist whose job was to augment the federal army in the event of mobilization.

The role was evolving and there'd been some changes in the past few months when, as a result of decisions made in Berlin, the Ministry of Defense had been ordered to shift some heavy equipment—such as Gedern's Marder—to the Territorial Army, which had traditionally been made up of foot soldiers. Gedern had been enthusiastic about the new vehicles—anything was better than walking.

Gedern's father had also been enthusiastic about the change his son reported at a family dinner.

"Good, good," the elder Gedern had said, banging his big workman's hand on the table for emphasis. "Now that there is some kicking power in the territorials, Berlin won't give so much away to the goddamned foreigners."

"Watch your language, please," Gedern's mother had said.

"The military is not going to get involved in policy making," the soldier Gedern said. He read the newspapers nearly every day and was always impressed to hear, from his own mouth, the kind of important-sounding language he could find on the editorial pages.

"Don't be an ass," his father came back.

Gedern's mother put her fork down sharply, and it clattered off the edge of the plate. Gedern's father didn't notice the rebuke.

"Military power is important because power is all there is," the father went on.

"What would the territorials say? It's not like we are all of one mind, anyway," the son said. He was still chewing his food, shoving bits of meat around in the gravy on the plate. When he looked up, he saw that his father had stopped eating and was leaning forward, one hand clutching the base of a tall beer glass. There were cuts across all the fingers, grime that resisted soap in the pores on the sides.

"Don't you know what's going on?" the father asked.

The job lecture again, Gedern thought.

Gedern shared a universal attitude with young people the world over: he tolerated parents who were not, in his opinion, very wordly, and certainly not his intellectual equals. But he had to be careful how far he pushed the old tyrant; without a job that could support him on his own, he relied on his parents.

"We're being taxed into poverty to rebuild the east—all their goddamned cheap roads. . . ."

Gedern's mother got up from the table. Her husband watched her retreating back, lowered his voice.

"All their fucking worthless utilities and buildings. Then, on top of that, we're being invaded by filthy immigrants. It's getting so you walk down the street, you can't even hear a conversation in German."

He paused long enough to pick up his fork and stab a fat, dripping sausage, which he waved in the air, like a baton, when he continued.

"The country is full of smelly Arabs, Serbs with one leg shot off in their civil war; lazy, stupid Poles; big, fat Russians looking for toilet paper; skinny blacks carrying their children around on their backs." He shook the sausage in his son's face. *"That's* why you don't have a job."

The younger Gedern chewed patiently. He'd heard the tirade before and knew there was another part coming.

"And then, when all these bastards get here, our government pays them for *not* working, provides them an apartment, everything that I have to work my ass off for."

The old man had built up a head of steam, and Gedern wished for his mother to return to calm the old fascist down.

"And you think bringing Marders into the Territorial Forces is going to reverse all that?" the son had asked sarcastically.

"You just watch," workman Gedern had answered. "You just watch."

Just then a shadow filled the hatch. "Who's in there?"

It was Brufels—an Unteroffizier, or sergeant—Gedern's squad leader and the commander of this vehicle.

"Gedern."

"So what you waiting for, Herr Gedern? An invitation to start this thing up and get the heater going?"

"What's going on?" Gedern asked as he squeezed forward to switch on the electrical system, the first step in getting the vehicle moving. Brufels, the NCO, was only a year older than Gedern, and Gedern liked to bait him occasionally by dropping "sergeant" from his speech.

Brufels leaned into the dark cavity of the Marder's troop compartment. "Well, I heard that there are paratroopers landing twenty, twenty-five kilometers south of here, near someplace named Karlshofen, and we're going out to contain them."

"So this is part of an exercise? A readiness test?" Gedern asked.

Brufels shrugged.

Gedern hit the starter, which whined a bit before turning the engine over. He climbed out of the driver's hatch and slid off the front of the vehicle, the cold steel sucking the body heat out of his legs.

"What paratroopers?" Gedern asked, a little put off that Brufels didn't give him enough credit to recognize a war game when he saw one.

Brufels climbed out of the commander's hatch and onto the deck of the machine to check the mounting of the twenty-millimeter gun. "Probably Americans," he said over his shoulder. Gedern, on the ground, made a circuit of the vehicle, checking the tension on the tracks.

"And they're jumping now?" Gedern pressed.

"It'll all be over if you don't get moving," Brufels said. "Hand me that tool box."

Gedern struggled to get the heavy box up on the vehicle's steel side. He had the strange sensation he sometimes had in dreams, where everyone around him knew something he didn't know and wasn't likely to learn.

"Aren't they just on maneuvers?" Gedern asked again. It seemed so obvious that it was almost a joke to talk about it.

"That's what they'd like you to think," Brufels answered. He looked down at Gedern, grabbed the handle of the tool box. There was a tense note in his voice that Gedern could no longer ascribe to the squad leader's unhappiness at being rolled out of bed. "You want to let them have the run of the country?" Brufels went on. "A replay of the last fifty years?"

This is incredible, Gedern thought. *He's as bad as my old man.*

If it was true that there was some danger, then certainly the Bundeswehr would respond with its active duty alert forces. The reservists weren't supposed to be called up until there was full mobilization, when the whole country was threatened. Ten years ago, with huge Warsaw Pact armies poised on the border, he would have had no trouble believing. Now, it was just too much. Gedern, faced with slim evidence that something exceedingly unlikely was happening, simply refused to believe. He decided that, despite Brufels's rantings, this was just a drill.

As Brufels left to talk to the platoon leader, a young soldier named Himmets came up and shoved his own bag into the rear door of the Marder. Gedern dropped into the driver's hatch, found his bag, and pulled out the earphones to his portable tape player, which he slipped on. Brufels would flip if he knew that Gedern was listening to American rock and roll instead of doing his maintenance checks.

Fuck him, Gedern thought. *The little Prussian.* He jacked the volume up a notch and slapped his thigh in rhythm.

Someone tapped him on the shoulder. Gedern, startled, turned around expecting a chewing out from the squad leader. But it was only Himmets. He took his headphones off.

"Excuse me," Himmets said.

What a kid, Gedern thought.

"What do you think we're going to do?"

Gedern looked around. There was no one on the deck of the Marder, no one else inside, no one listening. He was about to vent his anger at the whole organization, but when he looked at Himmets he realized that the teenager was scared.

"Nothing," Gedern said. "We'll probably drive out of here and sit on our asses someplace for a few hours. Lose just enough sleep to make you tired for the rest of the week." He smiled, but in the sickly light of the park spots that filtered down into the hatch, he could see that Himmets was not comforted.

It took them less than an hour to get moving, mostly because they'd been on maneuvers over the weekend, just a few days before, and because their maintenance program, the heart and soul of any mechanized unit, was tightly run. They drove south on the shoulder of Highway 71 as it curled away from Bremervörde, but the headlights of the civilian traffic, though light at this hour, played havoc with their night vision.

Gedern couldn't understand why they had to drive with their blackout lights on, as if they were in the field. It wasn't as if the passing cars couldn't tell there was an armored convoy on the road. But within a mile or so they moved off the main road and onto secondary roads, still heading south, as far as Gedern could tell. He concentrated on maintaining convoy distance from the tiny lights in front of him that marked the rear of the Marder ahead.

"Prepare to stop." Brufels's voice over the intercom startled him. There was no noise from the troop compartment, where everyone was asleep, and Gedern could easily imagine that he was out driving alone.

The vehicle ahead pulled off to the left side of the road, and Gedern anticipated Brufels's instructions to go to the right. He'd already begun to swing the squared-off nose of the Marder when Brufels told him to turn.

"Leave it idling under those branches," Brufels said, indicating a stand of neatly cropped fir trees a few meters off the road.

Yeah, yeah, yeah, Gedern said to himself.

Brufels got out of the vehicle, then returned a few minutes later to tell

Gedern to shut the engine off. When he did, he became aware of the sound of aircraft overhead. He wasn't sure how far the Marder had come, but he didn't think there was a major airport around.

It was impossible, down in the thick trees, even to guess where the aircraft might be. Gedern stood in his hatch and stared upward, trying to catch a glimpse of the planes in the sporadic moonlight, but the sound was already fading.

"I can't see a thing," someone said from behind him. It was Himmets, who'd climbed up into the vacant commander's hatch. "Usually you can see the lights and stuff on the planes."

"They're gone, now," Gedern offered. The two men sat quietly. A short distance away, they could hear the NCOs and officers talking. Turning around in his hatch, Gedern could see the outline of Himmets's form against the sky, but he couldn't see Himmets's face, and the younger man said nothing. For some reason, perhaps because Himmets was only nineteen, or because the younger man had only served in the reserves, Gedern felt obliged to comfort him. "I told you we'd come out here and just sit around," Gedern said. Himmets didn't reply, and Gedern's comment hung lamely in the cold air.

Gedern was about to light a cigarette, against standing orders to maintain light discipline, when a truck pulled off the highway and approached the parked armored vehicles. The driver switched his headlights off but left on the parking lights, which seemed incredibly bright in the woods. There was a stir near where the platoon NCOs had been standing, then Sergeant Brufels called to them.

"First squad, give me three men."

Himmets woke another soldier, then joined Gedern on the ground. "Aren't you supposed to stay with the vehicle in case you have to move it?" Himmets asked.

"Fuck that," Gedern said, tightening the drawstring at the bottom of his parka. "I want to see what's going on."

His feet were already numb. They walked to the truck, where Lieutenant Stoddard, full-time shopkeeper, part-time platoon leader, was standing on the open tailgate. Stoddard was holding a pistol, as if expecting an unruly mob.

It's freakin' Napoleon, Gedern thought.

"We're going to unpack ammo," Stoddard said, as casually as if he were talking about unloading furniture.

Gedern sucked in his breath, a small, involuntary alarm. It was not all that unusual to roll the vehicles out of the park in a practice alert; it was quite another thing to load live ammunition. Even in his days on active duty, Gedern saw very little live ammunition. He remembered that their American allies were constantly amazed that the Bundeswehr didn't carry live ammo, even when patroling the old East-West border. The Americans attributed this, he had heard, to a denial of the threat from the East.

Gedern's NCOs had told him that carrying live ammunition was dangerous: trigger-happy or jumpy soldiers could get someone killed, could even start an international incident, if left to handle live ammo. Gedern was sure that Stoddard knew all this as well as anyone, but he didn't want to be the only one of the group to speak up.

Stoddard waved his pistol as he spoke. "I need three men, no, four, on the truck."

The two men nearest Stoddard eagerly pulled back the canvas flaps, and Gedern could see that there were indeed cases of ammunition on board: dull green boxes of machine gun ammo, wooden crates of rifle and pistol ammunition, and, near the front of the bed, the bulky metal cans of linked twenty-millimeter ammo for the Marder's big guns. He looked hard at Stoddard for some clue as to why they were doing this, but when the little lieutenant met his gaze, Gedern looked down. Stoddard was a blowhard, but Gedern wasn't about to challenge a man who was waving a pistol.

Gedern joined the line waiting for cases of machine gun ammo to be handed off the tailgate. Soon there was a lot of talking in the woods; the men were all awake now and wondering aloud what was going on. Stoddard stood to one side, giving unnecessary instructions.

There was quite a lot of noise as the men broke open the crates and slapped the metal boxes into the racks inside the vehicles. After the tracks were loaded, the soldiers began to load their individual weapons. When Gedern squatted beside his Marder to load magazines for his assault rifle and pistol, he found that he was sweating.

"Do you suppose it could be true?" Himmets asked. "What Sergeant Brufels said about paratroopers?"

Gedern counted the rounds as he slid them home in the aluminum magazine. Pack them too tightly and they'd jam.

"Oh, there may be paratroopers," he said. "But it's probably just maneuvers. You know, ordinary training stuff. After all, if we were about to be invaded, we'd have heard something about it before now. There'd have been talk about it on the television, in the papers. Brufels is just bullshitting us, trying to scare us so we'll take him seriously."

Himmets considered this for a moment, then held up a single cartridge between thumb and forefinger. "You're probably right," he said. "But this part," he said, shaking the metal casing, "this part is strange."

They heard more aircraft, which were invisible below the horizon to the south. When it came time to move again, they increased the interval between the vehicles—a step taken when contact with the enemy is imminent—and rolled toward the low growl of the invisible airplanes. In less than thirty minutes, they pulled off the road and onto a dirt track that led into some woods. Sergeant Brufels had one soldier dismount to guide the vehicle through the trees. They pulled into a position that, as far as Gedern could tell, was no different or more significant than any other patch of woods they'd seen—except for the sounds of the aircraft.

Gedern fell asleep with his head resting on the foam pad that lined the edge of the hatch. He was awakened by some voices in the woods ahead of them and came to in time to see a flashlight bobbing through the woods. Behind the flashlight, and only a dozen meters in front of Gedern's vehicle, a car sat with its engine running, its headlights shining toward the hidden platoon.

"Hold on there."

The voice had come from among the platoon's vehicles, out of Gedern's sight. He craned his neck and saw Stoddard, their platoon leader, on foot and moving to meet the man with the light.

Stoddard's flashlight picked out a Bundeswehr captain approaching through the trees. When the man got closer, Gedern recognized him as the regular army's liaison with their unit. He must have followed them from the motor park.

At last, Gedern thought, *someone is going to straighten out these goofy fucking part-timers.*

"These vehicles have been moved illegally and must be returned at once." There was no alarm in his voice; it was more like the officer was struggling to be tolerant of some teenagers he'd caught in a prank, something serious but pardonable.

Gedern noticed that the captain directed his comments to the platoon, which was dispersed in the woods but not invisible. Lieutenant Stoddard walked up to the army officer, picking his way along behind the circle his flashlight threw to the ground. Stoddard held his drawn pistol at his side. The captain was alone.

"I'm under orders to keep these vehicles here and await further instructions," Stoddard said, his breath clouding the cold air. He did not salute or address the captain properly, as Herr Hauptmann.

"And where did those orders come from, Herr Leutnant?" The captain was a good seven or eight inches taller than Stoddard. The tension in his voice had the flavor of exasperation; it was not fear of the little man before him.

"We are going to repel an airborne invasion," Stoddard said, motioning with his head to the clearing behind the bigger man where the automobile sat idling.

Gedern couldn't believe it. The paratroopers—and the sound of the planes made him believe there *were* paratroopers—were landing close by, and here they sat like ambushers, weapons locked and loaded. He looked around him, feeling a tangy bile of panic rise from his stomach, from his groin. Surely he was not the only one who saw how dangerous this was, how this nutcase Stoddard was going to get them in real trouble. But

Gedern could see only the shadows of some of his comrades watching the drama before them.

The captain snorted through his nose, dismissing Stoddard, then stepped past the lieutenant. "You are here because of illegal orders. I am taking charge of this unit."

It's about freaking time, Gedern thought. *Now we can go home and back to bed.*

"You men start those vehicles," the captain continued. "And prepare to return to your base. Where is the platoon sergeant?"

The shot sounded small and inconsequential, not even a car backfiring. The captain stumbled, then turned to face Stoddard, who moved forward and shoved the big man backward. The captain fell, and Stoddard trained his light on the man's face, which registered surprise. Before he knew what he was doing, Gedern had climbed out of his vehicle and approached the prone figure, as did a couple of the others. Then one of the men who'd taken his place beside Stoddard, a mean little sergeant who was new to the unit, skipped forward and kicked the captain hard in the side. The body didn't move. They stood around him for a moment, a group of seven or eight frightened and suddenly confused men half-lit by a couple of flashlights.

Gedern was struck dumb. This was unbelievable, a nightmare. Stoddard was a madman, and all they had to do was seize his weapon and turn him over to the proper authorities, and that would be that. They could all return to what they'd been when the sun set the evening before: law-abiding citizens.

No one moved.

Gedern watched Stoddard, who, for all his imbecility, knew this was a turning point. A mighty bridge lay behind him in flames. At his feet, the old order, in the person of a captain who'd been rousted from his warm bed on a winter night, lay bleeding onto the icy brown leaves of the forest floor. Now was the time to seize the reins.

"Get rid of the car and the body," the lieutenant commanded. Four men moved to do his bidding.

"We have a mission to do," Stoddard said, cocking his thumb back over his shoulder where the sound of airplanes suddenly grew loud again, as if on his cue. There was no trace of fear in his voice, no irony when he added, "*We* will be the saviors of Germany."

3

. . . .

THE FIRST SIGN OF TROUBLE, MARK ISEN WOULD LATER RE-
member, was when he couldn't raise the German exercise controllers on
the radio.

"No sign of them on the ground, either?" Lieutenant Colonel Spano
asked after Isen explained the problem.

"No, sir," Isen said. "They dropped off the DZSO and left."

The Drop Zone Safety Officers, in this case a captain and sergeant first
class from Spano's headquarters who'd flown to Germany on a commercial flight in advance of the main body, were supposed to be on the
ground to vector the planes to the right place.

"And they weren't at the first linkup point, either. But there's supposed
to be another group at the oh-be-jay," Isen said, referring to the mission
objective by its standard abbreviation.

"How about Team Black?" Spano asked.

Team Black was the second command group, made up of the battalion
executive officer and the assistant staff officers, which stood ready to take
over from Spano's Team Gold if the first string should be wiped out. The
XO, heading the advance party, had also arrived in-country a few days
ahead of time with several staff officers to coordinate feeding and sup-
plying the Rangers.

"Nothing from them, either, sir," Isen answered.

"OK, get the word back to Regiment and let's move out. I'll tell the lead company to stay on their toes. Now that we don't have the controllers to run interference for us, I don't want to waltz into some frau's backyard."

Isen passed the word to the battalion communications officer, a Signal Corps major who was part of the staff, to use the satellite linkup to get word to Regimental headquarters, back in the States, that the unit was on the ground and continuing the mission in spite of the glitch. Spano got on the battalion command net and told the commanders of the three rifle companies to move out toward the airfield, some ten kilometers away. When it came time for the command group to move, Isen helped his two radio operators out of the ditch. The young men spent a few seconds adjusting their heavy loads.

"Ready?" he asked.

"Ready, sir. Let's boogie," Sergeant Gamble said.

Isen's place was near the battalion commander, so the two could stay on top of the situation and react to whatever might happen. But Spano was uncomfortable with too many people walking clustered together, so Isen kept a good fifteen meters behind the colonel as they moved. He found that in the moonlight he could see better without the night vision goggles he carried, which threw off his depth perception and limited his peripheral vision. Isen hooked his thumbs into the shoulder straps of his rucksack and leaned into the weight, feeling his body warm with the exertion. They would stop in ten minutes or so to allow the men to remove their outer layer of clothing, otherwise the soldiers would be drenched with sweat, and then would freeze when the unit stopped again.

Isen looked up just as the moon swept from behind a cloud. He could see only two or three men. Even as the operations officer of the battalion, the commander's chief operational advisor and assistant, his scope of immediate control—the men beside him whom he could direct with the sound of his voice—was no greater than it had been when he was a brand-new lieutenant. In fact, the problem was exacerbated here, since he was expected to be able to control the rifle companies comprising the five-hundred-man battalion as tightly as if he could speak to them all. The radios made that possible, but there was a fine art to using electronic wizardry to direct men in extreme circumstances, such as in the pressure of combat. Isen knew a lot of officers who frustrated themselves and their subordinates by trying to make the radio a substitute for direct control, when all it could be was a link to subordinate leaders.

Out in the dark, it came down to trusting the squad leaders and platoon sergeants, the lieutenants and captains who would make it all happen. In the final analysis, it wasn't so much a matter of directing people to do things as it was channeling their efforts. Leaders could point the unit in one direction or another, but success or failure was largely determined

FIREFALL

during the hundreds of hours spent coaching, teaching, guiding on field exercises and on the ranges back at Benning and wherever else the unit trained. If the soldiers didn't learn their task there, then they would be lost when things got hot. If the plan worked, the credit was theirs. If it all fell apart, Spano and Isen would take the blame, and rightly so.

Several hundred meters ahead of where Major Isen mused about the philosophy of control, Private First Class Tim Brennan watched a green-tinted world through the lens of his AN/PVS-7 night vision goggles. His team leader, Sergeant Handy, raised his right hand, palm open, and the fire team stopped. In a routine practiced hundreds of times, the Rangers turned outward, securing the little pie-shaped piece of ground defined by their five-man formation. Brennan had the goggles for this mission because his was the lead team in the lead squad in the lead platoon, out in front of Charlie Company and the whole battalion. The men always took their work seriously when they were out in the woods, moving as carefully as if the next tree might hide an enemy. But tonight the mission was particularly important. Lieutenant Hawkins had told them they were the point of the spear.

Brennan knew exactly what this halt was about, and to confirm it, the soldier just ahead of him dropped his rucksack, peeled off his cold weather parka and stuffed it into the waterproof bag inside the ruck.

There was comfort in the patterns they followed, in the rehearsed and endlessly repeated drills and procedures. And although Tim Brennan felt as if he would never measure up to the demands of this soldier's life, he was able to act well enough, when he knew what was coming, to satisfy almost everyone. Except for himself. And Lieutenant Hawkins.

Before he strapped on the substantial weight of gear that he and his fellow soldiers were obliged to carry, Brennan weighed only a little more than 145 pounds. He stood just under five seven, with the fair skin and pale blue eyes that would have identified him as an Irish American even without the name. His voice tended to the high end of the scale, and it still broke on him from time to time, so that he was never sure, as he opened his mouth, when he was going to sound like a teenager just into puberty.

When he arrived at Fort Benning and his assignment to the Rangers, his First Sergeant had asked why he joined, and Brennan responded—as did many soldiers new to the unit—that he came on board for the adventure. His squad leader at first suspected that Brennan actually had something to prove—to his father, to himself—about his manhood. That had alarmed the NCO because it was a recipe for disaster he'd seen before: young men who joined the Rangers for someone else's approval didn't make good soldiers. The motivation had to come from within. And although Tim Brennan—who had less than his fair share of self-confidence—would

· 39 ·

have been surprised to hear it, the noncoms who watched him struggle to assert himself, however meekly, thought that Brennan's motivation did come from within. The kid wanted to do a good job.

Brennan swung the bulky goggles, scanning the nearby trees for any movement. Although the set weighed just over a pound, it always made him feel as if he had a tremendous head cold, and he moved ponderously, as he imagined a dinosaur might look for food. Except that he could see in the dark, thanks to American technology.

When half the team finished removing a layer of clothes, the other half started. Even out in the cold and dark, Brennan was fairly content. His needs were simple: he wanted to know what was going on, and he did know because they had rehearsed everything they were expected to do on the ground. Every mission they might be called on to perform had been broken down into a series of tasks, whether it was as simple as having the whole unit adjust winter clothes to something as complicated as securing an airfield. Each man had an assigned part, and in training, one practiced that part (and learned the role of others, just in case) until it became a drill.

For the most part, Brennan appreciated this—it gave him a secure feeling knowing that there was a plan originating somewhere echelons above his level. At other times he resented it, since it reduced everything to rote. But whenever he was out in the woods at night, and he could see only the few squad members nearest him, he was glad to know that there were captains and majors and a colonel getting paid to worry about what the mission was and whether they were in the right spot and how fast they should be going. All Brennan had to do was get his parka off, pick up his weapon, and stay alert to what they might walk into.

He knew that in wartime his position would be dangerous—he would be one of the first to walk into the enemy—but that didn't bother him this night. He was content to move along and do his part, hustle and play the game, and daydream about getting into a warm barracks somewhere and digging into a hot meal.

He occupied himself with such daydreams for the rest of the move and during the halt near the edge of the airfield that was the battalion's objective. That stop was longer than it was supposed to be, and Sergeant Handy crawled around to each of his men to tell them what the problem was. The German controllers who were supposed to meet them before the assault on the airfield were not around, and no one seemed to know where they were. But eventually the call came to move again, and Brennan's squad shifted to their blocking position at the north end of the airfield, which lay empty in the moonlight. Brennan could see patches of old snow caught in the fences around the perimeter, but there was no opposing force to fight.

"I don't know what the hell happened to this mission," Sergeant Handy confided to Brennan and a soldier named Charis, Brennan's partner for the two-man fighting positions they were digging.

"Well, the bad guys aren't here, and the controllers aren't here," Charis said. "Maybe we showed up a day early."

Handy chuckled with the two privates. "So I guess you think you'll get to sack out until tomorrow when the real thing goes down, right?"

"Something like that," Charis said.

"Well, that's a no go, cause I'm taking your sidekick here out on a little patrol," Handy said, indicating Brennan. "That means you'll be pulling some wide-eyed security the whole time we're gone. You got that?"

"Yes, Sergeant," Charis said. "Just call me Mister Alert."

Brennan left his rucksack beside the shallow hole that he and Charis had been digging and followed Handy to the next fighting position, then to the squad leader's position, where they got instructions as to where to leave and where to reenter the perimeter as they checked the woods in front of the platoon. Handy had two other men, besides Brennan, with him when the small group moved forward of the platoon line and into the dark woods. Brennan was a few feet behind Handy, stepping lightly through the thin undergrowth, not so much because he thought there was someone out there who might hear them, but because he knew the sergeant would get angry if the soldiers didn't play the game the whole way.

Brennan heard the metallic clank over the sounds of his own breathing. He was so startled that he stopped walking, causing the soldier behind him to stumble into him.

"What the hell?"

Brennan held up his fist. The men behind him froze, but Sergeant Handy, who was in the lead and thus not watching them, kept moving.

"Sergeant Handy," Brennan whispered. Nothing. Brennan took a few long steps forward and touched Handy on the shoulder. When the sergeant turned around, Brennan was about to say that he'd heard something when the sound came again.

Clank.

It was close, too. Twenty, maybe thirty meters away. Brennan dropped to one knee, a little proud that he'd been the one who'd noticed it. But now he wasn't sure what they should do. He wondered if Sergeant Handy would want to go find out what was making the noise or if he'd go back to the platoon or if he'd radio for help. As he wondered how one was supposed to sort out all these choices, Brennan was startled by a voice almost in his ear.

"Sounds like a truck." One of the others, a specialist named Reidt, had crawled up next to where he and Handy were kneeling. "A tailgate or something."

Brennan looked back to where the other man in the patrol lay flat out on the ground, his rifle in front of him in the prone firing position, pointed in the direction of the noise in the woods. It seemed to him that everyone else knew what to do. Brennan got down too.

"No," Sergeant Handy was saying, "it sounds like the hatch on an armored vehicle."

"The OPFOR got tanks?" Reidt asked.

"I think so," Handy said, recalling their briefings on the opposing forces, or OPFOR, for this exercise. "Armored vehicles, anyway. We'd better go check it out."

That's it, Brennan thought. *He just decided. Now how does he know if he's doing the right thing? Did someone tell him to go crawling around after every noise? Don't leave until you make eye contact with anything suspicious out there?*

"Brennan, you come with me," Handy said. "You two," he said to Reidt and the fourth soldier, "stay here. If I'm not back in an hour, you go back to the platoon."

Brennan moved off behind the sergeant, who circled around to the right of where the sound seemed to originate. When Handy got down on all fours, so did Brennan, though he could see nothing beyond his team leader's backside.

Then, suddenly, they were at the edge of a small clearing, and there were two or three men speaking German somewhere ahead of them. Handy moved to one side, and as Brennan came abreast of him, the sergeant pressed his lips almost to Brennan's ear.

"See it?"

Brennan strained. Both men wore their night vision goggles, but Brennan was having a hard time making out anything among the trees. Then he saw the clear horizontal line that defined the deck of an armored vehicle some thirty meters in front of them. He nodded excitedly.

"Those guys we hear must be on the other side," Handy whispered. "Let's move up some."

Brennan turned to face Handy, bumping his headset into his team leader's.

"Watch where you're going," Handy said. "OK, you know what we're looking for, right?"

Brennan hesitated. He was ready to follow Handy anywhere, but the sergeant, true to form, was making the most of his chance to train his men to think like leaders.

"Uh . . ."

"Acronym, Brennan."

"SALUTE, Sergeant," Brennan said, recalling the guideline for information sought in a reconnaissance: size, activity, location, unit, time, equipment.

Brennan hated stumbling in front of Handy, who seemed, to the young PFC, the model soldier.

He could feel his heart against his ribs, hear it against his eardrums, and he realized he was holding his breath. He had to remind himself that this was a game, this wasn't the real thing. No one out here wanted to hurt them. *This could even be fun*, Brennan told himself. He followed Handy again, lifting his hands and knees and imagining himself a big cat stalking prey. Quiet.

Handy stretched out flat under a low bush, sliding effortlessly, noiselessly into the perfect position. When Brennan tried to squeeze in, he snapped a tiny branch. He contented himself with staying a few feet back.

Yeah, this is pretty cool, Brennan thought. *We got the drop on these guys.* It was quite possible, he allowed, that he was too much of a worrier. He'd been told, by his father, by teachers, and coaches and, in his short time in the Army, by nearly every NCO he'd had contact with, that he needed to be more assertive. All that prompting was one reason he'd joined the Rangers in the first place, thinking that by associating with forceful, confident men, he might himself become one. So far, it hadn't worked out all that well. He was still pretty much of a subdued loner, and putting himself in a group where the young men tended to be loud and aggressive only made him seem more quiet by comparison. He didn't fit in, but he was determined to do a good job.

Handy backed out from under the bush. "Marder," he said.

"What's that?" Brennan asked.

"German Marder, like our Bradley."

"Oh." As Handy ticked off the details that fit the SALUTE format, Brennan concentrated hard, knowing that he'd be quizzed by the sergeant when they returned to the platoon.

The two GIs moved in a low crouch for a few meters, not in the direction they'd come from, but on another route back to link up with the other two Rangers. Brennan was looking down, trying not to step on anything that would make noise, when he heard something in front. He looked up, past Handy's shoulder, and saw a man standing not more than fifteen feet away. Handy was looking down. The other man—Brennan could see him clearly in his night vision goggles—was armed with an assault rifle and had frozen, as if he'd heard the two Americans.

Brennan's voice seized in his throat and he didn't know whether to warn Handy—who was walking straight toward the apparition—or keep quiet and hope they could pass. In the second of hesitation, the other man acted. He must have caught some dim glimpse of the Rangers and been frightened, perhaps, by the grotesque outline they presented with the Cyclops shape of the night vision goggles on their heads. The other man turned to run, but in liquid slowness, Brennan saw that the rifle was still pointing at Handy.

The muzzle flash was incredibly bright in the darkness, magnified by the goggles to a frightening intensity that made Brennan crouch forward. Instinctively, he brought his hands up to his face, smashing the goggles against the bridge of his nose. The green field of vision was now somewhere up on his forehead, and nothing was clear except for the short choppy moans, like pain being sucked inward, that came from somewhere out in front of him.

Then Brennan was on the ground, the goggles hanging from their strap around his neck. He'd dropped his weapon and he scrambled to find it, diving forward and coming up with a mouthful of dirt and wet leaves. He fell across the stock of the rifle, knowing that he should shoot at the retreating shadow but that he had only blanks. The weapon was muzzle down and by the time he turned it around and got his glove-thickened finger into the trigger guard there was no sound but those moans and a rustling on the forest floor just beyond where he knelt.

"Fuck, shit, fucking, shitting, mother*fucker!*"

The voice was Sergeant Handy's, but then again it was not. It belonged to some tortured twin.

"Sergeant Handy?" Brennan said.

"The motherfucker *shot* me," Handy said, gaining some control over his voice, bringing it down.

Brennan reached for his flashlight. Handy slapped it away.

"Don't turn that thing on. You want them to come out here and get us?" he seethed.

Get us? Brennan thought. *This is incredible.*

Clearly the exercise was over. He had go get Handy back to the perimeter and get the controllers to yank those crazy bastards from the OPFOR.

"Live ammo," Brennan stuttered. "He had live ammo."

"No shit, he had live fucking ammo," Handy said. "And I'm not going to give him a chance to come back here and use it again."

The sergeant was tearing at the compress strapped to the suspenders of his load-bearing equipment. Brennan reached down and helped him.

"I saw him standing there," Brennan said. "He was listening, like he heard us, maybe. Next thing I know, he's turned around, ready to run, but he shoots first."

"You saw him?" Handy asked.

Brennan, jolted by adrenaline, didn't catch the drift of the question.

"Yeah." He looked down at Handy, but the sergeant's face was unreadable in the darkness. "Where're you hit?" Brennan asked.

"Hip," Handy said. "Right hip."

Brennan's goggles were still useless—the muzzle flash blanked the viewers—and would be for a few minutes. He struggled to apply the dressing, looking for the dark hole in Handy's jacket whenever the moon slid out from behind a cloud, while Handy watched for the shooter, who might return at any minute. "What'll I do if he comes back?" Brennan asked.

Handy, still in charge, didn't hesitate. "Put your bayonet on your rifle. If the bastard comes back, run him through."

Brennan moved as if in a dream, reaching down to the scabbard, unsheathing the blade and fixing it to the muzzle of his weapon. He couldn't imagine using it to stab someone.

"C'm'on, let's get the hell out of here."

Incredibly, Handy was on his feet, one arm pressed tightly against his side, his rifle unfamiliar in his left hand. He stepped off again, and Brennan took a quick look around to see if they were being followed.

I wasn't much help there, Brennan thought. He wanted to make up for his slow reactions by being more careful than ever to watch for pursuers, but the constant pirouetting to look behind them just slowed Handy down.

"C'mon, Brennan," Handy said. "Let's get the lead out and get the hell out of here."

Paul Gedern was asleep in the driver's seat of his vehicle when the shot woke him. He jerked his head up, bumping it hard against the steel rim of the hatch. He pushed the hatch cover up with his hands and peered out, wondering, as he did so, if what he'd heard was another gunshot. A soldier he recognized from one of the other platoons came running out of the woodline just a few meters away from Gedern's position. In a flash, the platoon leader and platoon sergeant, as well as a couple of other NCOs, were on the man.

Gedern was frightened. Normally, no one carried live ammunition. Now there was too much of it around, and too many people willing to use it.

A few minutes later, Lieutenant Stoddard made his way from vehicle to vehicle down the line, talking to the track commanders over the heads of the drivers. Gedern knew what was coming: a lecture on safety and responsibility. He was just thinking about what a dolt Stoddard was when the platoon leader reached their vehicle. Sergeant Brufels was in the commander's hatch, up above Gedern's head and just out of sight.

"They're out there," Stoddard said. "Goetz exchanged shots with them."

Gedern couldn't contain himself. "Exchanged shots? I heard only one shot," he said.

Stoddard had both hands on the front edge of the Marder's steel hull.

He hadn't been talking to Gedern and didn't seem to appreciate Gedern's intrusion, but was unsure of what to say.

"You were asleep," Brufels called down from the commander's hatch. "You couldn't have heard everything."

Gedern could say nothing to this. He had been sleeping. But he wasn't about to give up.

4

WHEN LIEUTENANT KEN HAWKINS HEARD THE DISTANT POP of a gunshot, his first thought was that one of his men had smuggled live ammunition on the exercise, a not unprecedented move that could get a platoon leader relieved.

"What the hell?" the soldier beside him said.

Hawkins was checking the positioning of his platoon's machine guns when the report rolled down on him through the cold air. Then he was on his feet and moving to the sound of the fire so quickly that Keefer, his radio operator, lost sight of him.

Hawkins quickly found Sergeant Bishop's position, which he'd left moments before.

"What was that?" Hawkins asked.

Bishop was trying to raise Sergeant Handy on the squad radio, a small, off-the-shelf-technology version of a policeman's walkie-talkie.

"Sergeant Handy took three men out to check the woodline," Bishop said. "Next thing I know, I hear this shot, and I can't get him on the radio."

Bishop looked up at the lieutenant. "You called the CO yet, sir?" he asked. The CO was the commanding officer. In Charlie Company, that meant Captain Dettering, Hawkins's immediate superior. Even if the old man didn't hear the shot, Hawkins knew that he had to let Dettering know what was happening.

At that moment, Hawkins realized he didn't know where Keefer, his radio operator, was.

"Shit."

Captain Dettering had given him an imaginative chewing out on the last field problem for getting away from his radio. What had started off as a successful movement—Hawkins had led the battalion to the right point at the right time—was quickly falling apart. If he'd heard the shot, Dettering was already on the horn asking for a report.

Hawkins looked at his watch. It had been less than two minutes since he'd heard the shot. Time to act.

There is a saying held in high esteem at the Infantry School (in spite of its ungrammatical nature), which is taught to all leaders who wear crossed rifles: Don't Do Nothing. When time and circumstances call for action, leaders act.

Unfortunately, the aphorism makes no provision for bad judgment.

"We need to go out there and get them," Hawkins said.

"I think we should give them another couple of minutes," Bishop said. "Keep trying on the radio."

But Hawkins was already on his feet. "Send a man with me," he said.

"Right away, Lieutenant," Bishop said. "I'll send a man to look for Keefer, also."

Hawkins, already moving into the woodline, missed the sarcasm. Bishop picked two soldiers from the positions just next to his and sent them after the lieutenant. "Just stick with him," he told them. "Don't get lost, and don't get shot."

Keefer showed up a few minutes later, blowing hard.

"Is Lieutenant Hawkins here?" he asked Bishop.

"You just missed him," Bishop said. "He took off into the woods." Bishop took the handset from Keefer, knowing that he had to notify Captain Dettering. As he was composing his report, Sergeant Handy and his three men came out of the woodline down at one end of the platoon area.

Mark Isen passed the radio handset back to Gamble and jogged a few steps to catch up to Colonel Spano, who was practically running toward the Charlie Company sector.

"Dettering will meet us behind his company," Isen said. "He got a sitrep a few minutes ago from one of the squad leaders: the team leader who went out on the recon, Sergeant Handy, has a flesh wound in the hip. He was shot by somebody he thinks was a German soldier."

"He hurt bad?" Spano asked.

"Not too, apparently. He made it back pretty much under his own power." Isen paused to catch his breath. "What the hell could be going on with the OPFOR, that they're shooting live rounds?"

Spano went on for a few meters, as if he couldn't comprehend the question. "Probably just some nut with live ammo," he said at last.

"We got another problem, too, sir," Isen said. "Hawkins is out in the woods with two soldiers, looking for this patrol that already made it back."

"Did Dettering call him back?" Spano said.

"That's the problem. Hawkins took off without his radio operator," Isen said.

"Jesus H. Christ," Spano said.

Isen knew that Hawkins had done the same thing not a month before, but he didn't say anything to Spano, who probably didn't know. Isen was more concerned with what they were going to do with a wounded soldier. Ordinarily, the controllers on the ground would have ambulances ready to evacuate any injured jumpers. But since Isen hadn't been able to raise the controllers, and there was no sign of them at the objective, he was temporarily at a loss.

Captain Bill Dettering, the Charlie Company commander, met them on the open slope just below the end of the runway, behind his company strong point in the woods at the north end of the airstrip.

"How's your wounded man?" Spano asked him.

"Very lucky, sir," Dettering said. "The bullet missed hitting any bone and passed through about two inches of flesh, mostly on his butt, on its way out. My medic has the bleeding under control and there should be no problem moving him."

"Soon as we find an ambulance," Isen said.

"So who the hell is doing the shooting up here?" Spano demanded.

"Sergeant Handy said that he and one of his men spotted a German Marder in the woods about six, seven hundred meters in front of our position," Dettering explained. He got down on the ground and held a hooded, red-filtered flashlight over a map of the objective area. "Right around here." He took off one glove and pointed.

"OPFOR?" Spano asked. The question was directed at Isen.

"The opposing forces for the exercise are supposed to be on the same frequency the controllers would be using. But nobody's up on that net," Isen said.

"But they're supposed to have Marders, right?" Dettering asked. "They're mech guys, aren't they?"

"Yeah, they're mech guys, but that doesn't explain the shooting," Isen said.

"Maybe the guy who shot Handy wasn't supposed to be out there," Dettering offered. "Maybe he was a civilian or something."

Spano stood up, clicking off his pocket flashlight. "Well, if we can't get them on the radio, there's only one way to talk to them," he said. Then to Dettering, "Let me have the guys who were out there with Handy. I'm going out to make face-to-face contact with these people."

Isen looked up from the map. "We could wait until it got light, sir," he said. "If there's some trigger-happy German out there, why take a chance on startling him again in the dark?"

"I'm not going to startle anybody," Spano said. "I'm going to be shouting at them all the way up to the side of their track. If they shoot me, it won't be an accident."

As they waited for Charlie Company to round up the soldiers, Spano went to the company command post, or CP, to check on the wounded Sergeant Handy. When they were alone, Isen spoke to Dettering. "Hawkins still out there?"

"Roaming around with no radio," Dettering said, venom in his tone.

"He's been out there—what?—twenty minutes?" Isen said. "He'll get back."

When the three soldiers who'd been with Handy drew close, Spano came up out of the woodline.

"Which one of you can lead me and Major Isen back to this vehicle you saw?"

Guess I'll be tagging along, Isen thought.

The men hesitated. "Well," one of them said after a moment, "I'm the only one who really saw the thing, sir. These other guys didn't come all the way forward with us."

The soldier who spoke was on the small side, and even if he hadn't been whispering, as he was supposed to do out in the dark, Isen guessed that his voice would have been quiet.

"Did you get a look at the guy who shot Sergeant Handy?" Spano pressed.

"No, sir. I mean, yes, sir. I saw him standing there, but I couldn't see his face or anything. I thought he was with the others, but I really couldn't tell. I lost him when he ran away."

"After the shooting?"

"Yes, sir. Well, actually, he started running before he pulled the trigger. He kind of turned away but left his weapon pointing forward for a second. That's when he pulled the trigger."

"What's your name, son?" Spano asked.

"Private First Class Brennan, sir." His voice was even, but he was clearly shaken up by the events of the last hour.

"OK, Brennan," Spano said, stepping up to the paratrooper and slapping him lightly on the shoulder. "Let's go on up and see what the problem is with these people."

Isen left his radio operators with Dettering, instructing them to let the other company commanders in the battalion know what was going on at this end of the airstrip. He and Spano walked ahead of the battalion commander's radio men, with the still-jittery Brennan just a few steps in front of them. Spano had an interpreter of sorts, a young Ranger from

Bravo Company who, as the son of a career soldier, had attended high school in Germany and claimed to speak the language fairly well.

They moved away from the Charlie Company positions, down a gentle slope where the trees thinned out. Isen figured there'd probably be a streambed or a road at the bottom. When they'd traveled about five hundred meters, Brennan held up his hand. Spano and Isen approached him.

"We're within a hundred meters or so, sir," Brennan said.

"Good, good," Spano said. He touched Brennan's arm. "You're doing fine." Then he turned to Isen and explained his plan.

A few minutes later, Mark Isen and the Bravo Company Ranger, a strapping twenty-year-old named Haslem, were crouched behind a cluster of thin, leafless trees while Lieutenant Colonel Spano stood a few meters away.

"OK," Isen told Haslem.

"*Achtung,*" Haslem called. "*Nicht schiessen! Wir sind amerikanische Soldaten, auf einer Uebung mit der deutschen Bundeswehr. Einer von unseren Soldaten ist verletzt.*"

At first there was no response, and Isen wondered if Brennan had been able to duplicate the movement he'd made with Handy. Isen guessed that after the shooting, if not before, the Germans would have men out on the ground to protect their position. But it could be that the Germans had moved off; or it could be that Haslem's German wasn't all that great. Then there was a stirring up ahead, a whispered conversation.

"*Zeigen Sie sich!*" the voice called.

Haslem leaned around Isen so that Spano could hear him. "They want us to show ourselves, Colonel," Haslem said.

"Tell them I will if no one shoots at us," Spano said.

Haslem translated. More hurried conversation, then a different voice. "*Sie sind ausser Gefahr.*"

"Here goes nothing," Spano said. He stood up and turned on the flashlight hooked to his suspenders.

If they want us dead, they've got at least one of us, Isen thought.

"*Hierherkommen.*"

"They want you to come forward, sir," Haslem whispered loudly.

"Ask them who they are," Spano said.

"*Wer sind Sie?*

"*Wir sind von dem Territorialen Kommando,*" the voice came back. "*Wir sind mit dem Schutz dieses Gebietes beauftragt.*"

"They're Territorial soldiers," Haslem said. "The other was something about keeping the area, no, protecting the area, the land or something."

Spano seemed satisfied, and he began to walk forward.

For an instant, Isen was struck by the absolute lunacy of what they were doing. He had expected to be maneuvering the battalion against a notional enemy under the control of umpires from the German Army. Instead, he was hiding in the dark and the cold, as if trying to surrender, wondering if, in the next few seconds, he would see his battalion commander get killed.

Spano had gone no more than ten meters or so when two or three more lights appeared in the woods. There were men around him, talking loudly in German and shining their flashlights on the American colonel. Things were getting hairy and Isen couldn't sit still any longer.

"You stay here, Haslem. If I call for you, come down there. If something bad goes down, you beat feet back to call Captain Dettering. Tell him to circle the wagons and start calling for help. Then you get back inside the position, you hear?"

"Yessir."

Haslem sounded calm enough, but in the little light available, Isen could see the wide disks of the soldier's eyes. He didn't want to be left alone, and he didn't want to go down to deal with the guys who might be shooting live ammo.

"Pretty weird shit, huh?" Isen said.

The levity worked. Haslem snorted a small laugh. "I'll back you up, sir."

"I'm counting on it."

By the time Isen reached Spano's side, the Germans had figured out that Spano didn't speak their language. There was a short junior officer, a lieutenant, Isen thought, haranguing Spano in English.

"We understand exactly what is going on, Herr Colonel," the lieutenant was saying. "You are here illegally. You think that your history of occupation gives you the right to do anything you wish."

"What the hell are you talking about?" Spano said, his voice rising.

However stressed they were by the *Alice in Wonderland* quality of the last few hours, Isen figured that he and Spano were in no position to get in anyone's face. He knew somehow that the lieutenant was baiting Spano, trying to get him to lose his temper. And it was working.

"We are here at the invitation of the federal government, and have coordinated this exercise with the proper authorities in the Bundeswehr," Isen said as evenly as he could. He kept his eyes on the lieutenant, who'd tilted his head back so that he was looking up at Isen along the line of his nose.

"Who are you?" the German demanded.

"I am Major Isen, the operations officer for the U.S. Army Rangers sitting right through those woods."

Isen got a reaction with that. The two men standing beside the lieutenant stepped back and peered at the black wall of trees, as if they expected a bayonet charge at any moment.

"And who are you?" Spano said. He'd gained control of his temper and was on the offensive.

"I am Leutnant Stoddard, Kommando der Territorialen Verteidigung, and this is my platoon." He waved one hand behind him, where Isen noticed for the first time that there was a large armored vehicle, probably the Marder Handy had spotted, in the trees farther on down the slope.

"The rest of my company is dispersed throughout this area, also," Stoddard added.

"One of my men was shot here about an hour ago, *Leutnant*," Spano said, emphasizing the man's rank. "Can you explain that to me?"

Stoddard tilted his head back again to give Spano that odd gaze, and Isen wondered for a moment if the German was nearsighted. "You are here illegally," he said, letting his right hand rest on the hilt of his pistol. "We don't want you here."

Behind Stoddard, the two other soldiers shuffled uncomfortably, looking now at the woodline, now at the Americans. Isen estimated the distance to the little officer, wondering if he could disarm the man if the German decided to pull the weapon. He was just about to demand an ambulance when another figure came up behind the German soldiers.

"Kehren Sie zu Ihren Fahrzeugen zurueck."

The two soldiers standing beside Stoddard were startled by what was, judging by the tone in which it was delivered, a command. Isen watched them recede into the darkness, back in the direction of the vehicle in the woods. Another figure came into the uncertain light of the flashlights. He was taller than Stoddard and Isen, and older than the lieutenant. Isen couldn't see his rank but it didn't take much to figure out who was in charge.

"Why are you even bothering talking to these men, Leutnant?"

Stoddard took his hand off his weapon, looking for a moment as if he might say something. Instead, he turned back and stared at the Americans. The new arrival turned his attention to Isen and Spano and addressed them in nearly unaccented English.

"So, you are the intruders."

"I am Lieutenant Colonel Spano, commander of the Third Battalion of U.S. Army Rangers, and we are here at the invitation—"

"And I say you are intruders," the other man interrupted. Isen could see his shoulder boards now: three black pips of a captain, or Hauptmann.

"You are here illegally, and that makes you invaders, infringing on German sovereignty." There was no trace of excitement in his voice, no anger. He was merely stating the facts, as calmly as one might correct a misguided student.

"That's ridiculous," Spano said. "Our countries have been allies for fifty years, *Captain*."

The reminder of rank had no effect on this German officer.

"Your country was allied with the puppet government in Berlin, but all that is about to come to an end."

Spano turned to Isen in exasperation. "Do you know what the hell he's talking about?"

Isen couldn't have been more lost had he been asked to translate Greek. He shrugged, feeling as if he'd let Spano down somehow. Maybe they should change tacks.

"One of your men shot and wounded one of my soldiers," Isen said. "Our man needs medical attention."

The German captain turned to Stoddard, who looked helplessly lost.

"Your soldiers opened fire on my men, who were merely defending themselves," the German captain said.

Spano stepped toward the German, as if to give his response forward momentum. "That's bullshit." He spit the words out, and Isen knew that the colonel was holding back a string of oaths that would normally mark this kind of flare-up.

He wasn't exactly sure what triggered it, but some sort of dull alarm tripped in Isen's head. He had a brief glimpse—like seeing your opponent's next few chess moves—of what the Germans were trying to do.

"Colonel," he said to Spano, tugging at his boss's sleeve. Spano was still leaning forward. *"Sir,"* Isen said, grabbing Spano by the arm and pulling him back a few feet.

"They don't know that we're not carrying ammo," he whispered in Spano's ear.

Spano showed the Germans no reaction, but played the scene out perfectly.

"Look, Captain—what's your name?"

"Schrebel. Hauptmann Schrebel."

"Yes, well, Captain Schrebel," Spano said, removing his helmet and lowering his voice out of the range of confrontation. "I have a man who is in need of medical attention. That is my first concern as a commander. I'm sure you can understand that. Why don't we get that straightened out first?"

"Agreed, Herr Colonel. It will be light soon, and I will be getting further instructions about this situation. Why not bring your man to the road that runs down this way from the east side of the airstrip, and I will arrange to have him evacuated to a hospital."

"I would appreciate that. Then I would like to meet you, or your superior, perhaps at that same spot, later on this morning," Spano said.

"Once I receive instructions from my superiors, I will let you know how we will proceed," Schrebel said pointedly. Then, softening a bit, he added, "I'm sure we can work this out."

Spano put his helmet back on his head and buttoned the chin strap. "I'm sure," he said.

He hesitated a second, and Isen thought he was waiting for Schrebel and Stoddard to salute, which they didn't. Then he turned and headed back up the hill.

"I wouldn't have returned their fucking salutes anyway," he said to Isen when the two of them were a few meters away. "Let's get on the satellite link and find out what the story is with these people."

Captain Schrebel watched the two Americans disappear into the woods, which were just beginning to lighten with the approaching dawn.

"I don't think they're armed," he said out loud.

"Sir?"

He turned to Stoddard, who stood with his perpetual look of bafflement.

"I don't believe they have ammunition, live ammunition, for their weapons. That is why the major pulled his commander away."

Schrebel looked back to the woods.

"And that is why this gamble is a good one. They are at our mercy. In a few hours we will have our forces in position and we will demand their surrender."

"Should I call for an ambulance, Herr Hauptmann?" Stoddard asked.

"No. Send a military vehicle to pick up the American. And make sure he is treated as a prisoner of war."

"Yes, sir."

5

· · · · · · · · · · ·

MAJOR MARK ISEN WATCHED TINY BUBBLES FORM ON THE inside of his canteen cup, which meant the water was finally warming, though it was far from boiling. He rocked forward from his squatting position onto his knees to peer at the small chemical fuel tablet, called a heat tab, that burned beneath the cup. The tab was almost gone.

"Not gonna get any warmer than that, I guess," he said to no one in particular.

He tore open the pouch of hot cocoa mix, as well as the instant coffee, creamer, and sugar that came with his MRE, or Meal, Ready to Eat, and dumped them in the tepid water. The mixture lumped together on the surface, resisting his efforts to mix it.

"I think it's getting colder," Sergeant Gamble said, looking up at the sky. Gamble sat a few feet away, holding the handset from his radio, idly watching Isen. He was waiting for the promised response from Ranger Regimental headquarters back at Fort Benning. The signal platoon had set up the portable satellite link, a small radio connected to a folding dish that resembled a spiny, stripped umbrella. The two men on this rig were at the other end of the airstrip, and they would call Gamble as soon as they got something.

To Isen had fallen the responsibility of reporting that they had evacuated a man with a gunshot wound. He had explained the odd encounter in the woods to three different people, ending with the Regimental adjutant. Even then, the best they could do was tell Isen to wait while the Regimental Commander—who was out in the field observing training— was notified and the staff back at Benning tried to figure out what had happened to the controllers and Team Black, and if there was any truth to the fantastic claims made by the German officers Spano had encountered in the woods.

"I think there's a cold front moving in today," Isen said. The weather forecast had been part of the operations order he'd issued to the company commanders. "It'd be unusual for this part of the country, but we might even get some snow tonight."

Gamble groaned. The tall, extremely thin Gamble—who reminded Isen of a black Ichabod Crane—was a Florida native with a near fanatic hatred of cold weather.

"Then we better catch some z's during the day, sir," Gamble said, smiling. " 'Cause I'll be up all night walking around, trying to keep my ass warm."

Gamble's radio sputtered a bit, and the sergeant immediately put the handset to his ear. Isen stood and walked over to listen, but all Gamble had to say was, "Roger, out."

"It wasn't the call from the States, sir," Gamble said. "That was Charlie Company. They said Major Hallam just came walking down the road from where those German vehicles are parked. He's coming down here now."

Hallam, the battalion's liaison officer, had traveled with the executive officer to Europe a week before the jump to work out with the Germans the details that were necessary for an operation such as Solid Steel.

"This is getting too weird," Isen said. "Maybe he'll be able to tell us what the hell is going on."

He sent a runner down to the Alpha Company area, where Colonel Spano was checking the position and telling the soldiers everything he knew about their situation, which wasn't much.

A few moments later, Hallam came out of the woodline about a hundred meters from the battalion command post, walking fast, eating up the distance with nervous strides. When Isen stood and waved, he began to jog forward, his hands on the straps of his rucksack, elbows tucked into his sides.

"You OK, Pete?" Isen asked when Hallam got closer. Hallam's eyes were red-rimmed, his face unshaven.

"Shit," Hallam said, ignoring Isen's question. "I heard that they shot one of our guys."

"Yeah, somebody did. Sergeant Handy, from Charlie Company," Isen said. "He'll be OK. They picked him up a couple of hours ago, him and one of the medics, to take him to a hospital."

Hallam seemed to be only half-listening. His eyes skipped back and forth, trying to watch everything at once. "Mark, I don't know what the hell is going on out there," he said.

"Hold on." Isen looked around for Colonel Spano, who was approaching from the opposite direction. "Hang on to the story so you don't have to repeat it."

Isen went to his ruck and got out a small spiral ring notebook. He'd been thinking about the lengthy investigations that were sure to follow this incident, and he was determined to be as prepared as possible to give his version of things.

"Pete, glad to see you're back in one piece," Spano said as he approached his subordinates.

"I'm glad to be back, sir," Hallam said, although there was no relief in his voice. His agitation was apparent, and Spano looked at Isen, as if for an explanation. Isen shrugged.

"So who are the guys in the woods?" Spano asked.

"They're Territorial Forces, sir," Hallam said. "Kind of like the National Guard back home." Hallam swallowed once, pulled at his scarf. "They say we're invaders."

To Isen it looked like Hallam had somehow gotten the idea that all the problems they were having were his fault, as if something he'd done wrong in his coordinating meetings had brought on this whole mess.

"Yeah, I heard all that stuff," Spano said. "What's the real story?"

"It's hard to tell, sir," Hallam said. "Everything was going fine until we were getting ready to position the drop zone safety party. Some of the Territorials came and took me with them to a local base, an armory or something, and wouldn't let me go out, wouldn't let me make any calls. The XO and the other guys from Team Black were there, too. They treated us pretty well, but the XO was calling them ten kinds of motherfucker for interfering. We weren't allowed to call anyone, and we sure weren't going anywhere."

Hallam took a drink from his canteen. His hands were shaking.

"Then, last night, they came and got me. Brought me out here. I think they had some sort of split between the regular army and these guys," Hallam went on. "I do know that these guys are pissed off—at us, at the government in Berlin, at lots of things. They kept hammering at me, telling me they're serious about taking their country back, Germany for Germans, that kind of stuff." He looked up and met Isen's eyes, then Spano's. "They got a shitload of ammo out there, and I think they knew what they were doing when they let me see it. They sure look like they're getting ready for the real thing."

"What else did you see?" Isen said, holding out his map of the area. "Show me on here."

"I was blindfolded just before they brought me in," Hallam said. "They drove me in a car . . . I think it was along here." He put his finger on

Highway 71 from Bremervörde. "They made us get out to get blindfolded and walk in the last little bit. But I saw some stuff over here." He touched the map uncertainly. "I saw at least four Marders back in the trees, some sort of big wheeled vehicle, like a recon car with a machine gun, and some trucks, one fuel truck, maybe two or three others. At least one of the trucks had ammunition on board."

"How many soldiers?" Spano asked.

"A platoon in here," Hallam said. He'd taken a pen from his pocket and was pointing with its tip. The talking was calming him, and he concentrated on making good estimates as to what the Rangers were facing.

"I heard some other guys off in this direction, too." He traced a line that curved around the Charlie Company strongpoint at the north end of the airfield.

"So they're at least covering our strongpoints," Spano said.

Isen watched Spano, bent over the map, studying what was now a tactical problem. Except that this was no longer an exercise. The Germans—whoever they were—showed every sign of deadly seriousness. The Americans, dressed for mock battle, had no ammunition. Isen and the others were completely at the mercy of whatever the other side wanted to do.

Spano must have been thinking along the same lines.

"Mark, I want to send some stuff back to the States," Spano said. He sat down on the ground and looked off into the woodline.

"First thing, tell them everything that Pete here just told us. Especially about his being held against his will, blindfolded, all that."

"Yessir," Isen said.

"Then I want you to work up a request for an immediate airmobile operation to get all of us out of here. They'll have to bring the helicopters up from down south, maybe Frankfurt, and that may take a while. Unless we can get the Brits or the French to bail us out."

Isen nodded as he wrote. There was a time when American military compounds dotted the whole German countryside, and a call for help could have been answered easily.

"Don't forget to get them to check into what's going on with Sergeant Handy, the XO, the guys from Team Black, the controllers."

"Right."

"And then I want you to work up a request for an ammunition drop."

Isen stopped writing for a moment and looked up. Spano met his gaze.

"In case we have to fight our way out of here," the colonel said.

6

THERE WERE THREE MEN ON THE SIDEWALK OUTSIDE THE OF-
fice building across from the Hauptbahnhof, Bremen's ornate train station, and a fourth in a car at the curb. George Rhone, a major currently
detailed to the Heeresnachtrichtendienst, army military intelligence,
drove past his usual parking space, across the cobblestone square in front
of the station, and pulled to the side of the busy street. Rhone shared an
office in the building with three other intelligence officers, all of them in
Bremen to monitor the activities of the German People's Union. Specifically, the officers were there to gather intelligence on the reported mach-
inations of that party to gain control of the Territorial Forces based in
northern Germany.

Over the past five weeks the staff had pieced together an alarming
picture of a political party determined to have its own military force.
Rhone had drafted and redrafted several memoranda for his boss, a full
colonel—Oberst—named Martle, to send to the Ministry of Defense in
Berlin, warning of GPU agitation in the ranks of the Territorial Forces.
Rhone's boss, a conservative fourth-generation soldier, had sent the papers back to Rhone each time with instructions to modify and temper the
language of the report. Rhone did as he was told, more and more convinced that Martle and his forebears had lasted so long in the military
profession because they never did anything worth noticing.

Rhone left his car at the curb and backtracked a full block before entering a small cafe to use the public phone. He dialed the office number, which rang only once.

"Oberst Martle."

Rhone listened for a few seconds for the almost imperceptible click, beep, or buzz that would mean someone else was listening.

"It is Major Rhone, Herr Oberst."

"Rhone, where are you?"

Rhone considered the question, decided that there might be someone listening after all.

"I'm at home, sir," Rhone lied. "I made it a few blocks, then my car broke down."

"Listen, George," Martle said. "They're on to us. The GPU sent some men here this morning to shut us down. They're waiting to pick up you and the others when you show up this morning."

"And you're able to talk?" Rhone asked.

"They're not in my office, and the idiots didn't do anything about the phone."

"Are they making their move now?" Rhone asked.

"It looks that way from here," Martle answered.

Rhone chewed his lip, wondering how much he wanted to talk about the situation on this phone line, wondering, quite suddenly, if he should have trusted Martle all along.

"Look, George," Martle went on, "you and I had some disagreements about this, about how far they would go."

The colonel paused, and for a moment Rhone thought the older man might apologize.

"But I don't want you to fly off the handle now," Martle said. "Don't be an alarmist."

Rhone was astounded. "Sir, you said that men showed up there this morning and detained you in your office. And they're waiting for the rest of us as well."

Rhone heard a brittle tremor of indignation in his voice and took a breath before he continued. "What kind of sign do we need that these people are serious about taking over the government?"

"I hardly think that entering our office constitutes a full-scale coup, Herr Rhone," Martle said, laughing a bit and switching to that silky smooth, there's-nothing-to-be-alarmed-about voice that insisted there was never any trouble, never anything worth upsetting the Ministry of Defense. Rhone had met the same frustrating stumbling block when he raised the alarm about the transfer of armored forces to the Territorials some months back.

"For all we know, they've done nothing else but detain us for questioning," Martle continued. "There are no signs of widespread challenges to the government."

"They have no right to detain anyone," Rhone said, his voice sharp with anger. "They are not officers of the law, are they?"

"No," Martle answered.

Rhone was about to say that as far as he could determine, the GPU had in mind a broad campaign to undermine the government in Berlin—he'd written an extensive information paper on the plans—when it occurred to him that Martle might order him to come in, or keep quiet, or return to Berlin.

"We must not overreact," Martle said again, his voice pleasant.

Rhone looked out the window of the shop to where two of the men from the sidewalk were checking his parked car. While Colonel Martle was telling him to keep calm, the GPU was looking for him. Rhone believed that the GPU knew that he had uncovered a great deal about their most secret activities. While Martle, with his natural predilection to downplay every threat, might be useful to them—assuring Berlin that there was no cause for concern—Rhone's knowledge of their plans was dangerous. Their cause would be better served if he was not around to spread the alarm.

"I must go, Herr Colonel," Rhone said into the phone. He could hear Martle's small voice still talking as he placed the receiver back on its hook.

Rhone stood away from the glass as he watched, through the front window, the two men circle his car. The automobile was rented, part of his cover while he worked in Bremen; but if they knew his car, they no doubt knew where he was staying.

"Do you have a back door?" he asked the proprietor, an old woman who looked him up and down. Rhone's *hochdeutsch*, his high-German accent, and the absence of a local, north German accent stuck out here and gave him away as a cosmopolitan, an educated man. Nevertheless, the woman turned one chubby wrist outward, indicating with her thumb the door to the kitchen.

Rhone thanked the woman and took his time walking behind the counter and into the steamy back room. The door let out on an alley, which he followed for several meters before finding another alley at a right angle that led him out onto the parallel street. Rhone found a cab and, dismissing the idea of returning to his hotel room—which might also be watched—he told the Turkish driver to take him north, out of Bremen along the highway that led to Bremerhaven and the North Sea.

They had gone only a few kilometers out of the city when Rhone told the driver to leave the autobahn. After driving for a few hundred meters on an intersecting road, Rhone had the driver turn around on the median strip. He watched out the back window to see if any other cars did the same thing. Satisfied that no one was following him, or at least that there was no tail right behind him, Rhone had the driver let him off on a side street, where he found another pay telephone. He dialed a number that would ring in Berlin, in the Ministry of Defense.

Rhone had to tell his story several times, repeating it for officers up the chain of command. Finally, Brigadier General Holtzen, who had overall responsibility for the mission in Bremen, got on the phone. Rhone repeated everything he'd said about what had happened in Bremen to Martle and, presumably, the other officers as well.

There was a considerable pause at the other end of the line.

"Where are you now, Herr Rhone?" the general asked.

"I have left the city," Rhone said, watching the front door of the shop in which he'd found the phone. "I'm in a northern suburb."

"The GPU has not announced the campaign against Berlin that we've been expecting. This may not be the beginning of armed resistance, but it is not an isolated incident, as Oberst Martle suggested."

Rhone was barely breathing. *I was right,* he thought, *about their conspiracy.* But there was no sense of relief or vindication, just a powerful sense of alarm that rolled over sickeningly in his stomach.

"Of course, you have not been briefed on everything that is going on," Holtzen said. "But right now I need you to do something for me up near Karlshofen."

"We got somebody coming into the area, sir," Sergeant Gamble said to Isen. "A civilian."

"Who's bringing him in?"

"He walked up on some guys in Bravo Company," Gamble said. "Asked to speak to the commander."

Isen walked around the little wall behind which he'd placed his radio operators to get a view west across the small airstrip at the sector manned by Bravo Company. It would be odd for a civilian to just walk up on that position, as there were no roads within three or four hundred meters of Bravo's front. The woods were thick over there, so if someone wanted to get to the American position, Isen reasoned, with the least chance of being seen by any Germans watching them, then the Bravo Company sector offered the best chance.

"I sent Hatley to go get Colonel Spano," Gamble said.

"Good."

As the hours had dragged into dawn and there was no word from the Germans, Spano had become increasingly agitated about the delay in getting an answer back from the States. And since Hallam's story about being held prisoner, he was worried about what might come of Sergeant Handy, the wounded Ranger, and the medic they'd sent out with him. Spano had been on the satellite linkup for the past fifteen minutes or so, talking to Regimental headquarters as well as the headquarters for the Army's Special Operations Command, the next higher echelon—which controlled the Rangers, Special Forces, and the army's elite counterter-rorist unit, the Delta force.

Spano made it back to the command post before the new arrival.

"Get those radios and weapons out of sight," Spano said to the few soldiers who made up the headquarters element. "This guy may be looking to see what we've got on hand in here, and I don't want to do him any favors."

Spano was angrier than he'd been before he left Isen to get on the radio, so Isen didn't expect any good news when he asked, "What did Regiment say, sir?"

"I talked to the Old Man, and he told me something is bollixed up in Washington between the State Department and the Pentagon. He's working on getting us out of here by helicopter, but he said the Chairman and the rest of the Joint Chiefs are against giving us ammo."

One of the things that amazed Isen about the part of the Army he'd recently joined, the Special Operations community, was how quickly things could get elevated to the highest level. Not that the deliberate shooting of an American GI by soldiers who were supposed to be allies was small business, but what had started out as a fairly routine exercise had suddenly become the concern of rooms full of four-star generals half a world away.

"So we're supposed to sit tight?" Isen asked.

"I suggested that I just put everybody in formation and march out of here," Spano said. "They could even send over some media crews to be here, just to make sure nobody takes any shots at us when we start to walk out . . . which, by the way, is one of the plans I want you to draw up."

Spano stopped talking when he saw two soldiers and the Bravo Company commander walking toward them. With the three GIs was a man dressed in civilian clothes.

"He's not dressed for a hike in the woods," Spano said.

And he wasn't. The man had on a raincoat over slacks and leather shoes. When the group got close enough, the Bravo company commander, a Chicagoan named Wisneiwski who towered above the three men he was walking with, spoke first.

"Sir, this guy came up to one of our positions and asked to speak to the commander." Wisneiwski was exasperated, and looked as if he'd be just as happy beating up the German as standing in front of Spano. "When I got there, he said he wanted to speak to the battalion commander."

The German listened as Wisneiwski made his explanation. Isen figured that, like many Germans, this one could speak English. He looked to be about Isen's age—thirty-five—with the thin build of a distance runner. His shoulders were narrow, almost pinched, an effect exaggerated because he held his body shrugged against the cold. He waited for Wisneiwski to finish, watching the Americans through round, gold-framed glasses.

"Colonel Spano?" the German asked in English.

Spano had been ready to speak, but the man's use of his name threw him for a second. Spano glanced down—just to make sure—to where his rain gear covered his nametag.

"How did you know my name?" Spano asked.

"My superiors in Berlin told me about this exercise, and they sent me to see you."

Spano shot Isen a look. *I'll bet.*

"How'd you get in here?"

"The forces around you have not completed their encirclement," the German said. "And at any rate are looking for people trying to get out, not people trying to get in."

"And who do you work for?" Spano asked.

"Could we talk privately, Herr Colonel?"

Spano remained unconvinced. "Search him," he said to the two soldiers.

One of the men patted down the German for weapons. "He's not packing, sir."

"OK, you can leave us alone now," Spano said to Wisneiwski. "I'll fill you in on anything worth hearing."

Wisneiwski, obviously still suspicious of the German, nevertheless touched his helmet with his fingers in an informal salute. "Rangers lead the way, sir."

"All the way," Spano replied.

When the other GIs left, Spano turned to the German. "I'd offer you a chair, but we're a little Spartan out here," he said sarcastically.

"Herr Colonel," the visitor began. He hesitated, looked at Isen.

"This is my operations officer," Spano said. "He'll be listening in also."

"Yes, of course."

The German came to attention as he spoke. "My name is Major George Rhone. I am a military intelligence officer assigned to the Ministry of Defense, here in northern Germany on a special assignment."

Spano simply nodded. He wasn't giving out any information.

"The units that are surrounding you are part of the Territorial Forces, our reserves, if you will," Rhone said. "Apparently they are under the control of the German People's Union, a right-wing political party that has its strongest support up here in northern Germany."

"So what's their beef?" Spano asked.

The German blinked at the slang but grasped the question nevertheless.

"The GPU claims that the government in Berlin has always been a pawn of the Americans, and that exercises conducted on German soil by foreign armies are a breach of German sovereignty."

"Isn't the GPU that racist party?" Isen asked. After he said it, he thought that perhaps he could have been a little less blunt—they were not sure whom Rhone was representing out here—but the hours and the strain of a tense situation were beginning to tell.

"Yes," Rhone said without hesitating. "Their platform is 'Germany for Germans,' but it is actually a backlash against the foreigners here. People are angry about the economy; angry that, in spite of the years of slow or no economic growth, we still allow so many foreigners to seek asylum in our country. The GPU plays on those fears to promote xenophobia and militancy against the federal government."

"I've read about them in the press, seen some TV reports," Isen said. "They're like neo-Nazis, aren't they?"

"They made a great show of publicly ousting all the professed Nazis from their ranks a few months ago, but most of those people are still involved with the party. It was a public relations move to calm the fears of the middle class and make the GPU more attractive."

"What does this have to do with us?" Spano asked.

"There are some people in the intelligence community—and I am one of them—who believe that the GPU will make an overt challenge to the government in Berlin."

"What do you mean by 'overt challenge'?" Isen asked.

"The GPU has been secretly stealing military equipment from Bundeswehr and Territorial Force stockpiles. My superior believes that the GPU was responsible for the disappearance of three Bundeswehr officers sent recently to arrange for the transfer of some equipment out of this part of Germany."

"They've been stealing enough to challenge the regular army?" Spano asked, somewhat incredulously.

"The evidence of that is surrounding your unit here," Rhone said quietly.

Spano clapped a fist into a gloved hand. "Are you saying that we jumped in here at the invitation of the German Army and wound up in the middle of a showdown between the federal government and some whacko right-wing hooligans?"

"Well, Herr Colonel," Rhone said slowly, afraid of further alarming this agitated American commander. General Holtzen had sent him to put out the fire, not to stoke it. "The Bundeswehr is more than capable of dealing with an armed insurrection," Rhone said. "And, as you say, you were invited here by the legitimate government. You will be protected."

"Why weren't we warned about this?" Isen asked.

"I'm not sure of that, Major," Rhone said.

The three of them stood for a moment, the Americans surprised, trying to make sense of what Rhone was telling them.

"So where's the cavalry?" Spano asked.

This time, Rhone did not comprehend the idiom.

"Why isn't the Bundeswehr out here protecting us?" Spano demanded. "We've been here for almost twelve hours; we had one soldier shot, on purpose, I believe. I'm missing half a dozen people who were supposed to be here on the ground, and we haven't seen a trace of the controllers for this exercise."

"I don't know about that," Rhone offered. In fact, he did know something, or at least was in a position to speculate. Control of military and civilian communications—radio, television, telephone exchanges—was a key part of GPU plans. Further, he suspected that there were GPU sympathizers in the ranks of the regular army, which might explain why the controllers had disappeared. But Rhone couldn't feed the suspicions of the American officer. Holtzen had told him to let the foreigners know what was going on and keep them from doing anything to provoke the GPU. The general had said nothing about what was happening elsewhere in the country.

"I talked to my superior at the Defense Ministry," Rhone said. "He is aware of the problem out here and is taking steps to correct the situation." Rhone didn't know that to be exactly true, but he did know that Holtzen was a man of action, and he wouldn't be sitting on his hands.

"Why should we believe you?" Spano asked.

Rhone wondered if Spano sensed that he, Rhone, was stretching the truth about Holtzen's response. He decided Spano was just being cautious, and he had a right to be indignant, considering their treatment so far.

"I would think that the deliberate shooting of one of your men is enough evidence of the GPU's bad intentions, Herr Colonel," Rhone answered.

"No," Spano said. "I mean, how do we know you're not working for the GPU? Are you going to ask us to turn ourselves over to those people out there?"

Rhone started to speak, caught himself, began again. At no time since Holtzen had given him the mission to inform the Americans had he considered that they might not listen to him. The Americans had always been allies.

"No, sir. But I am going to ask you to refrain from taking any actions that might be seen as hostile."

Isen spoke. "Such as?"

"Such as trying to leave without their permission, until the federal government can get you out of here." Rhone looked around. The nearest soldiers were the radio operators, and they were obscured by the wall. "Such as requesting ammunition."

Spano said nothing, and Isen took his lead.

"I know that you do not routinely carry ammunition on these exercises," Rhone said. "I spent quite a few years training with American units here in Germany."

Rhone tried a comradely smile, but the two Americans remained silent.

"I am not sure that they"—Rhone indicated the woods and the surrounding Germans—"know for certain that you are armed only with blank ammunition. I would not want to broadcast that fact."

"I don't like him," Spano said to Isen when the two men walked away from the German. "He's a staff weenie who talks like a freaking politician."

"I guess there's at least as good a chance that he's working for the GPU as there is that he's telling the truth," Isen said. He and Spano had retreated behind the low wall that hid the radio operators, leaving Rhone under the guard of one of the soldiers from the headquarters section. Isen was drawing little squares on a page of the notebook he held open in his palm.

"We have a couple of courses of action open to us, I guess," Isen said.

Spano put his back against the wall and crossed his arms. "Go ahead, I'm listening."

"We could play it completely passively, which seems to be what Regiment wants us to do, and what Rhone has told us to do. Maybe Rhone is GPU, sent here to warn us so that they could avoid shooting. I mean, it wouldn't do their cause any good to shoot up a bunch of unarmed Americans, even if they do claim we're invaders."

"If that were the case, why would he claim to be from somewhere else?" Spano said. "Why not just say he's with the GPU?"

"Maybe they want to save face," Isen said. "They want to look like they're ready to fight—that would appeal to the militants—but it would be stupid to take on the U.S. Army. Maybe the GPU figures we'd be more likely to listen to a Bundeswehr officer."

Spano thought about that for a moment. "OK," he said chewing his bottom lip. "That's the most passive response. What are some others?"

"The most extreme would be to get a bunch of ammo and try to fight our way out of here," Isen said. "But that would be foolish, since they've got armored vehicles and big guns and the ability to maneuver all around us. And we really don't have anywhere to run to, as far as I know."

Spano stared hard at the ground around the toes of his boots. He continued, "If we call for an ammo drop, and the guys in the woods get hold of just one misplaced case of live rounds, they'll know what's going on and they'll take that as a hostile action, no doubt. That just might be the excuse they're looking for to pounce." He stopped for one beat, two. "Then it's Little Big Horn time."

"We might have the Air Force load the ammo and keep it ready to go," Isen said.

"As soon as we get approval," Spano added. "But the boys in Washington are having a little trouble believing that we're in that much danger."

Spano was frustrated at the lack of response from his superiors back in the States. For some reason, Isen found himself thinking about the defenders of Corregidor, who lived on wild rumors that help was on the way even as the Japanese closed the noose in early 1942. He pushed the image away. *You're getting a little panicky, Mark,* he told himself. *It ain't time to start picking out coffins yet.*

Spano was still silent. Isen's job was to present his commander with feasible alternatives, then carry out the one the old man chose.

"Here's what I recommend, sir," Isen said. His commander looked up.

"First thing, we need to get on the phone and tell them what this Rhone guy told us. We have to try to talk our way out of here, first."

Spano nodded.

"While we're talking, we need to get the Air Force to rig up an ammo drop and keep the stuff on hand near here, close enough so that we can get it if we have to call for it."

"Lead time might be tight on that call," Spano said.

"Yes, sir, it might," Isen agreed. "Then we send this guy Rhone back out of the position with the news that we're just going to sit tight, no need to get alarmed and all that. Meanwhile, we prepare defensive positions here in case we wind up with the ammo, having to defend ourselves."

Isen drummed his fingers on his leg as he tried to concentrate. He was getting a bad feeling. *Gotta shake that attitude before the troops catch on,* he warned himself, forcing his mind back to the task at hand.

"Finally, we make up contingency plans for E and E out of here."

Spano studied his deputy. Isen had suggested the possibility that the soldiers might have to split up to escape and evade, that is, run away in small groups to some safe haven. The theory was that small groups are harder to track and more men would make it to safety. But it also meant that Spano would be relinquishing command: in effect, leaving his men to their own devices much as the captain of a sinking ship who calls, "Every man for himself."

"That's a hell of a suggestion, Mark," Spano said. He wasn't angry, just stunned.

"Yessir," Isen said. "But if what this Rhone guy is telling us is half true, we're in a helluva fix."

"We are that," Spano said. "We are indeed."

The next problem came when Rhone refused to leave the shelter of the Rangers' perimeter.

"What do you mean you won't leave?" Isen asked him.

Rhone squatted by a small fire some of the headquarters soldiers had built. Spano had allowed each company a few warming fires behind their positions. Since the Germans knew where the Ranger strongpoints were located, the fires didn't give away any vital information beyond that the GIs were cold.

"The GPU was already looking for me this morning," Rhone said. "I am not sure what they have in mind for me, but it can't be good."

"Well, you certainly can't expect to stay here," Isen said. "For one thing, you don't have the equipment, the winter clothes."

As if to agree with Isen's point, Rhone started shivering. Under his raincoat he had on only a dress shirt. He pressed his arms around his thin chest but did not answer.

"Besides, we want you to tell them that we're going to sit tight until this thing gets straightened out," Isen said. "There's no reason for anyone to get ugly."

Rhone stared into the fire. "They will kill me," he said.

"What makes you think that?"

Rhone stood up and brushed off his pants. His clothes smelled of wood smoke.

"I have been studying them for several months, Major . . . is it Isen?"

"Yes."

"Interesting name," Rhone said. "At any rate, in that time I have discovered some very disconcerting things, about their party, their aims, the designs of their leaders."

"So tell me," Isen said.

Rhone looked to the woodline, where snowy crescents in the shadows of trees shone a brilliant white in the winter sun. He thought about all the reports he had filed with his superiors, about how they had been ignored, about how his predictions seemed to be coming true.

Rhone did not consider himself a brave man. He'd spent almost his whole career working behind a desk, shunning intelligence jobs with field units because he loathed living outdoors. Yet he had surprised himself that morning when he agreed to risk capture to try to get through to the Americans—he could have told Holtzen that he couldn't find the position, or that GPU units had the place closed off.

Now he was in a position where he had to decide if his mission—keep a lid on the situation with the Americans—should come before his personal safety. If he told Isen everything he knew about the GPU's plan for a violent overthrow of the government, the Americans might panic, might try something that would give the GPU an excuse to attack. But if he did not tell Isen, the Americans would turn him over to their captors. He had decided more than a week ago, when one of his informants had turned up in an unsightly pile on the ice below a Weser River bridge, that the GPU knew about his activities.

"I am not at liberty to tell you everything, Herr Isen," Rhone said. "But

I do know a great deal about the GPU and can be of assistance. And, as you point out, I am obviously not dressed for the weather. If I came here on behalf of the GPU, which is what you are implying, don't you think I would have had the foresight to dress warmly?"

Isen shoved his hands into the large pockets on the sides of his parka. "I'll see what the old man says."

He found Spano a few minutes later by the signals platoon, monitoring the silent net that connected him to the States.

"Anything yet, sir?" Isen asked as he approached.

"Nothing," Spano said. "Is your friend gone?"

"No, sir. That's what I came to talk to you about."

Isen related Rhone's tale, allowing that the story about the clothing, though a good one, might have been a planned bit of trickery.

"Still, I think we should keep him here," Isen said. "He may have a point about the GPU. Besides, what harm can he do in here if we keep an eye on him. He isn't armed, doesn't have a way to contact them."

"You're looking at it the wrong way, Mack," Spano said. "You're trying to come up with reasons we shouldn't send him back. I want reasons we should keep him, see? What do we get out of it? Why should we take the chance, when he serves no purpose for us?"

Spano had a point, Isen thought. But there was something about the German's argument to stay, sincerity born, perhaps, of fear. But that wasn't going to sell it to Spano.

"He might be telling the truth, sir," Isen said. "They might kill him."

"Sorry, Mark. I have to put the battalion first."

Isen studied his commander's eyes, which were red above his chapped, unshaven face. For hours he'd had the feeling that things were going to get worse before they got better, and it was important to keep all lines of communication open between the two of them. Still, there was something about Rhone. Isen wondered if he didn't just feel sorry for the guy, a "staff weenie," Spano had called him, caught out in the field.

"But that would mean that we're weighing a guy's life up against the fact that his being around might *not* help us."

Isen knew immediately that he'd gone too far. Spano leaned forward, narrowing his eyes.

"They're coming up on the horn, sir."

It was one of the radio operators, holding up a handset to Spano.

Isen listened to the tiny clicking of the encoding device switches in the satellite link radio as he watched Spano scribble in a notebook. The colonel had little to say; he mostly listened. It was over in less than two minutes.

"Let's move over a bit," Spano said to Isen, inching away from the signal operators.

"That was Colonel Schauffert," Spano explained when they were out of range of the soldiers' hearing. "He just finished talking to the Chief and the SECDEF."

Good ol' Cracklin' Charlie, Isen thought, *no doubt raising seven kinds of hell with the Secretary of Defense, the State Department and the Pentagon.*

Colonel Charles Schauffert, whose feisty, if not abrasive personality had earned him the nickname "Cracklin' Charlie," was commander of the Ranger Regiment, all three battalions of the Seventy-fifth Infantry.

While it was easy for Isen—and no doubt for the rest of the battalion—to believe that they'd been waiting for instructions for an unreasonable amount of time, it was much more likely that Schauffert had his people back in the States jumping through hoops, looking for information and solutions. Isen sometimes thought that Schauffert was out on the lunatic fringe. Still it comforted him to know that they weren't forgotten, that the old man had the ball. *Something* would happen.

"Looks like the shit is hitting the fan, Mark," Spano said.

Isen let out a long breath; that could mean a lot of things.

"The news is that the German People's Union is confronting the Berlin government over the legitimacy of this exercise—Americans on German soil. I guess there are a lot of Germans who don't want us or any other foreigners around anymore."

"Wish they'd told us that day before yesterday," Isen said.

Spano managed a hint of a smile. "Ain't that the truth?"

"Anyway," he went on, "Berlin asked Washington to delay making any public announcement of our predicament. The Germans think they can get this problem under control without inviting the world to see their dirty laundry."

Spano looked up from his notes. "I guess the GPU stands to gain a lot of publicity if this thing goes according to their plan."

"Which is?" Isen asked.

"Nobody's sure," Spano said. "The President has agreed to hold off, for twenty-four hours, on going public with this thing—provided nothing else happens to us. The Chief said that after that, he's going to come down hard on these goons."

"It'll take that long—longer, maybe—to come up with a contingency plan to do something to get us out of here," Isen said. He found it difficult to be impressed with rhetoric while they were hanging it all out ten thousand miles from home.

"Colonel Schauffert reminded me to keep everybody out of our perimeter," Spano said. "I'd be surprised if the GPU didn't know that we have only blank ammo, but on the off chance that they think we're armed, we'll do what we can to preserve that uncertainty."

"So, since Rhone is already in," Isen said, "I guess he's not going anywhere."

"Right."

*　　*　　*

Thirty meters away, Major George Rhone was seized with another fit of shivering, and he wished again that he'd had time to bring his winter uniforms and sleeping bag.

He understood why Holtzen had sent him, but he didn't believe the Americans were going to let him stay. *If they haven't kicked me out by nightfall, I'll probably be so cold I'll be begging to go to the GPU,* he thought. If the Americans did kick him out, the GPU would most likely shoot him. If he stayed with the Rangers and the GPU attacked, the Americans would be massacred. *Not a lot of good choices either way,* he admitted to himself.

Tim Brennan stabbed at the frozen ground with his small entrenching tool.

"This is fucking ridiculous."

Without looking up, Brennan knew that his partner, Mike Charis, had stopped working again and was getting ready to give his opinion on some aspect or another of their orders.

"This ground is frozen hard as my head," Charis said, waving the entrenching tool around. "If we're gonna mess with those clowns in the woods, why don't we attack them so *they* have to dig in?" Charis, although shorter than Brennan, was built like a fireplug; the small shovel looked like a child's toy in his hands.

In spite of his fatigue, Brennan had to laugh. "I'll be sure to mention that to Sergeant Bishop," Brennan said. "Maybe the colonel just didn't think of that option, you know?"

"I should have taken that job with the Old Guard," Charis said, referring to the Army's ceremonial unit at Fort Myers, near Washington. "I'd be sleeping up in some barracks, pulling one hour shifts in the Tomb."

Brennan looked at his partner. Old Guard soldiers were uniformly tall, like a race of supersoldiers. It was obvious to both of them that Charis didn't fit the bill. Brennan knew what was coming and gladly played the straight man.

"Is that right?" Brennan asked.

"Yeah," Charis went on expansively. "They'd have been happy to get a good-looking dark green Ranger like me."

Charis referred to black soldiers as dark green, whites as light green, and Brennan believed that that was truly how he saw things.

"But then I found out that the fancy uniform comes with white gloves," he continued.

Brennan couldn't resist. "So?"

"Shit," Charis said, dragging the word out. *Sheeet.* "You'd have me wearing white gloves out in public, having all those people thinking I'm a *virgin?*"

Early on in his assignment to the Rangers, Charis had gotten wise to all the cheerleading that went on around the battalion. He figured out, as a private, that most of the puffery was for the sake of the privates. As an eighteen-year-old, he'd been dazzled by all the buttons and dials the paratroopers got to wear on their uniforms: the colorful flash behind the jump wings, the black beret, so carefully shaped and shaved of lint, with its green and blue flash and the centered metal insignia and Latin motto *Sua Sponte,* "Of Their Own Accord," that spoke of their volunteer status.

Once he was in the unit, however, he noticed that the officers and NCOs, even while joining in all the posturing, went about it in a different way. They shouted "Hooah," a sort of guttural lodge cheer, as frequently as did the young soldiers, and they blustered about Ranger this and Ranger that, but there was something self-deprecating in it all. They also reminded one another that jumping from airplanes was a tough way for thirty-five-year-olds to get around. And if the First Sergeant made a comment about how much he absolutely loved sleeping out in the rain for the fifteenth straight year, the sarcasm was less a comment on his toughness than on his sense of reality.

Charis didn't become cynical: he knew that young soldiers had to be enthusiastic, had to be cheered on and made to think that they are a cut above regular soldiers, the grunts in leg land. Otherwise it would be difficult for them to do the things asked of them in this unit. The older soldiers believed just as strongly in what the unit stood for, they just showed their enthusiasm in different ways.

Charis was somewhere in between: he shouted "Hooah" with the best of them, but he never lost sight of the seriousness of what they were about. And he never missed a chance for a laugh.

"Hooah," Brennan said in response to the joke.

"Hoo-ahh," Charis replied, drawing the word out, as if it made some sense. "Yes, indeed, hoo-ahh."

"You're supposed to be digging, not laughing and jacking off." Sergeant Bishop, their squad leader, came up behind them. "What kind of progress are you two heroes making?"

"Oh, we're doing great, Sergeant Bishop," Charis said, kicking at the crisp dirt in what was supposed to be an armpit-deep two man fighting position. "In another ten hours or so I should be able to get my feet below ground. But if it's all the same to you, I'm going to stop once I get in deep enough to shelter my pecker. OK?"

"I wouldn't worry about that, Charis," Bishop said. "I reckon the marksmen ain't been born that can hit that little target."

Bishop turned to Brennan. "How you doing?"

"I'm fine, thanks, Sergeant Bishop," Brennan answered honestly. People had been asking him that all morning. *Either I should be more upset about what happened to Sergeant Handy, or everybody in this platoon thinks I'm a wimp.* Brennan wasn't sure which answer was correct.

"You guys toss your blank adaptors in here," Bishop said, holding out an empty plastic meal bag. Each man surrendered his adaptor—a small red attachment that fit over the end of the rifle to make it function with blank ammunition—dropping it into the proffered bag.

"What's the word, Sergeant?" Brennan asked.

"Colonel Spano says the Germans out in the woods don't know if we have live ammo or not, so he doesn't want them to see these things on your rifles."

"Oh," Charis said.

"Are they a threat to us?" Brennan asked.

"As a matter of fact," Bishop said, "they just might be." The NCO then told the soldiers everything that had been passed down through the chain of command about their situation, which was just about everything Spano knew. Colonel Spano believed that keeping the troops informed kept down the rumors and helped the men handle the stress, and themselves, better.

"We're going to be digging until we can fight from this position," Bishop said. "Now I want you two guys to go around and collect canteens from the other guys. Take them to the edge of the airstrip, where you'll see a little building with a control tower. Keep to the woodline and go to that building—it's no more than three hundred meters—and fill up everybody's canteens."

"OK, Sergeant," Brennan answered.

It took them almost ten minutes to round up the squad's empty canteens, which they strung on a piece of cord like a day's catch. They found the building easily enough, a small administration building just slightly larger than the base of the two-story tower. There was a little bar inside, with several tables. A sign marked Toiletten pointed to the back of the room. Several other Rangers on the same mission were crowded in the tiny hallway.

"You guys from Charlie Company, right?" one of the soldiers said to Brennan.

Brennan nodded.

"What about the guy who got shot?" another soldier asked. "He hurt bad?"

Brennan looked up at the speaker, who he thought was from Alpha Company. There was something in his voice besides concern.

"Nah," Charis snorted. "Took off a piece of his butt, but he moved out under his own power."

Brennan had filled the string of canteens he was holding, but Charis was taking his time, socializing as if they had all day.

"Let's go, man," Brennan said.

Charis held another canteen under the single tap. "Last one," he said.

Brennan turned to leave, but their inquisitor was in the doorway. Brennan hadn't noticed how large the soldier was—his shoulders almost filled the doorframe.

"We heard that the guy was with the one who got shot didn't do shit," the man said.

Brennan froze, felt a sickeningly familiar emptiness somewhere behind his stomach. It was the schoolyard—any schoolyard he'd ever entered—all over again, with some bully demanding his lunch money.

How did he know it was me? Brennan wondered. He felt something working its way up the back of his throat, some response that he knew, based on a thousand bad experiences in just this situation, would be entirely inappropriate and might even lead to his getting a beating.

"What the fuck would you have done, dickwad?"

It was Charis, moving through Brennan's peripheral vision, heading for the door as if it weren't blocked. "I suppose you'da shot him with your blanks."

Brennan waited for the hammer to fall, but a couple of other soldiers in the room laughed, and the big man just flexed his hands.

"You wanna get outta my way?" Charis said. "I got women to do, places to go."

The big man backed out of the doorway, Brennan completely forgotten. He pushed his eyes together, straining for a comeback for the short black soldier who'd just brushed him off.

"Let's go, man," Charis said over his shoulder. Brennan followed him outside. They'd gone no more than ten steps when they heard, "Yeah, well, fuck you, man," from the doorway behind them.

Charis laughed.

"Something wrong, men?"

They looked up to see Lieutenant Hawkins in front of them, heading for the same building. He'd heard the comment from the doorway.

"No, sir," Charis said, smiling. "Just some rock-head from Alpha Company shooting his mouth off 'bout stuff he doesn't know about."

Hawkins nodded, unconvinced.

"Private Brennan," Hawkins said, leaning forward a bit at the waist, as if talking to a child. "Bad morning, huh? Are you OK?"

Hawkins used the same mock solicitous tone the Alpha Company soldier had used. There was no doubt in Brennan's mind that Hawkins thought he was a pussy.

"I'm fine, sir," Brennan said flatly.

"Good," Hawkins said. "We wouldn't want you to be too upset, would we, Private Charis?"

"No, sir, we wouldn't," Charis said. "But my man Brennan is hanging tough."

"I'm sure," Hawkins said, moving beyond the two soldiers toward the building that housed the water source.

Charis and Brennan walked a few more meters before Brennan spoke. "Thanks, man."

"For what?" Charis said, and that was that. "Say, listen."

He turned halfway back to the building and put one hand up to an ear, as if straining to hear.

"Hey, sir," Charis said in a fair imitation of the bully's deep Texas twang, "you wouldn't happen to know who was the dipshit lieutenant who got himself lost this morning, out in front of the perimeter without a radio?"

Brennan broke up. "You're nuts, man," he said. "I can't believe you don't get your ass kicked more often than you do."

"Me either."

As the two men made their way back to their squad area with their burden of water, it began to snow.

7

MARK ISEN LEANED OVER THE RADIO FREQUENCY KNOBS TO block the falling snow as he tried another channel.

"Still nothing, sir," he said. "I'm sure they're jamming us."

"Those bastards," Spano said. "They're escalating this thing." He turned to the signal officer. "When did this start?" he asked.

"Just in the last ten minutes, sir. They haven't been able to touch the satellite stuff, though."

"The thing that alarms me about this," Isen said, sotto voce, "is that it might mean they've been bringing up additional equipment all day. If the electronic stuff just arrived, maybe they've also brought up more armored vehicles."

"Anybody hear anything? Any of the companies report hearing anything?" Spano asked.

"No, sir," Isen said.

"If they're coming, what the hell are they waiting for?" Spano asked. "Not that I want to take on those Marders with my pocket knife."

"It could be that they launched this thing, this coup, prematurely," Isen offered. "I mean, ideally, everything would have gone down at once. Surprise attack. But Rhone said stuff's been breaking over a period of time. He mentioned some Bundeswehr officers missing. Then there's Team Black, then Sergeant Handy, then a lull. Maybe they have to wait to consolidate their political position before they launch in here."

"Well, that's a fucking hopeful assessment," Spano said.

"I could be wrong," Isen said, "but I've come up with a plan of sorts."

"What have you cooked up now, Major?" Spano said. There was no trace of the anger he'd felt with Isen over Rhone's presence.

"I think I ought to walk out there and tell these people that we need hot chow, some coffee, stuff like that. Meanwhile, maybe I can get a look at what's out there, what they have."

"Why you?"

"Well, they've already seen you and me, so they'll know who I am, and I figure you ought to stay with the troops," Isen said.

"In case they haul you away and lock you up?"

"Something like that, sir."

"OK," Spano said. "But don't try anything cute out there. If they know you've found something, you're dog meat."

"Roger that, sir," Isen said. "You want me to complain about the radio jamming?"

"Nah," Spano said. "Fuck 'em. They won't turn it off, and I'd just as soon not give them the satisfaction of knowing that their stuff is working."

Isen rounded up Haslem, the German-speaking soldier from Bravo Company, and a Ranger from the headquarters element named Gore, and set off for the road that led from the airfield's one building into the woods where the Germans waited.

"You guys keep your eyes peeled," Isen told the soldiers. "When we get back we'll talk about what we saw, how many vehicles, what kind, all that. But don't get caught looking around, or they'll be pissed."

The three men walked abreast on the narrow track, heading into the blowing snow that was coming down heavily now. They could see no more than a few meters, and the whiteness lifted sound away from them, so that they seemed quite alone.

When he thought they might be close, and because he didn't want to startle an armed sentry, Isen yelled "Hey, we're coming to talk to your commander." Then, to Haslem, "Repeat that in German."

Haslem got a response almost immediately.

"He said stay here," Haslem translated.

Isen turned to the other man who was with them. "Back off a few feet and kind of move to the side of the road. Don't get out of sight. If anything goes wrong, hightail it back to the perimeter, hear?"

"Yessir."

They waited five or six minutes, with Isen straining to see through the gray-white gloom that blew sideways on the road, cutting streaks across his vision. Finally, two dark forms appeared just ahead of them.

"Colonel Spano?" came the question in English. "Is that Colonel Spano?"

"No," Isen said. "I am Colonel Spano's deputy. Who are you?"

"I am Leutnant Schorr. I am to take you to our commander."

"Would that be Captain Schrebel?" Isen asked, remembering the name from the morning's encounter.

"No."

As the two men came closer, Isen saw that the one doing the talking was a big man, six feet, easily 230, 240 pounds, wrapped up in a military issue parka as well as several decidedly unmilitary scarves, a big pair of bright blue mittens, and a red ski cap pulled down low over his ears. He surprised Isen by smiling at the Americans.

"And your name is?" Schorr asked.

"I am Major Isen. Are you taking me to see Captain Schrebel?"

"No, sir," Schorr answered. He smiled again, and Isen thought of all the jolly bakers he'd seen in German shops during the years he'd spent in this country. Even without the red cap and scarves, Schorr would have a hard time appearing to be anything other than a light-hearted civilian.

"Come with me, please," Schorr said, holding one arm out to where the road behind him disappeared into the swirl. Isen walked beside the German officer, while the two Rangers followed.

"Your men have sufficient clothing to protect them from the cold?" Schorr asked solicitously.

Isen was suspicious and wondered if the Germans were simply trying some new approach to find out about the Rangers' predicament. He looked at Schorr's broad, concerned face and had to remind himself that these were the people who'd shot Sergeant Handy.

"We could use some hot food," Isen said, trying not to sound desperate.

Schorr nodded in agreement. "Yes, yes, of course."

Schorr and the soldier with him led the Americans along the fast disappearing road that sloped gently down. Nothing marked the point where Schorr turned sharply into the woods. Isen looked around, trying to get his bearings in case they had to find their own way out in a hurry, but all about him was a moving dull whiteness, as if they'd been submerged in stirred milk.

Less than a hundred meters into the woodline, they came upon what must have been Schorr's command post.

"This is your platoon?" Isen asked.

"No, Major," Schorr said. "I am a company commander. It is not all that unusual in the Territorial Forces for a *Leutnant* to command a company."

Schorr pulled back the flap of a tent that had been camouflaged with evergreen branches and was now covered with snow. Isen stepped inside, half-expecting to come face-to-face with someone who outranked Schorr. What he found instead were three NCOs, two of them as big as

Schorr, sitting around a folding table and drinking from steaming canteen cups. They were as startled to see Isen as he was to be in their midst.

Schorr came into the tent, struggling to squeeze his bulk past Isen without shoving him.

"This is Major Isen," Schorr said convivially to the men at the table. "Let's give him something to drink."

He turned to Isen. "Would you like some coffee, hot coffee?"

Surprised once again, but tempted, Isen thought about his soldiers outside.

"Do you have enough for my men?" Isen asked.

"Certainly, certainly," Schorr said expansively, the gracious host. One of the NCOs handed Isen a remarkably clean aluminum cup half full of steaming liquid, while another one carried two more cups outside to where the two Rangers Isen had brought along waited. Schorr went over to a trunk on the tent floor and produced a silver thermos. He held it over Isen's cup and smiled. "Schnapps?"

"No, thank you, I don't think so," Isen said.

As Schorr poured a generous portion into his own cup, Isen studied the lieutenant. He was at least as old as the captain they'd met in the morning, and his physical condition didn't bring to mind the words *field soldier*. Isen had seen plenty of men like Schorr in the reserves back home, and he wondered, with the company commander and NCOs sitting inside a tent and drinking schnapps, what kind of shape the company outside might be in.

The scene inside the warm tent reminded Isen more of hunting trips with his father than of any field problem he'd ever experienced. This was what Isen had expected when he heard that they'd be working with some German reservists for Operation Solid Steel. He looked down into the coffee. *Maybe all the hours since the jump have been a bad dream,* he thought.

Isen heard a vehicle pull up outside the tent, and in a panicky flash he thought that he shouldn't have let the two soldiers out of his sight. They might have been carried off already. Isen and Schorr made for the door at the same time, both still carrying their cups. Isen hesitated, and Schorr bumped into him heavily.

"Excuse me, Major," Schorr said. His smile no longer had any hint of amusement. The NCOs were quickly putting their cups away, and the steel thermos of schnapps had disappeared.

Isen emerged from the tent behind Schorr but could see nothing beyond the lieutenant's broad back. Schorr brought his right hand up in a salute, while he balanced his drink against his left leg.

"Sir, I have the American second-in-command here with me," Schorr said.

Isen stepped around and saw Schorr was addressing a pinched-faced little man, a colonel, Isen thought, who'd just emerged from a staff car. He had on the same parka that Schorr and the others wore, although the colonel's looked as if it had just been cleaned and pressed. He spoke sharply to Schorr.

Isen couldn't follow the German, but the words had an immediate effect on Schorr, who brought his heels together and dropped his hands to his sides. A few drops of coffee slipped from the cup and made a brown hole in the snow.

The old man shifted his bird gaze to Isen and switched to English. "Come here," he said.

Isen wished he had an option other than responding to the man's acid tone, but the truth was, he didn't . . . at least not any good ones.

"What is your name?"

"I am Major Mark Isen of the United States Army, and I must say we protest the treatment we have been given here. Your men are interfering with a training mission—"

"That is quite enough, Major," the old man said. "Your presence here is *exactly* the issue," he said, pressing the words out through tightened lips. "Our government says that you have no right to be here."

"But this whole exercise was coordinated with the Ministry of Defense—"

The colonel cut him off again. "Which is in Berlin. I am not talking about the puppet government in Berlin, I am talking about the freely elected representatives of the people's will—"

He stopped, apparently in midsentence, and studied Isen through eyes half-closed.

"Tell your commander," the colonel went on, "that he is in a precarious situation, and that the only thing keeping us from crushing your tiny unit is the German People's Union's dedication to a peaceful resolution to this problem. You will surrender your unit to us upon my command. Until then, you will stand by for instructions."

"And if we refuse?" Isen asked.

The colonel pulled his gloves on tighter. "Then we come in to get you and take you out by force."

Mark Isen followed his guide back through the woods to the road, now thick with snow, and turned toward the airfield and the Rangers' perimeter. There was little chance that they could be resupplied by air in this weather, even less of a chance that they could be lifted out by helicopter. He thought about the prospect of turning the battalion over to the Germans, specifically, to the GPU, in the midst of its power struggle with the government in Berlin. It went against everything he felt, everything he knew about keeping control and unit integrity, but as he walked along the road a few steps ahead of the two Rangers who were accompanying him, he thought about all the other youngsters out there in the cold and knew that there was no way he or Spano should ask for ammunition and force a fight with these men in their armored vehicles. It would be a bloodbath.

"What's the scoop, sir? Did you learn anything?" Haslem asked, his voice muffled by the olive drab GI scarf he'd wrapped around his face. Isen studied the boy's eyes for a moment and knew that he couldn't risk the deaths of these soldiers. Better to turn themselves over and wait for the State Department or someone else to bail them out. It would be humiliating, but they would all get out alive.

"They told us to stand by," he told Haslem. "And I expect they'll want us to just turn ourselves over when they call."

"Sounds good to me," Haslem said. "We'll be out of chow soon, and I'd rather not hang around to reenact the Valley Forge thing."

As he expected, Isen found that Spano was harder to convince.

"God*damn*, Mark, I can't just turn over my whole command to these people," Spano said when Isen had explained the German colonel's demands.

"Well, you could get the Chief to OK it," Isen said, "once you explain that we're running low on chow and we're in the middle of this snowstorm and the SOBs have given us an ultimatum."

Spano took off the issue watch cap he'd put on in place of his helmet and scratched furiously at his close-cropped hair.

"What are our other options, sir?" Isen went on. "We certainly can't resist them if they come in here. We're not armed, and even if we were we wouldn't have much of a chance against those Marders. No one is going to be able to come in and pull us out of here, not by air, at least, not in this soup."

Spano looked up, but there was no sky to be seen above his head, nothing but a few feet of falling snow.

"The best we can do, perhaps, is to agree to leave, but on American trucks, in control of our own units," Isen said.

"Let's get that Rhone guy over here," Spano said. "See what he says about what these jokers have in mind before I call back to the States again."

Isen sent a man to get Rhone, whom they'd stashed in the one building within the perimeter. There was no power in the control building, and thus no heat, but it was out of the wind. When the German came up to them, still in his street clothes, his lips were blue, his ears and his cheeks chapped by the cold.

"You been inside?" Isen asked.

"Yes, thank you," Rhone said. "It is still quite cold, but I am much more concerned with helping you in this dilemma. As I said—"

"Look, Major," Spano snapped, "here's the deal." He recounted the story Isen had just told him about the GPU demands. He didn't ask, at the end, what course of action they should take, he just let the dilemma hang there between them.

Rhone shoved his hands deeper into the pockets of his raincoat.

"Even if we believe that they will guarantee your safety," Rhone said, "which I don't believe, by the way, they will make a spectacle of your surrender. The GPU is very ... what you Americans might call media savvy. They will have television crews here, they will insist that your men are disarmed, they will make it look as if the United States Army has willingly surrendered. They'll use it to show the people that the GPU is the real power in Germany."

"And if we don't agree?" Spano asked. "Do you believe that they'll come after us?"

Rhone was seized by a fit of shivering that passed in a few seconds. Isen looked down at the German's shoes, which were soaked through with snow that had melted in front of the fire. Outside again, his feet would be in danger of freezing. Spano's expression showed, Isen noticed, neither sympathy or disdain. He merely waited for an answer.

"I believe it is worse than that," Rhone said. "I don't think they have any intention of taking you out of here peacefully."

"What if we don't put up a fight?" Isen asked.

"Let me explain," Rhone said. He was seized by another fit of shivering, his head bobbing on his thin neck, like a doll being rattled by a child.

"Let's go over to the fire," Spano said impatiently.

The three of them walked around the low wall where the soldiers in the headquarters element had built a fire against the base of a concrete block wall. The soldiers backed off out of earshot.

Once Rhone had settled down a bit, Isen pressed him further.

"You mean they'll attack us even if we don't put up any resistance?"

"Yes, I am afraid so," Rhone said. He rubbed his hands together and watched the small flames as he spoke.

"The GPU, and in particular, their leader, Deitrich Jaeger, does not look on this as a standoff between your unit and their forces," Rhone said. "To them, this is an opportunity to show the German people that they are a serious group, a force to be reckoned with. What they do with you is of consequence only as far as it affects that goal. They have another agenda, too: it is important for them to be seen as Germany's saviors. That is how they trumpet their cause—after all, to be against saving Germany is to be beneath disdain. I believe they will use you, use this opportunity, to answer that need."

Rhone stopped, waiting, apparently, for this to sink in with Spano and Isen.

"So if they can make it look like we're fighting them, if they can make this a shooting war, then they look like the good guys," Spano said. "Fighting off the invaders and all that."

"Yes, sir, I am afraid that is correct," Rhone said.

"All the more reason," Isen blurted, his voice a little more shrill than he'd intended, "for us to cooperate. We don't want to give them any excuse to fire us up."

Spano squatted down by the fire and shoved a small cardboard box, a discarded meal wrapper, into the flames. He looked up at Isen, then at Rhone, then back to Isen before he started speaking again.

"That's the point Major Rhone is trying to make," Spano said. "They've already got everything they want—they've got us here. They'll keep stringing us along with phony deadlines—'stand by for instructions,' isn't that what the man said?—until they're good and ready, with all the political pieces in place. All they have to do then is pull the trigger and fabricate some story about how we started shooting first. What we decide is of no importance to them."

Isen felt his jaw go slack. Spano, who had always seemed to Isen the very model of rational thought, had apparently bought into Rhone's description.

This is insane, Isen thought. *Just freaking unbelievable.*

"You're telling me that they've surrounded a bunch of unarmed men and they're going to start shooting? How can that possibly help them?"

"They control all the news that goes out of here, Major Isen," Rhone said. "Only their version of the story will survive."

Isen felt an odd compulsion to laugh, a panicky flutter in his belly.

"So you're saying we should arm ourselves?" Isen asked. "That would just give them the excuse they need."

"No," Rhone said. "I'm saying that they will attack as soon as they have consolidated their strategic position. We must not let them control events. Your government must intervene here."

"What about Berlin?" Spano said.

"They will not move fast enough," Rhone said. "I have already told you how my reports on GPU activities have been ignored because the Ministry of Defense has its collective head in the sand. When morning comes, they will still be considering what to do, and those Marders may well be running through your positions."

Isen felt a pressure behind his eyes, as if he had a sinus headache. Nothing in his years of experience had prepared him for this free-for-all. He looked at Spano, who still squatted, pushing tiny bits of paper and wood into the flames. Spano would have to make the call, finally. The folks at the Pentagon might hem and haw and demand more information, but Spano was the man on the ground, and in his hands were the lives of the hundreds of soldiers who waited in the white stillness that surrounded them.

"Mark?" Spano said.

Isen shook his head slightly. *My job is to make recommendations,* Isen reminded himself. *I've got to help the boss weigh these things, consider the possibilities.*

"Well, one thing's for certain, sir," Isen said. "We've got to make the higher-ups understand the seriousness of the spot we're in." He paused while he grasped for other options, but he was having a hard time pulling things together. He kept seeing those big Marders coming through the forest at his unarmed men.

"And I was going to say we could try to drag things out. Tell the Germans that we need more time to consider our options, talk to our superiors."

"But if what Rhone here says is true, that would play right into their hands," Spano said. "They'll come when *they're* ready."

Spano stood, stretching out his long frame, coming to rest with his hands on his hips, thumbs hooked into his pistol belt. "We're caught in the web, and we're just waiting for the spider."

"So we should call for the ammo?" Isen asked.

"That's what I'm thinking," Spano said.

Spano got back on the secure satellite net—which the GPU, with its fairly unsophisticated equipment, could not jam—and explained the situation to Colonel Schauffert, the Regimental commander, and General Charles, the Chief of Staff. They told Spano that they had assembled enough airlift to take his men out of the airfield, but that the weather, as Spano guessed, made that impossible. During the afternoon, while the snow built serpentine drifts across the open spaces, the commander of the last American armored unit still based in Germany had begun to assemble a convoy of trucks with an armored escort to come and get the Rangers. But the German authorities were holding up permission for those vehicles to move. The GPU had just announced that the Bundeswehr officers who were to have been the controllers for Operation Solid Steel were being held by GPU forces. Berlin felt that those officers' lives were in danger if the American convoy tried to run a GPU roadblock.

Spano brought up the ammo request and got assurances that the supplies would be loaded—but held pending further discussion between the Pentagon and the White House. Spano signed off the disappointing transmission by saying that he would try to delay the Germans as long as possible.

Mark Isen curled up just after midnight, having left instructions for his radio operators to wake him in two hours, or whenever word came from the States. He fell asleep immediately but slept fitfully, shivering in a makeshift cover of poncho and poncho liner. He thought about his sleeping bag, sitting somewhere on an Air Force pallet that was supposed to have been delivered by a German Army truck during the exercise. At one-fifteen, Sergeant Gamble shook him awake.

"Major Isen. Sir. Wake up," Gamble said.

Isen opened his eyes. The snowstorm had abated somewhat, though some flakes still came to rest on his face as he pulled at the small opening through which he'd been breathing.

"What is it?"

"Charlie Company just caught some people snooping around inside the perimeter," Gamble said.

Isen sat upright. "Colonel Spano know?"

"Yessir," Gamble said. "He's already on his way down there."

"You didn't wake me right away?" Isen demanded.

"Yes, we did, sir," Gamble answered. "Colonel Spano was already awake. I don't think he slept at all."

Isen dressed hurriedly and pulled on his boots, which he left unlaced as he jogged the twenty meters or so to where Spano was already questioning the Germans.

There were two soldiers, both of them very young, both dressed in uniforms that were too light for the weather. They knelt in the snow, two Rangers standing behind them and holding them prisoner with what Isen knew were unloaded rifles. But the Rangers' bayonets gleamed dully under the flashlight. Lieutenant Hawkins was also with them, standing behind the two prisoners.

"We saw some people moving around behind our platoon," Hawkins was saying as Isen approached. "We chased them, but they split up in the snow. At least two of them got away, but we nabbed these two."

Spano turned his red-filtered flashlight on the captives, who looked away from the light.

"I'd have shot them—" Hawkins began.

Isen made a chopping motion at his neck, and Hawkins remembered they weren't supposed to reveal their lack of live ammo.

Spano was bent over, peering into the faces of the two youngsters. He directed his remark at Hawkins.

"They wouldn't have been much help to us then," he said. He stood up, gave Hawkins a flat look, then turned to Haslem, who'd become part of Spano's command group.

"Ask them what they were looking for," Spano said.

The Germans remained silent under Haslem's questioning. Since each of Haslem's sentences sounded different to Isen's ear, he wondered if the soldier's German was strong enough to get what they wanted.

"Why don't we ask Rhone to question them, sir?" Isen asked.

"OK."

Rhone joined them in a few minutes, wrapped in a poncho some soldier had loaned him to cover his thin raincoat. Isen explained the situation. Rhone nodded once and walked behind the soldiers.

"Wonach haben gesucht?"

One of the soldiers tried to turn around to look at Rhone, but the major pushed his shoulder so that he was facing front again.

The two men said nothing, so Rhone leaned closer to them, almost whispering. Isen noticed Haslem straining to keep up with what the German officer was saying. Finally, one of the youngsters spoke.

"Wir wurden befohlen, fest zustfellen, was vor uns war."

Rhone straightened, then walked around the men until he was in front of Spano. Isen thought that Rhone glanced at Haslem, the only American around who spoke any German, but it was hard to tell in the red light reflected off the snow.

"They were looking for ways to bring their vehicles through the woods, Colonel," Rhone said.

Spano said nothing. Then Isen asked, "Why would they tell you that?"

"I told them we were going to hold them in the forward-most positions," Rhone said.

Isen looked at the two Germans again. They were very young, perhaps eighteen. They looked nervous, maybe a bit guilty about getting caught, but neither of them looked terrified. *I probably look more scared than they do,* Isen thought.

"Looks like Major Rhone's call is beginning to make sense, Mark. If they were just gonna wait until we turned ourselves in, why would they risk sending a patrol into our area?"

Isen didn't have an answer for that. He felt uneasy about the way things were unfolding, but he dismissed it as nervousness about the morning, about what might be an impending attack.

Spano waved Isen over to him. "The truck convoy won't get here before the morning, if it can move at all, and nobody is going to be able to fly in here," Spano said. "I'm going to call for the ammo."

8

LIEUTENANT KEN HAWKINS LOOKED SOUTH FROM THE WOOD-line out across the open airfield that had been the previous night's drop zone, and guessed that he could see no more than thirty feet. The snow came down steadily now, the wind twisting and turning the flakes in white skeins that moved every which way across his field of vision. His night vision goggles were useless in this weather, but the snow picked up and reflected whatever ambient light there was, making the field a little better than pitch black.

Charlie Company held the northern point of a triangle centered on the airfield and described by the positions of the three rifle companies. Hawkins's platoon was occupying the line facing north while another platoon got ready to recover Charlie Company's share of the ammunition that was to be dropped onto the airfield by U.S. Air Force planes flying up from Frankfurt.

Although Hawkins had been embarrassed when, on the first day, he'd been caught off in the woods without his radio, he felt as if the capture of the two German infiltrators by his platoon had put him back on top. When his platoon was passed over for the recovery job, Hawkins told himself that it wasn't as important as manning the fighting positions. And, in spite of his misgivings about what might happen in the morning when they were armed and squared off against the German vehicles, he had regained some of his confidence.

He made his way back through the woods to his platoon, where he walked the line, checking on and talking to the soldiers.

"Make sure your men keep dispersed," he told his NCOs. "And keep an eye out for any chutes that miss the drop zone. We don't want anybody getting hit in the head with five hundred pounds of ammo."

Hawkins flitted nervously along the line, talking to the soldiers, asking them how they were; whether their feet were dry; how many meals, of the three they'd been issued before departure, they had left. His concern was genuine enough, but it was clear to his NCOs, at least, that a lot of his talking was nervousness.

"Who's this?" he asked, coming up behind two dark forms lying outlined against the snow.

"Charis and Brennan, sir," Charis answered.

Hawkins hesitated for a moment, long enough for the soldiers to notice.

"You men OK?" Hawkins asked. "Your socks dry, and all that happy horseshit?"

"Yes, sir," Charis answered. Brennan said nothing.

"You OK there, Brennan? Too cold for you out here?" Hawkins asked.

"I'm doing just fine, sir," Brennan answered.

"They gonna have any chow on this drop, Lieutenant?" Charis cut in.

"I don't know," Hawkins replied, his voice joking again. "I asked for forty blonde Air Force babes to jump in and help us keep warm, so that's what I'm going to be looking for on the drop zone."

"I hear that, sir," Charis said.

"You guys keep an eye peeled for those chutes," Hawkins said. "Don't let one of them drop on top of you, hear?"

"Roger that, sir," Charis said.

When Hawkins had moved away again, Charis whispered to Brennan, "Why don't you ever talk when he's around, man?"

"He hates me," Brennan said, as if it were the most obvious thing in the world. "He thinks I'm a dud. And that thing with Sergeant Handy didn't help my stock any, either."

Charis considered his friend, who was as inscrutable in the darkness as in the full light of day.

"Man, you just worry too much," Charis said. "Just go with the flow."

"Yeah, go with the flow."

Charis peered into the gloom and the trees before them. "Besides," he said after a pause, "Lieutenant Hawkins is just like you and me, really. Ain't none of us been in the shit, so none of us know how we'll act. You know?"

"I guess so," Brennan said.

*   *   *

At three-thirteen the Air Force enlisted man who'd been on the ground with the safety party the first night turned on the homing beacon he'd placed on the center of the airfield, then turned for the edge of the strip where Isen and Spano waited with their radio operators near the control building. The first pass came exactly on schedule at three-fifteen while the airman was still trying to make his way to shelter through the thick blue-white drifts.

The sound of aircraft engines rolled in on the falling snow, thrumming louder and louder until the lead aircraft passed directly overhead, followed, fifteen seconds later, by another.

Major Rhone came running out of the building, crashing into Isen. "What's going on? What have you done?"

"That's our ammo," Isen said. He felt a little like giving in to panic himself.

Rhone stared up at the sky, though nothing was visible there as the aircraft sounds faded and the planes came around for another pass.

"Good God," Rhone said.

Lieutenant Ken Hawkins stared up into the snow, trying to see some sign of the cargo planes lumbering a few hundred feet overhead.

"Listen."

Sergeant Bishop was beside Hawkins, and he'd raised himself out of the prone position and was half-facing the woods before them.

"I think I heard something out that way," he said, pointing outside the perimeter.

"That would mean they overshot the drop zone," Hawkins said uncomfortably. The ammunition was supposed to be delivered to him by the other platoon, but if some of the bundles fell to the north of Charlie Company, someone would have to go after them. Maybe even race the Germans for them.

"I didn't hear anything," he said to Bishop.

It took the aircraft three and a half minutes to turn around for the second pass over the drop zone. It was easy to follow the sound, a distant buzz that dragged around them until it was in the southern sky again. When the planes approached the southern edge of the airfield, the woods south of the Rangers' position erupted in flashes of gunfire that lit the snowy horizon in blinking gold and gray. Bright tracers stabbed upward, and the lines of fire were visible all over the battalion's perimeter.

"Holy *shit*," Hawkins said.

"Holy shit is right," Bishop said.

A few seconds later, just as the firing tapered off, Bishop heard sounds out in front of them again. This time, it was unmistakable, and even Hawkins could hear the heavy bundles of ammunition crash through the trees. Though the sounds were generally muffled by the snow, several large limbs snapped as the aluminum pallets sped for the ground.

Bishop faced his platoon leader. "The ammo is out in front of us."

"Some of it is," Hawkins said. "Maybe there's enough of it behind us, out on the airfield."

"We should ask the CO, sir, if he wants us to go out after it. The sooner we move, the better," Bishop said.

Hawkins strained to see into the impenetrable woods. "I guess you're right." He hesitated for another few seconds.

"I can get my squad ready to move out, sir," Bishop prompted.

Hawkins came back from somewhere else. "All right," he said. "I'll talk to the old man."

By the time Hawkins returned from the company CP, Bishop had his two fire teams up and ready to move.

"We need to haul back as much ammo as we can," Hawkins said, "and we'll leave a couple of guys out there so it'll be easier to find on the second trip."

"If we have time to make a second trip," Bishop said. "I have a feeling our friends out there are going to try to stop us."

"Yeah," Hawkins said quietly. "Let's get going."

"I had the men fix bayonets," Bishop said. "You might want to go ahead and do that yourself."

"Right," Hawkins said.

Sergeant Bishop began to walk forward into the wall of snow and dark trees, his men stepping off behind him, keeping their interval. Ken Hawkins felt them go past him as he bent over the cold muzzle of his rifle, his hands shaking slightly as he slid the bayonet to its stud.

There was so little sound in the thick evergreens that Tim Brennan kept turning to make sure he wasn't alone in the woods. He could see only the "cat eyes" on Charis, the man in front of him—little strips of phosphorescent tape on the back of his helmet. He followed them as Charis followed the man in front of him. Since they weren't the lead team, the soldiers didn't have the goggles. The plan was that they would advance about fifty meters or so, then would get on line and comb the woods for the chutes and ammo.

"Here."

The voice was very low—the whole squad knew that the Germans were not far away, and that someone on the other side had already fired at the American aircraft.

Charis halted in front of him, so Brennan stopped. He heard rustling ahead of them, and he moved up carefully. Another soldier had come across one of the bundles, and he was using a small penlight as he worked the straps holding the crates to the pallet. Charis and Brennan joined him, and soon they were stacking the green cans of rifle and machine gun ammunition in the snow. The wooden crates protested noisily, and the handles on the metal cans clanked and squeaked so that Brennan was sure that they would be discovered at any moment.

They spent about five minutes unpacking the boxes before Sergeant Bishop came for them.

"Who's this?" he asked, coming upon them in the darkness.

"Charis, Brennan, and Spinello," Charis answered.

"All right, listen up," Bishop said as he knelt by the soldiers. "We're going to start hauling back the first load. I'm gonna leave you guys— Charis and Brennan—out here so you can guide us in when we come back."

"Great," Charis said.

"Somebody's got to do it," Bishop said. He felt no need to explain his decision, but he wasn't beyond acknowledging that they were getting the short straw.

"At least we won't have to haul all this crap back," Brennan said.

"That's the spirit," Bishop said. He sent them out another fifty meters to the forward-most pallet they'd found. On the way they passed four men from the other fire team heading back to the company, each carrying as many as six or seven of the cans.

"Since when did you get so friggin gung-ho?" Charis whispered when they were alone.

"I think the cold is getting to me."

Brennan bent over to inspect the dark rectangles spread on the snowy ground.

"These things feel like AT-4s," he said. "They should have carried these back first."

"Why's that?" Charis asked.

"'Cause these things can stop one of those Marders," Brennan said. He sat down on one of the crates that held the shoulder-fired antitank missile.

"Maybe we oughta—"

Charis was interrupted by the sound of voices. He turned to the rear, back in the direction of the Ranger perimeter.

"Did you hear that?" he asked.

Then the voices came again, slipping through the trees and the veil of snow.

"*Abstand halten. So dicht aneinander werden wir nichts finden.*"

"Shit," Charis said. "What do we do now?"

Brennan slid off the crate to the ground. That was precisely the question he wanted answered. "Let's get some ammo," he said.

Charis grabbed two green metal boxes he found with his foot, and Brennan grabbed two more. They walked backward a few meters, then knelt in the snow. The voices were getting louder.

"They're coming this way," Charis said. *"They're coming this way*, man."

Brennan looked up at his friend, all but invisible in the darkness. Brennan was frightened, a nightmarish I-can't-believe-this-is-happening fear, but Charis was worse—he seemed about to panic. And something told Brennan that wouldn't be a good thing for either of them.

"Look, just open one of those boxes and load a couple of your magazines," Brennan said. He pulled off his mittens, which dangled from his sleeves at the end of their retaining strings. He got the ammo box open easily enough, but his fingers were going numb as he fumbled with the packing material.

"Schau das mal an!"

A bright flashlight came on by the pallet they'd just left, and in its glare Brennan saw four or five men.

"Munition."

He looked down to where he'd managed to pry loose one small cardboard box of live rounds. Beside him, Charis was emitting a sound like a low groan in the back of his throat.

Brennan thought, *Shit, they're gonna hear us.*

"Be quiet," he hissed.

Then suddenly he could see Charis's face, eyes wide, mouth open, as the light played over them.

"Dort, ich sah 'was!"

The alarm in the voice reached Brennan, who dropped to his belly and pulled Charis down with him. With great difficulty he began to crawl backward through the thick snow and dead fall of branches, dragging the ammunition can and the boxes he'd freed and his rifle and mittens. He pinched a handful of fabric on Charis's pants leg and tugged at him.

Charis was frozen in place.

"Let's go, c'm'on," Brennan said.

Charis was on all fours, moving noisily along beside Brennan. He didn't seem to have any of the ammunition with him.

The first rounds crashed into the trees ten meters or so off to Brennan's right, but even the ground seemed to shake with the fire, incredibly loud in the still forest.

Brennan looked up. There were at least three lights playing on the woods now, swinging back and forth like crazy white eyes. Charis was facedown on the forest floor, his shoulders drawn up tight, his hands over his face.

Brennan was startled with a perfect clarity of vision. He was out of himself, and he apprehended the scene in its entirety: the swinging lights and the Germans behind the white muzzles of flashlights, Charis on the ground a few feet away, pinned in place by terror. Brennan didn't consciously think about what he must do next, he merely acted. He rolled over onto his back, dropping all but one of the cardboard boxes onto his chest. He tore the box, then slipped a hand down to his ammunition pouches and the empty magazines there. He cut his finger on the sharp metal clip that held the rounds together, but no blood came—his cold hands were drained. The bullets clicked into the magazine, and he could hear each one of them seating as he pressed against the spring.

The trees above his head were lit now by the probing lamps, and he could hear someone breaking brush close by, on the side.

They're trying to get around me.

Still no panic, just a clinical appreciation of the move, which he admired as he might a skillful chess maneuver. It made good sense.

Brennan rolled over on his stomach, fumbled the rifle up to his shoulder, tapped the magazine once against his palm and jammed it home.

Charis had pulled his knees up, so that he was crouched in the snow like a Muslin at prayer.

One of the white disks approached, a flashlight found Charis, and Brennan could see the German soldier take aim. Brennan brought his own rifle up, lifting the muzzle over the black shape of Charis, and pulled the trigger.

Nothing happened.

And then everything happened at once. The German's weapon fired, one, two shots, point blank range, at Charis. Brennan reeled up, felt the cold cold air flood his open mouth, pulled back the charging handle and shoved it forward. From somewhere there was a low growl that climbed to a scream, then the muzzle of Brennan's weapon split into tongues of fire, and the German fell away into the darkness.

Brennan stepped forward, knelt beside Charis. There were at least two more flashlights around them, and he fired at them until the Germans turned the lamps out. Brennan couldn't tell if the GPU soldiers were still advancing or not. As he strained to hear, Charis began to groan.

"Oh, my head," Charis moaned. "It's my head."

Brennan bent over and reached for the top of Charis's head, pulling his hand away from a hot streak on his buddy's helmet. He rolled Charis over, unbuttoned the man's chin strap and yanked the helmet clear.

"Owww," Charis moaned.

Brennan put his hand out, expecting the worst, but he felt only the bristly stubble of Charis's hair.

"If he hit you, your helmet saved you," Brennan said, his voice squeaky with fear. "We gotta move. Now." He grabbed Charis under one arm and yanked him backward, moving only about ten meters before he stopped to listen.

"Maybe they took off," Brennan said, trying to reassure himself and

Charis. He felt a sheen of sweat on his neck. There was no sound other than the heavy pumping of his heart. He was strangely exhilarated, like nothing he'd ever experienced.

"You OK?" he asked Charis.

"I guess. You?"

"I think I pissed my pants," Brennan said, feeling no embarrassment. Charis didn't answer.

"Could have been worse," Brennan said. "I could have crapped myself."

"We gotta get back," Charis said. He had regained some of his composure, but there was an unmistakable urgency in his voice. He didn't want to stay in the woods any longer.

Brennan picked up some of the boxes scattered in the snow. "We're supposed to guard this ammo," he said.

"Bullshit," Charis hissed. "We were supposed to be here to guide another party in. Nobody told us to guard anything. There's no telling how many of them are out there." He turned and scanned the trees, which were just starting to show blacker than the surroundings in the first hint of predawn light.

Brennan went on as if Charis hadn't spoken. "We've got to hurry, they may come back right away." He handed Charis two of the little boxes of ammunition. "Here, load these up."

Ordinarily, Brennan would have been surprised if Charis, or anyone else, listened to a suggestion of his on any matter. Now, even with their lives at risk, Charis acquiesced—unhappily, but without another word. He removed a magazine from the pouch on his belt and began loading the brass cartridges.

Brennan watched for a few seconds before he finished loading another magazine for himself. Then he stood slowly, scanning the area for movement.

"Let's not stay in the last spot they saw us," Brennan said. He had no clue where the ideas were coming from, but he felt the need to do something, to take charge, as Bishop would most certainly have done. "Let's move to the other side of the pallet so we can get the drop on them if they come back."

Brennan led the way toward the clearing where the ammunition pallet had splintered a tree, trying to walk in the footprints they'd already made. He was visited by a sudden fear that he wouldn't know what to do once they found another position. Which way should they face? What if the Germans rode up in an armored vehicle? What if they came back by the dozens?

Then his foot struck something and he fell to his knees. He put out a hand, hoping to find one of the ammunition cans they'd dropped.

It was the soldier he'd shot.

The man lay face up, arms flung wide, legs bent under his torso at a grotesque angle. A few moments ago, Brennan had shot this man without even thinking about it. They'd been racing to see who could pull the trigger first, and Brennan had won. But the dead man seemed not at all related to the threat and the fear Brennan had felt in the short fight. Now he was harmless, pitiful.

Brennan shook his head to clear his muddled thoughts. The German's light was still burning, buried in the snow so that only a dull glow showed through. *That was stupid,* Brennan thought, *walking around with those lights glaring.*

And all at once he realized that these soldiers were just as scared, just as confused as he was, and just as likely to make mistakes. He turned to Charis, who followed grudgingly.

"Just over here a little bit," Brennan said, his voice showing more confidence than he felt. "We'll go around to the north side—their side— and wait for them to come back. If there's too many, we'll lay low, OK?"

Charis didn't answer. He was too badly scared to weigh the choices, but not so frightened that he failed to notice Brennan's new role.

"Just follow me," Brennan said.

As soon as Ken Hawkins heard the gunfire behind him, he knew he had to go back in a hurry.

"Drop it all here," Hawkins told his NCOs. "Have your guys load up as many magazines as they can. We've got to go back and get those guys we left there."

Sergeant Bishop was surprised at how quickly Hawkins made the decision. For a moment, he wondered if Hawkins knew that it was Brennan out there. But then he was ashamed of the thought and he went to work loading magazines and exhorting his men to greater speed.

"We should send someone back to the company to lead another squad out so they can pick up the rest of this ammo," Bishop told Hawkins.

"Good idea," Hawkins said. "Do it." The lieutenant seemed just as agitated as before, but at least he was making decisions now.

Hawkins grabbed several boxes of rounds and began loading his own magazines as he talked to his two squad leaders.

"We'll head a little to the right of where the pallet is," Hawkins said. "Just so we don't walk up on any surprises. You got the azimuth, Sergeant Bishop?"

Bishop, whose squad was first in order of march, had used dead reckoning to figure out where, in relation to the company area, the ammunition had fallen: a particular compass heading for so many meters, measured by pace count.

"Ready, sir," Bishop said. He was anxious to get back and find Brennan and Charis, but he was just as determined to approach the area carefully, so as not to walk into any unpleasant surprises.

As the two squads picked up their traveling formation, with the men spreading out in small wedges among the trees, it occurred to Hawkins that he should have consulted with his commander.

"That thing still jammed?" he asked Keefer, his radio operator.

"Yessir," Keefer said. He'd been carrying around the dead weight of a useless radio in the hopes that there might be a break in the electronic jamming.

Well, at least we're doing something, Hawkins thought. *And I can't get chewed out for not having my radio along.*

As they walked, Hawkins thought about all the things that might happen in the woods ahead of them. At the infantry school, they'd taught him to plan for contingencies, and in the Ranger battalion, that philosophy was reinforced again and again. He knew he should be able to fit just about any possibility into one of several categories—if they were hit first, if they saw the enemy first, if they got ambushed—and he should be able to plan according to those categories. But Hawkins found the situation overwhelming—anything might happen out there. He had no indirect fire support, no communication with higher, no way to call for reinforcements or even for medical help beyond what his platoon medic could provide. The range of bad outcomes stunned him, and coupled with his own fear of failure, made him find the whole thing daunting. Every step took him deeper into a situation he felt unprepared to handle.

Given the ability to remain objective, he would have known that he was leading some of the best-trained soldiers in the world, that they were, in all probability, going up against some reservists with a fraction of the training and experience the Rangers had. But there was no logic, and instead of harking back to his most basic training as an infantry officer—think ahead—he went back to his football days, and he concentrated on remaining preternaturally alert, believing that he could react to whatever he found out there, and do so quickly enough to save his men and the mission.

None of these decisions were conscious, and the thought processes, overwritten with fear and nervousness, were not part of any pattern. Still, Hawkins managed to calm himself a bit, just enough to keep him moving forward into the gray woods.

Brennan touched Charis lightly on the arm when he heard the noise. It was there, then it was gone. Brennan cocked his head, opened his mouth to equalize the pressure and strained to hear it again.

I'm losing it, Brennan thought. *Maybe Charis was right, no one told us to stay out here.*

He blinked, touched his chapped lips with the tip of his tongue, struggling to breathe silently and quiet his heart.

There.

No more than a faint *brush, swish* that floated around the dark vertical lines of the trees.

Brennan tilted his head back. The tops of the trees were clearly visible now against a paling sky.

Brennan and Charis had positioned themselves just to the north and west of where the ammunition pallet lay broken on the forest floor. The soldier Brennan had killed lay south and east of the pallet, and it sounded as if the people moving through the woods ahead of them were going back to that spot, as Brennan had predicted.

"Can you see them?" Charis whispered.

Brennan got up on all fours, raised his head. The sounds were a tiny bit louder now, and more steady, but he could see nothing. He got to his knees. Nothing. Then there was something that might have been movement, and suddenly he saw the shoulders and helmeted head of a man glide above some undergrowth twenty meters away. Brennan stayed perfectly still and counted two, three, four more. He lay back down next to Charis, pressing his mouth up to his buddy's ear.

"There're at least five of them," he said, "heading back past the pallet."

"Looking for us," Charis said, his face almost in the snow.

"Or setting up an ambush," Brennan countered, "for whoever comes out next."

"They might not come back for us," Charis said. "Our guys, I mean."

"Of course they'll be back," Brennan said. "And we can't let them walk into an ambush."

"I was afraid you were going to say that," Charis said.

The two soldiers waited another few minutes before climbing out from under their covering of boughs. Brennan led as they walked east, then turned south in the snowy footsteps of the German patrol.

They walked for five meters, then stopped to look and listen. Another few meters, another stop. When he stopped the third time, Brennan could hear Charis's breathing behind him. He turned around, leaned close, his voice no more than a breath.

"You OK?"

Charis nodded, then shook his head slowly. *No.*

Great, Brennan thought. He realized that he'd come this far without any clear idea of what he was going to do when he found the Germans. And it would be hard to convince Charis, who actually outranked Brennan, to continue if he could not tell him what their plan was.

Brennan held up his pinched thumb and forefinger. *A little bit more*, he signed. He noticed, for the first time, that it was now light enough to see

Charis's face. The other soldier's eyes were wide open. He worked his mouth, without sound, then nodded. *OK.*

I wonder what I'm leading him into, Brennan thought.

When Brennan turned again, he saw what he was looking for.

Two boots, the legs not quite visible, the owner obviously lying face-down and looking away from where Brennan and Charis approached. Brennan's hand shot up. *Freeze.*

OK, he thought, *OK, I've found them, now what?*

Brennan stood still for what seemed like minutes, but was probably only five seconds or so.

No, I've only found one of them, he considered. *I've got to find the rest.*

Brennan backed away from the boots, taking Charis with him, circling to the east, farther away from the ammunition. Brennan reasoned that if the Germans were lying in ambush, the kill zone would no doubt be near that pallet.

As the two Americans moved back, they found themselves on a slope, a bit higher than the Germans in front of them. Charis crouched down behind some thick undergrowth and motioned to Brennan. It was almost full daylight.

"If we had some grenades, we could do 'em all," Brennan said.

Charis was amazed. "You want to take on a whole patrol?"

"We have to," Brennan said, "if our guys come walking this way, looking for us. . . ." It simply hadn't occurred to him that there was another option.

Charis rubbed his eyes with one finger. Brennan noticed that his partner had developed a tic—part of his right cheek jumped periodically, as if trying to shake off an insect.

"I say we go around them and head back," Charis said.

"We should wait a little while, maybe," Brennan said, unsure.

"What for?" Charis demanded. Even though he was still barely whispering, there was a noticeable change in his voice. "You have no idea what they're doing back there at the company. You don't *know* that they're coming for us," he said, leaning forward even farther. "And if you guess wrong, we're dead."

Brennan suddenly felt immensely tired. It was dawn of their second day in Germany, and he'd had no more than a couple of hours sleep, caught in small bits, in almost seventy-two hours. Fatigue covered him like some smothering ooze, settling in his joints, his neck, his legs. But something told him it wasn't time to rest. Not yet.

Charis was angry and scared; neither of them had any experience like this. Besides that, Charis had been shot at point blank range. What would that do to a man?

He's right, Brennan thought, *I'm acting like I'm Audie Murphy.*

But even as he considered leaving the area, some nagging thought rolled over in him like a stone. They wouldn't be at all surprised, back at the platoon, if he came crawling back. Especially Hawkins. And the lieutenant would say something every chance he got.

The Germans below them spoke.

"Bereitet."

Brennan crawled furiously to where he could see some of the German patrol. Most of them were still invisible to him, lost amid the trees and snow-draped branches. But there was something else out front. Movement.

Rangers, Brennan thought.

He and Charis were behind the German ambush line, and the Rangers were approaching from the front. Approaching the kill zone. Brennan took a second to look over at Charis, who'd moved up beside him and saw—judging by his expression—what Brennan saw.

Brennan was seized with a giddy feeling, as if all time, all of his life, had rushed funneling downward and was now focused on this hard crystal point.

With no more control over his actions than he experienced when he stepped out of an airplane in midair, Brennan stood and ran down the hill at the Germans from behind, screaming hard, up from his belly.

"Yahhhh. . . ."

Sergeant Bishop fell to the ground with the first popping noises of gunfire ahead of them. His first thought was that they'd walked into an ambush, but then, as three, four, five more reports came to them, he knew that the shooting was up ahead and not, apparently, directed at them. He pushed himself up into a crouch and darted forward to his point man.

"What do you see?"

"Nothing," the soldier answered. "Not a thing."

After the briefest of pauses, another rifle, then a third weapon that wasn't familiar. With that, Bishop realized that the first two were M16s, which meant that Brennan or Charis or both of them were up there shooting.

Lieutenant Hawkins reached them as the firing withered.

"See anything?" he asked.

"No," Bishop replied. "But at least two of those weapons were M16s." He turned to his lieutenant. "That means our guys are out there."

Hawkins got up on a knee. The forest ahead of them had dissolved into a watercolor of varying shades of gray. Visibility was fairly good here where the trees thinned out and the forest bent upward on a hill, but even in the light there was nothing to see.

"We'll go on," Hawkins said. "But let's swing around to the right a little, so we're not walking directly up on where the shooting was." He tapped the magazine in his rifle. "They might be waiting for us."

When he looked up, there was movement in the trees ahead of him. Hawkins brought his rifle to his shoulder; Bishop and the point man did the same.

There, a vague shape coming toward them, green against the gray and black of the wet trees. Hawkins's thumb pressed the selector switch from safe to fire.

"It's Brennan," Bishop said.

Hawkins held the sight picture another second.

"Sir," Bishop said, placing his hand on the stock of Hawkins's rifle. "It's Brennan."

Hawkins let the muzzle ride down with Bishop's insistent pressure. Then he could see Brennan and Charis.

"Just wanted to make sure," he said.

The two soldiers were almost on top of their comrades before they saw them. When Brennan stopped running, Charis bumped into him.

"Damn," Charis said. "Are we glad to see you guys."

"You all right?" Bishop asked.

Brennan nodded. Nauseated, he bent over, hands on his knees, and spit on the ground. Nothing else came.

"Let's get out of here," Hawkins said.

"What about the ammo, sir?" Brennan said. "It's right up there a little bit."

"Who were you shooting at?" Bishop asked.

"There was a German patrol waiting to ambush you guys," Brennan answered, his breath still coming in sharp bursts.

"But we got them first," Charis said. "Actually, Tim got them, I just joined in at the end."

Brennan saw Hawkins look at him, then at Charis, then back to him. "They're dead?"

"Yessir, three of them," Brennan said. "A couple got away." There was no triumph in his voice.

"Five of them?" Bishop asked. "There were five of them?"

Brennan nodded, and Bishop blew through his teeth, a low whistle.

"All right," Hawkins said. "Let's go up and pick up another load of ammo. We aren't hanging around, though. They'll be sending more people out."

Sergeant Bishop raised his hand, motioning for his men to follow.

Lieutenant Hawkins stepped past Charis and Brennan. "See if you can find your helmet, Charis."

9

A GRIM RAY SPANO REPORTED THE CONTACT BY THE CHARLIE Company patrol, adding that he was preparing to defend his position in the event of German attack.

They'd lost several pallets to the GPU in the scramble that followed the drop. The most significant losses had been part of the ration load and most of the mortar ammunition. Isen helped Spano prepare notes on the losses for the transmission, and the operations officer stood by as the colonel listened to the men on the other end. When the conversation was finished, Spano tapped the radio handset against his leg while he stared at the ground. Finally, Isen could wait no longer.

"Well, sir?"

"Well," Spano said. He seemed to be searching for the right words. "If you were thinking that it couldn't get any worse, you were wrong."

Spano turned the handset over to the radio operator. There was no doubt that the soldier had heard Spano's pessimistic report, and, things being what they were, with everyone avid for information, the word would be around the battalion soon.

"Let's go over here, sir," Isen said. He steered Spano away from the little knot of headquarters people huddled in the lee of the block wall.

"What exactly did Colonel Schauffert say?" Isen asked.

"He said that they're trying to get some air support up here, some antitank helicopters and stuff, but nobody can fly in this mess." He looked around forlornly, the portrait of a man expecting the worst. Tiny snow-flakes stuck to his eyelashes.

There wasn't much more to say. Without air support to fight off the German armored vehicles in the woods around them, the Rangers stood little chance. Since the airdrop, the Rangers were armed with a mix of antiarmor weapons: the German-made Karl Gustav rocket, the ninety-millimeter recoilless rifle, and the lightweight AT-4s. These could stop a Marder with a well-placed—read lucky—hit on the flank or rear, less likely with a frontal shot. But that kind of shooting needed more room than the close woods offered, and it would be difficult to get good shots off if the Germans came on in a rush, snapping shut the noose on this small perimeter.

"And the Germans are apparently no closer to letting any convoys come up from the south to help us. Colonel Schauffert said that the State Department is involved, but now there's some question about loyalty. Seems that the authorities in the south, the ones holding up the convoys, some of the police organizations and maybe even some of the regular army units, aren't quite ready to side with Berlin over the GPU."

We're fucked, Isen thought.

Spano sat down heavily, kicking his boots out in front of him.

Isen felt the urge to rant against what was happening, to scream and shout and punch someone. But his job was to think, not to panic. He was supposed to think and provide advice and somehow help Spano get them all out of this mess, with or without help from the outside. Isen balled his fists inside his mittens and pushed them deeper into his pockets.

"This fucking weather is killing us," Spano said.

He was right, of course. All the fancy communications equipment in the world couldn't get aircraft to fly in this weather, at least not the kind of close-support missions they needed. Their electronic wizardry was humbled out here, and they became simply a battalion of soldiers shivering through a snowstorm. For all their grand technology, they were cut off by the storm, as isolated as the Grande Armée on the road from Moscow.

The weather had to break soon, Isen believed, but even if it did, their problems wouldn't end there. They were still ignorant as to what was happening in the rest of the country. He believed that American units could eventually fight through to them, but there would be a critical period, twenty-four, maybe forty-eight hours, where they would have to go it alone. If the Bundeswehr sided with the GPU against them, if the police wouldn't let the American convoys roll, then even clear weather would leave them as they were now—stuck in the middle of a hostile country, friendless, vulnerable, and all but alone.

Behind the wall, the Rangers were huddled in their parkas, barely moving, like thickly wrapped scarecrows riding out the storm. The snowfall seemed to have slowed, but the wind had picked up, so that one could hardly see across any open space for the white horizontal streaks drawn across the ground. Isen recalled a night in his stint in the Army's Ranger school, at the tail end of a cold January, stuck up in the hills above the mountain camp in north Georgia. A half dozen students had been evacuated for cold weather injuries, but the instructor with Isen's patrol, a hard-bitten twenty-six-year-old from Minnesota, had different ideas.

"No one is wimping out of this fucking patrol," he'd told Isen and the group. Although this rattled the students a bit, since they were completely subject to this man's control, it turned out he wasn't just trying to scare them. The buck sergeant had a point to make about the hard reality of the footsoldier's lot. And there was something else, too.

"Look, men," he said to them after he'd pulled them into a little circle of shivering, almost shapeless forms. "If you guys think that you're cold, don't you think the bad guys will be cold too?"

He'd been right, of course, though the lesson was hard to swallow while they were playing at war. But in his combat experience, Isen had told himself more than once that the other guy was just as scared and uncertain as he was, maybe even more so. He turned to those thoughts as he squatted next to Spano.

"Sir," Isen said to the colonel. "Remember I told you about going in that tent with that company commander, and all those guys were sitting around drinking coffee and schnapps?"

"Yeah," Spano said.

"Well, I figure there's a good chance that there are a lot more of those tents out there by now," Isen went on. "I'd be surprised if the troops sat around all night in those cold steel tracks while the NCOs and officers get toasted in warm tents."

Spano looked at him, weighing the argument. "Rhone seems to think they're likely to attack soon."

"We haven't heard any vehicles moving into attack positions, and we're certainly close enough to hear the engines."

"Go on," Spano said.

Isen had a fleeting sensation that Spano was losing his ability to concentrate. Maybe it was the cold. *Maybe it's me*, he thought.

"So if they're sitting around in tents, then this weather is an opportunity for us," Isen said, aware that he was about to step beyond some important line. "No one told us—specifically—that we have to wait for the Germans to make the first move."

Spano studied the younger man's face for a moment. "No sense waiting for them to come to us, right?"

"That's exactly what I had in mind," Isen said somberly. "That's exactly it."

*   *   *

There was a lot of work to be done under difficult conditions, but the Rangers were glad to be doing something. The hours of sitting around, interspersed with the deadly serious crackling of gunfire during Brennan's fight, had set on edge the nerves of every soldier in the wide perimeter. The plan that Spano and Isen drew up in the morning at least got the soldiers' minds off the specter of impending disaster.

Spano called the company commanders in and told them that they were going to do something to take away the GPU's offensive capability. But they could not take any direct action until something happened. Defining that something would be the hard part.

Isen told the commanders to establish positions, using one of the three squads in each of their three platoons, as close as possible to the German positions. That would put one third of the Rangers' strength right in the pocket of the GPU. These men were to pinpoint and record the exact location of every vehicle they could spot—paying particular attention to the Marders and other offensive vehicles—as well as the German tents and fighting positions they could find. The soldiers would establish a hide position from which they could keep an eye on the Germans, and stash in those positions most of the antitank weapons the Rangers had secured after the ammo drop. If the Germans started to make threatening moves, the Americans would hit them first, before they got a chance to roll.

"The risks are pretty obvious," Isen said. "Our guys will be on the ground next to these vehicles, and the only advantage we'll have to even the odds is surprise."

"What if we're reading them wrong?" Gene Wisneiwski, the Bravo Company commander, said. "I mean, what do we know about their intentions?"

Isen started to speak, but Spano raised his hand. He had excluded Rhone, the German major, from the meeting. Spano would be the one to make the call, and he wanted to avoid giving the impression that he'd been unduly influenced.

"Based on what I've learned about their overall objectives, I don't think they're about to let us out of here."

The company commanders were quiet for a few moments.

"There's one other thing." Bill Dettering, the C Company commander, spit tobacco juice between his feet, then wiped his mouth with the back of a gloved hand. "How will we know if they're going on the offensive? I mean, what if they crank up the engines and start backing up? That could mean that they're pulling out, or it could mean that they're moving to an attack position somewhere else."

"Mark and I discussed that one, and I discussed it with Colonel Schauffert," Spano said. "This is where the biggest risk comes in. There's a chance that we'll fire them up when they have no intention of attacking. . . ." He let that comment hang, as if he were only part way through the sentence. But Spano and Isen had decided that there was little they could do to get this one right. "If we think about the alternatives—hold fire until they start shooting or risk shooting them early," Spano said, "I have decided that we're going to go with the second."

He let the point settle for a few seconds.

Ray Spano was not a melodramatic man. He was not given to theatrics, and he wasn't acting when he talked about the consequences. "I will take full responsibility for this decision," he said. "These people have demonstrated that they're willing to shoot us. I have determined that we are in grave danger here. We will use force when we feel threatened. And that's that."

That wasn't all, of course. There were lots of questions about the timing of the reconnaissance—they couldn't afford to have everyone moving around the perimeter at once. The company commanders suggested, and Spano agreed, that the squad occupying the forward position should be rotated fairly often. It was going to be tough to stay on the edge out there, lying still in a snow cave and watching a bunch of shadowy, stationary vehicles.

But those were all answerable questions, things that could be worked out and planned. Finally, the tough questions would have to be answered by the captains and the lieutenants and the sergeants they were about to send off into the snowy woods to find and face the black shapes that waited there.

Brennan was glad that his squad, which had been through enough in the previous two days, didn't get the first rotation out in the woods. One of the other squads spent the time from eleven until after two crawling around in the deep snow out near the German positions, pinpointing the location of as many armored vehicles as they could identify.

As Brennan rested in his fighting position and watched the snow blow across the trees, steady as a painting, he imagined how difficult it would be to find even those big vehicles in this weather. Normally, the squad doing the reconnaissance would follow a design, crawling back and forth in a pattern that suggested the petals of a flower or described a circle around the objective. But in this poor visibility, it was likely that a soldier would get disoriented, doubling back, counting the same vehicles two or three times. It would be up to the squad leader to sort out what he found and hand it over to the next squad in the rotation. The second squad to go out would build snow caves where the Rangers would wait, guarding the German vehicles before them, watching for some hostile sign.

Brennan was glad he missed the day out in front of the line, but he knew that meant he and his squadmates would get the first shift of night duty. Brennan wasn't sure that Charis, his partner, was up to it.

For several hours the normally talkative soldier had been silent in the position the two men shared. He didn't even complain about the cold. Brennan let him alone for a while, but finally tried to draw him out.

"It's going to be cold out there tonight, man," Brennan said. "Sitting around in those snow caves."

This got no response, so he pressed on, thinking he'd try one of Charis's favorite subjects—baiting Lieutenant Hawkins.

"Remember when we went on that exercise in Alaska, and Hawkins's snow cave collapsed on him in the middle of the night?"

No response.

Brennan was sitting on the edge of the shallow hole the two men had scraped in the snow and the frozen ground. Although the drifting snow had not filled their position any faster than they could bail it out, the white ridges made it impossible to see to the front if one stood in the bottom. So they were obliged to sit above ground. Yet, even with his body exposed, Brennan was not all that worried. In the enveloping snow it was easy to imagine that he and Charis were the only two people in the whole countryside. The whiteness pulled a cocoon tight around them, filtering sound and all but a dull light that seemed to come from everywhere and nowhere.

Brennan looked down at his friend. He figured Charis was angry with himself for his performance out by the ammo drop. Brennan was not anxious to take on the role of Charis's counselor—that seemed like something that one of the sergeants should be doing. But they were alone, Charis was his friend, and besides, the two of them would soon have to depend on each other again.

"What's eating you?" Brennan asked.

"You mean besides the fact that I was a complete dud this morning?" Charis asked.

Brennan was about to argue with him, but Charis's voice had some tiny hint of that humor—self-deprecating, to be sure, but humor nonetheless—that would help him deal with his problems.

Maybe he'll work through this, Brennan thought.

"I was just thinking about how wrong everybody was about you," Charis said. He got to his feet and stood next to his partner. "Especially the legendary Hawk Man. You turned out to be quite a . . . fighter."

"I was scared to death the whole time," Brennan said, looking away.

"Yeah, but you still did *something*," Charis answered.

Brennan thought about the men he'd shot less than twelve hours ago. They'd left them out there, of course, three bodies tossed against the snow like misshapen dolls, looking nothing at all like men. When Brennan thought of the figures, he was visited by a line whose source he couldn't recall, something about man as *the paragon of animals*. Yet the bodies stiffening in the snow and cold left him thinking that perhaps being human was, for all that, not such an exalted position.

"I don't know what happened to me out there," Brennan said. "It was like someone else was doing it all."

Like a movie, he thought.

Tim Brennan couldn't reconcile the image he had of himself with what had happened out in the woods.

"No matter where it came from, man," Charis said, "you were doing it."

No, Brennan thought. *A fluke. I couldn't do it again.*

"You're the guy I want with me, my man," Charis said.

Brennan looked at him, his face a model of wide-eyed surprise. "No," he said. "Don't start counting on me every time." He smiled, trying to make a joke of it.

"That's the way it works, man," Charis said. "You lean on me, I lean on you."

The two men sat uncomfortably with their truths until Charis could no longer stand the silence.

"I'll tell you one thing, man."

"What's that?" Brennan asked.

"If I'd known that things were gonna get this hairy—with a good chance of me getting shot—I'd have gone ahead and gotten that big-ass tattoo you talked me out of."

They were chuckling over that when Sergeant Bishop came up behind them. "Doesn't sound like you guys got much sleep."

"We got some, Sergeant," Charis said.

Bishop was showing signs of strain, Brennan decided. His eyes were red-rimmed, his mittens sooty from whatever fire he'd been allowed during daylight hours. Like the rest of the Rangers, he hadn't washed or shaved since they'd jumped. It took heat tablets to melt snow for water, and no one was about to indulge in such a luxury. Still, his first question was always about their well-being, and his briefings were just as careful and complete.

"We move out at fifteen-thirty," he said. "That will give us a little while to get into position before the sun goes down. Once we're out there, second squad—that's who we're relieving—will brief us on what they know about the German positions and will show us where everything is."

"You mean where the vehicles are?" Charis asked.

"Where the vehicles are and where our ammo is," Bishop answered. "The idea is that if they start to come after us, we're going to fire them up first."

"Fuckin' A," Charis said.

Brennan wondered how they were supposed to know it was an attack if the Germans didn't start shooting first. Who would tell them to fire? But he figured that his superiors had probably already addressed this concern and must have come up with a good, solid plan.

They moved out as a squad, then broke into their smaller fire teams once they were a few meters in front of the perimeter. They were met in the woods by guides from the second squad who took them where they needed to go without a bunch of thrashing around. Brennan and Charis inherited a small hollow scraped out of the snow behind a large fallen tree. Inside, the soldiers they were relieving had drawn sketches of what they'd found in their sector.

"These three are Marders," the soldier-guide told them, pointing to little rectangles he'd drawn on a crude map fashioned from ammunition packing material. "These are trucks, and these are tents."

"Tents?" Charis asked.

"Yeah," the soldier replied. "That's where they've been for hours."

"Can't say I blame them," Charis joked. "If I had a tent I'd be in it, too."

"So the idea is to get them while they're still in the tent?" Brennan asked.

"Or at least before they get their vehicles fired up," the soldier replied. "We got six AT-4s here," the soldier said. "About a dozen grenades and some flares." The ammunition was laid out under the cover of a pine bough someone had cut from a tree. The dark green cannisters and boxes were stark against the snow.

"You're supposed to take the AT-4s and crawl up there," the soldier said, indicating a small rise that was just visible through the underbrush and the snow. "From there you'll be able to see them."

The two newcomers surveyed the area silently.

"Look, I've gotta go. My squad is pulling out. You guys need to know anything else?"

Only about a million things, Brennan thought. They were just a few dozen meters from the Germans, it was still snowing, it was getting colder and would be dark soon. And Brennan still wasn't sure if he'd know when to shoot.

Looking about, Brennan saw how close panic could be.

"No, I guess not," Brennan said. "Thanks, man."

Alone again, Charis and Brennan checked their weapons and loaded their belts with grenades while they waited for Sergeant Bishop to send them forward. They didn't have to wait long. They reached the small rise, which, in spite of the falling snow, was marked with footprints and the signs of crawling men. Brennan kept his head pressed almost to the ground, taking care that he couldn't be seen. He was in control of what he was doing, but he was not ready for what he saw.

The two Marders sat side by side, separated by only ten or fifteen feet, in the woods below them. Brennan couldn't believe how close they were. He could hear voices, but saw no one moving about. As he studied the silhouettes, trying to memorize their positions and the attitudes of their twenty-millimeter guns before the last light faded, he thought about advancing on those machines, but he couldn't picture it.

Paul Gedern rotated his shoulders, which were beginning to ache from the effort of keeping them shrugged against the cold for the past hour. He was sitting cross-legged on an ammunition crate inside the overcrowded and overheated tent he and his squad had erected behind their Marder, and he was doing his best to look inconspicuous. He was certain that Sergeant Brufels, his squad leader, was going to send them all outside at any moment. He figured that they should all be on guard; the Americans had shown themselves willing to fight. But the leaders couldn't seem to agree on what to do. And in the meantime, if the NCOs and officers thought it was all right to be dry and warm, that was good enough for Gedern.

A soldier Gedern didn't recognize, a new man from the adjacent squad, was playing straight man for Brufels's pontificating.

"Don't you think it's dangerous to antagonize the Americans?" the soldier asked.

"They have been the source of strain between two halves of our country since nineteen forty-five," Brufels said. "They deserve everything they get."

"They are dangerous, though. Powerful," the soldier pressed.

"They had an impressive army at the end of the war in the Persian Gulf," Brufels allowed. "But they took it apart. No, they *tore* it to pieces to save the money they'd been spending on it all along. Now they're left with virtually nothing. Berlin did the same thing to the Bundeswehr, using the money to feed and house all the damned *auslaenders* they so foolishly let in."

Gedern caught himself shaking his head slightly. The xenophobic rhetoric was familiar, and the talk went round and round, from theoretical to paranoid and back again, all the while moving further and further from the reality of what was happening. Gedern thought the debate sounded as if it should be in a school, a mere discussion of hypothetical events. They were talking as if the problem existed somewhere else while, just outside, their combat vehicles sat loaded, ready to make war against the Americans.

But Gedern was not about to become engaged in the talk. That ass Brufels would just send him outside on guard duty.

"I heard that the Bundeswehr is joining our cause," Heidt said. The eighteen-year-old had managed to look interested for both hours that Brufels had spouted the GPU line about "Germany for Germans."

"I wouldn't be surprised," Brufels said in a tone suggesting that perhaps he was responsible for the alliance. "And that would be the final act. The Americans wouldn't dare make a move against the whole German armed forces."

Gedern wanted to ask where Heidt had gotten his information, since they'd all been together in the woods—with only the chain of command to rely upon for news—since this thing began. But he didn't want to confront Brufels or draw attention to himself by making comments about the army's loyalty to the Grundgesetz, the basic federal law, or the military's historical mistrust of politicians. It wouldn't convince Brufels, and it would only land Gedern outside the damned tent. Gedern settled deeper into his overcoat, flexing his cold fingers inside his pockets, wondering what the Americans were doing to keep warm.

He must have fallen asleep sitting up, because when Stoddard burst into the tent, Gedern fell off the ammo box, his hands still pressed down into his pockets. At first there was no shape to the voices, no sense of what they were saying, just volume. But after he shook his head and opened his eyes to see the lieutenant in the yellow glow of gaslight, he began to understand.

"Berlin has declared the GPU illegal," Stoddard was telling Brufels and the others. "They are running scared of us, but we are too big now."

He's smiling, Gedern thought. *He's enjoying this, as if we were heading into some soccer match.*

"What are we going to do?" Brufels asked. He too had been sleeping, and his hair stuck out from his head at unlikely angles.

"The GPU is going to march on Berlin and throw them out," Stoddard announced, as if it were the most obvious thing in that world. "That's what we should have done a long time ago."

Gedern felt his mouth working. These fools were talking about anarchy, about treason and a violent overthrow of the government.

They'll throw our asses in jail and lose the key.

He looked around, hoping that someone with some common sense would announce that it was all a game. But the soldiers around him were no more willing to resist than was Gedern. They were green stalks, pushed this way and that by whatever breeze blew through.

"But first we have some little business to attend to here," Stoddard said. "The party will soon announce to the public that this American force was sent here to help the Berlin government interfere with the people's will. We will neutralize the Americans first."

Gedern scrambled to his feet, his head going light from the sudden move, from the odd phrase. *Neutralize? Neutralize? What does that mean?* But he didn't interrupt his sergeant and the officer.

"We have the honor of leading the advance," Stoddard told Brufels. "We are to destroy everything in their perimeter."

Gedern felt swept away. Then he thought about the infantrymen in the woods, who would be no match for the giant armored fighting vehicles.

"Gedern," Sergeant Brufels called. "Get her fired up."

Gedern stood still, his mouth working silently. Shocked by the calm announcement that they would soon start fighting, he felt himself distracted, wishing he had a few moments to gather his thoughts. The earth had shifted under him, but he did not know how to name the thing.

"Gedern," Brufels said loudly. "Get your ass moving."

"Yes, Stabsunteroffizier," Gedern said.

And so he turned and stumbled out of the tent, his head reeling with concerns over what was to come. Much later, in a calm moment, he would see the sticking point. In a few quick seconds, Stoddard had put the Territorial Forces at the disposal of the GPU, and Gedern and the others had simply followed orders.

Yes, Stabsunteroffizier.

Spano and Isen got the word about Berlin's actions more than an hour before the Germans outside the perimeter heard it. The trouble was—how were they to interpret it?

"The State Department says that they're no more likely to attack us than they were earlier," Spano told his assembled company commanders. "Some guy who has the chief's ear is even saying that they'll probably take some of the assets they have here away for other stuff."

Spano paused, looked up from the little flip book in which he'd taken notes during his latest round on the SATCOM. He wondered if he looked, to his young commanders, as confused as they looked to him.

"Colonel Schauffert, on the other hand," Spano said, "has allowed that they might try to get rid of us so that we pose no threat to their rear. Or they might do it to show the people—the vast majority of Germans who are undecided about whom to support here—that they can handle the Americans."

"Then we're dusted."

Spano looked around slowly for the source of the comment. Captain Tommy Lee Chang, U.S. Air Force, the Tactical Air Controller for the battalion, met Spano's straightforward gaze.

Chang, who'd flown dozens of sorties in the Gulf War, had been through his share of tough spots. He wasn't one to panic, and Spano was convinced that all that was showing here was frustration. Chang could talk to the whole world on the sophisticated radios he and his men carried, but the aircraft couldn't fly close air support without some degree of visibility. So, for the time being at least, Chang, his men, and their radios were just so much dead weight.

"Well, we'd certainly be in for a fight," Spano said.

Bill Dettering, who commanded C Company, jumped in. "Don't be too sure that we won't give them enough of a beating to get them off our backs," Dettering said. He didn't like Chang, didn't like the implication that all was lost. "With or without Air Force help," Dettering finished.

Chang, feeling hamstrung and useless, didn't take the insult lightly. "Fuck you," he said.

Dettering bristled, was about to speak.

"Knock it off," Spano said, surprised at how quickly his anger flared. "The last thing I need is for the people I have to count on to start acting like a bunch of fucking teenagers."

Dettering managed to look sheepish and angry at the same time. "Sorry, sir," he said.

"Sorry, sir," Chang said.

Wisneiwski, B company's big, pragmatic commander, ignored the spat. "Maybe we should try to take them out, or as many of them as we can. Then they can't use this equipment to overthrow the legitimate government."

"That's a good point, Gene," Spano said. "But it isn't our place to get in the middle here. If we do anything, it will be to protect this command."

Spano looked at his watch. He had no idea how long the GPU had had the news about Berlin's actions. He wanted time to talk about their options with his commanders and with Isen, but time was short, and when time was critical the law was: rule by decree.

"I want you to move your platoons forward. Be ready for anything out there—don't get caught flat-footed." He flipped the notebook closed. "If they come at us, if they threaten us, we'll hit them all at once. The object is to get them before they have a chance to get us. You know the rest of the drill."

As Spano listened to the few questions they still had, and as he watched Isen field the questions competently, he had the strange sensation that what was happening wasn't real. Where Isen and two of his company commanders had been in combat before, Spano had not. He and Isen had been in a couple of firefights in Mexico, but he'd never been involved in anything larger than a shootout—and in most of those he had even or better than even odds on his side.

Things were different this time. He'd always thought that the minutes before going into action would be somehow different from other times—suspended, dramatic, fat with anticipation, like movie minutes. But for all the anxiety and worry, these minutes were like any others in that they were connected to the mundane. He was still aware—perhaps more aware—of other sensations. He knew he'd have to talk to his radio operators and brief them on what he wanted. He had to repack his ruck in case they had to move quickly. He wanted to change his socks, which were damp with perspiration.

He figured that Isen would be steady but one or two of his company commanders might get rattled, and he would have to reassure them. There were a million details to think about, but the single most unnerving thing was his concern that he might start a fight that didn't need to be fought.

When he dismissed the company commanders, Spano pulled Isen aside.

"Did they tell us to hit them first, sir?" Isen asked.

"You know what deniability is, right?"

Isen nodded. Sometimes superiors granted approval by not withholding it, with the understanding that the subordinates—who were in the only position to know what was required—would bear the burden of responsibility if things turned out badly.

"Colonel Schauffert told me he didn't buy this crap that the Germans would leave us alone out here," Spano said. "There were already pictures on the TV news over here of those guys that Brennan shot this morning. The story is that we're the hostile ones."

Spano pulled his nine-millimeter pistol from its holster and checked the action.

"Schauffert said that I was the one who knew what was going on here, and that he trusted that I knew enough about the political implications of a fight to keep us out of one if possible. But finally it comes down to protecting my men."

Isen nodded. If things turned out badly, if their attack proved suicidal or contributed to a larger conflict, Spano would bear the blame personally. Isen looked at his commander and tried to memorize what he was seeing and hearing against the day he might have to testify as to Spano's state of mind, about the actions that led to this decision.

"I don't believe for a minute our intelligence was so bad that no one knew all this shit might happen," Spano said. He sucked his lips back against his teeth. "I think some asshole at State or at the Pentagon let us get stuck out here." He looked at Isen, a small, ironic grin working the corners of his mouth. "I'm just afraid I won't be around to find the SOB so I can kick his ass."

Throughout his career, in a dozen different school-setting discussions of the limits of force, Isen had never imagined that such an assumption— that the men on the ground should make the final call—could come to this. Spano had to be free to act, to protect his command. But if ever there was an illustration of the cliché about the tail wagging the dog, this was it.

Spano was a man tormented, but his biggest fear was for the soldiers who'd been entrusted to his care.

"When we go, we're going all out," Spano said. He hitched his webbed belt, adjusted his helmet. "We've got to get the first licks in," he said, " 'cause this may be our only chance."

*　　*　　*

Ken Hawkins was on, and he knew it.

"This is it, we're going to take it to them, really fuck 'em up before they even get out of their fart sacks," he told his squad leaders. He'd given them a thumbnail sketch of what he wanted them to do when they got the word, a fairly simple—in terms of its planning—attack. Execution was another story. It would be tough to pull off, nearly impossible if the Germans moved first or got wind of what was going on. That was the contingency on which Sergeant Bishop wanted to concentrate.

"Are we going to establish a rally point for the platoon out by our jump-off position?" Bishop asked. *In case we get our asses kicked*, he thought.

"Huh? Yeah, yeah," Hawkins said. "We'll make the hide position our initial rally point. But tell the boys to head back to the company if . . . if they need to."

Ken Hawkins was not a stupid person. He knew that there were other ways to approach this business. He imagined some of the other platoon leaders were very methodical in their briefings, using all the time available to go over in minute detail every contingency, every possible outcome. But Hawkins believed that combat was largely a matter of will, and he believed it was his responsibility as a leader to infuse his men with what he thought of as the "warrior spirit." He would never be so "Hollywood" (the Rangers' all-purpose term to describe the love of show over practicality) as to name this warrior spirit, or even mention its existence out loud, but he believed in it, and he believed it was a factor. Some people had it, and some people didn't. And just as it was the responsibility of some officers to plan logistics and coordination, it was the job of some officers to imbue soldiers with the will to fight.

Ken Hawkins, who had only recently heard shots fired somewhere other than a rifle range, was sure that his approach to the coming fight was the correct one. And in pursuing what he saw was the right way, he saw himself as no different from the planners, the detail men like Isen, or even the old man, Colonel Spano.

"Any questions?" he asked his squad leaders.

Sergeant Bishop looked at his peers, most of them already lost in thought, outlining in their heads the plans they would brief to their soldiers. He wondered if any of them saw the dangers in Hawkins's seat-of-the-pants approach, and he wondered if, once again, he was letting the fact that he didn't like Hawkins interfere with his judgment.

"OK, then," Hawkins said. "We move out in fifteen minutes."

"Rangers lead the way, sir," two of the squad leaders said automatically as they rose and headed back into the darkness and to their men.

"Something bothering you, Sergeant Bishop?" Hawkins said.

"Oh, I don't know, sir," Bishop said. "It's not exactly a situation from the textbook, is it?"

Hawkins felt sorry for Bishop. First he'd lost Sergeant Handy, a top-notch junior NCO. And he had to contend with that loser Brennan in his squad, which had to be like playing with a handicap. On top of that, Hawkins had heard that Charis—also one of Bishop's men—hadn't exactly covered himself with glory that morning either. Hawkins figured that Bishop was turning to his platoon leader for reassurance.

"It'll turn out OK, you'll see," Hawkins said. "This will all be over in a day or so, and they'll be wanting to make Hollywood movies about us." He snorted a laugh at his joke. "Say, who do you think they'll get to play my part?" Hawkins asked.

"I don't know, sir," Bishop said. He turned and moved off through the deep snow to where his squad was pulling watch in the hide position. *But if the Germans hear us coming and get those Marders going,* Bishop thought, *it'll make for one goddamned short movie.*

Tim Brennan moved forward slowly, careful of his footfalls even in the muffling snow, guarding against making noise with his load of antitank weapons. They dog-legged around a German listening post, slipping in behind the ineffective GPU security.

Bishop's squad, which included Brennan and Charis, was to be support squad in the attack. They would move into position alongside the German vehicles they'd found in front of their sector while one of the other squads in Hawkins's platoon set up nearby. The two groups would form a right angle, with the Germans in the crook. Bishop's squad, augmented with all of the platoon's machine guns, would open up first and would keep firing until Hawkins determined it was time to rush into position. The support team would then lift their fires while the other squad rushed across the objective area to finish off anyone who'd survived the initial hail of bullets and antitank rounds.

The concept was simple—they'd done it hundreds of times as a team, but always against target silhouettes. Now they were going to face men who would shoot back. There was still a chance, Brennan knew, that they wouldn't engage the Germans. Spano, through his chain of command, had made it clear to every soldier that they weren't out here to provoke a battle. But they would respond to the first sign of aggression. They would strike hard and fast and finish the fight on their terms. The nuances of the distinction were lost on most of the soldiers, who were concentrating on the coming fight as if it were inevitable.

When he first heard the noise, Brennan clamped down with his elbows on the slings of his rifle and the AT-4s. A few steps later, he heard it again. There were a couple of seconds where he thought it might be the Ranger in front of him or behind him, but then it came again, clearer and closer, small and frightening.

The point man, two in front of Brennan, had already stopped and gone to one knee. Sergeant Bishop moved past Brennan, on his way up to the front, to see what was going on. As he moved, he touched each soldier on the arm.

Bishop and the point man put their heads together—Brennan could see them clearly through his night vision goggles. Then Bishop raised his arm and signaled. *Follow me.*

Brennan glanced off to his left as he moved again, out where the Germans were supposed to be. All at once he could pick out shapes, two men walking away from him, carrying something between them. When they spoke, Brennan sensed the Rangers stopping. From his vantage point, Brennan could now see that he was looking at the side of one Marder. Brennan looked up for Bishop, waved the sergeant toward him.

When Bishop joined him, Brennan lifted his arm to show the Marder. When he looked back along his arm as Bishop turned, everything changed.

The two men were on the deck of the nearest Marder, hurriedly pulling a tarpaulin off the twenty-millimeter gun mount.

"Pop 'em," Bishop said clearly.

Brennan dropped his load and shouldered one of the AT-4s. He had the same sense of incredible alertness that had visited him when he and Charis had surprised the German patrol. His hands worked on their own, detached, as if he were watching someone else remove the covers, arm the weapon. Everything was sharply focused on the simple task. *It's easier this way,* Brennan thought. *I just do what I'm told.*

"What's going on?"

Hawkins had come up beside them, speaking in a taut whisper.

"What are you doing?" he whispered, indicating Brennan's hands on the antitank missile.

"Look," Bishop said. "They're uncovering the weapons."

More Germans were moving about now, running back and forth between the tent and this vehicle. Brennan thought he could see more men moving in the background, where the recon had located three other Marders.

"Shit," Hawkins said too loudly.

Brennan cringed, expecting the noise to attract attention. But the Germans were talking among themselves now, hurried and agitated.

"Shit," Hawkins said again. "Maybe they're just checking the guns."

"Look at all those guys," Bishop said. "They haven't moved around this much the whole time they've been here." He paused. "They're coming after us."

"I gotta call the old man," Hawkins said, lifting the small commercial radio—called a brick—that each of the leaders carried. So far, the bricks seemed impervious to jamming.

"He said we have to make the call out here," Bishop said, putting his hand over the lieutenant's radio.

Then they heard the even whine of a motor as the rear door on the nearest Marder opened.

"*Schnell, schnell, los, los!*" *Quickly, quickly. Let's go, let's go.*

While Bishop and Hawkins went at it, Brennan watched the front. Some German soldiers were inside the vehicles, tossing out ration boxes and sleeping bags. Others were cracking open ammunition crates, sliding the small cans across the open metal door.

The engine in the nearest vehicle coughed, then one, two, three more in line. Brennan stared hard into the night. Beside him, his leaders were locked in indecision.

"I say we shoot," he heard Bishop say.

"I don't know," Hawkins said.

"You want to wait another minute until they open up with those fucking guns," Bishop seethed.

Brennan stepped to the side a few feet, so that he could see inside the open rear of the Marder. He couldn't be sure, but he thought he saw a soldier fixing the muzzle of his weapon to one of the side firing ports.

Brennan raised the bulky weapon and sighted on the vehicle.

Behind him, he could hear Bishop say that something was bullshit, while Hawkins kept repeating some indistinct phrase.

Brennan settled his finger on the trigger, tightening slowly. The German soldier inside the vehicle crossed the reticle pattern.

He drew in a breath, let it halfway out.

Charis was at the trail end of the squad, close enough to see Hawkins and Bishop, but too far away to see what Brennan was doing. He reacted immediately when the rocket, dragging its bright tail of flame, cut through the trees and into the open back end of the Marder. He pulled his night vision goggles—which were blinded by the flare—away from his face, raised his rifle, and began to fire at the shapes he saw in the light of the furiously burning vehicle.

The flames lit an *Inferno* circle of madness as the Germans scrambled this way and that, unsure of what to do, dying for their hesitation. No one was even returning fire as the Rangers sent their volleys into the GPU position. Someone popped a flare, and Charis saw some men on his right, the Rangers who'd been in front of him, break for the vehicles. He brought his weapon to port—diagonally across his chest—and high stepped through the snow.

Brennan circled around the burning Marder, giving it and the light a wide berth. Only a few of the Germans were returning fire; most of the ones he could see were intent on getting inside the remaining vehicles. When he passed the light he saw that the doors to the other three Marders in this position were also open. He left the cover of the woods and ran toward the second vehicle in line, catching up to a German who was running in the same direction. Brennan yanked a grenade from the side of his ammo pouch, knocked off the safety and tried to stick his trigger finger, bulky in the glove, into the pull ring. He ran with his arms in front of him, did a short hop when he thought he was going to drop his rifle, and overtook the German who was running for the same vehicle.

The other soldier stumbled; Brennan went to his knees, felt the snow kick up in his face. The German, sprawled facedown, tried to get up, but Brennan jumped on the man's back. He felt the grenade pin give way and he tossed it, awkwardly, with his left hand, at the troop door of the second Marder.

An elbow came up and caught him square on the nose, lighting the inside of his skull with painful shards. The soldier below him scrambled free and ran without looking back at Brennan. He made it to the Marder just as the grenade went off.

Someone had Brennan's shoulder.

"Get up, get up."

It was Charis, and Brennan was halfway to his feet when another explosion—this one at the back of the third Marder—bowled them over.

Gedern had just opened the driver's hatch over his head when the first explosion rocked the German position. The white light and sound boiled over the hull of his vehicle and fell on him from the opening above his head. Behind him, Sergeant Brufels was screaming at the other men to get on board.

Gedern strained to turn around, but Brufels yelled at him.

"*Get moving*," Brufels shrieked as he raised the troop door. "Go forward, whatever you can do, just get moving."

Gedern slammed the Marder into forward and raised himself so that he could see out of the open hatch. A dark figure ran across the front of the vehicle, just a few feet away. Gedern, trained for years to be careful of the dangerous machine he drove, instinctively smashed the brake pedal, then the accelerator.

Something hit him in the head, fell to his lap. He looked down quickly, then back up to make sure he split the trees in front of him. Then the image, caught in the uncertain light of flares floating outside, came back to him.

It was a grenade.

On his lap.

Gedern straightened his legs, banging his head against the coaming, and felt the grenade slip between his thighs. He let go the steering column and reached for it, sure that he was going to be killed at any second. He grabbed the top of the fuse, lost it for a second, found the round hardness of the grenade body and thrust his arm out of the open hatch.

Some part of the fuse hung up on the wool of his glove, and the grenade did not leave his hand. He shook it furiously, as if he were being stung by some insect, and heard the grenade bounce off the sloped front of his Marder. It exploded underneath the vehicle as Gedern rolled forward. The shock wave terrified him again, but then it passed and he was still alive.

Gedern made a hard left, thinking to go back to where the Americans were overrunning the platoon.

"What are you doing?" Brufels screamed. "Hard right! Turn, turn!"

Gedern swung the Marder around again, and he heard the small machine gun, mounted on the rear deck, open up on the Americans behind them.

"We will get inside their perimeter," Brufels—his voice barely recognizable for rage and fright—told him.

Gedern tucked his head back down inside the vehicle, tried to use the vision blocks and decided he couldn't see. When he raised his seat again and the cold air caught him, he felt an uncomfortable wetness. For a moment he thought the grenade in his lap might have wounded him. Then he realized that the wetness was not blood, but urine.

The sound and light started in the Charlie Company sector, and Isen and Spano moved in that direction when they heard the first reports.

"I can't get anybody," Isen said as he worked the push to talk on his hand-held radio. "They must have switched frequencies."

Spano—who was just a shade over six one—was making better progress through the deep snow than Isen could manage. He was heading for the open airfield, the shortest distance—and the most dangerous route—to Charlie Company.

Isen pumped his legs hard, trying to bring his knees up above the tops of the drifts, but it was like running in heavy surf. He'd gone only a few meters and already his thighs felt leaden and the sharp air singed his lungs.

Spano was more than ten meters ahead of him now, and the distance was increasing. Something in Isen sank as he struggled through the snow and fought his own ineffectiveness. There was no power in him. He fell forward, put his arms out in front of him to break his fall, but his hands shot through the deep snow. Then he was facedown in it, had a mouthful of cold wetness and the tangy taste of blood from where he'd bitten his lip. He grunted, struggled up, thrashed his way to his feet, though it was like trying to gain a foothold on water. He got his head up and saw Spano's back, still moving toward the woodline.

Must go forward.

He reached the edge of the airstrip, where the trees along the woodline had kept the snow from piling too deep. The going was easier here, and Isen managed to jog along parallel to the woodline in the direction of Charlie Company. He could see Spano, halted now ahead of him, looking back.

"C'mon Mark," Spano said calmly.

Isen's chest heaved. His legs were soaked with melting snow, his front and back covered with sweat from the exertion of fighting his way through the deep drifts. *Damn,* Isen thought, looking at his commander. *He doesn't even look winded.*

"Helluva run, eh?" Spano said as he got closer. Isen could only breathe sharply in response.

"Sounds like the shit hit the fan up here in Charlie Company," Spano continued.

In spite of Isen's fear and the thousand things that crowded his mind about what might be happening just a few hundred meters away, he could see that Spano was as calm as he might be on a field problem back at Benning. Isen wondered if the old man had a grip on what was happening. His soldiers, foot soldiers, were taking on armored vehicles in the dark woods just ahead of them, and Spano was talking about the difficulty of running through the deep snow. Then Isen knew that was how he should be. No panic. Command presence.

"Sure does," Isen managed to say.

Then they heard one of the big twenty millimeters, the main gun of a Marder, open up behind them, in the Bravo Company sector, and Isen felt the fear claw at his throat, and he could do nothing to keep back the dismal thought, *We cannot hold here.*

The two men began moving forward again, and Isen had time to wonder where all their radio operators were. He looked back to see the soldiers still mired in the snow, fighting to keep at their posts.

The Marder came out of the woods from the right, accelerating as it gained the little open space beside the treeline. It jigged left, then right, only thirty meters ahead of them, its engine and transmission screaming as the driver pushed it hard.

Isen froze, an eternity of seconds as he tried to wish the vehicle away from them.

But it turned, and he could see the long barrel of the twenty-millimeter gun, and the head and shoulders of the vehicle commander. He imagined he could hear the man as he spotted the Americans. Isen could not make his legs move.

To the left was the deep snow of the open airfield. There was no way they could run through that faster than the vehicle could go. To their right lay the woods, where the undergrowth threatened to hold them up while the Germans worked their guns on the darkness.

In front of him, Spano moved to the center of the track. The Marder accelerated, and while it was not clear that the Germans had spotted them, it was clear that they were about to be run over.

Isen heard something come up from his chest, a frightened moan squeezed out as all his muscles tensed.

Spano moved again, drawing his pistol.

Isen watched with the dumb fascination of an animal caught in the headlights of an onrushing car as Spano raised his tiny pistol and began firing at the Marder bearing down on them. Isen could not hear the reports over the engine, but he saw the expended shell casings fly off dully over Spano's shoulder.

Then the Marder exploded.

In a painfully bright second, like a photoflash, Isen saw the turret pull away from the vehicle hull, white hot flame spitting out of the new gaps in the machine's body. It came forward, then turned crazily into the snowbank, where the sound of secondary explosions of on-board ammunition mixed with the hiss of flame meeting snow.

Isen was on his knees, with no idea of how he'd gotten there, when Spano turned around. The colonel used his left hand to open the flap on his holster, shoved the weapon into place.

"Got him," he said.

Just beyond Spano, two Rangers emerged from the woodline beside the Marder, one of them still shouldering the body of an expended AT-4 he'd used to make the kill.

And Isen began to laugh, a snorting sound mixed of fear and panic and relief that shook up from his gut.

"Jesus," he said. "Jesus H. Christ."

The Marders burning in the woods made it easy to find Charlie Company. Isen and Spano, trailed by their exhausted radio operators, made their way forward cautiously, not wanting to startle any nervous Rangers. Neither of them were prepared for what they found.

There were three Marders on fire in what had been the German position, two of them burning violently. Spano could see men moving about behind them, outside the immediate circle of light. He and Isen waited until they could identify the men as GIs.

"Whose platoon is this?" Spano asked as he moved forward.

"Lieutenant Hawkins's, sir," the Ranger answered.

Isen looked around at the destruction. There were at least fifteen bodies in the snow, caught in various poses of flight or panic. As far as he could see, none were American. It looked as if the Charlie Company platoon had completely surprised the Germans here—even catching some of them in the tents behind the vehicles. Isen looked up when he heard Hawkins approaching.

"They were getting ready to move on us, sir," Hawkins said before Spano had a chance to talk. "And I remembered what you said about our not wanting to be surprised. I didn't see any other way."

He was talking fast, nervous after the fight, after—apparently—initiating the contact.

"You guys shot first?" Spano said.

The light was tricky here, shadows jumping across their faces, the snow picking up and throwing back bright spots. Isen couldn't see Hawkins's expression, so he stepped up beside Spano to hear what the lieutenant had to say.

Hawkins hesitated, and Isen got the impression that he was trying to guess what Spano wanted to hear. One second stretched to two, then three. Spano tired of waiting.

"It's ancient history now, Hawkins," Spano said. "I didn't want us to shoot *second,* but I need to know. For the sake of argument, you might say."

"Yes, sir," Hawkins said at last. "We shot first."

Spano breathed quickly, deeply through his nose in what might have been a sigh. "OK, son. OK."

"I'll get sitreps from the companies, sir," Isen said. The battalion commander nodded.

Hawkins shifted back and forth on the balls of his feet.

"Go ahead and get back to your platoon," Spano said.

As he watched Hawkins turn back to where the Rangers were beginning to destroy whatever German weapons they found, Isen wondered if anyone would ever know the truth of what had happened here.

10

. . . .

PAUL GEDERN HAD STARTED OUT INTO THE OPEN SPACE OF the airfield without knowing what he was doing. When he realized his mistake, he tried to turn the Marder around, but the vehicle would not pivot in the deep snow that had drifted into high ridges like sand dunes. The thick hull smashed back and forth, a black bull in a rodeo stall, until there were tight walls of snow on either side.

"Back up," Brufels yelled from the commander's hatch.

"I can't see," Gedern answered.

"I'll tell you where to go," Brufels said.

Gedern wanted to repeat himself, but of course Brufels would know that the driver couldn't see behind the vehicle. What Gedern meant was that he was afraid of going backward—blind—toward the woodline where more Americans probably waited for them.

They pulled out of the drifts and Gedern could feel—through the controls—small trees give way behind the Marder.

"Driver, left turn," Brufels said. The panic was beginning to recede, and the sergeant was giving the proper commands again.

The nose of the Marder swung around dutifully, and Gedern could see the relatively clear track that ran in the lee of the woodline. He hoped that Brufels would let him run for the nearest German position—they were still in among the American units—when something exploded ahead of them.

· 125 ·

"It's another Marder," Brufels said.

From his driver's position, Gedern could just make out the indistinct shape of the hull, now capped with yellow-white fire. He wondered who'd been in that vehicle.

"Pull into the woodline here," Brufels said. "Left turn."

Gedern turned to where the trees made a dark curtain at the field's snowy edge, then made a small loop so that the nose of the Marder was pointing back out into the open area, into the center of the American position. He kicked the engine to idle and strained to see who might come up on them in the darkness.

"We're inside their perimeter," Brufels said. His voice, calm now, sounded far away in the earphones of Gedern's headset.

"But it won't be long before they come looking for us," Gedern added. He paused, wondering what Brufels was planning. "Maybe we should get out of here," he added.

"We will, but not before we do some damage to them," the squad leader said. He turned to the troop compartment and gave instructions to two of the four soldiers there to dismount and check the woods immediately adjacent to the Marder.

This is lunacy, Gedern thought. *They massacred us in our platoon position. Now there are only six of us, and he expects us to fight them.*

When the other soldiers were out on the ground, Gedern heard Brufels climb out on the deck of the Marder to look for damage to the guns.

I could drive away, he thought. *Throw Brufels off by accelerating, then run over the miserable shit.* He looked to his left, where he could just see the burning Marder, the flames licking upward, lighting the trees.

"Don't you think we should leave before they find us again, Stabsunteroffizier Brufels?" Gedern ventured.

"We will, Gedern," Brufels said. "But first we have a job to do."

Gedern shifted uncomfortably in his seat, in his wet trousers.

He was emboldened by something—fear, the knowledge that they could all be dead in a moment, or the realization that things were finally out of control.

"But you saw how quickly they wiped out the whole platoon," Gedern said, trying not to whine. "What can we do alone?"

"We were surprised out there," Brufels said, angry now. "Our security was lax and they attacked us first. But they used their one advantage. From now on, we will be in control."

The squad leader squatted on top of the hull beside Gedern's hatch. "It's normal to be afraid," he said solicitously.

"I'm not afraid," Gedern said quickly. "At least no more afraid than anyone else." He licked his lips with a cotton-dry tongue.

"But this is stupid." He looked up, trying to see Brufels's expression in the blackness. "Why are we even fighting these people? There's no reason it should have come to this."

He braced for a tirade from the squad leader, thinking that he would welcome the fight, that he still might push Brufels to the ground—it would take only a small shove—and take off in the Marder.

"You are resisting the truth," Brufels said. "We've been telling you all along that the Americans were dangerous, that they don't respect German sovereignty, that they want to control us still. Didn't the attack prove that?"

Gedern wasn't sure what the night had proved, except that combat was terrifying and confusing. He could not see how anything so chaotic could have at its root something that pretended to be rational, like the GPU arguments about sovereignty. But it was too much. Gedern couldn't, by himself, resist all the Brufels, all the Stoddards, and still keep himself in one piece.

"We're going to fight from here," Brufels was saying above him in the gloom. "We'll fight our way out of here and inflict as much damage as we can."

"Yes, Stabsunteroffizier," Gedern said.

The first explosions of the firefight woke Major George Rhone, who'd been sleeping inside the small control building, wrapped in a poncho liner loaned him by a generous Ranger. He jumped up, pulled the nylon blanket around him and darted outside, where he ran into a GI who was standing in darkness by the door.

"Where you going, Major?" the soldier asked.

"What's going on?" Rhone demanded.

"Sounds like the shooting's started," the soldier said. He had a thick drawl that made his speed too slow for the circumstances.

"Who started shooting? What's happening?"

"Well, now, I don't really know, sir," the Ranger said. "I imagine we'll find out soon enough." He spit into the snow, and Rhone caught a whiff of chewing tobacco. "I do know," the soldier continued, "that you're supposed to stay put."

Rhone had been staring at the far edge of the airfield, where a big fire was lighting up the low clouds. He turned to the soldier. "What did you say?"

"First Sergeant said for me to keep you here, Major," the soldier said. "You're not allowed to wander around." He paused. "No disrespect sir. I guess maybe they don't want you getting hurt."

"But I might be able to help up there," Rhone said. "I can talk to those people on the other side."

The Ranger looked over to where the fires, visible now through the trees some half mile away, burned brightly. They could hear the small popping sounds of distant gunfire.

"Sounds like they're past the talking stage, sir," the GI said.

Rhone stomped his foot, turned around and went back inside the building, where he kicked the wall in rage and frustration. His street shoe, wet for almost two days, came apart where it struck the wall. He felt the sole flap down so that it hung below his foot.

"Damn," he said. Then louder, "Damn, damn, damn this all to hell."

He paced back and forth in the dark room for ten minutes or so, pausing on every rotation to look out the window at the fires in the distance. Then he heard the American outside speaking to someone. He walked to the doorway, shuffling to keep the sole of his shoe under his foot. There were red flashlights visible a few meters from the door. When the lights got closer, he saw that several wounded were being carried into the shelter.

"You got some company, Major," the guard said to Rhone as the first two Rangers came in carrying a makeshift stretcher—a poncho slung over two rifles—and its burden of an American soldier. The GI's head was thrown back, and he sucked air violently through his teeth. The man's legs hung over the edges of the poncho. One foot was missing.

Rhone stepped outside as several medics began to work on the soldier. His guard watched him.

"Had to get out of the way in there," Rhone said. The guard nodded. The sight of his wounded comrade had changed his attitude, and Rhone reminded himself that, to this American soldier, at least, he was a German, and therefore just like the GPU troops on the other side of the trees.

Then the prisoners came up. Two of them led by one GI, three more with two Rangers watching them. Rhone's guard, who seemed to be the ranking man, had all the prisoners sit, hands on their heads, in a line along the bottom of a low brick wall that ran from the doorway.

Rhone shuffled his odd shuffle over to the prisoners and began to question the men. He got only as far as "What happened out there?" when he felt a sharp poke in the back. He turned to see his guard standing behind him, bayonet leveled.

"I don't think it's good for you to be talking to them, Major," the guard said.

"If I can find out how their units are lined up against us," Rhone said, hoping the *us* wouldn't grate, "we'll have a better chance of getting out of here."

The soldier studied him for a moment, looked down at the prisoners, then back to Rhone.

"OK, I guess it'll be all right. But tell 'em if anybody moves too fast, there'll be a few less of 'em around to see the sun come up. Right?"

"Got it," Rhone said.

He turned to the prisoners and told them to be quiet and still. "Or I'll have this American shoot you," Rhone said.

A few of them were wounded, all of them were badly frightened and clearly believed that the GI would kill them if Rhone gave the word.

"I am Major Rhone, of the Bundeswehr, and I am going to ask each of you a few questions."

He pulled them aside, one by one, and asked what units they were with, and what had happened in the woods, and what they knew about the plans their leaders had made. More than half of the Germans—and all of them privates—cooperated with him. One told him to fuck off, another apologized before saying that he didn't think he should tell Rhone anything.

"Why's that?" Rhone asked as innocently as he could.

"Well," the soldier said, "you're with the enemy."

And so it went. By the time he finished talking to them, there were eight GPU soldiers sitting along the wall. There was only one diehard in the group, and one who was so badly frightened that he could barely speak. Most of them lost whatever enthusiasm they'd had for the fight. Every once in a while, Rhone could hear the crackling of small arms fire in the surrounding woods, and he believed, more strongly than before, that he could save some lives if he could just talk to the German soldiers out there.

"I have to talk to Major Isen or Colonel Spano," Rhone told the guard.

"I'll let them know first chance I get, Major," the GI said sarcastically. "But I'm kinda busy right now."

"But I can save some lives if I can get out there and talk to the GPU soldiers. I think I can talk them into stopping the attacks."

The Ranger looked at him, as if he were waiting for Rhone to make a case.

"I can save lives on both sides," Rhone said. "These men," he said, pointing to the prisoners, "these men know that this fight is crazy. That it doesn't have to be this way at all."

The GI seemed to waver a bit as he considered his counterparts at the wall.

"They're all smart enough to know that shooting is only going to make things worse. And it's not going to help Germany any."

Rhone felt the familiar clawing of frustration as he tried to make the obvious clear. How could anyone *not* see that fighting was a stupid, wasteful, immoral way to effect change?

"You've got to let me go find Colonel Spano," Rhone told the soldier. "We don't want any more of your buddies winding up like that poor guy in there." He pointed to the open door, where the eerie red lights still bobbed and shook as the medics worked on the badly wounded Ranger. "Take me to him, if you don't trust me."

"I told you I'm busy," the GI snapped. But he mostly looked confused, and tired, and, in spite of his bravado, he also looked frightened.

Come on, Rhone thought. *Come on. I can do something out there.*

The report of the twenty-millimeter gun was unmistakable—great hammer blows of sound that shook the air. The Ranger guards and their prisoners crouched instinctively. The Ranger who seemed to be in charge turned away from Rhone to spot the gun's muzzle flash, its signature.

Rhone stepped backward a few meters, retreating into the darkness. Then he turned and ran, leaving the sole of his shoe in one of the first footprints he made.

"They're over there," Brufels yelled. "I can see them, I can see them!"

He had fired two short bursts of the twenty millimeter at targets only he could see. Gedern, startled by the noise, was now even more terrified that the Americans would know exactly where they were. And there was no way they would leave the Germans undisturbed.

"You should have seen them run," Brufels narrated into the intercom. "We'll get them moving with this baby."

"We should move, Sergeant," Gedern said.

"Why should we move?" Brufels asked. "They'll be the ones running, you idiot. What infantryman would stand up to a weapon like this?"

"One with an antitank rocket," Gedern said.

Brufels snorted, and Gedern expected to hear something about showing fear. Instead, the sergeant leaned into the troop compartment and ordered the two men still inside to get out with the other two, who were already on foot, checking the area around the vehicle for infiltrators. The men got out reluctantly, and Gedern could hear them curse as they fought through the deep snow. He wouldn't be surprised if all four men were hovering just out of Brufels's sight, waiting for their chance to get back to the warmth of the Marder.

The first shot was inconsequential, like a sharp rap on the side of the Marder's armor. But that was followed quickly by a burst of automatic fire, then another as three or four weapons opened up. Brufels was screaming for the men to come back to the vehicle.

Gedern pulled himself up to peer out of the driver's hatch, then dropped back inside when a half dozen rounds spanged off the glacis plate in front of him. He pulled the hatch shut, remembering the grenade.

The muzzle of the twenty-millimeter gun was only a few feet above the driver's hatch, and its report reached down and shook Gedern inside the hull, even with the hatch closed. Brufels fired wildly, moving the barrel right and left.

"Move out," the squad leader screamed into the intercom.

Gedern threw the Marder into gear and smashed the accelerator. The sudden jolt banged his head against the pad behind him, and he strained against the shock and the blackness outside to see out of the vision blocks, which, even in daylight and from a stationary vehicle, was a little like looking at the world through a soda bottle.

"Left turn," Brufels said.

Gedern couldn't see well, so he tried to imagine where they were. The open space at the center of the American position was in front of them, and Brufels wanted him to turn parallel to the woodline that surrounded the airfield. This would turn their vulnerable flank to the center of the Rangers' stronghold; but since the Americans seemed to be everywhere, it probably didn't matter much.

"Where are the others?" Gedern managed.

"They're gone," the sergeant said.

"Did you see them?" Gedern was shouting, fighting to be heard above the sound of the straining engine and the intermittent slamming of the big gun.

"They are lost, Gedern. Just keep driving."

Gedern could see very little, and the snow was plowing up over the front of the vehicle, cutting off everything that the darkness didn't hide. It was impossible for him to notice that he was not driving parallel to the woodline, but was veering left into the trees. So he never saw the stand that stopped them, large pines and spruce packed tight as a fence.

The Marder was moving at almost twenty miles an hour, and though it did considerable damage to the trees, it came to a dead stop. Gedern's head bounced off the pads set in between his vision block periscopes, exploding in a white burst of pain through his eyes and jaw and neck. There was an insistent yammering somewhere deep behind his nose that eventually became Brufels's voice.

"What the fuck are you doing? What the fuck are you doing? Get us out of here. *Now!*"

Gedern blinked at the pain, could see nothing, wondered if he was blind. Then he realized that something was blocking the periscopes. He popped his hatch and slid upward to find the front plate thick with evergreen boughs.

"I'm going to back up," he said. His voice sounded funny, so he reached up to his face and found that his nose and mouth were bleeding, and a thick, slippery coat of dark blood was already seeping into the neckline of his shirt.

The left track slipped, so the big vehicle tried to pivot toward the open space of the airfield. Gedern fought it as Brufels shouted instructions at him.

The first rocket came in low, climbing only a few feet as it streaked the hundred or so meters from its firer toward the Marder. Gedern, who caught the signature flash as he struggled to see what was hanging up the vehicle, had time only to think that he was going to die before the missile burned over the back deck and exploded in the woods nearby.

He worked the steering and accelerator frantically, but the Marder seemed to settle more deeply into the ruts made by the spinning tracks.

"I can't get it out," Gedern screeched through the intercom. Behind him, he heard Brufels open the commander's hatch and drop down onto the deck.

He's getting out, Gedern thought. *The motherfucker is going to leave me, too.*

He kicked at the floorboards, trying to push himself through the hatch above, getting his parka caught up in the controls. He was like that, half in and half out, when the Americans peppered the Marder with small arms fire.

Gedern found the seat and shoved himself out of the hatch, rolling headfirst down the sloped front of the vehicle and into the torn branches there. He got to his feet and began moving at once, away from the vehicle. He'd managed only a few steps when he saw the second rocket ignite in the woodline some distance behind him. Gedern had time to throw himself behind the sheltering trees, and then the Marder was hit. There was a sound like a great searing, and a pure light shot through the open hatch where, seconds before, Gedern had been hung up by his clothing.

His first instinct was to lie low, but within a few moments he could hear the Americans advancing on the burning wreck that had been his Marder, and he thought they'd seen him climb out and would look for him. He crawled backward for a few meters, out of the circle of light thrown by the flames, then stood and began to move slowly, parallel to the woodline. He knew that at some point he would have to head back through the woods in order to escape the American perimeter, and that he would have to do so soon, before it got light. But he was disoriented. He had no idea how far he had come from his platoon's original position. He was still bleeding heavily, and his shirt, soaked with sweat inside the Marder, now threatened to freeze to his skin. And he was unarmed. His pistol, still in its holster on the floor of the driver's space when he climbed out, was probably a puddle of molten steel.

He moved slowly, then was startled by how close the Americans were when he heard them again.

"If they got out, they're close by."

Gedern stopped moving, stopped breathing. He was afraid to turn his head, even though he doubted the Americans knew where he was.

Then one of them was in the clearing beside the woods, no more than thirty feet away. Gedern could just see him silhouetted against the snowy field behind. The man was turning his head, scanning the trees. Then, in profile, Gedern saw that the GI was wearing goggles.

They can see at night, Gedern thought. During his time in the regular army, Gedern had seen some of the sophisticated equipment the Americans used even at the squad level, and their night vision devices were legendary. Gedern remembered reading about their performance in the Gulf War, when the Americans maneuvered as if it were daytime while the Iraqis were blind.

He's looking for me. Suddenly, the thought of trying to escape was too much for him, and, in the next instant, he decided to surrender. He didn't think the Americans would harm him, and the charade would be over. He would have nothing more to do with those GPU fools like Brufels and Stoddard.

But he had never considered how difficult it would be to surrender. If he simply stepped from the woods, the GI might open fire. The man held his weapon at the ready, and it was certainly loaded and off safe. If he called to them, they might think it was a trap. They could simply back up a safe distance and fire into the woods. They had to be at least as frightened as he was, and ready to shoot if they felt threatened.

Gedern was at a loss. He couldn't go forward, and he couldn't go backward. He couldn't fight, and he couldn't surrender. He waited, scared and alone.

The American moved on a bit, a few steps at a time, until he had gone about fifteen meters along the woodline. Then someone called him, and he trotted back toward the Marder. Apparently they decided the quarry had entered the woods there to try to make it back to German lines.

Gedern stepped closer to the clearing, looking left and right. The Americans appeared to be gone. He moved into the open and put his hands in the air to show that he was unarmed, in case any of them were watching. When nothing happened, he dropped his hands and thought about following his pursuers.

When he turned around again, there was a man coming toward him in the open.

Gedern reached up quickly and immediately regretted the sudden movement as the man dove for cover.

"*Nicht schiessen,*" Gedern said. What little command of English he had left him. "*Nicht schiessen, ich kapituliere!*" *Don't shoot, I surrender.*

The man didn't move. Gedern closed his eyes and fumbled for a prayer.

"*Kommen Sie hierher,*" the figure commanded. *Come here.*

Gedern advanced, opening his eyes. He pushed his hands farther up into the air. "*Ich bin unbewaffnet,*" he said. *I am not armed.*

Only after he used the German phrase did it occur to Gedern that the man before him had also spoken German. Perfect, unaccented *hoch deutsch.*

"Who are you?"

"I am Private Paul Gedern, a Territorial Forces soldier."

"Is that your vehicle back there?" the man asked.

"Yes." Gedern suddenly felt extremely tired, and he wanted more than anything for this ordeal to be over.

"Are you an American?" Gedern asked.

"No, I am a major in the Bundeswehr," the man said. "Major Rhone. I am here with the Americans."

There was something odd about the man's look, Gedern decided. When the two drew closer together, Gedern saw that the man was in civilian clothes. And he was holding one foot on top of the other.

"I wanted to surrender to the Americans, but I was afraid they would shoot me first," Gedern confessed.

"I will take you back."

The man looked confused, and Gedern got the distinct impression that he was lost also.

"Did any others from your crew make it out?" the questioner continued.

Gedern thought about Sergeant Brufels jumping off the deck of the Marder. "I don't know," he said. Then, "No."

"Come with me," the officer said. They walked side by side for a few minutes, the major limping noticeably.

"Are you injured?" Gedern asked.

"No," Rhone answered. "I lost my shoe."

"Oh," Gedern managed. He was walking along beside an unarmed man in civilian clothes who had just taken him prisoner, after having participated in a plot—however short-lived—to take over the country by force. And the man had no shoe. He wondered if anything would surprise him.

"Are you an Ossie?" Rhone asked. Many of the men who'd found their way into the GPU were Ossies, easterners from the now-defunct army of the German Democratic Republic.

"No. I was in the Bundeswehr before I joined the Territorials," Gedern said.

"How did you become involved with the GPU?" Rhone asked.

"How does anything happen?" Gedern said. They went a few more steps. "It wasn't as if one day we all came in and said we were going to ... going to . . . ."

"Overthrow the government," Rhone finished.

"That's not the way they see it," Gedern said.

"Oh?"

"They are out to save Germany for the Germans," Gedern said. He'd heard the phrase hundreds of times, and it had never much rattled him, because it sounded so sensible. But he had never figured that, in execution, it would mean a civil war. He shook his head.

"What is it?" Rhone wanted to know.

"How did it get this screwed up?" Gedern asked.

"I'm not sure myself," Rhone answered. "But what we have to worry about now is how to get out of this mess before more people get killed."

Gedern looked at the man beside him. He couldn't see the officer's face, but he'd struck a chord. Why couldn't those fools in the GPU be this sensible?

Gedern was about to speak again when he heard a faint shuffling behind them. He turned around in time to be blinded by the muzzle flash of a pistol. Two shots, and the Bundeswehr major went down.

"Shit. It's a civilian!" It was Brufels.

Gedern staggered back, holding his eyes. "What are you doing?" he demanded.

"Rescuing you, you ass," Brufels said.

His chance to escape was gone, and Gedern knew it immediately.

"Let's go," Brufels said.

He didn't want to go. He wanted to turn himself in to the Americans and be done with it all. But the first step—resisting—was so difficult and unfamiliar. When Sergeant Brufels turned into the woods, Gedern followed meekly. Unarmed, unhappy, and swept away by forces he did not understand and could never control, Paul Gedern did what was expected of him and followed his leader.

Renegade German Army Units Attack Americans; U.S. Army Rangers on Maneuvers Are Surrounded

BERLIN, 26 February. (AP) Army Reserve units of the German Bundeswehr, apparently under the control of the right-wing German People's Union, have surrounded a battalion of American paratroopers near the city of Bremen. Some reports indicate that German and American soldiers may have fired on one another, but restrictions on travel and communication in a section of the country largely controlled by the ultrarightist political party have made reporting difficult.

A government spokesman in Berlin announced this morning that the German People's Union has been outlawed by the Bundestag, the German Parliament, under the provisions of a federal law originally designed to fight terrorism.

Both the Ministry of Defense here and the Pentagon in Washington have refused comment on the reports of combat, but a spokesperson for the U.S. Defense Department did indicate that Operation Solid Steel, the joint exercise in which the Rangers were supposed to participate with the German Army, had been cancelled.

This morning, U.S. Air Force personnel at Rhein Main Air Base near Frankfurt said that American military transport planes had left the field yesterday loaded with pallets of ammunition rigged for parachute drop. Air Force spokespersons later denied the report as careless speculation by uninformed personnel. Press access to the base, and to Air Force personnel, has since been curtailed; however, a former Army officer now employed in this city has confirmed that the Rangers, a parachute unit, are frequently resupplied by air drops of ammunition and food.

Speculative reports in the European press about the intentions of the German People's Union have pointed to that party's increasing hostility toward the federal government. The GPU claims that the Berlin government is a puppet of the former NATO powers. The party has gained an alarming measure of popular support with its "Germany First" campaign, the cornerstone of which is a curtailment of the rights of foreigners.

The GPU, backed by the public opinions of respected economists, maintains that Germany is no longer affluent enough to keep its doors open for poor immigrants. The GPU blames these new arrivals, many of whom arrive penniless, for Germany's current economic woes. While the xenophobic backlash against foreigners has reminded many citizens of the Germany of the 1930s, the GPU denies links to the burgeoning neo-Nazi movement.

11

THE MORNING BROKE SLOWLY, PAINFULLY FOR RAY SPANO, Mark Isen, and the men of the Third Battalion, Seventy-fifth Infantry.

Two of the three rifle companies had been successful in catching the GPU off guard and had managed to destroy much of the German combat capability before it could be brought to bear. But Bravo Company had not been as lucky, and the GPU unit they faced had been quicker out of the blocks than their counterparts. While Charlie and Alpha companies were able to destroy almost three quarters of the Marders in the first few minutes of shooting, Bravo Company knocked out only two of twelve.

Spano's plan—putting one platoon forward—had, in the case of Bravo Company, split the friendly force. The GPU Marders rolled out and were immediately in between the major elements of the American rifle company. The big, unwieldy twenty-millimeter guns were not effective in the woods and the tight confines of the American position, but the coaxial 7.62-millimeter gun on the turret and the matching remote-controlled gun mounted on the back deck of each machine tore big holes in the Rangers' positions.

In the morning, the Rangers counted twelve GIs killed and another eleven wounded. Four of the wounded were serious cases, with one of the men lapsing periodically into unconsciousness. The German major, Rhone, had slipped away from his guards and had gotten himself shot.

He'd have frozen to death but for a curious Ranger who investigated some pistol shots in his sector.

Colonel Ray Spano had dead and wounded on his hands, no guarantee that the GPU wouldn't attack again at any moment, and no clear indication of what they should do from that point other than pray for weather clear enough to allow the Air Force to fly close support.

"I know that armored column will be coming for us now," Spano said. "These GPU assholes have opened themselves up on this one."

"Did we get any messages out before we lost the SATCOM?" Isen asked.

Three men of the battalion signal section had been killed and the satellite link radio had been destroyed when a lone German Marder had blundered into the battalion command post.

"I'm pretty sure my guys got off that first message," the signal platoon sergeant was saying. He was badly shaken, and had survived the attack only because he had been carrying one of his wounded men to the aid station when the Marder broke through. "We sent a sitrep that we were being attacked by armored units and that we were fighting back."

"Did you get an acknowledgment?" Isen asked.

"No, sir."

"We've only got to hang on for a few hours here," Spano said. "We can dig in, send out some patrols, bring our wounded in here to the building."

"What if they can't get through?" Isen said.

"Nothing is going to stop that relief column," Spano said.

Isen could easily imagine the rage that would sweep over the American military when the news got out, and he knew that the armored units to the south would be ready to punch through whatever tried to get in their way. But the reality was that they were all still in Germany, and a U.S. force couldn't go shooting its way through the countryside—even to rescue other GIs. And the armored column, like the air force, had to contend with the weather. Isen didn't think it was a good idea to sit and wait.

"I don't think we ought to rely on that, sir," Isen said.

"What are you talking about?"

"I believe that they'll do everything they can," Isen said. "But in case something else goes wrong, in case the weather stops them, we don't want to get caught just waiting around. We should be doing something."

"What would you suggest?" Spano snapped. "Walk out of here carrying our wounded? How far do you think we'd get?"

The old man was beat, but Isen didn't mind being in the line of fire. He just hoped Spano would get some rest soon.

"I'm not exactly sure, sir, what we should do. But I think we should examine the possibilities. I don't think we should wait for somebody else to make the first move."

Spano snorted through his nose. Isen pressed him.

"For one thing, with all the casualties Bravo Company suffered, we're too weak to hold the original perimeter. We'd at least have to tighten things up in here."

"All right, that makes sense," Spano said. "Let's circle the wagons a little tighter for now, consolidate the wounded." He rubbed his eyes with grimy fingers.

"Got it," Isen said, turning away to begin the work.

"Oh, and, Mark," Spano said, "better make some plans in case we have to unass this place. OK?"

"Right, sir."

"I still think the column will come," Spano said. "And it'll be just like the cavalry in those old movies."

"Right, sir."

The twelve-passenger black-and-white fixed wing climbed sharply out of the clouds that pelted Andrews Air Force Base and the nation's capital with freezing rain. One of the three men in the back, a captain and a aide-de-camp for the lieutenant general on board, tried to make himself as inconspicuous as possible in the seat nearest the forward bulkhead. He'd been an aide only a short time, but he knew, without anyone having to tell him, that aides weren't supposed to hear arguments between generals and senior officers. And that's very much what he expected to hear.

Another passenger, Colonel Charles Schauffert, commander of the Seventy-fifth Infantry, the U.S. Army's Ranger Regiment, chewed the inside of his lip as he watched the gray wetness slip by the starboard portholes. Thanks to the cabin lights, he could see the reflection of his close-cropped head and much abused boxer's face in the inside glass. Schauffert's natural expression was a scowl, and when he was agitated, as he was now, the scowl became a grimace almost painful to see.

"I can't believe things in Europe are that fucked up," Schauffert said.

"Believe it."

The other man in the aircraft was Lieutenant General Don Stomer, current head of the army's Special Operations Command, based at Fort Bragg, North Carolina. If Schauffert was the stereotypical paratrooper— the hard-bitten type-A personality always spoiling for a fight—Stomer was just the opposite, or at least as opposite as one could be and still function in the demands of the job he held. Stomer, whose staff referred to him as "The Surfer," was the epitome of the unhurried, easygoing officer who was rattled by nothing.

Early in his career as a paratrooper, Stomer had suffered a near-fatal accident when both his main and reserve parachutes failed to open properly. When he got out of the hospital twelve weeks later, then-lieutenant Stomer had decided that life was too short to get excited over little things. "On my way to the ground," he told friends, "I decided that I should have been enjoying myself all along. I didn't expect a chance to do it again."

Stomer had been upset—but not surprised—by what he and his subordinate had learned in their all-day meeting in the Pentagon. He turned in his seat to face Schauffert.

"They cut the guts out of the European command, starting right after the Gulf War and the collapse of the Soviet Union," Stomer said.

Schauffert knuckled his scalp. "Everybody knew that Congress went after the defense budget in a big way," he said. "But who knew it was this bad?"

"I suspect a lot of people knew a lot of details, but very few had a glimpse of the big picture," Stomer answered.

The two men had just attended an emergency meeting of the Joint Chiefs of Staff in which the Deputy Chief of Staff for Operations, a three-star general who'd commanded a division in Germany just before that unit stood down, gave them a bleak view of American capabilities in Europe.

"We have one brigade scattered across southern Germany," he'd said, tapping the map lightly, almost meekly. Schauffert thought the shiny tip of the pointer came down somewhere west of Munich, some seven hundred kilometers from Bremen. "And one cavalry regiment operating as part of the European Contingency Force, also in the south, near Ulm."

"Aren't they closer to northern Germany?" Schauffert had blurted. He wasn't in the habit of interrupting presentations by three-star generals given for the Joint Chiefs, but everyone in the room understood his anxiety—those were his boys out there in the snow—and indulged him.

"Yes, they are, Colonel," the DCSOPS had allowed. He was under the gun, and he didn't appreciate the sharpshooting. "But treaty restrictions limit their use."

Now, in the privacy of his aircraft, Stomer had told him that the U.S. Armored Cavalry Regiment that was part of the multinational European Force was not allowed to participate in combat actions without the general consent of the member nations.

Schauffert bridled at that. "I suppose I shouldn't be surprised," he complained to his boss, "that something set up by politicians and diplomats is that screwed up. How much sense does it make for us to field a combat unit and then hand over its control to a bunch of goddamned foreigners?"

What had seemed to Stomer like a typical Cracklin' Charlie outburst had in fact been a carefully chosen comment. Colonel Charles Schauffert saw the events of the last thirty-six hours as an historic opportunity for America—and the American military in particular—to gain center stage in a world no longer dominated by the superpower struggle. Given the choice between the power to intimidate and the power to persuade, Schauffert would always choose the former. But before he showed his hand, he wanted to know just where his boss stood.

"Sir, when I left the meeting, I had the impression that the Chief didn't expect the president to use the multinational force to spring our guys," Schauffert said to the window glass. He swiveled his bristly head around to face his boss. "Please tell me I'm wrong."

"I wish I could, Charlie," Stomer said. "There's a lot of pressure from the European community to keep a lid on things, to try to keep it contained."

"Is that what I'm supposed to tell those guys in Third Batt?" Schauffert demanded. "If somebody's shooting at them, then as far as they're concerned—and as far as I'm concerned—the lid *is* off."

"Look, the armored cav down south has been alerted and they're ready to roll. The Air Force is standing by to fly support missions as soon as they can see. But we still have to wait for Berlin to give the go-ahead. And the Chief believes we have to be careful about getting into it with the Bundeswehr, the regulars."

"And I say if they get in the way then we kick their asses too," Schauffert said, much louder than he'd intended.

Stomer's aide got out of his seat and knocked on the door to the cabin. The pilot let him in.

"If we back down, those guys are going to get wasted." Schauffert said, quieter now.

Stomer took off his steel-rimmed glasses and pushed the heel of one hand against his eye socket. Schauffert noticed the older man's shoulders sag a bit as Stomer leaned back. Outside, the gray clouds had given way to a bright, cloud-banked setting for the sunset.

"There's something else, too," Stomer said. "Something that the Chief wouldn't allow into the briefing." He looked up to see that the door to the cabin was closed. "There's a chance that the GPU has access to nuclear weapons."

All the more reason why we should be in charge, Schauffert told himself. *None of the fuckers should even be allowed to have nukes. We should take 'em all away. Toss 'em back if the natives give us some shit.*

"Naval intelligence has been tracking three warheads that were apparently smuggled out of Kazakhstan," Stomer continued. "They came from the old Soviet ICBM sites at Semipalatinsk and were shipped across the Caspian Sea to Iran, then out through the Middle East."

"And they think the GPU has them now?" Schauffert asked.

"One of them is still in Iran," Stomer said. "That's scary enough. Two of them dropped out of sight after leaving Jordan. The GPU has dropped some hints about what they have. Berlin is telling us that the chances are slim, but at the same time they're hedging their bets. They've been busy trying to locate a couple of ships the GPU controls that could be used to transport the warheads. The President thinks Berlin knows more than they're letting on."

"Jesus Christ," Schauffert said. He shook his head, trying to figure an angle that would make this decidedly new wrinkle work for him. "No wonder Berlin has been supercautious in responding."

"That's best-casing it," Stomer said. "Worst case is that they'll be completely paralyzed. They won't do anything and they won't allow us to do anything."

Stomer paused and looked out the window to where the sun cut blood-red bands through the western clouds.

"So you can see why we can't go riding around their country shooting things up. It would be better to let them handle it, if they can do it in time."

"What if they're too slow?" Schauffert asked. "What if they just don't give a fuck? I got five hundred guys out there who must feel like they're at the end of the earth."

Stomer slid forward in his seat and put his elbows on his knees. The pose was concerned, but there was no mistaking the steel in his voice.

"Look, Charlie, you don't have to tell me about commanding troops. I care about those soldiers as much as anybody. But that doesn't mean that rocketing in with guns blazing is in their best interest. There's an awful lot at stake here. This is something completely new, something the world hasn't seen at any time in history: outlaws with nuclear weapons."

For all his twenty-five years in the Army, Schauffert had had trouble controlling his temper. As a lieutenant, when people told him his anger was counterproductive, he simply wrote them off as wimps who were afraid to get riled up. As a colonel, he knew that sometimes he was his own worst enemy. But, in this situation as in so many others, Schauffert thought his anger righteous, not just the appropriate response, but the only response for the man of action, the true patriot.

"The whole problem, sir," Schauffert said in measured tones, watching Stomer's reaction, "is that we've been half-stepping all along, right behind the politicians and all the rest of the pussies who are afraid to make the tough calls, who are afraid to see things as they really are."

Stomer studied his subordinate. There were a few people around the army who would say—behind his back—that Charlie Schauffert was a nut case. Stomer had never had occasion to wonder before.

Schauffert saw no alarm on Stomer's face, so he barged ahead.

"We're the only ones with any real power left," he said, "even with everything we've had taken away in the last few years." Schauffert slid forward in his seat, so that his knees were almost touching Stomer's. *This is easier than I expected,* Schauffert thought.

"There's a real power vacuum in the world," he continued. "Somebody has to be in charge, lay down the laws. If we took control, at least made it known that we weren't going to put up with any nonsense, we wouldn't be having all this trouble with missing nukes and civil wars in all those fucked-up little countries. We could do a lot of good." He paused, realized the need for some dramatic ending. "We should step up and seize the reins. You know, 'carpe diem.' "

"That's 'seize the day,' " Stomer said coolly.

"Whatever. You get the picture, right, sir?"

Stomer stared out the window. It seemed to him that Schauffert, instead of concentrating on fixing the problem at hand, wanted to treat it as an opportunity to influence foreign policy. It was conceivable that the army, by shouting loudly enough about this incident (and the shouting would be justified, since GI lives were on the line) could influence the president to escalate the action beyond what he might otherwise. Such an action went against everything the American officer corps stood for.

But men were dying out there.

Stomer looked back at the expectant colonel.

"We're going to do whatever it takes to bring those boys out of there alive," Stomer said. "Beyond that, we'll let the President conduct foreign policy."

Generalleutnant Stefan Paul Graf was almost positive that he'd been duped, but he was not sure how he was going to find the responsible party.

The fifty-one-year-old Graf was the Inspektur des Heeres, Inspector of the German Army, equivalent to the U.S. Army's Chief of Staff. When news of the standoff between the Americans and the GPU reached the top brass, Graf had been finishing an inspection tour of troop installations in Bavaria, far to the south in Germany. He kept abreast of developments with portable communications gear, and he kept insisting to his boss, the Generalinspektur der Bundeswehr, the nation's top-ranking military officer, that he should be in Berlin. He had received messages, decoded for him by signalers from the Ministry of Defense, that he was not yet needed in Berlin and that he should complete his tour. So the ranking officer in the army kept to his original itinerary, which kept him out of the capital.

And then the evening news carried pictures of the shootings.

When Graf saw the footage on German television of the dead Territorial Forces soldiers and heard the GPU screed that accompanied the story, he was convinced that there was a plot to keep him out of Berlin. He sent a brief message that he was returning as soon as possible, then boarded his personal jet to fly to Templehof Airfield in Berlin, where his chauffeured Mercedes limousine waited to take him to the ministry.

"Is everyone else there already?" Graf asked his aide, an ambitious major named Waldhem.

"Yes, sir. Although Admiral Dorting arrived only an hour ago."

It was Waldhem's opinion that Graf had made a serious error in judgment by not coming directly to Berlin, in spite of the assurances made by various army types that the situation in the northwest was not going to get out of hand. Of the three flag officers who worked directly for the Generalinspektur der Bundeswehr, Graf was the most vocal in his criticism of the GPU. Three months earlier, Graf had warned the Minister of Defense that the continued transfer of sophisticated weapons to the Territorial Forces was a serious threat to the nation's stability. But the minister had patiently explained that the government no longer wanted to foot the bill for an active army to train full-time with these weapons. Better to let the reserves handle them at one-third to one-half the cost.

When that argument had failed to waken the government, Graf set out—within the small circles of the Ministry—to convince the nation's military leaders that the GPU was a dangerous group of anarchists. He'd been surprised at the cool reception his testimony had received, and he wondered if some of his peers wouldn't actually support the GPU bid to take over the government. Graf railed against the GPU and its racist policies every chance he got. This failed to endear him to his peers, who did not believe in alienating a political body that might someday hold the fiscal reins.

Major Waldhem moved in lower-ranking circles, where talk was looser, and he had heard more than one officer whisper that the other chiefs had bought into—or at least were tolerant of—the GPU view of Germany for Germans. The economic backsliding the nation had experienced over the previous five years had cost the military complex mightily, and some officers saw the GPU as an antidote for the shrinking budget.

"And what is the latest from Bremen?" Graf asked.

"Not good, sir," Waldhem said. In his hands he held a message he'd received just before he left the Ministry to pick up his boss. He'd folded and refolded the paper so often that it was already deeply creased.

"The GPU killed at least one officer who tried to interfere with their movement of armored vehicles near a town called"—he flipped his notepaper over—"Karlshofen. Also, the GPU claims to hold the officers who were supposed to be the controllers for Operation Solid Steel. Apparently they were kidnapped."

Or they went over to the other side, Graf thought.

"Is there any shooting going on?" the general demanded, anxious to get to the point.

"The Americans said that the GPU fired on some of their aircraft," Waldhem said. "And their Rangers sent a partial report that they were under attack only a few hours ago."

"What the hell does that mean?" Graf said. "What's a partial report?"

"The transmission was interrupted," Waldhem said. He had inferred two possibilities from this bit of news. Either the radio had quit working, or someone had destroyed it.

"Shit," Graf said. He looked out the window beside him at the cars they passed on the highway. His driver was pushing two hundred kilometers per hour, but that was fine with him; it was time he got to Berlin to find out what was going on. Which reminded him of the odd messages he'd been getting: stay away.

"What do you know about the signals officer who was handling my message traffic?" Graf asked.

"I haven't met him yet, sir," Waldhem answered. "He came on board just about a week ago."

Graf seemed as if he were expecting this answer, which made Waldhem wonder if there was something he should have been doing to keep his boss better informed. The aide glanced down at his notes, though he knew there was nothing helpful there. When he looked up, he saw another limousine, one that had passed them less than a minute before, slow down on the left-hand side of the car. Both vehicles had darkly tinted glass, and though the near windows on the other car were more than halfway down, it was still too dark inside to see what was there. But Waldhem had been trained to be suspicious in his efforts to protect his boss, and everything about the last thirty hours had heightened this paranoia.

"Driver, slow down," he said.

The sergeant in the front seat touched the brakes, and even before the other car slowed also, as he somehow knew it would, Waldhem was reaching out for his boss.

"Possible bandit on the left," he said, sending the two soldiers in the front seat into action. As the driver stomped on the accelerator and grabbed the radio handset to contact the security car behind them, the soldier on the passenger side turned around and knelt on his seat, swinging the stubby barrel of his submachine gun up behind his partner's neck to train it out the now-open left side window. This took less than two seconds, and in that time Waldhem reached out with both hands, grabbed Lieutenant General Graf by the wide collar of his military greatcoat, and threw the older, smaller man down to the floorboard.

Graf grunted in surprise, but Waldhem kept his hand on the old man's neck, pushing him below the level of the armor plating in the door panel of the Mercedes. The aide drew his pistol, saw the other limousine gain on them, glanced back to where the security car, with its four heavily armed soldiers, was closing the gap. The other car, the bandit, was also a powerful Mercedes, and though Waldhem was sure that they would be able to defeat whoever was on board, given a minute or two to bring power to bear, there were a few crucial moments where, thanks to the element of surprise, their chances were about even.

"You want me to shoot, sir?" the soldier in front asked.

Waldhem thought *Yes*, then hesitated as he considered that the other car had not threatened them. Could it be possible that they were joyriding fools?

And in that second of hesitation, Waldhem lost the fight.

The windows in the other car never came down all the way; whoever was inside simply thrust the muzzle of the American-made Mark 19 grenade launcher through the open part of the glass.

Major Waldhem's last thought was to tell the driver to brake, but the first grenade smashed into the post between the front and back doors of the limousine, while the second banged into the window where the glass met the door. The third grenade found the smoking hole and exploded inside the tight confines of the limousine just as it careened off the highway.

12

* * * * * * * * * * *

A S MARK ISEN WENT ABOUT HIS WORK OF DIRECTING THE
companies into a smaller, tighter perimeter, he watched the skies above
him clear. A half hour after the sun came up, the sky was achingly blue,
a perfect china bowl above the incongruous scene of burned vehicles and
blackened snow.

Isen had the medics move the wounded into the control building,
which had been serving as the informal headquarters. He pulled Bravo
Company, which had been the most badly mauled, in close to the building, leaving a security force in the woods to warn of attack. Spano also
directed him to reposition the other two companies' lines, since the units
were working shorthanded.

The Rangers sent out patrols that combed the area behind the positions
the GPU had vacated. When these patrols found nothing, Isen sent them
out again, farther this time, to try to locate the enemy. As unnerving as it
had been to be ringed in by armored vehicles, it was worse not knowing
where the Germans were.

As he followed Sergeant Brufels, who turned out to be a skilled foot
soldier, through the woods and back to GPU lines, Paul Gedern accepted
that the battle was not over for him. Still, he was determined to take the
next chance to make a break from these GPU idiots.

When dawn broke he and Brufels were hiding in a thicket that the light revealed to be no more than two hundred meters forward of the Rangers' position. But they were outside of the American circle. They moved quickly through the gray and white light to the road that, according to Brufels's map, curved around the airfield at a distance of two to three kilometers.

They flagged down a GPU truck and made their way to the center of Zeven, the staging area for the GPU offensive. The little town's square, marked in the center by a stone fountain surrounded by cobblestones, was host to an incongruous collection of modern military vehicles. Radar vans and trucks and command vehicles were scattered through the tiny streets and fighting to get through, each on their own important mission. The soldiers they saw varied from the motley collections of overweight men in ill-fitting uniforms that mark reserve and militia forces around the world to sharp-eyed platoons of light infantry.

Gedern trudged along behind Brufels, more than a little dazed by the experience of the previous night. He thought about asking to go to an aid station, if they could find one, but he was sure that Brufels would point out that he wasn't seriously wounded. Just being shaken up was more like malingering.

"You can get something to eat over there," a fat sergeant told them from the back of a truck loaded with cases of rations and black water cans. "Then report to the building on the corner of this street. Someone there will help you link up with your unit, or will assign you to a new one."

Gedern was happy to hear there was food around, and he followed Brufels to a courtyard behind an ancient house where some army cooks had set up a line to serve GPU soldiers. Once there, he began to look for friendly faces, wondering what had become of the rest of his company. His clothes still bore the smell of burned diesel and plastic to remind him what had happened to his platoon, and he wondered if the same thing could have happened to the company?

"I don't see anyone here from the platoon," Gedern said.

Brufels had a mouthful of *brocthen*, bread soaked in a runny stew that was probably left over from the previous day. He looked up and said something that sounded like "Nowunf camnee."

"What's that?" Gedern asked.

Food dribbled down Brufels's chin in a sickly yellow stream. "I said, no one from the company, either," he finished.

"Did we get beaten that bad?"

If Brufels suspected that his one remaining subordinate was on the edge of losing control, he did nothing to reassure the younger man.

"Things got pretty bad last night, that's for sure," he said, tearing off another large mouthful of bread and chewing with his mouth open. "But hell, I don't know, maybe the rest of the company is eating chow right now in some other field kitchen."

How can he be so calm about this? Gedern wondered. He watched the other man eat—nothing had affected Brufels's appetite—and then looked down at his own tray of food: a greasy broth over a slice of good bread that had probably been taken from one of the surrounding shops. All around him, other men were eating at the same determined pace with which Brufels attacked his food. Some of the men had obviously been in last night's fight: their clothes were scorched and torn, their faces blackened. None of them appeared to be wounded, and all of them were—as far as Gedern could tell—oblivious to what was really going on.

Gedern felt a twisting spasm in his intestines. They were going to do it again. The thought came over him all at once, fully formed, no hint of its approach. They were going to do it again and again, as long as it was necessary, until they destroyed the Americans or, more likely, the Americans and the Bundeswehr came and destroyed them.

He looked up quickly to where the clear winter sky, visible here as only a blue rectangle above the surrounding houses, suddenly seemed threatening. He was afraid of American air power, of German air power. The Americans had slaughtered fifty thousand Iraqis using nothing but their airplanes. What would they do to a group of disorganized part-time soldiers like the GPU?

Paul Gedern lowered his head, and his paper tray slipped forward in his loosened grip, so that the food leaked over the edge and dripped down on his fire-blackened boots.

"Hey," Brufels said, close enough to his ear that he could feel the spittle and food. "If you don't want that shit, I'll eat it."

A few kilometers away, a GPU unit that had not been involved in the night's fighting was preparing for the next round. Hauptmann Martin Loudenslaner, commanding Second Company of Flak Battalion 224, watched as his soldiers set up their fire-direction radar on a small rise some ten kilometers from the airfield occupied by the American forces. From where he stood he could not see the missiles: twelve infrared-guided Rolands, mounted on modified Marder chassis and boasting a six-kilometer range. These weapons, the same ones used in the regular army's Heeres Flak Truppe, the antiaircraft batteries, were dispersed on the spiny back of another small ridge, offset by two or three kilometers from the radars. As he watched his men perform, climbing over their vehicles, sighting the radars, testing the power, camouflaging the vehicles under the green and brown nets, he was pleased with his work.

Originally, the military council of the GPU had thought that air defense would be a large and significant hole in the party's military capabilities.

But then had come a sudden windfall with the transfer of the sophisticated missile systems to the reserves. Loudenslaner was one of the officers who believed that this highly technical equipment needed to be
manned by full-time soldiers. It took lots of practice to maintain profi-
ciency, to have any hope of bringing down a fast mover, a jet skimming
over the battlefield at five hundred knots only a hundred feet in the air.
But he had accepted his mission and trained his men hard. His soldiers
had even given up some of their own time—on free weekends and after
work—for extra training.

That was the wonderful thing about this new German solidarity. Before
the economic decline, most Germans had lost their sense of service to the
nation in the selfish excesses of materialism. Now, with the GPU, he saw
that his people could once again be selfless, could make sacrifices on
behalf of their country.

Loudenslaner was proud of his soldiers—now almost completely ready
for action—and proud of his five-month-old association with the GPU. As
far as he, or for that matter, any of the officers in the units actually doing
the fighting knew, the Americans below had been offered the opportunity
to surrender peacefully. They had opted to fight, prompted, no doubt, by
those frightened sheep in Berlin, who knew that the end was coming for
them and their reign, the end of their prostituting the Republic for the
NATO allies and the rest of the West.

"We're ready for systems test, sir," Loudenslaner's radio operator said.

"Very well," the captain replied. He watched the lighted indicator
board and imagined the stout black tips of the missiles rotating on their
firing platforms according to the commands given by the fire-direction
center.

"First test is green, sir," the radio operator reported.

"Yes," Loudenslaner answered. Off to the south, the winter sky, with
its thin cold clouds, stretched like a pastel cloth above the expectant
German countryside.

Gedern did not touch his food, and Brufels had to display a whole new
talent for speedy eating when an officer—Gedern didn't recognize him—
strode into the courtyard where the soldiers were eating and announced
that the meal was over.

"You men who were in the first and second companies step to the right
as you leave this courtyard," the officer directed. "The rest of you will
form with your units on the opposite side of the square."

That's it, Gedern thought, *the companies are no more.* He looked around,
hoping to see some familiar faces among the other men who were being
reformed into new units, other men from his company and its sister
company who were suddenly without units. When he and Brufels made

it out of the square, there were only fifteen or twenty men standing at the tailgate of the truck that waited there. Gedern recognized a few men, none of them friends.

"That all of you?" a fat private demanded from the shelter of the truck's canvas cover. He was old for a private, Gedern noticed, and very clean. And he didn't look tired. Gedern hated him immediately because he knew that the other man would not be going forward to find the Americans.

The private looked at the assembled soldiers through round glasses, as if he expected them to explain their disheveled appearance to him.

"What do you have for us?" Brufels asked. He had lost his own jacket with its insignia of rank, and was wearing instead a dirty private's coat.

"Just hold your water," the fat private said.

Brufels drew his pistol, tugging back the action. "I should shoot you, you fat fuck," he said.

The private, though obviously frightened, did not seem to believe that Brufels would actually shoot him. After a few seconds, Brufels lowered the pistol.

What a bunch of losers, Gedern thought. *How can we not be defeated?*

"We went out this far, sir," Sergeant Bishop said, using the tip of a mechanical pencil to point out, on the map, the farthest extent of his reconnaissance patrol.

"Nobody on foot?" Spano asked.

"No. But we saw some tracks that were fresh this morning, made after it had stopped snowing."

Isen watched as Bishop briefed the battalion commander, referring to a small green notebook he'd used to collect the information. The staff sergeant was tired, bone tired after the last three days and nights. But he'd been given the recon mission this morning and had done a first-class job. Isen didn't see the soldiers in Bishop's squad, but he knew that they had to be at least as tired as Bishop was, at least as close to the end of their considerable stamina.

"This was the hill where we saw the vans," Bishop said, pointing to a ridge several kilometers away.

"Recognize anything?" Spano asked.

"No, sir, they were just boxy green vans. We wouldn't even have seen them but they happened to be moving at the time."

"Did they have camouflage netting up?" Isen asked.

"It looked like that's what they were doing, putting everything under nets," Bishop said.

"What do you think, Mark?" Spano asked Isen.

"If they're putting them under nets, then the vehicles are meant to stay.

So they're not supply trucks dropping stuff off. My guess would be communications vans," Isen said. He chewed on the inside of his lip for a moment. "Course, they might be radar vans, too."

"Radar," Spano said. "Air defense stuff."

"Yessir," Isen answered. "They have to expect now that the weather is clearing that our Air Force, which already came in once in miserable conditions, will be back to hammer them so we can get some choppers in here to bail us out."

"Makes sense," Spano said, studying the map again. "Our guys have got to expect flak, don't you think?"

"The flyboys always expect the worst," Isen answered. "I just wish we knew what kind of things the Air Force had in the works."

The loss of the SATCOM had handicapped the Rangers more than almost anything else that had happened. Spano could not even learn what to expect from his superiors, what the next American move would be. He was not even sure, for that matter, if the folks back in the States had gotten his transmission that the shooting had started. His response was to expect the best, the dramatic rescue, with the humiliation of the GPU figuring prominently in the production.

"OK," Spano said. "So the flyboys can expect to be shot at. What can we expect on the ground?"

"Any signs out there of armored vehicles?" Isen asked Bishop.

The NCO took off his helmet and ran his hands furiously over the tiny black comb of hair that clung to the front of his head. "We didn't hear any tracks. A couple of trucks, maybe, but nothing heavy, you know."

"And you didn't spot anything?"

"No, sir."

"You think they're holding in an attack position?" Spano said.

Sometimes, before an attack, armored forces were marshaled in an area called an attack position, somewhere short of their objective or their jump-off point for the attack. It would make sense that, after the night's battle, the Germans did not want the armor in close to the Rangers until they were ready to launch an all-out attack.

"Could be that they're planning an air strike against us and they want to move their own guys out of the way. Another possibility is that they're getting ready to take on a U.S. armored force and need the equipment, or maybe they're expecting the Bundeswehr to attack," Isen said. "Maybe they're not sure what they should do next."

"And if the armor is gone?" Spano asked.

"Well, the Territorial Forces are mostly light infantry anyway," Isen said. "They call them *jaeger* or something like that; I did learn that much from the predeployment briefs about their army."

Spano twisted the toe of his boot in the dirty snow by his foot. "So what are the possibilities? They bomb the hell out of us, in which case we're pretty much screwed. Or they could come at us with light infantry, which would be the best scenario for us."

"Depending on the odds," Isen added.

"Depending on the odds," Spano agreed. "If they come at us with armor?"

"That's the scenario—the worst case—that we have to prepare for," Isen said. "I asked Major Rhone, and he said the GPU almost definitely has more armored vehicles available. The question is whether they'll save them to fight the Bundeswehr, for the move on Berlin, or to stomp us."

He drew in a breath, let it out quickly. "I think we should move."

"Move?" Spano said. "Where? How?"

"We can't fight those Marders again," Isen said. "Not here. They won't make the same mistakes they did last time."

"The Air Force will chew them up with the Specter," Spano said.

Isen knew that the USAF Specter, a prop-driven C-130 Hercules aircraft that mounted an impressive array of large guns, including a 105-millimeter howitzer that had been converted to an automatic, direct-fire weapon, could indeed make short work of any German armor unlucky enough to be caught out in the open. But they couldn't talk to the Air Force. Isen looked up at the empty sky.

"What if we don't have air superiority?" It was a rhetorical question. Without air superiority, the ungainly Specter would be an easy kill for any enemy aircraft. "What if they don't show up in time?"

Spano seemed almost incapable of entertaining the idea that they wouldn't be rescued. "Move to where?" he asked again.

Isen unfolded his map and pressed it up against the wall of the control building. He noticed that the original markings—boundaries, objectives, limits of advance—for Operation Solid Steel were still marked in color codes on the acetate covering, though the concerns of Solid Steel belonged to another life.

"There's a factory complex of some sort here," Isen said. He pulled his mitten off with his teeth and pointed with a finger. "It's not very big, so we wouldn't have to spread ourselves too thin," he said. "And it's not that far from here, a couple of klicks. Or we could move into this town here . . . Karlshofen."

"And how . . ." Spano began, his voice rising. He caught himself, pulled Isen by the arm farther away from where the soldiers inside might hear them. "How the fuck are we supposed to get the wounded there? The dead?"

Isen hadn't yet figured out how to move the wounded, some of whom were in great pain. But the comment about moving the dead made him wonder if Spano really understood that he was talking about desperate circumstances.

"Look, sir, I don't have an answer for that yet. Maybe we can use one of the vehicles we captured last night if they're not too shot up. The point is that we can't stay here. If the Germans come rolling back, we're going to be massacred. Or we'll have to surrender."

"Don't even fucking say that." Spano bit the words off angrily. "We're not going to surrender. We'll E and E first."

"In a hostile country?" Isen said. "There's no place to hide out there."

Isen saw that he and his boss were looking at the problem in fundamentally different ways. Isen was concerned with the worst case: what if the Germans launched another armored attack? Spano was hanging on to hope for the best case: the Air Force would be here soon to rescue them. And although Isen knew that it was very likely that Spano was right—every Air Force squadron remaining in Europe must be scrambled by this time—he didn't want to bet the lives of all their soldiers on that possibility.

"Look, Mark, don't freeze up on me here," Spano said.

And at that point Isen knew that Spano thought he was acting out of fear. The thought infuriated him, but he had a fleeting moment of doubt—what if Spano was right?

If I crack up, I'll be no good to him or to the command, Isen thought. He watched Spano closely. The old man was tired, but he was not hysterical and seemed to be in control of his faculties.

I wonder what I look like, Isen thought.

There was no sure way to tell, of course, if he was being overly cautious. He was beyond exhausted, had hardly eaten or slept for three days. During that time he had almost been killed, and he had seen the men he was responsible for fighting for their lives.

Jesus, Isen thought. *Would I even know it if I was losing control?*

Isen folded his map up again. The area around the airfield was so familiar to him now that he barely need to consult the map. "I'll talk to the company commanders; we'll pull into a tighter formation so we can hold here, sir," he said.

Not far away, Private Paul Gedern was trying to adjust to the idea that he would soon be attacking the Americans again. This time, he would not have the security of a steel hull to protect him from their fires.

Gedern lay in the snow alongside some ten other men, all of them complete strangers to him. He'd been sent as a replacement to fill a rifleman's slot in one of the *jaeger* companies of the Territorial Forces. The only person who'd spoken directly to him was the squad leader, a former East German NCO who'd warned him that malingerers would be shot.

"We go in five minutes," the squad leader said behind them.

Five minutes. Gedern wondered if that was how long he had left of his life.

Ahead of them, the woods continued down a slope that probably led to a streambed. Gedern knew, because he'd heard the other men talking, that there was a small rise on the other side of that streambed, and the Americans were somewhere on top of that rise, no more than a kilometer away.

"Check your magazine."

The squad leader, whose name was Ossen or Ossing—Gedern couldn't remember—was addressing him.

"I just did, Stabsunteroffizier." Even as the words were coming out of his mouth, he knew the response was the wrong one.

The sergeant crawled up next to Gedern and punched him on the side of the face. Not as hard as he could have, but hard.

"I don't care what you just did, you little shit. I said check your fucking weapon."

Gedern felt the now familiar rush of fear. *Stoddard and Brufels might have been assholes, but these people are dangerous.*

He took the magazine from his rifle, checked the round seated in the chamber and the ones visible in the dark magazine.

"What was your name again?" Ossen or Ossing asked.

"Gedern."

"Make sure you keep your fucking interval."

"Yes, Stabsunteroffizier," Gedern said. He thought about the other question he wanted to ask, then about the stinging sensation on the side of his head. He asked anyway.

"How close are we here?" Gedern asked. He'd been given a perfunctory briefing, and he wasn't sure that he understood exactly what the attack was to look like.

"A kilometer, a little less, maybe," the NCO said. "All we have to do is pinpoint their fighting positions." He pulled his lips back against his teeth and spat into the snow. He was close enough for Gedern to smell his foul breath. "Then we're going to use the mortars to work them over before we get in there and mix it up with them."

When the sergeant crawled off, Gedern pulled his legs up, grasping his knees in his hands. Somewhere out in front of him lay a resourceful enemy who'd had days to prepare defenses, an enemy who'd had the guts to attack—on foot—armored vehicles. And now here he was, about to walk into the fight, when he'd done nothing but drive a Marder since he finished his basic training two and a half years earlier. He looked around him, listening for some sound other than his own shallow, rapid breathing. Surely there had to be some armored vehicles left to support this push. Why had they been pulled back?

Gedern was suddenly seized with an urge to urinate. He crawled backward.

"Where are you going?" It was the squad leader, off to his right rear.

"I have to piss," Gedern said.

"You're not going anywhere," the NCO said, the bully menace in his voice unmistakable. "Do it right there."

Gedern knelt in the snow and unzipped his trousers with trembling hands. He faced away from the line, away from the Americans. As he urinated, he watched the woods just in front of him, where the snow scattered the sunlight and the wet trunks of the trees stood black against the brightness. He felt like crying.

"Hurry up, Gedern, you dickhead," his new squad leader said.

The collapse of the American perimeter had changed its shape from that of a triangle to something more like an enlarged, shallow crescent on the southern side of the airfield, with the control buildings nestled in the concave side of the American line. The ends of the curve were anchored by Alpha Company in the east and Charlie Company in the west, while the battered Bravo Company occupied the middle. Isen and Spano were banking on the open airfield, which now lay behind Bravo, inside the crescent, to help protect them from an attack from that direction.

Though the last platoons at each end of the battalion position had moved their fighting positions to give themselves all-around protection, there was no getting around the fact that the ends of the American line were exposed.

The GPU soldiers who'd been arrayed against the Rangers until the first attack, all of them Panzergrenadiers, or mechanized infantrymen, were used to riding everywhere and might have missed the importance of the shift. This was not true of the *jaeger* companies who, with Paul Gedern and other replacements loosely fitted into their organization, began to move forward late in the morning of the third day.

The move through the woods was completely disorienting for Gedern. He would walk a few meters, being careful to keep his interval with the men on either side of him, then lie down in the snow for five or six minutes. He suspected that someone was moving while he tried to remain motionless, but he couldn't see what was going on. He was terrified that they'd simply walk up on an American ambush, and although he did his best to control his fear, he felt as if he might turn at any moment and run for the rear.

Up, move forward, down.

The snow under his legs melted enough from his body heat to soak his trousers, and he could feel the moisture being drawn down to his socks, leaking into his boots.

Up, forward, down.

There was still nothing in sight, and Gedern couldn't even tell if he was going uphill or down. Nothing made sense to him. Not this stupid walk through the woods, not the fact that he was with men he didn't know and who didn't know him—and thus couldn't care less about his safety. It didn't make sense that they were advancing on foot when somewhere around here were armored vehicles that at least offered some protection.

Gedern wondered what would have happened to him had he been able to surrender to the Americans.

I'd probably get killed by German fire, he thought. The man beside him waved, and he stood up to walk forward again. *Now I'll just get killed by American fire.*

"I don't like the way this line has shaped up," Colonel Spano said.

His audience, Isen, Dettering, the Charlie Company commander, and Lieutenant Hawkins, one of Dettering's platoon leaders, all had their own opinions about the company's new position on the south side of the airfield, but they waited for the old man to finish.

"We're hanging out here on this end," Spano said. He looked at Dettering.

"How far out are your patrols going?"

"There's a dry streambed down about three hundred meters," Dettering said. "We've been running past that by another three hundred or so." He looked at his watch. "The next patrol is scheduled to go out in about ten minutes."

"What's out there now?" Spano asked.

Hawkins, whose platoon owned this sector, answered that question. "I got my observation posts down about halfway to that streambed. Two two-man posts, sir."

The observation posts were set out along likely enemy routes into the position. Their job was early warning. Hawkins had taken care that his OPs, as they were called, were well placed and well camouflaged.

Isen was not satisfied. He'd pointed out to Spano, as they walked over to the end of the battalion position, that the airfield was not significant and that they didn't need to stay just because they'd started there. The implication was that they should move to the factory area he'd located, or at least to the nearby town.

Spano waved his hand, and Dettering took his lieutenant and backed off.

"You don't much like this position, do you, Mark?" Spano said when they were out of earshot.

"No, sir, I don't."

"And you don't think we need to hang on to this area so that evacuation choppers would have this as a landing zone?"

Isen had considered this. "I think that's a concern for later on. Right now I'm more concerned with having anything left when the choppers do come."

Spano nodded slightly.

"But you understand," Spano said, "that as long as I listen to you and still feel like I have good reasons for staying here, that I should stick to my guns. Right?"

Isen thought about the Marder on the narrow track beside the woods and Spano's foolhardy gesture with the pistol.

"Yes, sir. I understand. You've got make the call," Isen said. "And it's my job to disagree with you."

"Sure, sure," Spano said. He put his hand on Isen's shoulder, squeezed once. "I'll tell you what. Let's go out and have a little look-see for ourselves, and if we can't fix things here, we'll talk about moving the battalion."

Isen knew that "fix things" meant to Spano's satisfaction. And the old man could grant or reserve his blessing as he wished.

"OK, sir," Isen said. "Let's take a look."

Isen motioned to Dettering and asked the captain to send along three men to provide security.

The time between halts was growing shorter, Gedern noticed, and there was a certain tension that carried from man to man, as if passed along with the hand and arm signals that told them when to stop, when to stand, when to advance. But there was still nothing visible in the woods.

Then he saw the bodies.

There were three or four of them, all in a small cluster amid some trees a few meters up the side of the gentle hill. Two of them were facedown, another's face was covered by the tails of a long winter parka, while the fourth stared skyward with frozen eyes.

They were German, Gedern knew immediately. He looked around quickly to see if he recognized the spot—which might mean these men were from his unit. But all the snowy woods looked the same to him, and his eyes kept coming back to the dead men. For a few seconds he stood straight up with his mouth open, wondering what had happened here, and so forgot to alert the others that he had seen something.

"Get down," the man beside him hissed.

Gedern automatically dropped to one knee, his eyes still fixed on the dead. Off to the side, he could hear the quick scuff of nylon storm pants as someone hurried toward him.

"What else did you see?"

It was Sergeant Ossen—Gedern was suddenly sure of the name—and he'd spotted the bodies. The squad leader knelt beside Gedern and pulled the private close to him so that they could whisper.

"I said, what else did you see?"

Gedern shook his head. *Nothing.*

"All right," Ossen said. "Let's see what's up there."

Ossen made a couple of short, furious motions with his arm, and the other soldiers in his squad, who apparently understood these signs, fanned out and took up firing positions. Ossen pointed to a soldier beside Gedern, then tapped Gedern on the chest and signed to both of them. *Follow me.*

Gedern—who wouldn't have thought it possible to be any more miserable—stood numbly, his rifle held too low across his thighs. He watched Ossen's back as the sergeant began a wide circle around the bodies, but he didn't move until the other soldier shoved him in the ribs with his rifle muzzle.

As he walked, feeling the cold wetness of his trouser legs stinging his flesh, Gedern considered that if he hadn't been the one to come up on the bodies, he wouldn't be moving forward again.

The slope below Charlie Company's corner of the sector grew steeper as Isen, Spano, and the company commander, each with his own radio operators, and the three security men moved away from the line. The trees were thinner here, in places spaced widely enough so that one could see for a dozen meters or so. Isen imagined the fight in these close quarters, in the terrifying dark and the swirling snow.

"Doesn't look like we can move this way," Spano said.

He was looking for ways to adjust the line to give his Rangers the best advantage that the terrain offered.

"Let's go up and make contact with the guys on OP while we're out here," the colonel said.

"That'd be this way."

Bill Dettering, C Company commander, headed off at an angle. Isen made a mental note of the change in direction. If they had to head back in a hurry, he wanted to know which way was home. As he squinted into the woods for invisible enemies, he wondered if the Germans were running counterpatrols.

Something moved off to his left, but Gedern kept on walking, too frightened to do anything but hold his breath and hope that it went away. In his rational mind, he knew that if they ran into Americans and the GIs saw them first, he might be killed. But his rational mind wasn't in control, and he kept putting one foot in front of the other, hoping that he wouldn't see anything—even though he had—telling himself that he'd seen nothing, hoping that whatever had moved out there was gone. He held his breath and walked.

When he chanced a look a moment later, there was nothing there. He scanned the trees, listened for soft footfalls in the snow.

Perhaps I did imagine it, he thought.

When he turned back to follow Ossen and the other soldier, they were gone.

*   *   *

"Thunder."

The soldiers in the observation post challenged them before Isen, who was in the rear, even suspected that they were close.

Bill Dettering gave the password. "Weather."

The security detail spread out forward of the OP without having to be told. Dettering and Spano got close enough to the soldiers to talk in whispers, while Isen hung back.

The Rangers had dug a fighting position, then had camouflaged their handiwork so that it couldn't be detected from any distance of more than a few meters. One of the men wore a pile cap under his helmet, with the earflaps pulled up—he had to be able to hear an enemy approach—and clasped ridiculously on top of his helmet.

"All quiet out here," Spano said, standing and moving toward Isen. "I want to go out a little farther."

"Don't you think we ought to wait for the patrol, sir? Bill said there'd be one along shortly."

Isen knew that he was making perfect sense. Even though there was no substitute for seeing the ground, Lieutenant Colonels had no business wandering around forward of friendly lines. Spano's job was to command, not to patrol the perimeter.

But the earlier encounter about moving to the factory sat heavily on Isen's mind. He wondered if he sounded as if he'd lost his nerve, wondered if he *had* lost his nerve.

"We'll be *fine*, Mark," Spano said.

He motioned for the three soldiers on the security team to move forward. Isen saw two of the privates exchange questioning looks. *Has the old man slipped his knot?*

Gedern heard them before he saw them, a single commanding voice floating down among the trees from the slope above him, followed by what might have been murmured consent. At first he thought it was Ossen and the other soldier, but then he caught at glimpse of the distinctive helmet profile.

They were Americans.

Gedern was overcome by a smothering fear. He was alone. He wanted to run, he wanted to throw down his rifle and surrender, he wanted to hide under the snow until these Americans and all the GPU had left the woods to its winter peacefulness. He wanted to do all this, but he could do nothing.

The Americans were moving toward him, down the slope, and would see him at any second. He crouched down in the thin undergrowth, took his weapon off safe, and held perfectly still.

If I surrender, I'll be with them when—and if—the Marders roll in on them, Gedern thought. *I can die here or in there.*

He looked around for Ossen, saw no one. He was afraid that he might have to shoot to keep them from shooting first. And he was afraid he might not be able to act.

Go away. He directed his thoughts at them, hoping to drive them back.

There were five or six of them, at least, Gedern thought, though it was difficult to tell because they kept good interval and so appeared and disappeared in the trees. They seemed to be heading down the slope at an angle, so there was a chance they might miss him completely.

Now there were at least six of them, close enough so that he could see their faces. They were moving in a wide wedge, so at least one or two of them would walk right up on him. There would be no chance to hide. His throat suddenly seemed too small to breathe through, and there were sharp, painful pinpoints behind his eyes.

He picked out the closest one and slowly shifted his rifle.

They had gone only a short distance past the OP, but Isen thought they'd seen enough. If they were going to run into a German patrol, there was a good chance it would be in the low ground at the bottom of the slope. He stepped quickly up to Spano and tapped him on the shoulder.

Go back? he signed.

Spano smiled, amused at Isen's concern, and held up his thumb and forefinger. *A little bit more.*

Then he turned downhill again.

The report startled Gedern, and he lost the sight picture with the first burst. All the Americans disappeared at once. He fired again, five, six rounds. Then, in the pause, he heard the crack of incoming rifle fire and the tiny ripping sounds as the bullets tore through the bare branches above his head.

Gedern was on his stomach, scanning the woods before him. He had no idea what had happened after he pulled the trigger, and it took him a few moments more to realize that the American fire was all high, and very little of it seemed to be going right over his head.

They don't know where I am, he thought.

With the first shot he had experienced a clearing sensation, and this heightened awareness continued as he watched two men from his squad set up an automatic rifle and begin firing into the woods. Gedern was on his side, watching the other two men when another GPU crew opened up with a light machine gun right beside him, startling him and adding to the terrible hammering that suddenly shook the woods.

*   *   *

Two bullets hit Mark Isen in the head. The impact on his Kevlar helmet
sent him backward, but not before one of the rounds skipped at the edge
of the helmet near his right ear, tearing a painful, though shallow, gouge
in the back of his neck. He lay on his back, eyelids skipping so that the
trees above him appeared and disappeared in flickering gray. There was
a lot of firing, and close by, another sound—deep painful moaning.

I've got to help that man, Isen thought. *I've got to get up.*

Then one of the soldiers from Charlie Company was crawling toward
him.

"You're going to be okay, man, you're going to be okay, man," the
soldier repeated. Even through his pain, Isen could tell that the youngster
was badly frightened. He shifted his eyes and saw the private, who
hunched his shoulders at each rifle shot. The man's voice trembled, but
for all that, he was still functioning. "You're going to be okay, man."

But Isen did not feel okay. He gulped cold air, tried to turn his head.

"Don't try to move," the Ranger said. "We're going to get you out of
here, but don't try to move."

Even wounded, it was tough for Isen to relinquish control. He felt as if
he should be giving the orders, more so because this soldier was so
obviously frightened. But he could not move his head. He pushed his
heels against the earth and strained his back against gravity, but he could
not move.

"I've got the major," the soldier shouted above the firing to a comrade
Isen couldn't see. "I'm starting back."

With that, the Ranger, who was no bigger than Isen, grasped the
wounded officer by his arms and began dragging him back to the American position.

Isen heard the crunch of grenades exploding down the hill as the other
Rangers tried to cover the withdrawal. Suddenly the young soldier was
kneeling. The trees and the ground swirled under him and over him as the
soldier lifted Isen onto one shoulder in a fireman's carry. With the sudden
movement, Isen began to lose his grip on consciousness. There was a sticky
sliding under his helmet, then the blood moved down his jaw and traced
the rim of his eye socket. As the Ranger carried him away, and just before
the eye blinked shut with warm blood, Isen caught a glimpse of a dark
bundle in the snow behind them that got smaller and smaller as the Ranger
moved purposefully through the fire, back toward friendly lines.

"Gedern."

The call was tentative, from behind him.

Sergeant Ossen crawled up beside Gedern, who sat on his haunches in
the snow, his feet splayed in front of him.

"Are you hurt?"

"No," Gedern managed. He hadn't taken his eyes off the stock of his weapon, which sat across his knees.

"What happened? Did you see them first?"

"No," Gedern said. He was angry that his voice was betraying him. "I mean, yes, I fired, but it was mostly them." He indicated the other GPU soldiers, whose firing had driven off the Americans.

"Are they gone?" Gedern noticed that Ossen didn't seem quite so fearless now that he thought there might be enemy nearby. That realization made Gedern hate the NCO even more.

"I think so," one of the other soldiers said.

Ossen raised himself to a crouch and moved to where a single American lay facedown in the snow. Gedern watched as the sergeant turned the body over carefully.

Another soldier came up and joined Ossen near the body.

"We need to get out of here," he said. "They'll be back for this body."

"Let me look for maps and stuff," Ossen said. The sergeant pulled open the man's parka, exposing the camouflage blouse underneath.

"I'll be damned," Ossen said. "This is a fucking colonel. I'll be god-*damned.*"

By the time Gedern got to his feet, Ossen had rifled the dead man's pockets, placing the contents on the unmoving chest. There was a map with smeared markings, a notebook, some pens and a wallet. Gedern watched Ossen, who had regained his disdainful air. The sergeant opened the dead man's wallet and a tiny packet of photographs fell out. Gedern stepped closer.

Ossen flipped over the first picture of two children, a boy and a girl sitting on a bench.

"Look at this," Ossen said, leering. He held up a photo—obviously a professional shot—of a beautiful dark-haired woman. "How'd you like to—"

Gedern was surprised at how quickly he moved. He stepped forward and shoved the stock of his weapon into Ossen's face, sending the NCO sprawling backward, arms flying.

"What the fuck do you think you're doing?" Ossen seethed through a bloody lip. He was doing everything he could to keep from yelling. "I'll fucking kill you, you little . . ."

Gedern leveled his rifle at Ossen's head, which was only a few feet from the dull muzzle.

"You . . . ," Gedern stuttered, started again, confused by the sudden rush of black hatred that swelled behind his eyes. "You miserable piece of *shit.*"

The other soldier made a move to bring his rifle to bear, but Ossen's hand shot up, stopping him.

"It's okay," Ossen said, narrowing his eyes at Gedern. "We have a sensitive one here."

I hate you for this, Gedern thought. *I hate you for this, I hate you. I hate.*

Mark Isen struggled mightily to swim out of the darkness and pain that muddled his head. He wasn't sure what had happened out in the woods—he only knew that he was hurt and that he was needed, and that was a powerful incentive for him.

He was on the hard floor, a medic bent over him, and Isen could see the blurry star of a pocket flashlight the man was using to examine the wound on the back of Isen's head. "What happened?" he managed.

"Looks like you guys got ambushed out there, sir," the soldier said.

"Everybody okay?"

The medic, a buck sergeant whose name wouldn't come to Isen, straightened so that he could look at Isen's face.

"Colonel Spano is dead, sir," the soldier said. "They went out and recovered the body a little while ago."

Something tightened in his chest, flowering darkly for a moment as he closed his eyes and pictured Spano's family. But then the soldier in him— the one with so much to do and so many people counting on him— pushed it back down.

"Tell my radio operators to send runners for the company commanders," Isen told the medic.

With the battalion executive officer—who was part of Team Black— already a prisoner of the GPU, Spano's death left Isen in command. He reached up gingerly and touched his neck where the medics had applied a combat dressing, and he wondered briefly if the company commanders would resist, telling him he was hurt too badly to command.

Can't have that, he thought as he struggled to sit up. His head went light from the sudden move, and another medic nearby offered a hand to help him.

"Anybody else hit besides Colonel Spano?" he asked.

"Just you, sir," the medic said. "The other guys are fine, far as we know."

Isen let his eyes come into focus slowly as he scanned the battalion aid station, such as it was. There were half a dozen men on the floor of the tiny building, a few of them hurt badly. He thought he recognized Major Rhone lying on a makeshift pallet made from a parachute.

There was much to do to get the battalion moved. Isen took a deep breath, thought once more about Ray Spano and his concern over the bodies of those killed, then began his work.

"Help me up here," he called to the medic nearest him.

13

SOMETHING HAD GIVEN WAY IN PAUL GEDERN; HE HAD LEFT some part of his old self in the woods next to the body of the dead American officer. He'd been terrified, ever since the shooting started, that some stupid civilian parading as a soldier—a Brufels or a Stoddard— would get him killed. When he met Ossen, he learned a new fear: he could be shot, deliberately, by a German, in the name of discipline. But now that fear had been displaced by a smoldering malevolence that was as near to homicide as anything he'd ever felt.

"Stay clear of Ossen," the soldier who'd been with them in the woods whispered to Gedern as they returned to GPU lines.

Gedern returned a flat, cold stare.

They moved back to an assembly area several hundred meters away from the American position, while other *jaeger* units stayed closer and kept an eye on the Rangers. In the rear, Gedern was issued extra ammunition and hand grenades.

"Do you suppose we're going to attack?" one of the younger soldiers asked no one in particular.

"What the hell do you think they're giving us all this stuff for?" an older man said sarcastically.

"Well, I don't see why we can't just sit here and wait until they give up," the youngster said. His cold fingers fumbled with the gleaming cartridges as he loaded magazines for his assault rifle. "Sooner or later they're bound to run out of food. They can't stay there forever."

"We can't afford to wait," the older man said. "If the GPU hesitates, then the people won't believe that we are serious, that we are strong enough to run this nation as it should be run."

A propagandist at every turn, Gedern thought.

The younger soldier did not answer this. Perhaps, Gedern thought, he couldn't comprehend the consequences. Or perhaps he had simply given in, as Gedern had, to things he could not control.

He studied the faces, most of them hidden by scarves and pile caps, of the men squatting around the open ammunition cans. They were all tired and cold, and most of them seemed taxed by the task at hand: loading enough ammunition for the coming fight. They were focused on the short range, on getting through the next couple of hours.

That is how it came, he thought. Inarticulate, soundless, Paul Gedern nevertheless saw what was happening. While the workers stayed focused on the next day and the day after that, on going to work and coming home from work, on the next payday and the next holiday, other men plotted for power, plotted to spread hate and violence.

It had all looked like everyday life, he thought.

Looking back on the incremental choices that had brought them this far, he found no breaking points. No one had told these men they were in power; no one said "I will follow you into the darkness." Yet here they were. The soldiers around him, trussed in scarves and dirty coats, reminded him of photographs of General Paulus's doomed army shivering outside of Stalingrad.

Gedern looked up at the sky, prayed for the strength to resist, for the luck to survive.

He caught glimpses of other formations moving forward to the jump-off point for the attack, and he heard the trucks delivering the mortar rounds to the pits they had passed on their way from the assembly area.

This will be a big one, he thought, wondering if there would be armor involved, or at least mechanized infantry.

They were to attack an hour before dusk, that much he knew. Had he been privy to all the planning, Gedern would have known that the infantry was to be used to find the gaps in the American position, a space where the remaining Marders—now idling in an assembly area—could stab through and get behind the GIs.

But Gedern only knew what Ossen told the squad: their platoon would have the job of clearing whatever fighting positions were left after the bombardment. The squad leader warned them to be careful about crossing in front of one another's fire. He looked at Gedern when he said, "We don't want any accidental shootings of our own men."

The file snaked quietly into a line facing the Americans, and they had to lie in the snow for another ten minutes until the whole company was ready to go. Gedern's trousers were completely soaked through by this time, and he could easily imagine the raw red burn on the front of his thighs, and how the skin would dry and peel. He shifted uncomfortably from side to side, trying to raise himself out of the snow a bit, and he wondered, with no little alarm, if one could get frostbite of the penis.

Two of the companies, it turned out, had taken it upon themselves to commandeer German trucks that were not too badly damaged in the fighting.

"The main priority is the wounded," Isen said. "Then whatever ammo we can carry. Then the KIAs."

Isen knew that the company commanders were watching him to see if he was up to speed. They had a right to be suspicious of a head wound, he thought, and they were all shaken by Spano's death. He did his best to win their confidence, and they seemed to respond, taking careful notes and asking good questions about the move to the nearby village. But just when he thought that perhaps he was going to be able to pull it off— assume command in the middle of combat in a highly fluid situation— Bill Dettering asked a tough question.

"Was this what Colonel Spano was planning?"

Isen put his hand to his forehead, where a deep bass drum of pain had lodged. He thought about lying.

"No," he said. "This was my idea. I think we'll have a better chance of defending ourselves in a built-up area than we do out here where their armor can get at us too easily." He blinked, and it hurt.

"What happens when the Air Force shows up here?" Dettering asked. "I mean, without the SATCOM we have no way of telling them where we are. Should we take off and leave them in the dark?"

"I don't want to leave them in the dark," Isen said. "But I feel that it's more important, right now, that we be able to take care of ourselves."

There were several heavy moments while they looked at him unhappily. Isen told himself it wasn't a lack of confidence in his plan, it was just normal worrying about what was going down.

He thought about saying something to the effect that he was in charge now. But that kind of melodrama wouldn't be in character for him, and besides, they all knew who was in charge. The seconds dripped fatly.

Gene Wisneiwski took off his helmet and looked up. "It's cleared up a bunch. You'd think those flyboys would be out here by now if they were going to help us out."

That was it. No more questions about command. Wisneiwski had spoken for them, sidestepping the issue.

"There may be political concerns keeping them from charging in here," Isen said.

He'd thought long and hard about the tough position the Berlin government was in. No doubt their American allies wanted immediate action, but if the federal government allowed an American-led rescue, that would be as much as admitting that Berlin had lost control—and that would be political suicide for the government, perhaps the nation. What Isen didn't count on was Berlin's concern over the loyalty of the armed forces. If the GPU could infiltrate and dominate the reserves to such a surprising degree, Berlin reasoned, wasn't that possible in the active army as well? Before the German military could mount a rescue, the high command had to be sure that the federal troops were loyal.

But all of that sounded lame to men who were busy counting their dead.

"The trucks will stage from here," Isen said. "Alpha Company will lead, followed by Bravo, then the trucks, then Charlie. It gets dark by sixteen-fifteen, and we'll move at sixteen-thirty."

"If we run into resistance," Dettering asked, "are we going to fight our way through?"

"Yes," Isen said. "I'm convinced that staying here is a bad move for us. A deadly move."

The captains shuffled their feet a bit. They were ready to go back and pass the orders along to their subordinates, to devise plans for their companies' individual roles. They would do as good a job as anyone could expect, under the circumstances, but he wondered what they thought.

Whenever Isen had drawn plans to execute one of Spano's orders, it rarely crossed his mind that the company commanders might have a serious disagreement about how things were being done. And if they did, in peacetime training, they voiced their opinion.

Now things were different. Spano was gone, and Isen knew that they thought of him as untried, which was the truth, at least as far as battalion command was concerned. He was surprised at how much he wanted their approval, or at least their confidence.

This bump on the head is making me dizzy, he thought. *I'm getting paid to command, not to be popular.*

"Check in personally on the radio no later than seventeen hundred," he told them. He didn't want to talk to radio operators, he told them, he wanted the commanders on the other end. "You're dismissed."

They turned all at once, stuffing their maps into their shirts or into the deep cargo pockets on the sides of their trouser legs, already planning their orders. They were good men, and he hoped they trusted him as much as he trusted them.

Bill Dettering turned back after he'd gone a few meters. "Rangers lead the way, sir," he said, deadly serious.

"All the way," Isen answered.

Then Dettering turned away, and Mark Isen, the unexpected commander, was left all alone.

Paul Gedern waited impatiently for the heavy *thunk-thunk* of the big mortars that would begin the attack. He was not at all anxious to stand up and move through the woods when there were sure to be American bullets heading in his direction, and he did not want to kill anyone or be killed himself. He was no longer even thinking of escape, he merely wanted to be warm. His trousers were soaked, and the skin on the front of his thighs seemed to be, as far as he could imagine it, frozen.

The sound of the first mortar startled him. He grasped his weapon tightly and pushed himself deeper into the wet snow, wondering about the chances of a round falling short. He counted, imagining the high arc, wondering if the Americans heard the report of the tubes also.

The second rounds were down the tubes before the first hit. Then there were the explosions, four, five, six of them close together. Then another volley from the big 120-millimeter mortars mounted in tracks somewhere behind them. He lifted his head, glimpsed one or two orange flashes through the trees.

There were men up there, no doubt trying to crawl under the earth for protection as the rounds came in on top of them. He'd seen what just one of those heavy explosions could do. Gedern lowered his head, wondered if he was the only one in the line thinking about the Americans.

Then they were up, moving forward, bent over at the waist as if in a rainstorm. Gedern felt as if he were approaching a great cliff in the dark: there was nothing ahead of him but menace and the dull *carumph* of the exploding mortar rounds.

The deadly flowering of fire was more visible now as the rounds struck home. The barrage was to shift as the advancing line got closer. *When will they move it?* Gedern wondered. *What will we find?*

Then the bursts moved, quite suddenly, and lessened. The woods were full of the smell of explosives, a sickly smell of chemicals and burned trees. Gedern crouched lower as the first blackened holes came into view.

The first American weapon to respond was a light machine gun of some sort, pattering away off to his right. He flinched, hesitated a moment, then ran to the base of a thick tree. He checked his left and right, where the others were doing as he was, advancing by small rushes from one shelter to the next.

Another few steps, past a black-rimmed shell hole, surprisingly small for the noise of the explosions.

Maybe they left, Gedern thought. *Before we even started shooting, maybe they pulled out and we won't have to find them.*

But then he heard an unfamiliar weapon to his left, and a sharp ripping sound that passed somewhere near his jaw. He crashed into another tree, trying to disappear behind its too-small trunk, then looked on, horrified, as small geysers of snow and dirt walked their way up to him and beyond as some machine gunner tried to get at him. He wondered if they knew about the colonel, if they could tell he'd killed their commander.

"Let's go, let's go," someone shouted, and Gedern took a tentative step from behind his tree, on the side away from where he thought the American gunner was located. He stooped low, so far forward in an effort to keep out of sight that he lost his balance and tumbled onto his face. The American gun came again, and Gedern looked up from the snow in time to see a man in his squad, no more than two or three feet away, get hit full in the chest. Bits of flesh and blood and bone exploded through the thick layers of clothing, splattering Gedern with a misty red gore.

Gedern rolled away from the sight.

"Let's go," came the insistent voice again.

If I stay here, they might not find me, Gedern thought. *I could tell them I was knocked unconscious.*

There was a sharp blow against his leg, then another, and he looked over his shoulder to see one of the junior NCOs kicking him.

"Get up, you sonofabitch, and get moving," the man said. "Or I'll shoot you myself." To make his point clear, the NCO lowered his weapon so that Gedern could see down the muzzle's dark mouth.

In this way, Paul Gedern advanced on the enemy.

Mark Isen hesitated for only a moment when the first rounds came in. *If we'd had a half hour more,* he thought.

But he quickly pushed aside his lament and went to the task at hand.

The Germans were engaging Charlie Company, which was to bring up the rear of their column. Isen made his way over to Dettering, who was calmly directing his platoon leaders on the radio while he studied the detailed sketch of his company position.

He lowered the small radio when Isen approached. "The barrage just shifted, sir, apparently right out of our position, but it's still hard to see what's coming up."

"Any track noises?" Isen asked, hoping that his voice didn't betray his fear.

"No. One of Hawkins's squads opened up on some men on foot."

Isen glanced out in the direction of the crescent-shaped line, which bowed to the south. Just a short distance away, men were fighting for their lives, trusting him to make the next move.

His choices were muddled, and he had only a moment to decide. If the German attack was coming in strength, Charlie Company could easily get cut up if he left them behind. On the other hand, if he committed his other forces to a counterattack, he might never be able to move again. There were a million things that could go wrong in the next few minutes, including, Isen thought, the fact that he could make a dead wrong decision.

"I'm going to tell Alpha Company to move on schedule," Isen said to Dettering. "I want you to develop this quickly and see if you're going to be able to pull back. If you need help, I'll have a platoon from Bravo back you up."

"Roger that, sir," Dettering said. Isen was amazed at the man's presence. They were about to execute one of the most difficult maneuvers light infantry could perform: breaking contact with the enemy and withdrawing under pressure. Yet Dettering was a picture of calm control.

"Just let me know when there's room for me to get out of here," Dettering said. "Once I start to move, I don't want to be running into the backs of those trucks carrying our wounded."

Tim Brennan was surprised to see that the men running through the woods toward them—appearing and disappearing in the trees—did resemble the pop-up targets on a rifle range. He crouched in the fighting position and fired at one close to him, something dark that skipped behind some brush just as he pulled the trigger, but saw no effect. Below him, Charis was cursing as he tried to use his bayonet to extract a crushed round from the chamber of his weapon.

"I can't fucking believe this," Charis chanted. "C'm'on, c'm'on, motherfucker."

"There doesn't seem to be too many of them," Brennan said. Then he realized that there might be dozens of them, advancing under cover. He decided not to say anything to Charis about that possibility.

"We're supposed to pull out," Charis said.

"We're supposed to pull out when we get the word," Brennan corrected him.

"What if we miss it? No one is coming out here to tell us shit," Charis said.

Brennan looked down at him. "They'll come," he said. "Sergeant Bishop isn't going to leave us stranded out here."

Off to their left they heard the loud, crackling exhalation of an exploding grenade.

"Die, motherfuckers," someone nearby yelled.

"They must be close if we're using grenades," Charis said, scrambling to a crouch. He leaned against the forward edge of their shallow fighting position, still holding his bayonet, his rifle still broken open at the breech. Brennan spied on him for a second, saw how terrified Charis was, wondered if there was any sense in both of them staying if only one rifle worked. He peered back over the barrel of his weapon, searching the wet trees for running forms, and was posed just so when something heavy and black came down on the side of his face, knocking him sideways in the hole and tearing his rifle loose from his grasp.

The German soldier jumped into the hole and kicked at him again, a big heel that found his eye socket, so that Brennan was able only to bring his hand up feebly, trying to pull his helmet down and find his weapon at the same time. He had one arm on the lip of the hole, trying to regain his balance. His right eye saw only red, and he turned in time to see the German find his feet and start to bring his long assault rifle around in the confines of the position. When the weapon got caught up in the dirt on one side, Brennan lashed out with his legs as hard as he could, falling dangerously lower in the hole as he left his feet.

There was an eternity of seconds as he fell, with the German, now above him, finding control of his rifle again and beginning to move it downward. Then Brennan saw Charis, behind the German, apparently unseen, standing with his bayonet and his rifle, as unmoving as the trees behind them.

Then the second was lost, and the muzzle of the German's rifle came down, dull gray and incredibly wide, and Brennan grabbed at it, but the weapon was out of reach. He blinked shut his one good eye, waiting for the noise and the surprise of pain, but instead there was a thick sound of impact, a grunt of exertion and one of pain, and Brennan looked up to see that Charis—his lips strained against his teeth in fear and the insanity of the moment—had the German around the neck and was stabbing viciously at the man's lower back.

The body fell heavily across Brennan's legs, but Charis left it there while he grabbed Brennan's rifle and looked for the dead man's comrades.

"Oh, Jesus," Charis said. "Oh, Jesus, oh, Jesus, Jesus, Jesus. How can the motherfuckers get so close before we can even see them?" he complained, his voice a knife edge of fear.

"Uhhhh," Brennan groaned. His face stung sharply where the cold air now washed a cut that extended from his eyes socket to his jawline. He pulled off his mitten and touched his face as lightly as he could with his fingers. The eye was swelling quickly, like a boxer's, and there was blood and water mixed with dirt on his skin.

Charis fired three rounds into the undergrowth before them, and they heard the men in the next position yelling something at the attackers.

"There's more of 'em," Charis said evenly.

Brennan looked up to see the stock of the rifle jumping rhythmically against Charis's shoulder. He pushed at the German with his feet and hands, struggling to get free.

Charis's rifle was still jammed, and it looked to Brennan, on a quick glance, as if all the prodding with the bayonet had only made things worse. He pulled two hand grenades from his web gear, snapped off the safety clips and straightened the pins before placing them on the lip of the hole.

Charis fired again. "Down there," he said.

Brennan followed the weapon to where he thought he could see something in the low shadows. He hefted a grenade, slid the pin out and threw a fastball down the gentle slope.

One thousand, two thousand, three thousand, he counted before the noise and the shock washed up the hill. He looked up in time to see two or three figures moving toward them from the right.

"Over there, over there," he shouted, smacking Charis's arm.

Charis fired, and the three men went down. Two of them got up almost immediately and were running now, firing from the hip. Brennan heard a couple of rounds slapping into the hole's dirt wall somewhere behind him.

"Shit, shit shit," Charis moaned as he tried to get a sight picture.

Brennan lobbed the other grenade down the slope. The Germans saw it coming and went to ground, but were up again in a moment, and Brennan realized he'd forgotten to pull the pin. He slapped at his belt, but there were no more grenades there. He turned around and spotted, with his one good eye, the rifle the German had carried into the hole. Charis was still popping rounds as he bent and picked it up, twisting its sling off the owner's arm. He thumbed the safety, brought the rifle up in time to see something move off to their left.

"Over there," he said to Charis. He had the barrel lowered, the weapon tight to his shoulder when he saw the movement again. He pulled the trigger just as Charis pushed the weapon up into the air.

"NO!" Charis screamed. "Those are our guys."

Brennan squinted his bad eye, shutting out the red haze, and tried to see with his good eye. Something moved, then he saw the distinctive shape of the GI helmet.

His first thought was that he almost shot a comrade. In the next instant he wondered what those men were doing.

"Are they pulling back?" he asked Charis.

There were two quick explosions near the next fighting position, and the noise reached them mixed with small arms fire—rifles and a light machine gun. Someone shot at Charis, who ducked after the bullet kicked up snow in front of him.

Brennan struggled to make sense of what was going on. He wasn't sure if the Germans were behind him or in front of him. He no longer knew if they had a position off to their left, didn't know what had happened to the Rangers there. His head felt too big for his helmet, his cheek and face were fiery with pain. He shot a look behind them, where he thought Sergeant Bishop might be, hoping that someone would tell them to move, or would at least tell them that the part of the line they couldn't see in the smoke and the failing light hadn't disintegrated. He saw no one back there, so he turned and stood shoulder to shoulder with Charis.

"Gonna be dark soon," Charis said.

"Yeah."

Paul Gedern fell down beside the NCO who'd been pulling him by the shoulder. The man let go of his coat, then crawled forward at a furious pace, hoping, Gedern thought, to see something of the American position.

There'd been some firing off to their left, hand grenades and small arms, and then their squad had gotten the word to move right, sidestepping, keeping—as much as possible—a constant distance from the Americans, hoping to find the point where the enemy line bent away so that the *jaeger* troops could hit them from two sides.

"I think this is it," the NCO said to Gedern.

He was young, younger than Gedern, who was only a private, and so anxious to find the end of the American line that he twice stood up too close to the Rangers' positions, only to be forced down again by rifle fire.

"Come up here," he said to Gedern, who crawled forward a few feet.

"Up here," the NCO said more insistently.

Gedern crawled forward to where he could see, remembering the seriousness with which the man had threatened his life.

"Up there," the man said, pointing.

All Gedern could see was the slight rise reaching away from them, the wet black trees and some lonely skeins of smoke. There was firing to their left, farther away now, but nothing to their front.

"I don't see anything," Gedern said. He hated this young man for his enthusiasm.

"Of course you don't," the sergeant said. "We've reached the end of the American line. In fact, I think we're past it."

Gedern looked back up at the seemingly empty woods, but was not convinced.

"What if they just haven't been engaged here?" he asked.

"Don't be stupid," the NCO said. "They'd be going down there to help their buddies."

"That's not right," Gedern said. "They'd keep their positions in case anything came out this way. They're not going to abandon their line and rush to wherever the shooting is." He'd learned that much in his time in the army, and as he thought about the Rangers and the cool competence they'd displayed so far, he was more convinced than ever that the Americans would hold their line.

"You don't know what you're talking about," the NCO said. It was more the challenge of a child who thinks he knows everything that's important than an admonition from a superior.

"Maybe not," Gedern admitted. *You asshole.*

"We've found the edge of their position," the younger man insisted. "This is where we need to send the Marders to turn their flank."

Gedern looked up in the woods again, weary of this guessing game but too scared to defy this fool next to him making all the decisions. The trees ahead of them thinned a bit farther off to the right, and the ground climbed a few more feet. Out there, a man in a fighting position would have a better view of the two sides he might have to protect. Something told Gedern that they hadn't reached the end of the American line, but he waited for the sergeant's next move.

"Let's go up there," the NCO said.

Gedern felt his eyes widen. "Up there?"

"That's the only way we're going to know what's in those woods," the youngster countered. He got to one knee, checked the safety on his weapon.

"I'm ordering you to get up," the sergeant said.

Fuck you, Gedern thought. He had that same sinking feeling of loss that he'd experienced when Brufels had kept him from becoming a prisoner. He got to one knee.

"Let's go," the sergeant said.

"You first," Gedern answered, surprising himself.

The sergeant narrowed his eyes a bit—in disgust, Gedern thought— before he got to his feet.

The effect was instantaneous. There was the now familiar popping sound, then a quieter bump, bump. The back of the sergeant's jacket tore open as the M16 rounds, tumbling through the torso, broke through jagged exit wounds. The sergeant fell backward, dead before he hit the ground, and was instantly still.

Gedern rolled over to his back and slid down the slope, away from the Americans and the dead NCO, wiping his face with the sleeve of his jacket. He could feel the blood there on his cheeks, in his eyes, and he threw off his gloves to get at it. But even when his hands came away clean, he knew he would always remember what it felt like.

He went only a few meters until he was alone, somewhere between the GPU and American positions.

Somebody else is going to have to find a place to attack, he thought. *I'm staying right here.*

"They're trying to get around us, but I think I got one," the GI said to Sergeant Bishop. "That should slow 'em down."

Three of Bishop's troops manned the last position on Charlie Company's left flank. Behind them yawned the gap left by the departing companies and the tiny road that ran true to the center of the shifting American position.

"We've got to hold on for a little bit longer, then it'll be our turn to move," Bishop told his men.

The NCO strained to see the spot where one of his men claimed to have shot a German soldier, but there was nothing visible in the underbrush. It occurred to Bishop that this was the most dangerous position in the company, perhaps in the whole battalion.

"I'll wait here with you guys 'til we get the word to move," he said.

14

* * * * * * * * * *

THE STRAIGHT LINE DISTANCE TO THE LITTLE VILLAGE OF Karlshofen was only about two kilometers due north from the *flugplatz*, the airfield, but the wounded, mounted on trucks taken from the GPU, had to go by way of the narrow, dog-leg dirt road that led east before it joined the main route. Isen was concerned because this route was exposed to view from the broad expanses of potato fields that lay to the southeast. Since the GPU mounted troops had been withdrawn, he had decided that the foot soldiers would keep to the woodline and that the trucks would make a run for cover, driving as fast as the little road and the blacked-out conditions would allow.

Isen was surprised when his operations sergeant, Master Sergeant Hendricks, told him that fifteen volunteers had stepped forward to drive the three trucks.

"Fifteen?"

"Yep," Hendricks said, tugging at his chinstrap. "No heroics either. These kids have grown up fast."

"Good thing," Isen said. "You figure out a way to choose who'll drive."

Isen paused in the ditch by the side of the road, waiting as the lead company stepped off for the village. The little cluster of trucks sat in the lee of the administration building while medics loaded the wounded.

"Stay here," Isen told Gamble, his radio operator.

He trotted across the dirt track toward the building. Over in the Charlie

Company sector, he could hear the ebb and flow of small arms fire as the GPU probed and Dettering's men worked to give the rest of the command time to get moving. And as he moved closer, he could hear the stretcher bearers talking to the wounded.

"Just going for a little ride," one of the medics was saying. "Got to find some better accommodations for you guys. Heat, running water, that kind of stuff."

No answer from the stretcher case.

"Hey, sir."

Isen looked up to the cab of the nearest truck, where a soldier from Bravo Company—McCartle? McCarthy?—was standing on the running board. Someone had removed the door on the driver's side.

"Ready?" Isen asked.

"Yes, sir," the soldier replied. "If I'd have known I was going to be doing some road racing, I'd have brought my driving gloves, you know?" He smiled at Isen, smacking a fist into the palm of the other hand.

A second soldier stood on the front seat of the same truck, arms and shoulders thrust through a hole they'd cut in the roof. His SAW, the 5.56-millimeter Squad Automatic Weapon, rested unevenly on what remained of the truck's canvas top. This soldier, who met Isen's eyes only for a moment, concentrated on his weapon, checking and rechecking the action.

Isen reached the rear of the lead truck just before the medics closed the tailgate.

"See you guys in town, OK?" Isen said.

One soldier, ashen-faced, his lips sickly pale even in the red glow of the medics' flashlights, blinked at the comment. Isen reached into the dark maw of the truck to touch the soldier's hand, but the boy's arm ended in a stump of bandage. Isen couldn't tell if the hand was still there or not.

The new commander, acutely aware of the risk he was taking, turned away.

"*Nein.* I'd rather walk."

Isen heard the accented voice before he saw Major Rhone, who was trying to convince one of the medics that he didn't need to ride. Rhone had been fortunate. One pistol shot had passed through the muscle of his left shoulder; the other shot had simply nicked his jacket.

"You're riding," the GI said. It was clear from the tone of his voice that he would spend no more energy trying to persuade.

"Major Isen," Rhone said as Isen drew close enough to be recognized in the gloom. "Won't you tell this man that I'm perfectly capable of walking to the village . . . we are going to Karlshofen, aren't we?"

"Yes, we are," Isen answered. "And you're going however this man says you're going." Isen nodded to the medic, who helped the reluctant Rhone climb into the back of the truck.

"Major," Rhone said. "May I ask what your intentions are in the village?"

"We have a better chance of holding off an armored attack—if it comes to that—than we do out here," Isen said.

"Did Colonel Spano want to move to the village?" Rhone asked.

Isen stared at the other officer but made no comment. It was possible that the German couldn't read him in the dark.

"What about the people who live there?" Rhone asked.

"Frankly, I'd be surprised if anyone stayed that close once the shooting started." *And if they haven't left,* Isen thought, *that'll be another problem to deal with when we arrive.*

"And how do you know the GPU isn't occupying the town?" Rhone went on.

"Because we took a look at it," Isen said. Then, after a pause. "Still glad you stayed with us?"

"I wouldn't have it any other way," Rhone said.

Isen left the trucks and jogged across the road and into the woods, where Sergeant Gamble and Hatley were waiting for him. Gamble had his ear pressed to one of the small radios. "The lead platoon is just outside the village, sir," he said.

Isen looked back over his shoulder to where the truck engines were starting to kick over. His command was spread over two to three kilometers, with an enemy force—possibly an armored force—close by. He could hear rifle and machine gun fire as one of his three companies engaged the pursuers, and just behind him, three truckloads of wounded Rangers were getting ready to make a sprint along an exposed road to the dubious safety of a village that may or may not contain civilians, that may or may not have been occupied right under the eyes of his recon squad.

"Feels good to be moving, doesn't it, sir?" Gamble said.

"Yeah," Isen said. *Just friggin' great.*

Leutnant Martin Schorr, the schnapps-drinking commander of the one intact company of Marders, sat in the tight fit of his commander's hatch, alternately listening to the radio and to the telltale rise and fall of small arms fire by the American perimeter. Someone came alongside.

"Anything yet?"

Schorr looked down to where another track commander—a neighbor of his from civilian life named Metzger—stood in the churned-up mud beside the black hull. Metzger always wanted to know what their orders would be, even before the orders came down.

"Nothing," Schorr answered after a noticeable pause.

"What do you think it will be when it comes?"

Schorr looked north, out into the gray woods before him. The north-south track that ran just behind the airport control tower was directly in front of him, pointed toward the American position. Off to the left was a stretch of scrub woods, crisscrossed by ditches and streambeds that effectively protected the American right flank from mounted attack. To Schorr's right, small fields divided by barbed wire fences on stout posts gave way to the wide open potato fields that lay south and east of the small airstrip.

"I think we'll go around to the right," Schorr answered, raising his arm. "Out that way." After the debacle of the surprise attack by the Americans, the GPU command had pulled Schorr's Marders back. Now they were about to be committed in a long swing around the American left, and Schorr was determined to husband the important resources.

Metzger, in civilian life a mean-spirited minor authority in the local power company, considered Schorr's call for a moment.

"Lots of open space," Metzger said, as if the thought hadn't occurred to Schorr. "Hate to get caught out there."

"I'd hate to be the Americans," Schorr said with some sincerity. He figured that Metzger might mention the misplaced sympathy to the battalion commander, but Schorr didn't much care. They were about to ride down a bunch of foot soldiers, and in spite of the fact that the American Rangers had done some severe damage to his and the other two companies, Schorr was convinced that the coming fight would go to the GPU. All they had to do was get the order to move, and that would come when one of the Panzergrenadiers out in front got word back that they'd flanked the American position.

"They deserve everything they get," Metzger said. He spit on the ground between his feet. Melodramatically, Schorr thought.

Metzger was the kind of man who had made the GPU a viable force. He was clever enough to function in the organization and help the party move toward its goals, but not so clever as to question, in any depth, the party's promises to the working class. Like most Germans, Metzger had seen more and more of his pay eaten up by the taxes levied to help pay for the reconstruction of the eastern sector. He had voted and demonstrated against the government's generous social policies, programs that doled out support payments and even housing to seekers of political asylum.

The liberal tendencies in Germany—nurtured in part by the nation's guilty conscience for the crimes of the Third Reich—kept the government from taking a hard line in cutting social programs. The result was that wage earners such as Metzger lost buying power while they did the same amount of work—in some cases more work. And all this time, the cost of housing shot up as Berlin tried to shelter refugees, and immigrants from the shattered east and from the Third World gobbled up the jobs.

Less than a year earlier, Metzger had attended his first German People's Union rally. Party spokesmen waxed eloquent about economic security for ethnic Germans, about planning and orderliness and control—all the national passions. As the night wore on and the speakers railed against debt, taxes and foreigners, the language grew more strident. Metzger had watched as party youth had lynched an effigy of a Turkish worker. At first he was repelled, but as the arguments piled up and the speakers harangued the crowd, Metzger began to see more merit in the party's position.

By the end of the night, Metzger, red-faced, chanting, whipped up and manipulated by GPU propaganda, had become what that party machinery was meant to create: an angry citizen ready to rationalize accelerated, even violent change initiated outside the due process of a free government.

After being startled by some rustling noises, Brennan heard the reassuring voice of Sergeant Bishop close behind them.

"Let's go. Move back, straight back."

"You first," Brennan said to Charis.

His partner climbed over the shallow back berm of their fighting position, crawled a few feet to the rear, and then called to Brennan.

"OK. Come on."

They continued like that for a few meters, alternating their movements as they slid backward through the snow, Brennan turning his head in exaggerated movements to bring his good eye to bear. The firing in front of them had abated somewhat, but that gave little comfort to Brennan, who didn't believe that the Germans had given up probing the position.

When they reached their squad leader's position, the two men stood, continuing their rearward movement toward the airport tower and—eventually—the village.

"Six, seven," Bishop said as they went by, counting to be sure everyone got out.

Brennan noticed two other Rangers come up on his left as he and Charis moved, then they drifted away a little bit so as to keep dispersed. Charis turned around once to make sure Brennan was still there.

Then there was movement to the right. Brennan looked for the distinctive and reassuring shape of the GI's Kevlar helmet, but he could see nothing, even with his good eye. He turned to see if Sergeant Bishop was behind them, wondering how long the NCO would stay back there, wondering how spread out the platoon might become if they kept moving at this pace.

"Charis," Brennan said.

"What?"

"Maybe we should wait for Sergeant Bishop."

"We're suppose to wait at the next rally point," Charis said, still walking. "You know the drill."

Charis moved faster, his equipment making small noises as he bounced along the track and brushed through the undergrowth.

Brennan shot another glance back, saw someone was walking a few feet behind him.

Finally, Brennan thought. *He caught up.*

But as he continued, he became uneasy again. He didn't recognize the man's gait, and in training he'd been told numerous stories of infiltrators simply following an unwitting patrol back into its perimeter. He had even, in a field exercise, done it himself, accompanying Sergeant Handy past the nighttime security of an "enemy" camp back at Benning.

After a few more feet, he chanced another look back. It was too dark to make out the soldier's face, even to see the shape of his equipment or his weapon, so they continued to walk in their file: Charis, Brennan, and the soldier in the dark.

Holy shit, Brennan thought, trying to remember what Sergeant Handy had taught him in that training exercise. *What the hell do I do now?*

Brennan moved closer to Charis, desperate for a plan, an idea.

"Count off from the front," he said.

Charis turned his head slightly over his shoulder. Men moving in a file frequently counted off to let the leader know everyone was on board, but usually the count came from the rear.

"Why?" Charis asked.

"Just give me a one count," Brennan insisted.

Charis got the message.

"One," he said.

Brennan turned around completely, and when the soldier behind him came closer than the six or seven feet he'd been maintaining, Brennan leaned forward and spoke right into his face.

"Two," he said.

The dark figure hesitated for just a fraction of a second, stopped completely, leaned backward, lost.

Brennan stepped forward and brought his rifle up from his hip, one hand on the stock, one hand behind the pistol grip, the bayonet thrust sharply forward, the flat of the blade turned parallel to the ground. He shoved hard, stepping forward as he did so, and felt the man's clothing give away. The soldier went down heavily, pulling the muzzle of Brennan's weapon down with him.

There was another figure behind the man Brennan had just bayoneted, and it took this man a few seconds to realize what had happened in the blackness ahead of him. But he got his weapon up before Brennan could.

"Charis," Brennan called. He went to his knees, yanking out the bayonet and hoping that the man behind would fire high. Brennan heard the rounds snap over his head as he brought his rifle to bear, flipped off the safety and pressed the trigger, arcing the rounds toward the muzzle flash on the trail. The second man seemed to leave his feet momentarily, as if he had hopped backward.

There were a few seconds of silence, broken by Charis's surprised voice.

"Jesus H. Christ," he said. He clicked on his tiny penlight. Brennan was on his knees in the snow, between the bodies of two GPU soldiers.

Charis asked the obvious question first. "How did you know?"

But Brennan couldn't answer that one. He got shakily to his feet, Charis stepping back to help him.

All at once the trail was lit by the explosion of a grenade, light and sound rocketing at them through the woods, knocking both men down. They crawled away frantically, setting off in two different directions before Charis doubled back, grabbed Brennan's shoulder and tugged him. When the ringing stopped, Brennan heard Charis speak.

"You OK?"

Brennan grunted. His face hurt again, the cut on his jaw burned in sharp points.

"Let's keep moving," Charis said.

The two men scrambled to their feet, saw more movement off to their right, answered a call in German with a half dozen rounds fired on the run. To their left, other Rangers were running also, crashing through the tangled, leafless undergrowth in the unforgiving dark.

There was no one at the rally point. Charis wanted to move on, but Brennan, in an agony of indecision, looked back again for Sergeant Bishop.

There were men in the woods around them; something had given way.

"They're going to get between us and the rest of the company if we don't move out," Charis said.

Brennan heard the words, but the alarm didn't register, and he wondered if he were going into shock. Then Charis had him by the collar and was dragging him, the two of them stumbling alongside the track that led to the airfield. Brennan had a vague sense that they'd passed the platoon rally point, but it was also empty.

Where is everyone?

There were more shots to their right, and now sounds to their left, men yelling in German and English. Charis held his rifle in one hand, by the pistol grip, while he kept the other clamped to Brennan's jacket.

"Keep moving, keep moving, don't stop, keep moving," he chanted.

They stumbled, Brennan fell, the muzzle of his weapon smacking his face where it had been split open in the fight. Charis was still pulling him, and he couldn't seem to get his feet. The pain in his cheek exploded in white hot splinters across his eyes, along the side of his neck.

All about them there were flashes of fire, ghostly yellow and white on the snow. Charis was running almost doubled over when they reached the airfield. The little administration building burned wildly, its roof already going in. Brennan felt Charis yank him sideways so that they could stay out of the light thrown by the flames.

There was a spattering of fire, like frying grease, and a Ranger running a few meters ahead of them went down in a heap. Charis leaped the ditch beside the little road, pulling his partner along with him so that both men wound up in a twisted pile of arms and legs. On the other side of the clearing, some GPU infantrymen were between the Charlie Company Rangers and the route to the village. There would be no more rally points.

"Stay down," Charis told Brennan. Then he crawled off toward the clearing to check on the Ranger they'd seen fall. Brennan pulled off a glove, put a hand to his cheek, and felt the sticky wetness of his own blood there on his neck and soaking the collar of his shirt and parka. Thoughts came to him with a viscous hesitancy. *I'm pretty fucked up.*

Charis crawled back quickly, all arms and legs thrashing at the ground like some inefficient insect. "He's dead," Charis said. "Let's get the fuck out of here."

Brennan could hear the impact of rounds in trees around them, angry metal hunting for targets. The firing had surrounded them somehow, so that now he wasn't sure where safety lay. "Which way?" he asked.

"Here," Charis said, crawling deeper into the woods.

But there was firing ahead of them, too.

"The motherfuckers are all around us," Charis said over his shoulder. "We gotta move faster." He paused to give Brennan a chance to catch up. When the two men were side by side, Charis asked, "You up to it?"

Brennan grunted his assent, trying not to think about the searing on the right side of his face, trying not to believe that they'd been overrun. He looked back over his shoulder and saw, in the light of the burning building, man-figures, awkward in thick winter clothing, shuffling toward them.

Leutnant Schorr keyed the mike and spoke on his company net. "They've broken. They're trying to get to the village and may have sent some units ahead. We're going to bypass the retreating elements by swinging around to the south. Then we'll hit them from the east before they have a chance to set in a defense."

He let go of the switch, envisioning the wild ride through the night, hoping that his luck would hold while his vehicles churned through the muddy and painfully wide-open potato fields that would lead them to the outskirts of Karlshofen.

"First platoon will lead. Keep out of the light from that fire at the airfield."

Schorr waited for his subordinates to acknowledge the transmission, then instructed his driver to turn right, to the south.

"Once we're clear of this cover," he said, "we'll be going as fast as we can to get into the village." He looked down into the tiny cupola, where he could see the gunner's arm working the control for the twenty-millimeter, running checks before the fight.

"We have to get there before they can get organized."

When Mark Isen trotted into the little crossroads town of Karlshofen—just a collection of buildings centered around a church and a small market—he felt like collapsing. He had experienced this before, where he'd simply gone farther than his body wanted to allow, and the exhaustion threatened to drop him where he stood if he paused for more than a few seconds. But it took him less than a minute of surveying the scene in the center of town to see that no one in his command was giving up.

Isen had assigned sectors to the companies based on a sketch of the town drawn by his recon squad. Soldiers from Bravo and Alpha companies were already at work preparing the defenses that might protect them amid the sturdy brick buildings.

"How's it look?" he asked the company commanders when they joined him in front of the market.

Alpha Company's Captain John Taylor spoke first. "No signs of any civilians. Looks like they unassed the place when the shooting started."

"Good. How's your sector?" Isen asked.

"It'll work pretty much the way we planned it, sir," Taylor said. "I can cover the woods from that school"—he gestured at a building behind Isen—"and a couple of the houses on the same street."

"How about you, Gene?"

Captain Gene Wisneiwski's Bravo Company had suffered the most casualties in the first fight, so Isen had assigned them a smaller sector in the defense. But because he trusted Wisneiwski's judgment, the company had pulled the critical assignment: the antiarmor ambushes that would close—must close—the roads into town.

"We're getting in place right now, sir," Wisneiwski said.

"Any sign of the trucks with the wounded?" Isen asked.

"They're all here," Taylor answered, looking up at the front of the building they stood before. "Parked right out back."

"Good, good," Isen said. In spite of the firing behind them, which hadn't tapered off and may have even picked up a bit, Isen allowed himself a bit of hope.

His plan was based on a couple of things he knew. A mounted attack would probably come from the southeast. The Marders—however many were left—wouldn't be able to get through the woods that lay to the south, directly between the airfield and the town. And because the woods extended for several kilometers to the south and west, Isen felt fairly confident those would be secondary approaches for the enemy. A dismounted attack by the *jaeger,* the light infantry, would either follow the route they'd just taken—directly north from the airfield to the town center, or it might swing around and hit Karlshofen from the west, directly across from the road entrance on the east side of the village, which Isen believed would mark the axis for the mounted attack.

"If it were me," Isen had told his commanders, "I'd come hard and straight and get here as fast as possible—drive the Marders from the southeast or the east. They don't want to give us time to get set up in here among these houses."

So he'd planned for Alpha and Charlie Companies to defend from the buildings and houses in town, while Bravo Company set up ambushes on the one paved and one unpaved road that came at the town from the southeast and east. Neatly trimmed hedges, some fifteen feet high and half that thick, not unlike the infamous Normandy hedgerows that gave defending Germans so much cover in 1944, paralleled that road.

Bravo Company's soldiers would use these and the woods bordering the fields for cover while they waited for the German advance. All of Wisneiwski's company was committed, almost half the men waiting with their Karl Gustavs and recoilless rifles and AT-4's for the tracks, with the other half there to protect their comrades from a dismounted attack. Isen had estimated it would take four or five hours to get the defense set up correctly. All around him and his two subordinate commanders, Rangers rushed back and forth in an ecstasy of preparation, for no one knew how soon the next hammer blows would fall.

"Major Isen."

Isen turned to Sergeant Gamble, his radio operator.

"It's Captain Dettering's RTO, sir," Gamble said, handing Isen the portable radio.

"This is two five," Isen said, shortening his call sign.

"This is two five kilo," a shaky voice came through. "I mean . . . shit, this is whiskey . . . two five . . . kilo. I, uh. . . ."

"Calm down, son," Isen found himself saying. There was an explosion somewhere near the speaker, and Isen thought for a moment that he'd lost the contact.

"Are you there, are you there?"

"I'm still here," the voice came back. "Two five is down. I can't find him, and I think he's down."

The "two-five" the radio operator referred to was Captain Dettering, Charlie Company commander.

"Where are you?" Isen asked. The kid was having too much trouble with the radio procedures, so Isen dropped them.

"I'm not . . ." The voice faded, came back in a rush of static, then dropped again. "It's falling apart."

"Calm down, now. Keep your head," Isen said. "What's falling apart?"

The soldier was screaming now, though Isen couldn't tell if it was panic or the competing sound of nearby gunfire. "The withdrawal, the whole fucking thing."

He clicked off, then came back up, quieter, but no more calm. "They're all around us, mixed in with us. I'm not sure I can get back."

"Look for Dettering," Isen said. "Then keep heading back this way."

"I don't know." The voice was weaker now.

"Are you wounded?" Isen asked.

"No."

"Then you keep moving this way, and don't stop, you hear? Do you hear me?"

There was a pause, then a "wilco" that sounded a bit stronger than anything that had gone before. Isen gave the handset back to Gamble. The sergeant had been listening, wide-eyed, the whole time, and now he watched Isen as if for some reassurance.

"John, tell your guys to watch for GPU mixed in with Charlie Company men when the Rangers start coming in. It doesn't sound like it's going to be too organized. Be careful."

"Got it, sir," Taylor said.

Isen looked at Wisneiwski, whose battered company was the linchpin of the defense.

"I better get back to my boys," Wisneiwski said.

Isen nodded, and the captain turned away. As he crossed the street headed south, Isen heard the distinctive pounding of a twenty-millimeter gun, the Marder's main armament.

The running firefight that had pursued Charlie Company out of its position by the airfield had washed over Paul Gedern, dragging him and a few others along through the woods, past the burning building and over the flat, scrub-covered stretch of frightening blackness that led to the southern edge of Karlshofen.

Gedern had run wildly, out of fear, without even thinking that they were in a footrace with the Americans, trying to beat the Rangers to the relative safety of the village. He had seen two men go down, shot through at close range by GIs they'd bumped into—literally bumped into—in the woods. Gedern had fired in the direction of some shadowy figures he thought he spied through the trees. But his shots were not aimed and were only intended to keep the GIs from being able to draw a bead on him.

The NCO who was leading—more or less—their headlong run had stopped just before a big clearing. Gedern, utterly winded, fell to his hands and knees, fighting the urge to vomit.

"This is it,' the sergeant said. "The Americans will have to go past this point to link up with anyone in the town."

All around him Gedern sensed, more than saw, the other infantrymen go into action. It was clear that they planned to ambush whatever Rangers tried to cross the open space. He lifted himself up slightly. Beyond the few trees, Gedern thought he could make out some wire fences and the dim shapes of a few buildings close at hand.

Someone was shoving him from behind.

"Who's this? Who are you?"

"Gedern," he answered. "Private Gedern."

His inquisitor leaned closer to him. He couldn't see Gedern's face in the dark, and the name didn't mean anything to him.

"I was sent as a replacement when my track was destroyed."

"Move over here, then," the voice told him.

Gedern crabbed sideways until he was behind a small berm at the edge of the field. After a few minutes, his breathing returned to something close to normal, and the disorienting blurring of his vision receded. Now he could see the clear outline of one low building, sitting at an angle to the line he occupied and at a distance of some thirty or forty meters. Beyond that was a taller building, partly obscured by the nearer one, which Gedern thought to be a house.

When the rush of his own breath faded from his ears, Gedern realized that the sounds of small arms fire and hand grenades had given way to an incomplete, suddenly unnerving silence. He wanted badly to ask someone where the Americans were. Were they in the village? Were they still making their way here? The most frustrating thing was not knowing, and Gedern was clueless.

We wait here in ambush, he thought. That much was clear. But then he began to wonder what they would do if no Rangers passed before them. He had a sudden mental picture of himself charging into the village, of American rifles winking at them from among the buildings, but he pushed it down in his mind, as if that might keep it from becoming true.

"There," Charis said, lifting his head a few inches off the ground. "I think I see a building over there, across the clearing. That could be the village."

Brennan was on his back, gulping air in quick, shallow gasps. His face was twisted in pain and he had no energy to raise himself to see what Charis was talking about. Yet, for the moment, at least, he'd lost some of the frightening sensation he'd had—as if the real world were slipping away from him. "How far?" he asked.

"Not far," Charis said, leaning over. "How's your face?"

Brennan groaned, touched his eye. "I'll make it, I guess."

"You're gonna be one ugly motherfucker, you keep smacking yourself like that." Charis looked back over the clearing. "We'd better wait a few minutes to see who's around here. We're going to have to cross this open area," he said. "And it could be hairy."

There was plenty going on around them: scattered shots behind them, noise in the buildings up ahead that Brennan hoped meant that the other companies were digging in, rustlings and movement and indistinct voices that came and went away at unknown distances and made Brennan all the more anxious to get going. The moving fight had washed up against the southern side of the town like some dirty, dangerous wave, and the Charlie Company Rangers—and undoubtedly some GPU soldiers—were at the edge of the malignant surf, tossed around, unsure of what was coming next.

"I think we should make a run for it," Brennan said.

"That's going to be dangerous," Charis came back, indicating the open area.

"It's only going to get worse," Brennan reasoned. "You know that those goons were all around us. If there weren't any ahead of us when we got up here, there'll be some up here soon. And they'll either try to get into the village, or they'll wait at the edge of this field or yard here— whatever it is—until we try to make a break for it."

Charis got up on one knee, craning his neck to look left and right, trying to see what he could at the edge of this open area on the south side of the village.

"Shit," he said. "I don't know, man. I just don't know."

"I don't know either," Brennan said. "I'm just trying to make the best guess I can."

The thought occurred to him that maybe that was the case with the NCOs and the officers, as well. No one of them had a crystal ball, either. The only difference, as far as Brennan could tell, was that their guesses were informed by experience and training.

As he sat still, Brennan realized that the pain in his neck and his face was leaving him, or he was becoming used to it. But it was being replaced by a terrible sense of dread at the prospect of trying to cross the open ground before them. Even if they made it to the building, they still had to get inside the perimeter—if indeed they had found it—without getting shot by some nervous Ranger. The hope that he'd felt when they'd first pulled out of their blocking position had now completely deserted him. He pushed himself off the ground and sat on his heels.

The voice came from behind, startling them both.

"Charis."

Charis tried to spin around quickly and bring his weapon to bear, but he fell over backward, feet tangled below him.

It was Sergeant Bishop.

"You talk too loud to be very good at this E and E stuff," Bishop said.

It seemed significant to Brennan that their squad leader had referred to escape and evasion, which is what you did to get out of enemy territory. It was an admission, as if they needed proof, that the withdrawal had fallen apart. Brennan looked behind the staff sergeant for other squad members.

"Anybody with you?" he asked.

"There's three of us, about fifteen, twenty meters down," Bishop answered.

"Our squad?"

Bishop shook his head.

Ten men, Brennan thought. *But there'll be some when we get to the village. They're probably in there now.*

"We're about to make a break for the barn there, or the house, whatever it is," Bishop said. "You guys ready to join us?"

It was a rhetorical question, of course. Bishop was their squad leader, they would move when he told them to. But there was a sense of relief there, too. Brennan and Charis both felt it. They didn't have to make the decision on their own. Someone else had made it for them.

"Sure, we're ready," Charis said.

They followed Bishop, crawling on a line parallel to the edge of the field until they linked up with the other two men. Characteristically, Bishop did not hesitate.

"I'll go first, then you two," he said, indicating the men from the other platoon. "Charis, you and Brennan bring up the rear." He handed them each two grenades. "If we can't get in right across from here, we'll back up, then try again off to the left. Got that?"

The four men grunted their understanding, and that quickly, Bishop had turned and was crawling, on his hands and knees, along the bottom of what looked to be a drainage ditch that ran from the barn to the woods.

"You probably should have gone first," Charis said.

"Nah, I'm OK now," Brennan responded. He popped the clips of his two grenades and straightened the pins out.

"Good idea," Charis said, attending his own grenades. "I hear anything that sounds like trouble, I'm heaving these babies and moving out smartly."

In less than a minute, it was their turn. Charis crawled into the ditch, which was barely wide enough to accommodate his hands and knees. Brennan watched him move a few feet, then got down and began to follow. He couldn't see anyone in front of Charis, but he'd heard no close shooting, and so he figured Sergeant Bishop must be making progress. He strained his one good eye to see the outline of the barn or house that sat opposite them.

There was no guarantee that the rest of the battalion was there waiting for them, for they'd heard very little from that side. The few things they had heard—a voice, the clank of metal, all of it coming unreliably over the snow—might be Charlie Company soldiers who'd gotten there ahead of them and were also milling about, looking for friendly positions. The more confusion there was, Brennan knew, the better the chance of their getting shot by their own side.

Progress was slow. Hand, knee, hand, knee, hand, knee. Ice and water had accumulated in the bottom of the ditch, and soon Brennan's gloves were soaked through. He'd adjusted his rifle sling so that the weapon hung suspended below his chest, and he wondered how fast he could put it into action if he encountered something. He paused, glanced backward. No one was following him this time.

He felt incredibly exposed, and he knew that anyone with night vision devices would be able to see them clearly, their backs exposed above the meager cover offered by the ditch. As he moved, fear knotted in his chest, and he cast nervous glances to the left and right, wondering if this was how he was to spend the last minutes of his life.

I just need to make it to those buildings, he told himself. *Just a little farther.*

"There. See them?"

The soldier beside Paul Gedern was convinced that he'd spotted movement out in the black yard before them.

"No," Gedern said. "I don't see anything." He studied the emptiness, dismissed the suspicion. Then he saw a shape, low to the ground and not identifiable as a man, but moving steadily toward the buildings.

"Yes," Gedern said. "I see it now."

Gedern knew what was coming next. This squad would open fire and kill the man, or the men, out there. But that wouldn't solve anything, and he'd still be trapped.

The NCO crawled up beside him.

"We're going after them," he said, as calmly as if he were talking about following someone down a street.

"What?" Gedern said.

"I don't think there's anybody at the barn, there. So we're going to rush these guys from behind. We've got the angle; they have their heads down and won't have time to react."

"I thought we were going to ambush them," Gedern said.

The NCO shook his head. "Then we're stuck on this side of the clearing and anybody in the village will know we're here. Better to get in among those buildings, keep up the momentum of the attack."

Gedern tired to swallow, but his saliva was oil thick. Already the others were up in a skirmish line, moving at an oblique angle to whoever was or was not in the ditch ahead of them. Gedern stood, tripped over a strand of the wire fence before him, and went clattering down.

* * *

Brennan pushed himself forward when he heard the noise, twisting his body so that he landed on his side in the narrow ditch. He had one grenade in his hand and was struggling to get the other hand free to pull the pin completely out when Charis, a meter or two in front of him, opened fire. Farther ahead, someone was straining a tense, "Move, move, move." He thought it might be Sergeant Bishop and he wanted to get up and run to whatever safety was offered by those buildings that loomed just ahead of him, just out of reach.

Quite suddenly, Brennan was seized by anger, a blackness like filthy water that welled up in him, building instantly to a terrible threatening pressure in his chest. All he could see was the chase that he and Charis and the others had just endured, the headlong run through the woods and the firing all around them, and he remembered suddenly the Ranger who went down by the burning building, no chance of getting up again, just down and dead instantly.

There were no words to vent this feeling, but violence was handy. He scrambled up awkwardly, planted one foot in the ditch and heaved the first grenade at ... there *were* men following, and the fastball of the grenade followed the pattern of Charis's tracer rounds, back toward the wood, but off to one side. *Were they that close to us?*

There were rounds coming back at them now, the muzzle flashes incredibly close, and Brennan heard several rounds ripping the air by his head. He fell flat into the ditch, counted after throwing the second grenade, *one thousand two thousand three thousand,* trying to force himself deeper into the earth as he counted.

The grenades went off, only a second apart, and there was a round, orange flash that shoved the breathy *crunch* before it over the back of his neck. In the next instant he was up again, on both knees this time, rifle at his shoulder, searching for targets. He thought he saw something moving along the ground, a man crawling, perhaps, and he fired, wildly at first, then more carefully, a three-round burst that stilled the movement.

"C'm'on, c'm'on, c'm'on."

Charis was ahead of him, farther along the ditch now, urging him to follow. Brennan swept the area again, shooting randomly, the rifle jumping in his tight grasp, an extension of the furies inside him. He willed his night vision—destroyed for the moment by the explosion—to return, but his good eye still swam in orange and red, so he gave up the shooting, stepped out of the ditch and ran as fast as he could toward the sound of his buddy's voice.

The first rounds of rifle fire came over while Gedern was still trying to disentangle himself from the wire that had snagged him, and so they sailed over his head, clearing him by a few feet. He rolled sideways, searching for the cover of the berm, and rolled into the body of the man who'd crossed the fence beside him. The one who didn't trip and give away their position.

The flash from the exploding grenades showed his comrades well ahead of him. Closer to him, also visible in the quick light, were the dark, still forms of the dead.

The rifle fire was still coming in—the Americans were off to his left front as he faced the shadows of the village—and Gedern felt the open space around him like a threat, like a promise of death. There was a lull on both sides, and without thinking much about what he was doing—all he wanted was the safety of the buildings before him—Gedern found his feet and began to run.

Then there was someone beside him, shouting, "*Vorwaerts—schnell.*" Let's go, let's go.

A third figure joined them, and then there seemed to be several more men running after him. All of them, Gedern thought, seeking cover by the brick buildings.

Gedern's foot found a rut at the corner of the wall, and his ankle flexed sideways. Pulling his weight at a dead run, he lost his balance and crashed into the unforgiving stone, into the sharp corner that loomed out of the blackness at him. Then, just as suddenly as he'd started running, he was on the ground, laid out, helpless, his face exploding in crystal skewers of pain where he'd smashed against the wall.

"Oh, *fuck*," he managed.

The walls around him were lit intermittently by fire, and the GPU soldiers rushing past him—there had to be at least ten—were shooting as they ran into the narrow passage between the first building and the second. When the pain slid back enough so that he knew he had to move or be stepped on, Gedern pushed up on an elbow, pulled himself along for one painful meter, then two.

Three men crowded, hesitating, at the corner of the nearest building. Beyond them shimmered the light and sounds of a nightmarish melee just beyond their little sanctuary: shouted curses in German and English, with sharp reports and the sudden, startling lights of flares bouncing off the walls all around them, belying direction, defying any attempts to make sense of what was going on.

"What's your name?"

The man next to Gedern was a sergeant, and he was talking to Gedern.

"Gedern."

"A replacement?"

"Yes," Gedern managed, gingerly fingering his cheeks to see what damage had been done to his face.

"That was a good job back there," the NCO said.

"What?" Gedern asked.

"Leading everyone over here on a run," the other man answered. "We had to gain this wall, this foothold, and we'd still be out there stalling if it weren't for you."

Gedern worked his mouth, but nothing came out.

15

THE GPU INFANTRYMEN WHO HAD PURSUED THE RANGERS OF Charlie Company from the airfield had also been taxed by the headlong movement, and having reached the outskirts of Karlshofen, they were at a comparative disadvantage: no one was waiting to help them through the lines. They collected haphazardly in two small groups, one at either corner of the American line, which faced south.

Gedern's group, to the right, or east, had gained a small foothold amid a cluster of outbuildings and one substantial barn that the Americans had excluded from their defensive position. The group at the western end of the line, another ad hoc organization under the shaky control of a junior sergeant and a badly wounded lieutenant, tried to form some semblance of a line in a muddy paddock and garden. The defenders here, the exhausted Rangers of Alpha Company, had only a slight head start in preparing for the fight, but were nevertheless more ready than their attackers.

Mark Isen had carried with him into Karlshofen the hundreds of worries of command. He worried that the GPU had a reserve to commit against his precarious foothold, fresh troops that could push his Rangers in disarray into the muddy potato fields outside of Karlshofen, where the Marders could shoot them to pieces at long range.

But the race was between opponents who were equally winded, and so the momentum hung, delicately balanced, while exhausted soldiers struggled against time to gain the upper hand.

*   *   *

Isen found the Alpha Company commander, John Taylor, as the captain was about to leave the little command post he'd set up in the doorway of a house on the east-west street that defined his sector.

"What's it look like, John?" Isen asked, leaning against the wall to catch his breath. He wished he could give Taylor more time to get his company settled, but they didn't have the luxury. It seemed fairly obvious that the GPU didn't plan on letting the pressure slacken.

"Two groups followed us down here, one at each end of my line," Taylor said. "My squads keep talking about platoon strength, but I was out and listening to the shooting, and I'd be surprised if either of them was that big."

"They within supporting distance of each other?" Isen asked. He was concerned that the two GPU groups, however small, could make a coordinated attack, covering each other's movement with small arms fire that would distract and disorient the defenders. Such an attack would have a much better chance of succeeding than the kind of piecemeal assault Isen was hoping for. It all depended on GPU discipline: were their leaders good enough to control their exhausted soldiers even after pursuing the Rangers for several kilometers?

Taylor rubbed his dirty face with the heel of his hand. "I don't think so, sir," he said. "I'm worried that they might have a reserve, though," he said.

"Me, too," Isen said. Cut off from their usual sources of information, the intelligence apparatus that used everything from satellite imagery to human intelligence—good old spookery—to form and pass on estimates of what they faced and what the enemy's intentions were, Isen and his Rangers were left to guesswork and conjecture.

Combat commanders in any battle, no matter how complete the intelligence picture, are finally left with some degree of uncertainty. They and their staffs consider whatever facts are available, along with all those difficult-to-name or unmeasurable things about the enemy forces: morale, confidence in themselves and their leaders, their will to fight. And from that uncertain stew of what was true and what might be true, the commander had to make decisions upon which depended the lives of his men.

Stranded as he was, Isen was not much better off than the battle captains of a century before, who could know things only by seeing with their own eyes or through the eyes of their scouts. Isen had no idea of the size of the GPU force facing them, and while the Germans hadn't shown anything to make him think that they had great resources at their disposal, it wouldn't take much of a reserve, Isen figured, to shove the Americans off of this real estate.

Over at the eastern end of the village, what remained of Bravo Company was preparing to fend off a mounted attack. The Alpha Company Rangers, arrayed about him in the houses and gardens and on the rooftops of this single street, were at the end of their endurance and their ammunition. And while training and conditioning and esprit counted for a great deal, Isen worried that it would not be enough to stop an assault by fresh troops.

Finally, Isen had to rely on the basics. "Let's go take a look up front," he said.

If it occurred to Isen that his predecessor, Colonel Spano, had been killed conducting just such a personal reconnaissance of the lines, it didn't show in the way he approached the platoon positions. Captain Taylor took care to keep himself between Isen and the known enemy positions, not because he was ready to sacrifice himself, but because he felt the battalion could better handle the loss of a company commander than of its new battalion commander.

At the western end of the street, one of Taylor's platoon leaders said that GPU soldiers were digging in the gardens and yard of a small house that sat by itself some hundred and fifty meters or so down the road.

Isen strained to see into the blackness. The batteries in his night vision goggles, like most others in the battalion, had begun to fade with the near-continuous use. Replacements were to have been on the drop zone with the advance party. "Have you been using the grenade launchers on them?" he asked.

"No, sir," the lieutenant answered. "We're down to only a few rounds per weapon, and I thought it best to save those in case they come at us all at once."

"You're probably right," Isen allowed, noting the confidence with which the lieutenant, a rail-thin New Englander named Jackson, answered. He was about to say something about wishing for more ammunition—the lack of it was keeping his mortars quiet, too—but thought better of sharing those concerns with his subordinates.

"You seen anybody else come up and join these guys?" Taylor asked.

"No, sir," Jackson said. "I got two guys up in this house—" he pointed to a building nearby that seemed to offer a view beyond the garden in question—"with a couple of the goggles that still work, and they haven't seen anybody join in."

Isen nodded to Taylor that he'd seen enough, and the two officers moved away from the forward-most positions.

"I have an idea that we might have to go get them first," Isen told the captain. "If we can get them out of those buildings, out of our pockets, at least, we'll deny them a jump-off point. That'll make it harder for them to make a coordinated attack."

"That's what I was thinking, too, sir," Taylor said.

At another time, Taylor, who had a keen wit, would have noticed how much like a sycophant he sounded with that comment. And no doubt he would have made jokes at his own expense. But his sense of humor had left him days ago, and as with everyone else, exhaustion had replaced all feeling.

"Let's go down the other end of the street to take a look," Isen said. "But I can see that you're going to have to put together a plan for clearing that garden, the house, and the yards."

"Wilco, sir," Taylor said.

Isen was thinking about contingency plans, in case they were forced out of the village, but he indulged himself for a moment: he didn't want to think about that just yet. Unless the GPU showed a greater resourcefulness than they'd demonstrated so far, the Rangers would be successful.

At least, I hope so, Isen thought.

The two men ducked behind another house, keeping the building between them and the enemy. The eastern end of the street was dominated by a large barn, the stucco painted a washed-out yellow that glowed a little with the ambient light. The GPU, a little more organized here, kept up a steady if ineffective exchange of fire with the Rangers from a position some hundred meters or so beyond the barn.

Taylor's Rangers had a team in the barn to keep the GPU from occupying it and to warn of imminent attacks. The Alpha Company platoon here had also used to full advantage two large brick houses—set back from the barn, closer inside the American position—that made good strongpoints.

"They're just buying time," Taylor remarked. "Something's going on over there."

"If they attack this end of the company sector," the platoon leader offered, gesturing with one arm, "I figure they'll avoid our defense, sidestep us to get across the street here, and work their way around behind us."

"That's assuming they know we only have one company here," Isen said.

The other two men did not respond.

"But chances are, they know that," he finished.

Staring into the darkness, Isen saw the same picture, the same opportunity for an aggressive enemy that he'd seen at the other end of the village. If the GPU could scrape together even a reinforced company or two, they could force the Rangers out of the village. And then the Americans might just be out of options.

"OK," Isen said. He tried to force the tiredness from his voice—he was assigning a combat mission—but his tongue felt thick, and there was a low buzz of uncertainty that went from his mouth to his brain and back again, like a low voltage current. He worried that his commands weren't sharp and clear: muddled commands made for bad planning and bloody mistakes.

"I want you to go over and force them out, John. All the ones close by, on either end of the street. You might use that barn as a jump-off point here, if you want. But we have to get them out of here. Bravo Company is tapped out. I think Charlie Company might be able to give you a squad or two to help out . . . I'll let you know. And I can put together a squad or two from the headquarters people."

Isen hoped the last offer didn't sound too desperate—he was throwing everything in—but the fact was that they were running out of bodies. He was committing his exhausted troops in a ground assault without benefit of supporting fires and without a clear picture of what the enemy was doing, or even how large a force the GPU had on hand.

The only thing the Americans had going for them was their aggressiveness. As he thought about the soldiers working around him in the dark, piling paving stones and furniture and firewood into makeshift barricades, checking weapons and fields of fire in a defensive position they had not seen in the daytime, Isen wondered how many more times he could call on that vaunted esprit.

The Rangers did not, as a matter of course, even practice the defense. The list of tasks they were charged to be proficient in, called the METL, for Mission Essential Task List, did not include defensive missions. The idea was that the Rangers would strike hard and early and be relieved quickly by a larger, more heavily armed force. As Isen watched two soldiers carry firewood into one house where they were shoring up their cover, he wondered about the wisdom of conditioning troops to think that their fights would always be short ones.

The NCO who'd congratulated Paul Gedern on his willingness to move forward under fire became suspicious when he saw how much ammunition Gedern still had in his ammo pouches.

"Did you shoot at anything?" he asked.

The men were squatting in the lee of a brick outbuilding that was just short of the big barn they'd spotted from across the clearing. Here they redistributed whatever ammo they had on hand, so that each would have approximately the same amount for the upcoming assault on the American positions.

Gedern decided not to answer the direct question. After a pause he ventured a question. "Will we have Marders in support of this attack?"

"You're the driver who had his track shot out from under him," the NCO said. When Gedern didn't respond, the NCO leaned forward, his face close to Gedern's. "Right?"

Though Gedern couldn't see him well in the darkness, which was cut only by a few meager flashlights, the man's breath was such that Gedern could easily imagine a mouth full of rotten teeth.

"Right," Gedern said.

"Yeah, the Marders are somewhere around here," the NCO continued as Gedern handed over three full magazines. "We'll probably hear them come in from the back or something."

Gedern didn't find the comments very reassuring. Obviously no one in the chain of command, or whatever was left of a chain after the footrace they'd just run, thought it necessary to brief the subordinate leaders. For all Gedern knew, he and the soldiers around him were out of contact and working alone.

That wouldn't surprise me, Gedern thought. He was with his third squad since losing his track, and each one was more haphazard than the last; he despaired of ever seeing any sort of apparent organization. They were being pushed again, rather than led, like some dazed, brutalized prize-fighter shoved back into the ring.

Paul Gedern wasn't read in on all the plans his superiors had, but it didn't take a genius to figure out that the GPU was ready to use up the tracked and light infantry units on hand in an effort to destroy the Americans in Karlshofen. There would be no letup. And while he felt that the Rangers—now digging in skillfully about the village just a few meters away from where he sat thinking about them—were doomed, it seemed to Gedern that he and the other GPU soldiers around him might be just as certain of getting killed or wounded.

Gedern believed that the GPU would win this battle, simply by virtue of having the heavier weapons. But he knew that the certainty of that outcome was no guarantee that he would be around to see it. What good would a new order in Germany do him? What would he care, once he was dead, that Germany was free of foreigners and asylum seekers?

Gedern felt the old bile rise in him, a dark anger at being used by forces out of his control. It mattered not a whit to the party or to the people in charge, not even to this foul-smelling young NCO before him, bent over his weapon in the dark, clothes wet, hungry, it mattered nothing to these people that Gedern had plans, that he wanted to marry and have a family and start his own business and live long enough to see his as-yet-unborn children grow into adulthood. No one cared for Paul Gedern's plans, any more than a farmer cared when his beasts balked at the cold winter air, any more than a worker considered that the machine at which he labored might be capable of desire.

Then the call came, and they were being herded again, called to the killing fields.

Gedern counted eleven men in the squad of which he was a part, and there seemed to be at least two more squads nearby, a smaller group—eight men at most—in front of them, crouched at the corner of the building closest to the Americans. They would be first into the storm. A third squad waited behind them to rush to a breach or replace the killed.

Gedern's squad crept slowly into the deeper gloom between the buildings, heading for a low brick wall that ran some twenty meters or so to the corner of a big barn that looked, in the scant light, dull white or yellow. Gedern's squad was to provide the fire support from their position near the barn, while the lead squad would make the actual assault. Gedern allowed himself a second or two of relief—at least they wouldn't be first.

Paul Gedern feared the Americans because they were smart and aggressive, as they proved in their preemptive strike against the armored vehicles marshaled in the woods. As he moved clumsily, painfully, through the garden, tripping over plant stakes, wrenching his ankle in one of several plastic window boxes that lay empty on the ground, he wondered if the Americans, beleaguered as they had to be, were even now waiting for them.

Gedern was the next-to-last man in the file that made its slow way to the support position. His shirt and T-shirt, soaked with perspiration from the run to the village, were now chilled. He had wanted to pull them off when they last stopped, but he'd spent the few minutes exchanging magazines and counting loose rounds of rifle ammunition, preparing for the next attack. He hoped this move would be fairly long, so that he could work up some body heat, but they moved only a few feet at a time, stopping often and awkwardly as the point man picked his way through the nest of fences and boxes of garden tools and benches.

They hadn't gone more than thirty feet before Gedern began to shiver, bone-shaking jolts that threatened to tear his weapon from his hand, to trip him, leave him helpless. He stumbled forward, tried to generate some heat by flexing at the knees, once, twice, rapidly again and again, but his teeth banged together painfully and he let out a small, involuntary moan.

The man just in front of him, who looked as terrified as Gedern was, turned around quickly. "Shut up. You want to get us killed?"

Gedern shook his head. His thoughts had a staccato quality, as if the shivering were shaking his brain. *If . . . I . . . could . . . just . . . get . . . this . . . wet . . . shirt . . . off. . . .*

They reached the barn without being discovered, and when he got close, Gedern pressed himself up against the broad reassuring wall, as if he might draw some protection from the steadiness of the building itself, its girth, its permanence. He pressed his face to the rough surface, trying to still the shaking. He could feel the clammy slickness of his undershirt stretched between his shoulder blades, wrapped around his abdomen.

The men in front of him were stopped, apparently waiting to take their places along a firing line that the young NCO still had to select. The whole thing might take thirty minutes, it might take an hour. In the meantime, Gedern was expected simply to wait beside the big barn.

Shivering.

One cold hand betrayed him and dropped the end of his weapon, the muzzle describing a quick arc as the rifle suddenly swung free in his other hand. He kept it from striking the ground—and making more noise—only by yanking his shoulder upward.

He studied the soldier in front of him, wondering, in his self-pity, if he was the only one who was this cold. He imagined himself succumbing to hypothermia, freezing to death.

The shivering came upon him again, shaking him upward from his legs, up through the cavity of his chest, where the movement forced out another groan, small and painful.

The soldier in front spun round again, grabbing Gedern by the throat with a strong hand, pressing the windpipe savagely. He barely whispered, but his voice was brittle with rage.

"If you make another sound, I swear I'll kill you myself."

It took all of Gedern's control to keep from gagging when the other soldier released him. He doubled over, elbows on knees, trying to force the spots out from in front of his eyes.

So cold, he thought, *so . . . cold.*

Gedern took a step backward, leaning into the cavity of a doorway he had spied earlier, swallowing in a vain attempt to soothe his throat. When he leaned against the door, it opened, and a tiny breath of air, slightly warm with the smell of manure and fertilizer, feathered his cheek.

He chanced another look along the side of the barn, straining to see if the squad had begun moving into its firing position. He could see no movement, and there was no sign of the mean-spirited NCO with the bad teeth.

Gedern pushed on the door, which swung inward quietly on well-oiled hinges.

I'll go in here and remove my shirts.

It was black inside, a deep terrifying blue-black that reached into his eyes to steal whatever light might be there. For a moment, Gedern was seized by a fear of the deep darkness and crisp silence. He opened his mouth and listened. The room was empty.

Once decided, Gedern moved quickly. He put his rifle down between his feet, unbuckled the chin strap on his helmet and set that down as well. He yanked at his parka sleeves, remembered to remove his mittens first, got the parka off at last, one sleeve lining flipped inside out. His wool shirt wasn't all that wet, he discovered, patting himself along the chest and arms, tugging it loose from the top of his trousers.

He pulled his undershirt—slick and cold as fish skin—over his head. Even the dusky animal smells of the barn couldn't hide his own stench, and for the first time in days, Gedern's mind turned to something other than warmth and safety. He thought about a shower. He thought about hiding in the barn until the fighting was over, until he could go home. He balled the wet T-shirt up and stuck it inside the loaded cargo pocket on the outside of his right leg, then bent over to find his wool shirt as his latest, desperate plan took shape in his head.

It was just then, naked to the waist, bent over with his hands plunged down into the inky darkness around his feet, that he heard the scrape of a boot on the floor above.

The three GIs who occupied the observation and listening post on the second floor of the big yellow barn had with them one of only three sets of night vision goggles that were still working in Alpha Company. The soldier who'd been on watch, peering through the high narrow windows at the yard below, had seen the GPU troops approach and had kept an eye on them as one of their number, an NCO, the Ranger figured, looked around for a suitable spot for a support or attack position.

"There, and there," the soldier said, pointing out to his team leader either end of the line of men he could see from his perch. The NCO, a corporal named Vaughn, depressed the push-to-talk on his radio and whispered the code word that said they had movement nearby. Then he turned the volume down so that no squawking inquiries would give away their position.

He leaned close to the soldier beside him, his lips almost at the man's ear. "Grenades," he said.

They spent the next few minutes preparing the half-dozen grenades they'd carried with them to the observation post, laying them out neatly, removing the clips, straightening the pins and pulling them halfway out. The window was wide enough for only one man to get his arm outside, so Vaughn picked up as many as he could, pressing two of them against his chest, holding another in his right hand. The second Ranger held the other grenades in the palms of his open and outstretched hands, serving them up to his team leader. Vaughn checked the window again and, spying his targets, he pulled the first pin. The other soldier stepped forward, scraping his boot across an uneven board in the floor.

Paul Gedern stooped over, hands out, trying to find his rifle, which came up in a mass of twisted wool shirt and parka. The hardness of it slipped in his grasp, the butt of the weapon striking the floor, and Gedern had a horrible fleeting image of the weapon discharging, shooting him in the chest. He bent down again, thrust one hand under the resistant wool of his shirt and found the stock just as the grenades began to explode outside.

Gedern hadn't been aware of the row of small, rectangular windows that lined the room some eight feet off the floor until the light came crashing through in a welter of glass and wood frame, spraying his torso with wicked shrapnel. He raised his hands to his face and rushed for the wall as the bursts continued. The thick smell of explosive rolled in through the holes, along with the screams of the wounded.

With the bright circles of the explosions still before his eyes, Gedern almost didn't notice the faint light that appeared on the wall opposite. It took him a few seconds to figure out what he was seeing: the beam from a small flashlight, a red flashlight. The lamp was being carried by a man descending the stairs, coming down fast, two at a time on the metal treads. Gedern brought his weapon up, heard some indistinct commands in English. He was terrified, and in his mind's eye the bottom of the tiny staircase was filled with charging GIs. But then he saw the dirty boots of just one soldier.

Gedern raised the butt of his weapon to his shoulder, and when he could see the man's torso, he fired. The American went down instantly, falling to the ground floor without ever touching, it seemed, the last steps. The red light spun crazily, went out.

Gedern turned to run, realized he couldn't see the door in the darkness, then turned back to face the staircase, where someone was calling down the steps. He took two steps forward, catching his feet in what must have been his own clothing, losing his balance and crashing into a piece of cold metal farm equipment that loomed up in the dark to stab his naked chest. Gedern fell to the floor, brought his hands up to the new puncture wound and rolled over on his side.

The Americans never saw him. They picked up their dead comrade and, after checking the outside, raced out the door. Gedern thought about calling them, but he could not find his voice.

I'll wait here alone, he thought. After a few minutes, he was no longer cold, and he was grateful for that and for the sharp images that came to him of his life before these troubles. In a little while he let go the pressure on the wound in his chest.

This is not so bad, he thought at last. *Not so bad.*

16

"WHAT HAVE WE GOT?"

Lieutenant Hawkins was leaning against the wall of a single-story house one street north of the buildings where the men of Alpha Company were fighting off an attack by the *jaeger*, the GPU light infantry. The big man's breathing, huge and ragged, reminded Brennan of a winded horse. Brennan and a handful of other soldiers from the platoon made a circle around the lieutenant. Inside that ring, two of the squad leaders, one missing his helmet, the other bleeding from a pattern of wicked cuts on his chin and throat, waited to help Hawkins figure out the next move.

"We got twenty men, Lieutenant, twenty-one counting you," Sergeant Bishop said, dabbing at his wounds with a balled-up field dressing.

"Any sign of Sergeant McNeely?" Hawkins asked, looking about for his platoon sergeant.

No one answered.

"OK," Hawkins said. "OK." He bent over, hands on knees, as if he couldn't think clearly standing up straight.

"I'd suggest we form two squads, sir. One with Sergeant Portalatin," Bishop said, indicating the other squad leader. "And one with me."

Hawkins nodded his assent. Then the hesitancy passed, and he assumed control again, as if Bishop's comments had helped him get kick started.

"Send somebody to find those trucks we brought here," Hawkins said. "That's the only place we're going to find any more ammo."

Bishop dispatched three men, under a corporal, to find some ammo.

"The rest of you get inside this house," he said. "We can use some light to check these weapons." He pointed to Charis and Brennan. "You two first."

Charis, who was closest, stepped up to the back door of the steep-roofed, brick and stucco house. There were empty window boxes stacked neatly beside the back door, waiting for spring, and the ubiquitous lace curtains in the square windows.

Charis produced a small flashlight with several turns of heavy tape around the body. He unrolled the tape, fixed the light to the handguards of his weapon, and switched it on. Then he brought his rifle up, ready to smash the glass on the back door.

"Just a second," Brennan said, leaning forward to try the handle. The door was unlocked.

Charis smiled. "Ready?" he asked Brennan.

Brennan summoned some tiny reserve of energy, of adrenaline. "Let's go," he said. Pivoting on one foot, he swung into the door frame, pressing his body close to the wall on his left. Charis followed immediately, sweeping the room with the narrow beam. They were in the kitchen, alone.

The two men made eye contact, a silent signal, and Brennan slid along the wall toward a doorway and the next room. It was also empty, as were the other rooms on the floor. Charis told the other men it was safe to come in, while Brennan shoved some furniture aside.

The Rangers sat on the kitchen's tile floor, legs spread, weapons across their laps. Sergeant Bishop kept watch at the rear door for his ammo detail, and another man watched through the windows at the front of the house.

"What's going on outside?" Charis asked the sentry.

"Can't see anything," the soldier replied. "Seems to have quieted down a bit."

"Maybe they pulled back," Charis confided to Brennan.

"They pull back," Sergeant Bishop said, "it's only to regroup for another attack. And you can bet it'll come before it gets light."

Bishop's mention of dawn made Brennan wonder what time it was. He glanced at his watch. It was only twenty-two hundred, less than six hours since they'd begun their move to this village. The withdrawal and escape and subsequent firefight seemed to have lasted for years.

"Check it *out.*"

The voice came from the tiny hallway that led off the kitchen. Brennan looked up to see one of his squadmates leaning against the wall there. The reflected glow from his red-filtered flashlight showed that he was grinning.

It wasn't an emergency, so only two of the others stirred themselves. "What is it?" one of them asked. Then, in a tone that could only mean they had discovered something vital, "Oh, *man.*"

Now there were three men, now four, then five pushing into the narrow hallway. Brennan hauled himself up as he registered some hope for what he might see there. He pushed into the crowded passage, standing on his tiptoes to see over his taller buddies. Their comments and adulation hadn't stopped.

"It's in perfect shape."

"Think it still works?"

"Looks like it to me . . . try it out."

Brennan squeezed sideways and, propelled forward by hope, pushed through the front of the tiny crowd just as the first soldier stepped in for the important test. Brennan was right there to hear the toilet flush.

"Yes!" three or four of them said in ragged harmony.

There were six men in the hallway now, and they formed themselves instantly into a line, removing their headgear to retrieve the extra toilet paper good field soldiers always carry in the helmet's webbed lining.

"This is gonna be great," the man behind Brennan said. "I haven't even unbuttoned my pants since we landed in this goddamn place. Now I get to sit down instead of squatting in the snow like a dog."

"Me, too," Charis joined in. "I was afraid my butt would freeze off if I dug a hole out there and dropped 'em."

"You should be afraid of getting your butt *shot* off, more likely," another soldier said.

Brennan noticed a tiny upswing in his mood, the first in days, and all at the prospect of being able to sit down—indoors—and defecate.

"That's two out of the three things that it takes to keep me happy," the Ranger just behind Brennan said as he unfolded a second packet of the toilet paper that came with the field rations. And although anyone who'd been in the army more than a few days had heard the joke before, they indulged him.

"What exactly do you need, man?" Charis prompted.

Two or three men answered at once. "All I need to make me happy is some tight pussy, loose shoes, and a warm place to shit."

In spite of everything that had happened, everything that promised to happen to them, Brennan smiled. The smile gave way to a small laugh that rolled around in his mouth a bit before he let it out. He breathed, laughed out loud just once, then leaned against the wall, in his neat line, waiting for his chance to participate in the kind of civilized undertaking that, as a civilian, he'd always taken for granted.

"Say," he said to Charis, who stood in front of him, bouncing on the balls of his feet as if he were about to collect a fat paycheck. "You think the folks at IBM get as excited about bowel movements as we do?"

"Don't be drawing any comparisons that might get me down," Charis said, half-seriously. "I'm almost in the right frame of mind for my big moment here."

After he'd taken his turn, Brennan made his way contentedly back to the kitchen. He sat down, so leaden in all his joints that if someone told him he would never feel rested again, he might have believed it.

As the men warmed, the snow and ice that had coated their uniforms and boots melted, sending dirty rivulets of water tracing patterns on the white tile. Brennan watched the floor, pressing his legs out straight in front of him, trying to stretch the knots from his calves and thighs. The heat in the house was not on, but he was much warmer than he'd been in days, and soon he began to feel the prickly clawing of that new warmth on his dirty face and hands. He thought he should clean the wounds on his face, then figured out that it could wait.

He closed his eyes, forced them open again, saw that nothing in the room had changed. Soon his body betrayed him, and the exhaustion, heavy as mercury, filled his limbs, hands, face. He felt his mouth go slack; he dreamed of hot coffee.

Then there were dancers. At first they were young women, all women, and they were doing some sort of folk dance, in costume, around a fire that singed his eyebrows as he leaned closer to watch. The women were all clean: clean hands, shiny braided hair, clean skirts white and red in the firelight. As Brennan stretched toward the heat he saw that they were wearing boots, little boots at first, that gradually took the shape, as he watched, of the big, muddy boots of soldiers.

A sharp pain in his side, and someone's hand over his mouth.

He woke with a start. The room was black again, and there was a dirty hand over his mouth.

"Quiet," Charis whispered.

Then he heard the footfalls again, the sound of his dream's muddy boots. It was coming from the ceiling.

Brennan fought his way back to alert consciousness, the confusion of exhausted sleep fell away, and he knew what was going on.

There was someone upstairs.

He remembered the house from the outside: steeply pitched roof with low dormers, windows on the side walls.

How could we forget to check the second floor?

As his night vision returned, Brennan saw a Ranger named Sparks, a SAW gunner, crouched in the middle of the room, staring up as if he might at any second see through the ceiling. Sparks had his weapon up and was preparing to fire through the plaster and wood at the noises upstairs.

"No," Brennan said quietly.

Sparks didn't look at him, but Sergeant Bishop, who'd come in to investigate, knew immediately what Brennan meant. There might be civilians up there, hiding out, terrified of the Americans.

Brennan stood and leaned close to Bishop. "I'll check it out," he said. He felt Charis standing behind him, ready to back him up, and Brennan was flooded with a sudden affection for the other soldier.

I'm glad I woke up, Brennan thought as he pulled tight and buttoned the chin strap on his helmet. He could imagine a whole family up there, perhaps an old couple, maybe a family with children, hiding in the dark, paralyzed by the sounds coming from below them, with no idea that the Americans might shoot through the floor.

He found the tiny staircase behind a narrow door he'd mistaken for a closet. He tugged the door open, snuck a quick look up to where the staircase turned back on a small landing against the front wall of the house. As he placed his foot on the first step, he looked back at Charis, who gave him a thumbs up and a lopsided grin.

Brennan suddenly remembered a television interview he'd seen during the Gulf War, with a GI who'd been processing Iraqi prisoners, giving them the first food and water they'd had in days, telling them that they wouldn't be shot by the Americans. Then there'd been a photo of some raggedy, half-starved Iraqis kissing the hands of a befuddled Marine. And the GI told the cameras, with the certain guilelessness of the young, how nice it was to be one of the good guys.

Brennan shook slightly, thinking about how close they'd come to killing innocent people here. That was something he wouldn't have been able to live with.

The stairs were solid, and didn't squeak, as he'd been afraid they might. Brennan turned on the landing and saw two doors at the top, one left, one right. When his head was level with the second floor, Brennan spied a tiny light under the door on the right. Wishing he knew a little German to reassure the people behind the door, Brennan stepped confidently onto the landing. Charis turned his back on the left door and braced himself on the top step as Brennan called out. "You can come out now. You're safe."

The *click-squeak* of the left door opening allowed Brennan only enough time to turn his head partway toward the sound before the snarling yellow muzzle blast reached well out into the hallway to the top of the stairs and Charis.

Brennan sensed, more than saw or heard, Charis flip down and back into the landing wall six steps below. The space was too small for Brennan to bring his weapon around, so he spun into the open door, holding the weapon before him like some battering ram. He'd removed the bayonet downstairs while checking the weapon, so that now—with neither hand near the trigger—the rifle was reduced to an unwieldly nightstick.

Brennan shoved, and there was a chorus of shouts, children's voices, and some small resistance in front of him gave way. Brennan, on his knees, found the shotgun and shoved it clattering out of the room. In the light from the room behind him, he could see that he was kneeling on the chest of a boy of about twelve. Brennan straightened, raised his fist and smashed it into the wall.

He heard them on the stairs, so he backed out to watch Sergeant Bishop and two other Rangers lift Charis out of a heap at the bottom of the stairs.

"He's alive," one of the Rangers said. "He's still alive."

The boy found his feet and stood defiantly in the doorway, glaring at Brennan and trying not to cry.

17

LEUTNANT MARTIN SCHORR LEANED DOWN INTO THE DARK interior of his Marder, keyed the intercom, and said, to the rest of the crew as much as to the driver, "Let's go."

The lead platoon leader called in the first checkpoint, and Schorr could see the other platoon following him. Though he commanded only eight vehicles now—having lost six in the first two days of fighting—the company still made a formidable force, and Schorr was certain that the sound of the diesel engines, carried to the Americans on the crisp night air, would shake the most stalwart heart.

Schorr's Marder broke out of the covering woods just a few hundred meters behind the tracks of the lead platoon. The commander could see the boxy shapes in front of him, intermittently reflecting light from the burning airport building.

"Swing out farther away from that fire," he called to the lead platoon leader over the radio. "The light is picking up some of your vehicles."

Schorr pivoted awkwardly in his hatch, his bulk resisting the effort. The trail platoon seemed to be coming up at the correct interval, though in the darkness it was difficult to tell. He felt the surge of pride that such movements always gave him—the impressive array of power and steel was moving at his command. Satisfied that they were proceeding as planned, he allowed himself a few seconds to stare at the flaming wreck of the field's administration building.

The *flugplatz* belonged to a private flying club and was run by some of the area's wealthier citizens. Schorr, who lived not far from here, had come out one Sunday to a small air show and been impressed at the number of luxury cars parked in the gravel lot. Now it was all gone, and the people who'd done so much work to bring this together had had nothing to say about it. As the platoon circled around the southeast corner of the airfield and then began the swing to the north, Schorr looked into the dark woodline for the first signs of the road that would lead them into Karlshofen. He glanced quickly toward the flames and wondered how many homes, how many barns and towns and farms would burn before this was through.

The first fence post they ran over jolted the Marder, but not enough so that anyone on board thought that they would have to stop. But Schorr, who had lowered himself so that only his head was above the hull, heard the scratching sounds on the outside of the hull and realized that they were dragging the barbed wire fence with them. He stood up, his feet slipping on the tiny seat, and tried to see what was happening. Outside the vehicle there was a terrific clawing of steel as the wire—there was quite a bit now, caught up in the wheels—and the bits of still-attached fence post banged against the hull.

"Stop," Schorr commanded.

He climbed out of his hatch, slid off the front of the vehicle, and trained his flashlight on the right side track. The wire had wrapped itself thickly around the road wheel axles on the front two wheels. On the left side, the damage was not as bad, but the tangle of wire clinging to the side was bigger.

"Get me the wire cutters," Schorr told his driver, whose head was visible above his hatch. It took the crew almost two minutes to produce the tools, while Schorr steamed and fretted outside and the vehicles of the trail platoon passed him. By the time he got enough wire off to continue, all of his Marders were out of sight. He decided to make up the lost ground by cutting across the circle he'd ordered the others to follow, even though that put him and his crew closer to the light.

"Left, left," he told the driver. Without his saying a word, it was clear that the driver did not want to venture too close to the burning building, where they would show themselves as a target for a side shot if any American antitank missiles were waiting for such an opportunity.

"Left, left," Schorr said again. He was frantic now, afraid that his company would go into action without him, or that they might become disoriented, overshoot the target and wind up scattered in the fields and woods beyond the town where, even with the help of a radio, it would be difficult for Schorr to police them up.

He was riding like that, standing in the commander's hatch, arms on the outside of the turret, straining to see, when the first pair of antitank rockets ignited off to his right. One streaked into the distance without exploding, but the second found a target somewhere in front of him.

Schorr grabbed the handset and called his first platoon leader.

"What's happening, one one, what's happening?"

There was no immediate response, but someone had the push-to-talk switch depressed on this radio net, because Schorr could hear yelling and indistinct commands being given over the company frequency. Then a voice came up and, without identifying itself, explained the problem.

"That was one one that got hit."

They were waiting in ambush along that road, Schorr thought. *Of course they would be, but how many of them could there be? How deep can their defenses go?*

Schorr believed that his breakthrough was inevitable. The Americans had only light and medium antitank weapons, and they could not sustain a rate of fire that would deny Schorr's company the breach of the lines. It was like a standoff between a crowd and a man with a pistol. The crowd would win, eventually, but what Schorr didn't yet see was that no one in the crowd wanted to be the first to die.

"Left, left, now right. No, not so much, now, that's it."

Schorr struggled to keep his voice calm as he directed his driver to take best advantage of the limited cover offered by the small folds and hedges that marked the edges of the fields here. In the commander's hatch, with the advantage of height, Schorr saw a good deal more of what was going on. But he couldn't see where the Marders, all of which had sprinted ahead of him, had joined the fight.

With his left hand he switched the radio to the internal frequencies of the two platoons he was now following, hoping to find some trace of them. There was nothing but static, and he supposed that the other platoon leader may have been hit, or had his antennae shot off.

"Over there, sir, to the left."

The driver had not raised his head above the protective shield of the hull but still had managed to see, through his vision blocks, the glow of flames reflected off the bottom of low clouds above the town.

He thought he saw flames off to his left, where the village would be, and figured that the infantry attack must be progressing. But he was looking for the long flashes from the muzzles of the twenty-millimeter guns. He was getting close to the dirt road that led southeast from the town, and would soon have to make a choice: should he charge ahead to where his vehicles were supposed to be, or should he move cautiously—and slowly—through the cover provided by the thin woods on the opposite side of the road?

Somewhere nearby a Marder opened fire. The report of the big gun was followed, within a second or two, by a strange crackling sound that he recognized as the splintering of trees beside his vehicle. His company was shooting at him.

Schorr dropped onto the seat, letting the hatch bang shut over his head.

"Cease fire, cease fire," he shouted into the handset. "You're shooting at me."

He'd seen the muzzle flash off to the right and behind him, just before he dropped into the small turret. But they were *behind* him.

"One three, this is one seven," Schorr called. The handset slipped from his grasp, and he caught sight of his hand in the dull light of the vehicle's interior. It was slick with blood.

One of the vehicle commanders of the first platoon came up on the net. Schorr thought the man's voice was shaky.

"This is one three, are you all right?"

Martin Schorr was, at almost all times, a calm man, someone who might be described by an American as easygoing. But the sound of the big rounds passing close by and the sight of his own blood—though he still couldn't feel any pain in his hand—had unhinged him.

"What the fuck are you doing back there?" Schorr demanded. "You're supposed to be in the fucking *town*."

There was a pause, too long, Schorr thought, to mean anything good.

"We're back here," the voice came up again. "We're all back here. There are antitank weapons all along the road."

So they had balked. A company of men in armored vehicles that could travel at thirty miles an hour, guns blazing, was being held up by some outnumbered infantrymen huddled, freezing, isolated, along the sides of a country road.

Schorr wiped his hand on the leg of his trousers without looking at it. *Fucking cowards,* he said to himself. Then he spoke into the handset. "First platoon, move forward."

There was no response. It occurred to the big lieutenant that he didn't know exactly who was on the other end of the radio. He did know that the platoon leader was dead, and it certainly seemed as if no one was in charge over there.

Schorr was seized by a sudden, deafening rage, and at that moment he felt capable of shooting members of his own command.

But homicide—or the threat of it—wouldn't get the village taken. And the sounds of the infantry battle, coming to him weakly from the village, were waning.

"Driver, right turn," Schorr said.

He brought his Marder onto the open road, in sight of the vehicles from his own platoons. All he had to do, he reasoned, was show them the power this weapon held when used correctly.

"Can you see me?" Schorr said into the handset, his voice even.

He got one affirmative reply. Then another. He waited, until, out of the darkness and the impersonal radio, he had heard from all the vehicles that remained in his battered company.

"Good. Now we will advance on the village. First platoon will go left at the crossroads. Second platoon will go right and set up a blocking position on the road to Bremen." He paused, calm once again. "Now, follow me."

All I have to do is make it to the village.

He popped the hatch and raised his head as his driver turned the vehicle around and aimed it at the flames still visible in Karlshofen.

"Slowly, at first," Schorr told the driver. He raised his hand, tasted his own blood. Turning around, he saw and heard the other vehicles trailing his, hesitantly at first. Then there were two of them moving out on his flanks, defining the wedge shape that would plunge into the Rangers' defenses.

"Faster," he told his driver as he settled farther down into the vehicle. The village was less than two kilometers up the road, and soon they would begin the sprint, the race that would end this uneven battle.

The vehicles beside him were staying tight, and he could see two more vehicles behind them. His troops were following him. It was going to work. They would make the village in time, before the exhausted light infantry had to break off their attack. Schorr glanced at his hand once more. He hadn't yet found the cut, but he was sure it was small, and the wound would make an interesting addition to the story of how he saved his faltering attack.

"Three of 'em in the lead wedge."

"I see 'em. I'll take left," the GI said, slowly traversing the wide mouth of his Karl Gustav antitank weapon. "You take right."

"Got it. Who's going to get the middle one? He's closer."

"Yeah, you're right. I'll get him first, then go back to the others."

18

THE LEADING EDGE OF THE U.S. AIR FORCE RESPONSE, IN THE form of six F-15C Eagles, cut into German airspace over the North Sea and made landfall above the blinking navigation light at windswept Dunhen. Close behind them were another half dozen planes, F-4G and F-14 Wild Weasel antiradar aircraft that had marshaled in England shortly after the Rangers first clash with the GPU. While the Eagles and the distant AWACS—Airborne Warning and Control Station—battle control crew searched the sky for enemy aircraft, the Wild Weasels made ready to deliver the first blow of the air battle against the GPU antiaircraft sites around Karlshofen.

The planes came in like angry angels, cracking the night with great peals of man-made thunder that shook every soldier tied down by gravity. Thanks to exceptional targeting data provided by satellite, the Weasels were able to launch their antiradiation missiles on the first pass, and though the German antiaircraft battery 2 Flak managed to fire three Roland missiles at their attackers, the air force pilots never wavered and the ridge occupied by the Germans lit up so spectacularly that it was hard for watchers to believe that mere men, a dozen mortals, could unleash such destruction.

Captain Tommy Lee Chang, the USAF Tactical Air Controller, ran to Isen in the small garden where the commander had set up his command post.

"We got Weasels on target," he began while still hurrying forward. "They're taking out those flak sites." His voice had the new energy of the saved. "I've got fair commo now; they just came up on one of my nets. I guess once they got in close—"

"What's behind them?" Isen interrupted. He was already dreaming of tank killers and rescue helicopters.

"There's a Specter on station over the North Sea, waiting to be called in," Chang said triumphantly, as if he had personally conjured the gunship out of the winter air. "And another ammo drop."

"Get over to the Bravo Company sector and talk to Gene," Isen told Chang. "Last word I got was that whatever Marders were out there had stopped, but that's where we'll need Air Force help. Alpha and whatever I can get from Charlie will have to handle the guys on the ground."

Chang turned and jogged into the night, his radio operator bounding along a few paces behind. Isen could still hear Chang's flat-footed run after he lost sight of him, and fast on that thought came the realization that the small arms fire had died.

"Get me sitreps from Alpha and Charlie," Isen told his headquarters people. He was anxious to go to each sector, but he was schooling himself to be patient. No sense taking off for one end of the line only to find out he was needed at the other. Besides, his subordinates now were captains, men who'd been around a few years and were themselves aided by competent First Sergeants; it wasn't like checking on green lieutenants.

While Sergeant Gamble and Hatley made the calls, trying to piece together for their commander a picture of what was happening in their tiny perimeter, Isen leaned back, his shoulders against the wall of the outbuilding where they'd taken shelter, and looked up. There was a corridor of stars visible between the close-set buildings around him, a strip of loveliness that seemed all out of place with what was happening around him.

Perhaps it was the thought of rescue that broke through to whatever hope he had left in him, perhaps it was the thought that, elsewhere in the world, under those same stars, life was going on without the madness that had embraced him and his men in the last few days. Whatever it was, he felt a tiny breakthrough, a shiver of something that wasn't yet relief, but was at least the promise of rest and safety. Had he been a private soldier, he might have surrendered to it, let himself enjoy it for a moment or two or ten. He took off his helmet, shook his head to clear it of weariness, and brought his eyes back down to the dark ground.

"What have you got?" he asked Gamble.

"Alpha Company stopped an attack over by that big barn we saw earlier. They think they got eight or nine enemy KIAs, one friendly WIA, and one prisoner," Gamble reported crisply. "Charlie Company has a platoon—it's Lieutenant Hawkins's—ready to use as a reaction force."

"What's their status?" Isen asked.

Gamble flipped open a notepad. "They've scraped together two platoons—twenty-one and twenty-five men. They also said that one of their guys got shot by a civilian."

"Shit," Isen said. "How's our man?"

Gamble was subdued. "Still alive, but hurt bad," he said.

Chances were that Gamble didn't know the identity of the soldier—that wasn't something that would be given over the radio. But it was clear from the sergeant's voice that he felt the loss. The battalion was too small, too tightly knit for any death, any injury, to be impersonal. They were all of them covered in loss, and Isen, who tried to look on his profession with more calculation than emotion, was nevertheless ready for retribution.

Isen set off in Chang's footsteps for the eastern end of Karlshofen. They had only been in the village for a matter of hours, but it was already ravaged. There were odds and ends of personal belongings in the street—clothing, papers, a single shoe—dropped, apparently, by the fleeing residents. Off to his left, a small barn or tool shed, set afire by a flare or grenade, burned slowly. Isen found Chang and Wisneiwski, Bravo Company's commander, at the last house before the road turned away into the darkness and the fields beyond, where the Bravo Company Rangers had turned back the Marders. The two captains huddled in the alcove by the house's front door.

"We got two of them, sir," Wisneiwski explained when Isen drew close. "The rest of them had stalled before that, like they didn't know which way to go. And they stopped dead when we hit the lead vehicle, just turned around and beat feet back out of range."

"What do you think their problem was?" Isen asked.

"They didn't have any supporting infantry," Wisneiwski said. "That might have left them feeling naked once they got in among those hedges and ditches."

"Any sign of them coming back?"

"We lost sight of them," Wisneiwski said. "You want me to go look for them, pin them down?"

"We can let Specter do that," Chang interrupted.

"When is he on station?" Isen asked.

Chang looked at his watch, turning his arm so that he could glimpse the face in the glow of fire from a nearby barn.

"Seven minutes."

Two thousand meters away, the remnants of Leutnant Schorr's Panzergrenadier company had found refuge in the lee of a long low hill that shielded them from the American position. Staff Sergeant Metzger, the senior surviving leader, had placed two sentries on the lip of the hill—an expanse of muddy potato fields—to give them warning if the Americans came looking for them.

"This is bullshit," one of the other squad leaders, a thick-necked factory foreman named Dorsch insisted. "We're not getting any support, the attacks are uncoordinated. This whole thing is a poor excuse for an operation."

He stopped short of saying that the GPU had left them stranded, or that the party had made a huge mistake in launching the attack in the first place. Dorsch knew, as did everyone else in the company, that Metzger was a zealous supporter of the GPU who mistrusted anyone opposed to the party, hated them with a rabidity most party members reserved for foreigners.

"The Americans are finished," Metzger said with more authority than he felt. "We can ride in there . . . ," he began, but the thought of Schorr's vehicle burning brightly just over the muddy rim of the hill behind them cut him off. Metzger was not an articulate man, and he choked on the frustration of one who cannot put into words what he believes to be true.

Had he been as educated as his dead commander, he might have told the other NCOs that the only way out was through: once launched on this course, there was no turning back. They would either defeat the Americans and then the Berlin government, or they would all be tried as anarchists and traitors. If they lived that long. But he was unable to muster the rhetoric, unable to convince, so he relied on other, simpler approaches.

"So you're saying that all those men—Schorr and all the others, died for nothing? Are you a coward?"

"I didn't stop going forward before you did," Dorsch countered, thinking of how the attack fell apart—and Metzger hesitated—after Schorr's death. But in fact, he was frightened. As would be anyone who had just faced flaming death in an armored vehicle loaded down with fuel and explosive ammunition.

"If the party fails, there will be no voice to speak out for Germans. We might as well turn Germany over to the foreigners," Metzger said, working himself into a familiar anger. "Give the whole fucking country over to those smelly Turks, to the goddamned Africans." He was leaning forward now, and Dorsch could feel his foul breath, his smoky hatred.

"You want to let them walk all over us?" Metzger pressed. "Is that what you want?"

But Dorsch had had enough of party slogans. He looked past Metzger's shoulder to where the men in his squad, just visible amid the snow, stood beside his Marder. They had sent him over here to get them out of any further attacks. They did not want to die, and like so many of the men who'd become entangled in the GPU plot, not by choice but by circumstance, they were not at all convinced that the government in Berlin was so misguided that its violent overthrow was their patriotic duty, that the situation was so critical that they were willing to trade the fifty or sixty years left of their lives so that some new caste could lead the nation.

Dorsch's men had urged him, with all the considerable sincerity that frightened men could muster, to get them out from under this death sentence. Dorsch, who was more afraid of dying than he was of Metzger, felt that responsibility heavy on him.

"We're not going forward," Dorsch managed. More clever than Metzger, he tried to leave the other man a way out, tried to avoid making him feel pushed into a corner. "We will stand our ground here, but we are not attacking again without support." He hoped Metzger would see that all he had to do was agree to wait for support, and no one would lose face. He was just about to repeat himself when Metzger struck him, closed fist, straight on his nose. Dorsch's head snapped back, and he felt the warm, salty spray of blood over his mouth. The ground swiveled below him, rushing up to strike him on the back, and suddenly Metzger was standing above him, pistol drawn.

Metzger, wide-eyed, shrieked, "You think I'm going to let you get away with this?"

But Dorsch couldn't answer; he'd had the wind knocked out of him in his fall. He had a second or two to wonder if Metzger would know this, would give him a chance to answer, to make good, to protest, anything to keep it from going to a ridiculous extreme. Inside his head, he heard his own voice, tiny, contained. *I don't want to die.* But his mouth moved soundlessly, and Metzger shoved the pistol at him.

Compared to the fast movers that had cleared its path, the Specter gunship—a weapons platform mounted in a prop-driven C-130 Hercules aircraft—lumbered into the battle area like an overweight boxer. Inside, its Air Force crew adjusted their screens to tone down the bright thermal image of the fire in Karlshofen, remarking that the glow was at the center of the American position. On the first pass from west to east, the crew identified the hot shapes of the Marders hidden in the folds of ground in the otherwise wide open potato fields.

"Come to one four zero," the weapons officer told the pilot. "Racetrack right."

The pilot swung the stubby nose of the airplane to the southeast, dipping one wing, rolling the belly out toward the targets. The automatic one-hundred-and-five-millimeter gun and the twenty-millimeter cannon came into line on the targets some eight hundred feet below.

The aircraft was so low that it appeared to climb straight up out of the distracting glow from Karlshofen. The Panzergrenadiers, watching the ground for Rangers approaching on foot, hesitated a few seconds before sounding the alarm. Had they been quicker, they might have saved one or two comrades. The Marders themselves had been doomed from the moment Specter had entered the battle zone newly stripped of enemy air defenses.

The twenty millimeter roared in a throaty voice, electronically steadied and even, and the tracer rounds darted from the aircraft like a divining rod, like a flaming saber shoved into the earth. The Rangers in the ambush positions closest to the enemy dared lift their heads up, but all they could see, over the edge of the hill before them, were the bright flashes of dying armored vehicles and the anticlimactic secondary explosions of on-board ammunition and fuel.

Stabsunteroffizier Metzger didn't remember leaving his feet or moving. One instant he was straddling Dorsch, about to shoot him, and the next he was on the ground some distance away, and the snow around him was lit yellow and red by the explosions of his nearby Marders. He worried that his leg was on fire, and somewhere he found the strength to roll over, trying to extinguish whatever flames there were in the snow. But the pain only worsened, and he decided that he was not on fire but merely wounded.

Afraid of the American patrols that would soon come out, he began to crawl away from the light, down an almost invisible draw that probably led to more mud and cold water. He heard a plane pass overhead, a sound too low-pitched for a jet, and he wondered if they'd been attacked by an American or a Luftwaffe aircraft. Whatever else he didn't know about the party and its plans, he knew that that distinction was crucial.

When the Specter opened up, its signature sound bouncing around the village, Isen thought that the first installment had been paid on the debt they owed the GPU. He was not a bloodthirsty man, and he wanted the fighting to end as quickly as possible, but for those seconds when he could hear the great ripping of the thousands of rounds cutting to earth, he was happy that the Germans were being made to pay.

"Get them to check out the assembly areas back by the air field," Isen said above the roar of airborne guns. "There's probably plenty of stuff back there to shoot at. And the fast movers should target anything on the highways headed in this direction."

Chang nodded vigorously as Isen spoke, deciding how he would put his commander's requests into mission orders for the pilots, calculating how much more station time they had and what ordnance they might be carrying.

Chang's handset squawked, and he put it to his ear. "The follow-on planes dropped more ammo," he said.

"Gene," Isen said to Wisneiwski, "after we get the all clear from the Air

Force, I'll want your guys to take a look out there, see what we hit, make sure that there's nothing threatening left close in. Then start recovering that ammo."

Isen was thinking about how to consolidate his perimeter and how to prepare his battalion for evacuation when he noticed Chang was yelling into the radio handset.

"Why is your station way the hell out there?" Chang demanded. "Over."

The captain listened unhappily for almost a minute. At one point he sank to a knee and pressed his hand to his forehead under the rim of his helmet.

"Standby, over," Chang said. Rising, he addressed Isen. "They're being pulled out of the immediate area," he said. "They're supposed to stand by out over the North Sea."

Chang was clearly confused—the person on the other end of the transmission obviously hadn't told him much about why the battalion was being left alone again.

"What the hell for?" Isen wanted to know. Some of the sick feeling was coming back in a rush, and Isen fought to control his anger, his voice. "Did you tell them the area is crawling with bad guys?"

"Yessir," Chang said quickly. He wanted the planes more than Isen, who, for a moment, was seriously dislocated. But the comment about the North Sea tripped something in Isen's mind, something he didn't want to discuss—just yet—with his officers.

"Fine," he said. "Tell those bastards to keep in touch in case the shit hits the fan again." A confused Chang shook his head and brought the handset up to his mouth.

"Get that patrol out there and back as fast as you can, Gene," Isen directed his Bravo Company commander. "Send a good-size group, in case they run into something."

"We bringing back enemy wounded, sir?" Wisneiwski asked.

It was a good question. The humane thing to do would be to care for enemy wounded in one of the houses in the village. But the Rangers were already stretched so thin as to make holding their own position risky—at best. Isen had been schooled for years about the implications of such choices by commanders. If wounded enemy soldiers died because he made a bad decision, he could be tried as a criminal by his own army. If that happened and he were captured, the GPU would do worse. And in either case he would have to live with himself. But their medical supplies were all but gone, and their own wounded required the constant attention of the medics.

"Administer first aid, try to make them comfortable, and leave them," Isen said. He hadn't meant for it to sound cold, but the picture was bleak:

exposed to the elements as they were, the wounded GPU soldiers would die if their comrades didn't come looking for them.

Isen pushed those thoughts from his mind: he'd made the best decision possible under the circumstances, and that was all the comfort he could take. In the meantime, he had another concern: why was the Air Force unwilling to come in and blow away the GPU? They had already established at least local air superiority, or else the Specter would never have been able to fly. So why were they pulling back? And what of evacuation aircraft? As he strode back along the street toward the center of the little town, he catalogued the possible reasons for such a decision.

Isen found Major Rhone in the house the medics were using as an aid station. The Bundeswehr officer was helping tend the wounded, following the instructions of an American staff sergeant. He was as tired as anyone else, and when Isen approached, he merely nodded.

"Were those U.S. or Luftwaffe aircraft?" Rhone asked. He was holding up the arm of a wounded soldier while the medic changed a dressing that was wrapped from the man's wrist to his shoulder. Rhone held the GI's bloody hand gently in both of his.

"They were ours," Isen said. He had wanted to question Rhone about the extent of GPU influence in the country, and particularly in the military. Isen didn't want to discuss, with his own officers, the possibility that they might be caught in the middle of a political debate over the use of force. But as he watched Rhone, Isen remembered that Spano had never completely trusted the German, had, in fact, considered the possibility that Rhone was sent in by the GPU to weaken the Rangers' position.

"Is it possible that the GPU might withdraw, might try to back out of this?" Isen asked.

Rhone gave him a strange look. "I think it's safe to say that they've gone too far to back down," he said. "There may be some sort of coup within the party, or it might fall apart on its own, but unless something like that happens, it is likely that the GPU will continue until defeated."

"So it's all or nothing for them, right?"

"I think so," Rhone said. The medic was finished with the dressing, and Rhone gently lowered the man's arm to the pallet they'd made from some bedclothes.

"What about Berlin?" Isen asked.

Rhone didn't follow the question at first. He sat back on the floor next to the wounded soldier, whose eyes were still closed in pain, and focused on Isen.

"Do you mean to ask about the options available to Berlin?"

Isen nodded.

"Well, this is not my area, of course. I was watching the GPU, but was not privy to government policy concerning them." He straightened his legs before him, and Isen noticed that he had replaced his civilian shoes with German-made boots. Isen didn't want to know where the boots had come from.

"I suspect that Berlin has a somewhat wider range of options. Obviously, the GPU has to be destroyed, but that doesn't have to be in battle. Things will go much better for Berlin if the GPU can be defeated without much fighting. Combat will only destroy German property, and the economy is in bad shape already."

The effort of trying to second-guess what was happening outside Karlshofen exhausted Mark Isen. He was supremely frustrated by the lack of information, and he desperately wanted to know what was going on. He'd received a message, through Chang and the Air Force, that replacement communications equipment was on the way. But until that equipment arrived and he was back in contact with the world, he had plenty to do.

"It'll be light in a couple of hours," he said. "I'm going to consolidate here in this town until someone comes to get us."

Captain Gerald Fitzsimmons, U.S. Army Special Forces, pushed his glove off the luminous dial of his watch and checked the time again. 0427. Three minutes until drop time, an hour to move to Karlshofen, and then, if all went well with the recognition signals, he and his team would deliver their charges to the commander of the Third Ranger Battalion, holed up in the little village.

Fitzsimmons and his HALO—high altitude, low opening—team had jumped just after dusk the previous evening, running off the back ramp of a C-130 Hercules almost two miles up in the frigid air. Wrapped in their electrically warmed suits and breathing from oxygen bottles—not because the air was too thin but because it was so cold—they had free fallen in a tight formation to eight hundred feet, where they deployed their steerable parachutes and glided to within a few hundred meters of the spot Fitzsimmons had picked out for their rally point.

After assembling the team and accounting for men and equipment, the Special Forces soldiers moved out to a prearranged point some six kilometers from where they landed. At twenty-nine minutes past four Fitz would activate the electronic beacon, signaling the plane that was to drop three more jumpers.

Fitzsimmons didn't know the identity of the men he was supposed to deliver to Karlshofen—he supposed he'd been kept ignorant for security reasons, in case he and his team were captured. Besides delivery of the commo equipment the team carried, his mission was to secure the immediate area and escort the second team—and that was it. He didn't get paid to ask a lot of questions.

Fitzsimmons punched in the coded entry that would set the homing beacon to its proper frequency. It could be turned on without the code, under duress, for instance, had Fitzsimmons been captured. The pilots were looking for a particular reply to their electronic interrogation of the machine, and the duress code would mean a scrubbed mission.

The little light marked INTERROG blinked twice, meaning that the second aircraft was on course for its pass. Since Fitzsimmons was supposed to recover the jumpers and move out quickly, the planners had opted for a low drop altitude for this aircraft, counting on the Green Berets to get out of the area before anyone could investigate the noise.

The captain turned his head to the side, thinking that he heard the plane's engines, but it was at least a minute too early, and the sounds were coming from the wrong direction. There was fighting going on in Karlshofen, and Fitzsimmons wondered how the lightly armed Rangers were holding up against the Panzergrenadiers they faced.

He'd been briefed on plans to evacuate his team if the operation came apart, but such a rescue would be difficult, almost impossible. His best hope lay in reaching the Ranger perimeter, where he would come under the control of the Special Operations Command back in the States. Fitz hoped the Ranger commander wouldn't come up with any hare-brained plans for him. The captain expected to be sent out on long-range reconnaissance missions to gather intelligence for higher headquarters. He didn't relish the thought of arguing with some lieutenant colonel who wanted the SF soldiers to join the line.

At the quick flash of the third interrogative, Fitzsimmons looked up. The C-141 Starlifter was in sight now, just above the treeline to the east, a black shape that appeared wingless against the just lighter sky as it swayed and skittered, adjusting its flight path and altitude. Fitzsimmons tilted his head back and, when the plane was overhead, saw the jumpers exit, trailing their chutes behind them in a fluttering tail. At five hundred feet, there was no time to use a reserve parachute, so each man's life depended on the main chute.

Fitzsimmons counted three, saw the canopies open briefly, then disappear as the backdrop changed from sky to the far woodline. He turned off the beacon, which was in his rucksack, and hoisted the heavy load onto his back. His team, with the three jumpers in tow, converged at the rally point in just over four minutes. Two of Fitzsimmons's men took the jumpers' parachutes to a shallow hole they'd scraped out and quickly covered the equipment with snow, dirt and branches. Anyone looking for the equipment could find it with little trouble, but the parachutes had to remain hidden only for a few hours.

"Captain Fitzsimmons?" one of the new jumpers said. He was just a shadowy outline, barely visible against the snow.

"That's me." His best guess about the identity of his charges was that they were Air Force guys, sent in to coordinate fires, or some other kind of specialists who could help the Rangers bring combat power to bear.

"I'm Colonel Schauffert," the dark outline said. "You gonna get me to my men, right?"

"Roger that, sir," Fitzsimmons replied, trying to hide his surprise. Half-turning to his point man, Fitzsimmons said simply, "Let's go."

As he walked, he watched his compass, checked the terrain against the route he'd memorized when they'd been locked in for planning, and wondered through it all why a full-bird colonel, the Ranger Regimental Commander, would jump into an endangered perimeter with just twelve other men. He thought about the French paratroopers avid to get into Dien Bien Phu as the Viet Minh closed the noose there in 1954, and he wondered if Colonel Schauffert was grandstanding.

Either he thinks he has to go down with the ship, Fitzsimmons thought, *or he's bringing up reinforcements.*

If Captain Fitzsimmons was surprised that the Regimental Commander had jumped in, Mark Isen was completely baffled. It made no sense to him whatsoever. He thought of the stories Ray Spano had told him about Schauffert.

Spano. Isen thought about his friend for the first time all night. Spano was dead, Schauffert probably didn't know it yet, and Isen had been making decisions without consulting his superiors. It was possible that he might have put more emphasis on using Chang's communications link— Chang had been in contact with the Air Force for a short while now—and it was possible that Schauffert had come to relieve him.

Schauffert was famous in the Special Operations community for his scalding handling of subordinates. But there was no margin in second-guessing; Isen had done what he could, and he was too tired to think about anything other than getting relief for his men.

Isen left the protection of the doorway where his radio operators huddled, prepared to meet Schauffert in the street. In a few moments he heard the *clink-brush* walk of heavily laden men and was able to pick out Schauffert's distinctive shape among the shadows. He was still thinking about how best to brief the old man when Schauffert reached him.

"Mark," Schauffert said, reaching for Isen's hand with both of his own. "John Taylor told me about the casualties, and about Ray. I'm sorry."

Isen was too surprised to pull his hand back.

"I need for you to show me around before we sit down and talk," Schauffert finished.

The perimeter was tiny, so it didn't take long for the old man to see most of it: Alpha Company's line and the positions of the failed *jaeger* assault; the two platoons reconstituted from the remains of Charlie Company; and several of Bravo Company's ambush positions, including the one that had stopped the attack hours earlier by knocking out the two

Marders. The last stop was the aid station the medics had established in a house one street behind Alpha's line. Here Schauffert moved slowly among the dozen badly wounded Rangers—the walking wounded, those who could still handle their weapons, had all returned to their units.

"How did you get to the village?" Schauffert asked when they were through.

"I decided that we'd have a better chance holding off the attacks from a built-up site rather than out in the open," Isen said. "We kind of made a run for it from the airfield. Charlie Company had a hard time getting out, and the Marders started hitting us almost right away." He paused, dizzy with fatigue and the effort of presenting a sensible picture.

There was so much to say about the steadiness of the men left behind to stall the GPU advance; about the resolution of the Bravo Company soldiers who crawled forward amid the hedges and ditches to lie in ambush for the onrushing Marders; about the casual heroism of the men who'd driven the trucks full of wounded on their crazy end-around to the village. But all the testimony moved about, just behind his tongue, in thick, mute eddies.

"We'd have been in a world of hurt if they'd been able to coordinate their attacks on the two flanks," Isen finished. He looked up at his commander's homely face, wondering how much Schauffert wanted to hear. The old man seemed impatient.

"The air strike came after they'd pulled back, but it kept them from launching another assault," Isen finished.

He had a great deal more to say, but Schauffert had seen, in the aid station, the most important testimony to what had been happening here. Isen felt himself drift away for a few light-headed seconds, his upper body describing an ellipse as he swayed with exhaustion. Then he came back to where Schauffert was still watching him.

"They wouldn't execute the other missions I asked for," Isen said. He was about to explain that he was talking about the Air Force when Schauffert interrupted him.

"I know," the colonel said curtly. "I have a few things to tell you about what's going on out there," Schauffert said, shrugging one shoulder to indicate the rest of the world.

Isen had a swift sensation that he was approaching something dangerous and just out of sight, as boaters might feel, through the fragile, tremulous deck, the falls just beyond the innocent curve.

"The Air Force is holding back because things are a little dicey between Washington and Berlin," Schauffert explained. "The Germans want to contain this as much as possible; defuse it, if they can, by outmaneuvering the GPU politically, undercutting their support among the people."

Isen heard Schauffert pause, saw him wait for some sign that Isen was following, but the younger man's head was reeling. For the past four days

Isen had been hanging on—barely—to a command threatened by a well-equipped armored force. He knew, of course, that politics and concerns about international power were holding up his rescue. But hearing all his suspicions confirmed did nothing to reassure him. He managed to keep his eyes focused on Schauffert's nose.

"You with me, Mark?" Schauffert asked.

"Yessir."

"I know this is all a bunch of mumbo jumbo bullshit, but it's affecting our plans for reinforcing you here."

Isen felt something inside him fall, as if from a great height. "Reinforce?"

"Yeah," Schauffert went on. "This is where we're going to start taking these guys apart. We're really gonna fuck 'em up."

The colonel paused again. He'd seen the look in Isen's eyes, a kind of vacuum that had built up back there in all that exhaustion. Schauffert liked Isen, and he wanted to throw him and the rest of the Rangers in Third Batt a lifeline. But that wasn't how the game was played, goddamn it. The Germans had given them the opportunity to kick some ass, show the Europeans that the Americans weren't afraid of taking charge, and Schauffert wasn't about to let the opportunity pass.

Schauffert had always been the hardass. It was a role that he'd carved for himself early on, and it suited him—most of the time—just fine. But he wasn't a machine, either. He had emotions, and he hurt for these kids. Hell, he was a father himself, of a seventeen-year-old girl and a sixteen-year-old boy. He knew that all around him were fathers and brothers and sons, all dressed in green and carrying weapons and depending on him and this tired major who stood before him—swaying like a drunk—to get them out of the mess they were in. These men were down, wounded, hungry, cold, tired beyond anything they knew about that word.

Too fucking bad, Schauffert thought. *When the going gets tough, and all that.*

"The SF guys brought new commo equipment in. We're going to get your wounded out of here, then we're going to use this village and that airfield back there—" he yanked his thumb over his shoulder; it was light enough now for Isen to see—"as soon as we get the go-ahead to bring in more troops."

"We're going on the offensive?" Isen asked.

"Fucking A right," Schauffert barked. "We got plans to bring an armored column up from the south, a Marine amphibious force in at the coast here, and we got fucking "Death from Above"—two battalions of Rangers and a brigade or two of those pussies from the Eighty-second Airborne who'll probably get all the goddamned press when this is over. We're calling it Firefall, Operation Firefall. They'll never know what fucking hit 'em."

Isen thought that perhaps the colonel's enthusiasm should be infectious, but there was nothing there for him. "When does all this go down?"

"Soon, soon," Schauffert allowed, dropping his voice. "First of all, the State Department and the CIA think that parts of the federal government over here have been compromised."

"Meaning?"

"Specifically, that GPU sympathizers have infiltrated the armed forces, the foreign ministry, some other agencies."

"Meaning that the Bundeswehr might not fight against the GPU?" Isen asked.

"Actually, it's worse than that," Schauffert admitted. He pulled off one glove, rubbed the back of his neck with that hand. "There are folks who believe that some units of the German military might actually fight against us."

Isen looked down at the ground, sidestepped left to a low wall that separated a garden from the sidewalk. "Mind if I sit down, sir?"

Schauffert joined him on the wall, and the two men sat with their legs tossed out before them.

"So we're supposed to hold out here until . . . what? Until we find out if the Bundeswehr is going to let us reinforce?" Isen asked, struggling to keep the anger out of his voice. "Until somebody in Washington or Berlin decides to hammer the GPU?"

"Yeah, that's what the pols would like," Schauffert said. "But things are already in motion. The President gave Berlin notice that we were coming in. The Air Force will be back on station soon, no matter what Berlin says. If the Germans can't fix things by then, we'll fix things for them."

Schauffert smiled briefly. "But there's another problem."

Isen put his hands behind him on the wall and looked up to where the eastern sky had begun to lighten. There were a few clouds visible, not enough to impede air operations, he thought. But then he remembered that they weren't going anywhere. They'd been battered and shoved around by a superior force, with little clue as to why the fighting was even going on, much less what was being done to rescue them. And now they were being asked to gut it out—and no promise of when help was coming.

It doesn't get much better than this, Isen thought. "What's the other problem, sir?"

Colonel Charlie Schauffert sat up straight on the little garden wall, the light expanding around him, and began to tell Isen about the missing nuclear warheads.

19

STAFF SERGEANT BOBBY PASCAL, UNITED STATES MARINE Corps, and two other squad leaders from his company waited anxiously outside their company commander's cabin on board the U.S.S. *Wasp*. They leaned against the bulkheads to steady themselves as the big ship, tracing an oval path in the North Sea some sixty miles from Bremerhaven, rolled on the winter swells.

"Hey, Pascal."

He felt a nudge in the ribs, a one-finger poke that had to be Wayne Bart. Bart, Pascal's bunkmate and sometime friend, held down a squad leader slot in the same platoon.

"So you think this carpet here," Bart said, scuffing his boot on the blue Navy-issue carpeting, "is so the flyboys won't hurt themselves when they come in off liberty all liquored up and fall down on the way to their condos?"

Pascal didn't answer, but he had taken note of the accommodations in officer country: the passage lined with comparatively luxurious two- and four-man staterooms for the pilots. These men, whose job was to ferry Pascal's squad and hundreds of other marines ashore, lived in an entirely different world from the grunts who were stacked up eight high on bunks deep in the ship.

"I don't care if they live in the freakin' Taj Mahal," Pascal said, "as long as they get me and my boys ashore, in the right spot, in one piece.

Besides, I think they put the rug in just this morning to make you jealous."

"They only let us up here when they want to show off," Bart said.

"Captain Cielli brought us up here to help carry stuff, just like he said," Pascal said. Bart raised an eyebrow at him, and Pascal knew that he sounded suspiciously like a party-line, a sycophant, a "lamb," in Marine Corps parlance.

Bart was about to say something when the hatch to the tiny cabin opened and their commander started handing out charts, maps, and photocopied sheets. Pascal and the others headed down a series of ladders that twisted down to the briefing room some five decks below. When they'd deposited their bundles by the podium, they joined the other NCOs filling the room up from the back, as if they were late for church services.

"You men in the last two rows come up front."

Captain Cielli, commander of D Company, had entered and was waving them forward to the seats immediately before him. The men did as they were told.

"Nobody's gonna ask for donations here," Cielli joked, trying to relieve the tension. "No volunteers needed for this show."

Pascal studied two maps tacked to the bulletin boards behind the CO. One was a map of the area around Bremerhaven, easily identified by the blue shock of the Weser River and the wide-mouthed bay beyond. The other was a street map, probably of the same area. On the floor beside the lectern were two or three pieces of plastic overlay, and Pascal expected that Cielli would use these during the briefing, fixing them over the maps to show objectives or boundaries or enemy dispositions—some sort of visual representation of the plan they were about to hear.

All around him, nervous, whispered conversations gave way to the fluttering of notebook paper as the NCOs and junior officers prepared to take notes. Pascal flipped to the first blank page and wrote, across the top, "Bremerhaven." On the same line, at the opposite side of the page, he put two question marks.

Captain Cielli started with an overview of the political situation in Germany that had led to the GPU's challenging the federal government. Then he talked about the predicament the Rangers found themselves in when they deployed to the continent for what they thought was a training mission. Without revealing anything he wasn't supposed to—for much of the situation was classified—Captain Cielli managed to convey the tough spot the soldiers were in. "It's kind of like Bastogne in there. You know, the Battle of the Bulge. From what I understand, they're holding on so we can get the rest of our combat power to bear.

"There are two phases, two objectives in Operation Firefall," he continued. "The most obvious one is the relief mission. Our part in that is to go ashore and secure the port facilities in Bremerhaven for the brigade mechanized force, which will close on the Rangers' position from the northwest. The second part comes when we join this brigade in a ground operation to crush the combat forces of this GPU."

From that large-scale picture, Cielli went into a fairly detailed warning order about the mission as it stood now. The *Wasp* carried four air cushion landing craft, or LCACs, in its huge lower deck. These would carry two dozen light armored vehicles to the beach, then return to ferry the artillery and support vehicles. The hundreds of combat marines, led by the rifle companies, would go ashore on the big troop-carrying helicopters, the CH-46 Sea Knights and CH-53E Super Stallions, all backed by the tremendous firepower of a half-dozen AH-1W Super Cobras. There were even a half dozen AV-8B Harrier jump jets, vertical takeoff and landing aircraft, for close air support.

"The planning staff still has this one, and more details will be forthcoming. Any questions so far?"

Pascal looked around for his platoon leader, but all the lieutenants were in the back of the room. He decided to go ahead and ask the commander himself.

"What if there's resistance on the beach, sir?"

Pascal's company was part of a Marine Expeditionary Unit, in this case an embarked infantry battalion with it support elements, which was not configured for a combat assault on a hostile beach. The MEU was too small for anything but raids and quick strike operations. Although it could spearhead an assault by a brigade, that brigade had to be close enough to lend support. The MEB, or Marine Expeditionary Brigade, that Cielli was talking about was still assembling in North Carolina.

"I mean," Pascall continued, aware that all his peers were watching him, "are we going to wait for the MEB? Do we have time for that?"

Cielli had asked a similar question of his battalion commander in a briefing a couple of hours earlier. He'd been told that there was a chance that they'd go ashore before the MEB was on station in order to distract the GPU, to draw off some of their combat power from the Rangers, and to show the Germans that the United States, once committed to military action, could hit in a variety of ways.

Cielli watched the eyes of the young squad leader as the NCO wrestled with the same question: what happens if we go ashore and run into something big? Cielli's boss, going for the black humor, had replied, "We're fucked." But Cielli couldn't do that to this roomful of junior leaders who had to talk up this mission in the deep holds of the ship, where his Marines waited to hear what their country was about to ask of them. Nor could he bring himself to throw out a lot of vague responses about air support and intelligence pictures of weak enemy forces.

Playing the cheerleader here was, he thought, somehow shirking his responsibility. There was a lot he could say about the poor training of the GPU, about the close air support that was available to the Marines, about the fact that the GPU was likely to shatter when they realized they were about to be assaulted by the whole U.S. Armed Forces. But Pascal knew all that, or could figure it out for himself. His questions were much more fundamental: are we going to be used for a mission we're not supposed to get? And is that going to get us killed?

Cielli hesitated for a moment, then let another two or three seconds roll by, heavily burdened with all the unspoken truths the two warriors—captain and sergeant—saw there. And then the captain stepped back into his role.

"If we get ordered in," Cielli said, "we're going in, and I feel sorry for the fuckers who try to stop us."

When it came to running his squad, Sergeant Pascal did not set much store with luck, premonitions, ESP, prayers, talismans, intuition, cosmic signs, or the interpretation of dreams. He believed in physical conditioning, clean weapons, meticulous planning, and USMC marksmanship training.

Pascal had told them the possibilities. They could run into a fully equipped territorial unit, complete with its own armored vehicles; or they might run into a few policemen.

"I bet we have to go in and rescue the Army before the MEB gets here," a bold private named Rawson said at the end of Pascal's briefing.

A few of the other Marines nodded their agreement.

"Sergeant, how far is it from the beach?" one of his corporals asked. "From Bremerhaven to this place where the Rangers are stuck?"

Pascal flipped up his map. "About thirty-five kilometers," he said. "Twenty-one, twenty-two miles, something like that."

"A morning walk," Rawson said.

"Not with all the stuff we're going to be carrying," the corporal corrected him.

The squad turned to Pascal. "That right, Sergeant? We going in loaded for bear?" one asked.

"No telling what we're going to find when we get there," Pascal said. "So we're going in ready for the worst."

Würzburg, Germany

Captain Theodore Roosevelt Kilgore, U.S. Cavalry, checked his watch again, holding it close to his face to help him focus. Twenty-one hundred. He'd been awake almost thirty hours now, ever since he'd gotten the alert call from the squadron operations officer, and he told himself for the tenth time that hour that it was just the lack of sleep beating him down.

He pressed the back of one hand against his forehead, which was chill and sweaty to the touch, then cupped his cheeks with both palms.

"Hundred, hundred and one, tops," he told himself.

He'd turned in at seven-thirty the evening before the alert, trying to head off the sickness—probably the flu—that had been stalking him for three days. But the morning call had defeated that plan. Since then he'd been running to mission briefs, hustling back and forth to the track park where his troop of M1A2 Abrams tanks and M2 Bradleys—the cavalry version of the army's infantry fighting vehicle—were loaded out and prepared for shipment by rail, at least part of the nearly five hundred kilometers north to Karlshofen.

There had been a frustrating series of delays as the missions changed, then the march orders changed. The uncertainty was compounded by the wild rumors that flew through headquarters quick as frightened birds: the Bundeswehr was going to ambush them, the GPU had control of the railways and had already sent one train of GIs off into a ravine, Washington had decided to surrender to the rebels all U.S. forces still in Germany. Kilgore and his junior leaders, his lieutenants and NCOs, did their best to squelch these wild stories, but the lack of solid information made that job difficult.

Unlike the men who'd manned their posts during the height of the Cold War, when there were 120 Soviet divisions within a three-day march of Wurzburg, Kilgore's men weren't all that used to alerts that smelled of real crisis. It wasn't unusual for the troopers to have four or five alerts and rollouts—all vehicles, weapons, ammunition—in a month, but there were no bad guys at the gates anymore.

These men of the Black Horse Regiment, the U.S. contribution to the pan-European contingency force, were the only unit on the continent that still served under the American flag. And more than one critic of U.S. policy in Europe wondered aloud if these men, with no "real world" combat mission to train for, still had the edge, the mental toughness for combat.

As the stories of GPU audacity grew more fantastic, Kilgore began to tell everyone he met that they were Territorial Forces, they weren't supermen. They're not supermen, he said again and again to anyone who would listen. *They're not supermen.*

"Sir, the lieutenants will be here in a second."

Kilgore snapped awake—he'd dozed off sitting straight up on the orderly room couch. First Sergeant Leonard stood over him, the strong overhead lights silvering his glasses and the top of his bald head.

"If you want, Captain," Leonard said, "you can do the first part of the briefing, the mission part, and I'll do the logistics and stuff. You look like hell, and you need to get some rest or you'll be worthless to us."

Kilgore blinked slowly, tried to swallow. There seemed to be some giant claw grasping the back of his skull, squeezing cruelly in time with his heartbeat. "I can get some sleep on the train," he said. He knew he was being hypocritical: he was always after his officers and NCOs to have a good rest plan while they were conducting continuous operations—which is what this load-out was fast becoming. Tired leaders, he reminded them again and again, make bad decisions.

Leonard looked down at him, his lips pressed in a tight line that might have been disapproval. For a second Kilgore thought that the First Sergeant might place his big hand across the captain's forehead to check his temperature, as one might do with a child. But Leonard held off. He knew, without having to touch, that Kilgore was sick.

The troops called the First Sergeant "Mother Leonard," not out of disrespect, but just as a way of acknowledging that he actually cared about them as individuals. He wasn't above giving them motherly advice, but no soldier in the collective memory of the unit had ever done anything but accept, with good grace, such offerings from Leonard, who stood an even six three in his olive drab GI socks.

Kilgore's platoon leaders entered in a noisy group, followed by his supply sergeant and the maintenance NCO that headquarters troop had attached to him.

"We get an up from the siding yet, Top?" Kilgore asked.

"Loaded the last tank about fifteen minutes ago, sir," Leonard answered. "I'll be going down there after this meeting to check the guard situation. I figure that most of the men can come back here and sleep in the barracks as long as we have a guard down there. We can stay by the siding if you think it's necessary, but it's awful damn cold out there."

"Sounds good," Kilgore said slowly, thinking about sleep.

The troop commander stood, which quieted the lieutenants. He walked to the bulletin board where Leonard had taped the maps, leaning his hip against the wall to steady himself. He squinted at the paper, noticed that Leonard—God bless him—had highlighted the route in yellow marker.

"Here's the rail route we'll use to go at least as far as Hannover," Kilgore said, tapping the map. "The word from on high is that we'll have to assess the situation again once we get there. Could be that we'll be able to take the train all the way to Bremen, could be that the GPU will try to stop us and we'll have to deploy."

One of his platoon leaders, a nervous second lieutenant named Bonham who was convinced he knew as much, if not more, than anyone else in uniform, interrupted. "It would take days to fight through all the way from Hannover to that little town . . . what's it called? Karlshofen?"

Kilgore was about to tell Bonham to wait until he asked for questions, but he allowed that the junior leaders were nervous.

"It might take a while, yeah. But we're going anyway. On the other hand, the GPU might back off by then, and we might just ride all the way in and all the way out without ever getting our boots dirty."

Kilgore didn't believe that—he knew that the Rangers had already been involved in some serious shooting—so chances seemed good that they'd do some fighting as well. But he had a great deal of confidence in his men and their equipment, and he believed they could accomplish whatever was asked of them.

He realized everyone was watching him, and he wondered if he'd fallen asleep on his feet. *I'd better listen to the first sergeant*, he thought as he focused again on the map. *Get some sleep.*

Suddenly someone was shouting in the hallway, and he heard a door slam. He turned around to see one of his staff sergeants, a feisty Puerto Rican named Herndez, push his way into the orderly room. Kilgore's first thought was that one of his soldiers had been hurt at the loading dock. Maneuvering the giant battle tanks onto flatbed rail cars that were barely wider than the squat armored hulls was tricky and dangerous business. Add to the normal perils the fact that it was dark outside, that the soldiers were tired and nervous, and the situation was enough to worry any commander.

Herndez was blowing hard as he stepped into the meeting. He was missing his hat and looked as if he'd run a good part of the distance. "Sir," he said, looking first at his platoon leader, then at Kilgore. "Sir, you better come down to the siding, there's some problem there with some civilian punks throwing things at us."

Kilgore wasn't sure why he thought of the question—maybe it was Herndez's description of them as "punks," that made him ask, "Teen-agers?"

Herndez shook his head and wiped the winter-air snot off his face with the back of his gloved hand.

"Skinheads," he said.

The headlights of Kilgore's vehicle, his "humvee," passed over what looked to be several dozen people pushing up against the fence that separated the railway siding from the street. Here and there he spotted a white T-shirt in the glare, or the pale white of a shaved head that gave the group its name. Kilgore's GIs stood on the opposite side of the tracks, with the loaded train cars in between them and the youths.

"The dickheads must be throwing bottles or something." Leonard said from the backseat, where he and two of the lieutenants were bouncing around. "Look at the troopers standing in the lee of those cars."

Just at that point several bottles curved into the air from outside the fence, sparkling into the brightly lit rail yard as they flipped end over end and splattered harmlessly on the tank hulls.

"We should throw bottles back at them," Lieutenant Bonham offered as Kilgore's driver brought the humvee to a stop behind the train.

"We should go out and kick some ass," First Sergeant Leonard countered.

Kilgore was quiet. The sight of a gang of teen-agers throwing bottles at his tanks didn't upset him very much, as long as he could keep his troops out of the line of fire until it was time for the train to roll. Nevertheless, there was something disturbing about the scene.

"Where are the fucking *polizei?*" Kilgore said.

There was no sign of the familiar blue and white police vans that should have been evident, nor was there any sign of the railroad security people who should have been inside the fence.

Kilgore climbed out of his vehicle and was met by a lieutenant from one of the squadron's other troops, a thin, nervous little man named Wilson whose birdlike movements and wispy mustache would have been better suited to a department store clerk than a cavalry officer. Wilson was apparently the only officer on site.

"They've been here for a while," Wilson said, his lip and mustache twitching slightly. "Thirty minutes or so. They didn't start throwing things until just a little while ago. We already had most of the vehicles secure, but they managed to get one of my men with a bottle."

"He hurt bad?" Kilgore asked as he surveyed the line of protestors outside the fence.

"Cut above the eye, sir," Wilson answered. "Bled pretty badly, but it'll be OK." He followed Kilgore as the captain made his way down the line of cars, on the side away from the crowd, at ground level. A bottle smashed on the deck of the tank above them, spraying them with pieces of broken glass.

"Umm . . . , sir," Wilson said tentatively. "I think you should see this."

When Kilgore met his gaze the lieutenant grabbed the handles at the end of the nearest car and swung himself up neatly. Kilgore followed, his eyes going slightly out of focus with the exertion of the climb.

I'm in worse shape than I thought.

Wilson crouched at the corner of one of the tanks, and when Kilgore joined him he scuttled along the back of the vehicle, moving closer to the skinheads.

"Up there," Wilson said.

Kilgore blinked his eyes, trying to clear away the tiny spots that had somehow accumulated there. They were in the bright light of the yard, and Wilson was asking him to look beyond that, into the shadows. "What is it?" he asked.

Even as he said it, he followed the line of WIlson's outstretched arm into the snow and darkness. As his eyes adjusted, he thought he saw something large, moving out at the ends of his vision. "What is it?" Kilgore asked again.

"About a hundred and fifty, two hundred of them," Wilson said. "I think they're getting ready to rush us." The lieutenant delivered this pronouncement in the same nervous voice he used every day. When Kilgore looked at him, he realized that Wilson, in spite of his less-than-awe-inspiring outward appearance, was completely cool.

"They have tools—maybe wire cutters—sticks, machetes, stuff like that." As he spoke, the weapons he named appeared in Kilgore's vision, suddenly visible in the weak light that reached up the hill from the siding.

"Holy shit," Kilgore said. "Holy fucking shit." He stood up and turned around, looking for Leonard or one of his lieutenants. The sudden movement sent his balance spinning, shifting the narrow perch of flat car deck he had available, and he avoided falling only by grabbing Wilson.

"First Sergeant," Kilgore called.

"Right here, sir."

Leonard was practically at his feet, quite a long, dizzying way down, it seemed to Kilgore. He paused, had time to think how lucky he was to have someone like Leonard. But he could go no further, couldn't find what he wanted to say.

Suddenly he felt Wilson behind him.

"Sir," Wilson said. The same voice that had always annoyed Kilgore now seemed remarkably steady, given the circumstances.

"You want First Sergeant Leonard to call back to squadron headquarters? Let them know we got big trouble brewing?"

Kilgore managed a "Yeah."

He closed his eyes momentarily—bad mistake—the train seemed to lurch under him. The wind that blew from the north, along the line of the tracks, was as sharp as blue ice, but Kilgore's T-shirt and blouse, under his field jacket, were soaked with sweat.

The bottles came in a tight pattern, flickering like renegade lights in the bright yard. Two of them smashed onto the deck of the tank where Wilson and Kilgore stood, spraying their backs harmlessly. But the third struck Wilson on the back of the head, just at the edge of his cap. He went down quickly, quietly, first to the bed of the rail car, then down the startling drop to the ground. Kilgore grabbed at him, came up with air, almost fell himself.

Something came alive in the captain, though the nausea and sickness still swirled inside him like a dark whirlwind every time he moved.

"Get that message off, Top," he told Leonard, who was already running for the phone. He steadied himself against the huge steel form next to him as he leaned out into space. Two soldiers were already helping Wilson stand. The lieutenant didn't seem to be hurt badly.

"Here they come, sir."

Kilgore didn't know where the warning came from, but he knew what it meant. He backed along the ledge behind the tank and turned around to face the fence. The two or three dozen skinheads by the fence were pushing the wire mesh, all together, fingers clasped in the steel, and the posts were already rocking loose of their concrete footings. Beyond them, still hidden in the grays and blacks of the middle distance, the larger crowd seemed to be moving too.

Kilgore had time to be surprised. The skinheads were not unlike the gangs that terrorized his own hometown, Los Angeles. Out there, the Crips and the Bloods were not large, centrally controlled organizations, but loose collections of small neighborhood gangs that simply shared a common name. But it looked to him as if the skinheads had organized this protest. There were several hundred people outside the fence, and Kilgore wondered if they would storm the yard. Something big was going on here, something that smacked of organization and planning. How did they know to pick this yard at this time of night?

But Kilgore hadn't the time to entertain his theories. The protestors, moving as one, came down the embankment just outside the fence. As the light caught more and more of them, Kilgore could see that they were armed: sticks and poles stuck out of the mass at weird angles; they heaved rocks, bottles, pieces of brick as they moved; and the whole thing was invested with a bubbling hatred that welled up into a mob voice. The fence before them was already reeling from the combined weight of the demonstrators leaning on it, and it didn't take a genius to see that the larger crowd would be able to push right through.

They yelled as they moved, a tremendous babble of German slogans and obscenities that rose and fell in threatening, featureless curves. Kilgore could make out "Americans," "war," and something about "the people's choice." His head reeled in a fever, and he had to brace himself against the cold steel tank to keep from falling off the rail car as he looked quickly left and right for some sign of his squadron commander, the *polizei*, someone who could help him defuse this mess.

"Captain."

It was Leonard's voice, and Kilgore turned around slowly, trying not to upset the feverish demons at war within him.

The first sergeant was holding a rifle, muzzle up, magazine locked into place.

"We have twenty men with rifles and a hundred rounds apiece down here," he said. "Enough to fight them off if we need to."

Kilgore swayed, felt his head and shoulders moving in a loose ellipse while his feet remained fixed to the car bed. He had a sudden vision of how ridiculous this was: almost delirious with fever, he was about to decide when to start shooting at a bunch of civilian thugs.

"Come up here," he told Leonard.

The big man climbed easily onto the rail car and stood beside Kilgore, the weapon at high port across his chest.

"We don't even know if they're armed," Kilgore said so that only the first sergeant could hear.

"Looks to me like they're about to bust down that fence, sir," Leonard insisted. "If they come pouring through, they might just beat these soldiers to death." Having said that, he looked hard at Kilgore, as if to say, *You going to let that happen?*

Kilgore had a hard time focusing. Leonard, who was close by, seemed even bigger than he normally did. The captain was vaguely aware that the soldiers, waiting in the shelter offered by the rail cars, were watching him. On the other side of the tracks, Kilgore could hear the protesting screech of the steel fence posts as they bent under the combined weight of hundreds of people.

"Give me that," Kilgore said, reaching for the rifle.

Leonard handed it over, and Kilgore aimed it well above the heads of the crowd.

"What are you planning, Captain?" Leonard asked calmly.

"Warning shots," Kilgore answered. But he was having trouble holding the rifle still. The barrel seemed inordinately heavy, and though he pulled the butt of the weapon tight against his shoulder, it still had a mind of its own as it swayed: now up at the stars, now dangerously lower.

"Better let me do that, sir," Leonard said. He took the rifle gently from his commander, then sidled out from behind the tank. "Just a few shots above their heads. Right, Captain?"

Kilgore nodded. "Careful, now. Wait until I give you the word," he said.

Leonard spread his feet, posed as if he were in a funeral honor guard, muzzle up at forty-five degrees, elbow cocked, face pressed close to the stock, waiting for Kilgore to say when. He was clearly visible, in the yellow glowing lights of the yard, to anyone in the crowd who looked up.

Kilgore blinked heavily, his eyelids moving in liquid slowness. The fence had given way in two places, and the more eager youths were scrambling up the shallow incline formed by the toppled barrier, pushing against one another to be first into the yard. Behind them, others brandished sticks and clubs. Somewhere in the back of Kilgore's fever-addled brain, a small voice warned him that he was in no condition to make such a decision.

The fence gave way with a sad groan. Two youths in sneakers and jean jackets were already running for the cars; one of them held a length of pipe. It was clear to Kilgore that they weren't going to stop at the tanks— they were going after the soldiers on the other side of the train.

"Fire," Kilgore said.

The report sounded small against the crowd noise. Kilgore looked over at the First Sergeant, who fired another burst into the air. But the rush came on.

There were young kids—and Kilgore's mind framed it just that way: these are just kids—all around the train now. A tall, dirty-looking youth in a leather vest had hold of Kilgore's foot, and the captain grabbed the fender behind him. As he did so, he turned to see Leonard, his rifle lowered, get hit with a flurry of rocks and bricks. The big soldier fell to his hands and knees on the thin shelf of rail car available to them.

"Top," Kilgore screamed. "Top!"

Leonard was only a few feet away, but there were three or four sets of hands between the men, and as Kilgore fought to keep his balance, some of the hands grabbed the big NCO's jacket and pulled him to the ground. Kilgore saw, in a few seconds that would be with him the rest of his life, one of the men on the ground draw a pistol and aim at Leonard's head. There was no sound above the screaming and uproar, but the pistol jumped in the shooter's hand, and a sudden spray of white smoke twisted out into the garish light.

Kilgore's feet were off the bed, and he kept from falling into the crowd by grabbing the loading chain that ran tight across the nearest tank. He felt hands on his legs, pulling him down into the chaos below him, pulling him down to where Leonard now lay, and Kilgore knew something that wasn't quite fear—it was a rejection of the mob's will. He wouldn't be pulled down.

He began to kick frantically with his big tanker's boots. He felt at least two of his thrusts find targets, and some of the hands gave way. He glanced over his shoulder—the man with the small handgun was behind him, drawing a bead on Kilgore's back. The captain tried to kick backward, but the shooter was out of reach. He let go the chain and dropped to the ground just as the first round *twanged* off the steel hull above him. Then the kicks came at him before he could gain his feet, two of them to his face. One eyebrow split open immediately, drawing a thick curtain of blood over his left eye.

Then the air above him tore open with the steel bright stabs of fire and light as his troopers, standing now on the decks of the tanks, opened fire on the crowd inside the fence.

Kilgore felt as if his head had been split, and he rolled over, pressing both hands to his ears. He heard the screams, and even as he felt the relief of knowing that he wasn't going to die at the hands of this mob, there was the unmistakable terror of knowing that there was at least one dead trooper, if not dead civilians, and that his mission had become even more complex.

20

TWO MORE SPECIAL FORCES TEAMS JOINED ISEN'S RANGERS AT Karlshofen before ten o'clock in the morning, two more sets of communications equipment to tie the surrounded GIs in with the outside world. One HALO team had been inserted just as Fitzsimmons team had been the night before. The other drove through the haphazard GPU roadblocks in a farmer's truck purchased by a particularly ballsy Master Sergeant who spoke German with the Prussian accent he learned from his German-born mother.

Isen and his operations officer, a captain named Norden who'd been Isen's assistant until Isen took the battalion, started receiving instructions from the planning cell back at Fort Bragg as soon as the Green Beret commo specialists got the sets up.

"They're bringing in a shitload of stuff," Norden said as he read from his notebook. "I guess somebody finally decided to do *something.*"

Although they had the capability to receive hard copies of the orders over the field equivalent of a fax machine, they had opted to receive the order verbally, over a scrambled signal, and to write down only a few facts that wouldn't mean anything if the notes fell into enemy hands.

"Both the other batts will come in first," Norden told Isen. "Followed by two brigades of the Eighty-second. And that's just the guys jumping in tonight. We're supposed to link up with the Marines and the cavalry, too. There'll be Special Forces teams inserted to keep an eye on GPU movement and help our guys pick the best routes."

Norden looked up from his book to see Isen standing above him, absorbed in his own notes. The major held his notebook open against his map and seemed to be consulting both sheets at once.

"You hear all that, sir?" Norden asked.

Isen didn't respond to the question, but the silence following caught his attention.

"What's that, Ron?" Isen asked.

"We'll have a lot of help here after dark," Norden said.

Isen nodded and went back to his notes. *Yeah, feast or famine.* "You get these points down correctly?" he asked Norden.

The captain stood up and looked over Isen's shoulder. The commander was reading Norden's notes on paragraph one of the order: enemy situation.

"Yessir," Norden said. "Far as I know. Something wrong?"

Nothing was wrong with the notes, Isen thought, nothing that he could see. But there was something that rested uneasy with him.

"They plotted the location of that cav unit, which is supposedly on its way north. And they even gave me a reading on the Marine battalion that's supposed to come ashore," Isen said. "But they only plotted one, no, two battalions of the GPU."

Norden wasn't following. "Yessir?"

"So that could mean a couple of things," Isen said, still studying the notes and map in his hands. Norden waited. When Isen looked up and saw the question there, he wondered if he should speculate in front of his subordinates. No sense in alarming Norden unnecessarily. Then he wondered if Spano had ever had those thoughts, if he'd ever kept anything from Isen because he thought Isen too junior, too inexperienced. He shook his head quickly to clear it.

"Where's Colonel Schauffert?" Isen asked.

"I believe he's over at the aid station, sir," Norden answered.

"Okay," Isen said. "You keep taking this down while I go talk to the old man." With that, he turned away toward the house the Rangers had commandeered for their wounded. When he found the colonel, Schauffert was bent over a wounded Ranger who'd slipped into a coma. The youngster had been shot at close range with a large-caliber weapon. Black, dried blood caked his throat and what was visible of his face.

"Sir," Isen interrupted. "Can I talk to you a second?"

Isen asked Schauffert about the dearth of information on GPU dispositions in the surrounding countryside. For the briefest of seconds, Schauffert looked uncomfortable. Then he stood, buckled his pistol belt and led Isen outside.

"It wouldn't be good security to give you a detailed picture," Schauffert said crisply. "You were told what you need to know. As for the rest, well, the fewer people who know how much we know—and how we came to know it—the better."

It was clear to Isen that he wasn't supposed to pursue this line of questioning. He looked down at the map in his hand. He'd made no marks on it—he'd learned that much about operational security when he was an ROTC cadet. Now, at his level, he knew that there was a lot of information that was kept from people because they didn't need to know.

Isen had, on more than one occasion, left subordinates ignorant because there was no compelling reason for them to be let in on some aspect of a plan. And with the GPU still around the town, there was a chance that Isen's notes could fall into enemy hands. He knew all that, and at another time, when he wasn't so exhausted, so frightened and beat up, he would have been able to agree with it. He would have answered Schauffert with a crisp "Yes, sir," turned on his heel and walked away.

But this wasn't one of those times.

Isen had been kept in the dark since he discovered that he couldn't make contact with the Bundeswehr controllers who were supposed to have been on the ground when he first jumped. Now, with Spano gone, he was responsible for the safety of these several hundred men, and he was tired of not being privy to decisions that might affect whether or not he could keep them alive.

Isen stood his ground, looked back into Schauffert's eyes.

"What is it, Mark?" Schauffert asked. But he knew precisely what the problem was.

"What's going on out there, sir?" Isen asked.

"You have the plan, Mark," Schauffert said evenly.

"So where's all the rest of the bad guys?" Isen said. In spite of his best efforts, he felt anger twisting loose inside him. "You expect me to believe that these are the only GPU units we're able to plot?"

Schauffert looked surprised, but Isen—assuming it was an act—became angrier, his rage fueled by the waste of men he cared for. "You expect me to believe that the whole fucking country over here has been turned on its head by two renegade battalions?"

Schauffert felt the anger rush up on him as if a dam had broken. All his life, whenever someone shoved him with one hand, Schauffert shoved back with two, then followed with a right cross. He was about to ask Isen just who the hell he thought he was talking to when someone bumped into him from the rear.

"Sorry, sir."

It was one of the medics, walking backward and holding up one end of a makeshift stretcher, a poncho slung between wooden garden stakes.

Slumped in the deep well of the stretcher was the comatose soldier Schauffert had been talking to some moments before.

"We thought it would be a good idea to move the dead out of there," the medic explained to Isen and Schauffert as he and his partner squeezed by with their burden. "It would bring down the wounded guys—the ones who can make it."

When the medics were gone, Isen and Schauffert were left face-to-face again, and Schauffert had had time to realize that he needed Isen.

"There are more formations out there," Schauffert said. "But the satellite shots aren't much good in helping us determine which are GPU and which are Bundeswehr."

"Can't Berlin tell us?" Isen said. His voice still had enough of an edge to call the question a demand.

"Information from Berlin is suspect," Schauffert said. He looked down at the ground, shifted his weight from one foot to the other.

"Somebody ambushed their Chief of Staff day before yesterday," Schauffert said. "Their security people think the leak is in their signals branch. The Joint Chiefs want us to verify everything we hear from German sources."

"Is it possible that their military is split? That some people support this GPU?"

"We don't know that for sure yet, Mark," Schauffert said. "But it looks like that may be the case to some extent."

"And the worst case scenario?" Isen asked.

But the question was rhetorical. Both men knew that if a large enough share of the German military decided to side with the GPU, Isen's command would be lost, the Firefall forces swallowed up.

"Look, Mark," Schauffert said. "I can understand how you feel. But believe me, I didn't jump in here to become a martyr." He paused, wondering how much of the broader plan he should confide in Isen.

"This could be a turning point in modern history, Mark," Schauffert said. "There's a power vacuum here in Europe, and pretty much throughout the rest of the world. No one can stand up to us, but if we're going to be in charge, we have to have the guts to take charge."

Isen was confused. He looked around. "Is that how you see this?" he asked. "As an opportunity?"

Schauffert considered his answer. *This is our chance to bring American power back to the continent, to seize the reins,* he wanted to say.

"This was an accident," he said. "Look, I have confidence in this plan, and I was willing to bet my life that I'll be commanding all three battalions from right here on the ground within the next eighteen hours."

Isen was barely mollified. "Right, sir," he said.

As Isen contemplated the forces that might be arrayed against him, the impressive Firefall plan suddenly seemed inadequate, and he began to think that Schauffert might just be the lunatic some people maintained that he was. But there was little he could do now except prepare for his role.

"I guess all we can do now is continue to march," Isen said.

Tim Brennan stumbled along behind the other men in the patrol, his face down, lifting his knees and watching the small bow waves of snow pushed out in front of his feet as he moved forward. Ever since Charis was wounded, he'd felt as if he'd had the wind knocked out of him. There was an empty feeling of uselessness centered somewhere below his sternum, a fear that he'd fuck up again, get someone else shot.

Click.

The man in front of him had snapped his fingers at Brennan, who looked up slowly.

Got to pay attention, he thought.

The other Ranger was tapping his head, asking for a count. Brennan passed the signal back, and a few moments later the count came up from the last guy. The man behind Brennan closed in on him, tapped him on the butt, and said, "Six."

Brennan lengthened his stride and closed on the man ahead. "Seven," he said.

The count was coming up from the rear, where Sergeant Bishop was located, to the front, where Lieutenant Hawkins was. Hawkins's mission was to find out what the GPU was up to over by the airfield. There had been some discussion, among the NCOs, as to how big the patrol should be. Bishop wanted to take just a few men with him, since it was broad daylight. Hawkins, who was more concerned about having the firepower to get out of a scrape, decided to take the bigger group.

Bishop had organized two teams for the patrol, and each team moved in a wedge-shaped formation. Brennan, point man for the second team, walked between and just behind the two men at the rear of the lead wedge.

The woods here were thick with stunted pine and oak trees, and the men kept a good distance between them. Brennan was supposed to watch the two men in front of him for whatever signals they might pass. Instead, he was looking down, replaying in his head everything that had happened back at the house to see if there was anything he might have done differently, something that might have changed the outcome.

Something rustled in front of him. He looked up to see another Ranger moving toward him.

"Pay attention, man," the soldier whispered emphatically. He was holding his hand up for a halt.

Brennan put his hand up quickly, then looked around to see if his team had become mixed in with the lead element because of his daydreaming.

Just as he knelt, another signal came back. The men in front of him were making slashing signs across their throats.

Danger area.

Brennan passed the signal back, then got to his feet. He'd practiced this drill—crossing a danger area—hundreds of times since he'd been in the battalion, but he'd never done it for real, with the possibility of someone shooting at him. Still, he knew his practiced role and didn't hesitate.

He moved forward and soon found Hawkins, then knelt beside the lieutenant as two other men from the rear team crossed the danger area—a wide firebreak in the woods, to check the other side. The narrow open space ran off in either direction like a white-carpeted aisle. Hawkins, who was busy studying the far side, didn't notice who was beside him until he turned to give Brennan the signal to cross. Hawkins started to speak, stopped when he saw who it was, blinked heavily, opened his mouth again.

He thinks I can't handle it, Brennan thought. *He thinks I fucked up and got Charis shot, and now I'm going to fuck this up, too.*

Brennan narrowed his eyes, forced himself to look away from his lieutenant. It seemed easier now, after the last three days, to hate.

"You OK?" Hawkins asked after a timeless pause of seconds.

If it had been Sergeant Bishop asking, Brennan would have assumed that the comment was sincere. But because it was Hawkins, he assumed the big officer was mocking him.

"You want me to cross now, sir?" Brennan asked, gesturing to the far side.

Hawkins hesitated for the briefest second. "Go," he said.

Brennan began running even before he cleared the few feet of brush between him and the open area. His trail leg caught up and he lost his balance for a few moments, so that his first steps were awkward—face down, arms windmilling in front of him as he struggled to keep his balance and hang on to his weapon. Straightening, he pumped his legs against the pull of the deep snow and made for the other side. He heard the engines just before he entered the sheltering woods.

Brennan threw himself into the brush, arms and legs flailing to turn him around for a look at what was behind him. About two hundred meters down the firebreak, a lone Marder had backed up into the open and was now moving away from the Rangers. Brennan looked across to where Hawkins was glued in place. When the Marder stopped, it backed into the treeline until only its twenty-millimeter gun was visible, poking out from the black trees. Brennan looked at his lieutenant, but Hawkins's face was blank.

Brennan shrugged his shoulders, miming a request for instructions. *C'mon, lieutenant, what the fuck do I do now?*

Hawkins had the familiar sensation he encountered when he had too many things to think about—like a juggler who suddenly realized he had too many balls in the air at once.

He reached for the radio handset and began composing a situation report in his head. But he didn't know how many Marders there were, nor what they were up to. He looked around for the Rangers carrying the AT-4s, the modest antiarmor weapons that would be their only defense if the Marders charged them. As he took the handset, he spotted Brennan across the way, looking at him quizzically.

Shit. I've got to get those guys back over here on this side, too, he realized.

He began to signal to Brennan, waving the handset around above his head. But then he wasn't sure if Brennan should try to run back or not. Where were the other two guys who were already across the road? Brennan had to collect them, too. How far into the woods had they gotten? How long had it been since he'd sent them across? Then there was that Marder, its gun pointing out into the trail like a black beak. He'd seen what the twenty-millimeter rounds could do against a building at the airfield. Now he worried about those same rounds ripping through the bush surrounding him. He inched away from the clearing.

Shit, shit, shit, he chanted to himself.

"What you got, sir?"

It was Sergeant Bishop, who'd come up from the rear, just as he was supposed to at a halt.

"I've got at least one Marder down there." Hawkins gestured, still moving backward. "Don't know what he's up to yet."

"You got men across the way?"

"Right," Hawkins said. He waited, knowing that Bishop would offer something.

The sergeant stood up to see over the brush to where Brennan knelt in the spotty cover. Bishop seemed unafraid. Hawkins was about to warn him about the Marder, about to tell him to get down, when the NCO spoke.

"We need to get those guys back over here before we take a closer look at our friends down the trail," Bishop said. "If something goes down, they're out of luck over there."

"Right," Hawkins said. He'd found his way into a shallow depression and was stretched out there now. "You bring them back over here while I call in a sitrep," Hawkins said.

Bishop wasted only one glance at his lieutenant, then stepped forward to where he could see Brennan.

Captain Dettering wanted more information. He told Hawkins to move closer to the Marder and try to determine what it was up to. Hawkins acknowledged the order and got off the air. He would have to turn right here, parallel the open track for a short distance before moving deeper into the woods to come at the Marder from the rear, its blind side.

He wanted to move quickly, but his assistant patrol leader, Sergeant Bishop, was off trying to recover the far-side security teams. Hawkins got to his knees and peered through the undergrowth. Though he was less than twenty meters away, there was nothing visible of the clearing. Hawkins inched forward, glanced to his right where he knew the Marder sat, waiting for a target.

When he looked up again, he saw a figure running toward him. It was one of the security men from the other side.

"Who's still over there?" Hawkins asked.

"Brennan and Sergeant Bishop," the soldier replied. "My partner is already over here again." He looked tremendously relieved, Hawkins thought, to be back with this tiny group.

The rifle shots jarred Hawkins, who rolled over onto his stomach as if someone were shooting at him.

"They're on the other side of the clearing," his radio operator told him.

Hawkins recognized the next shots—a group of three—as coming from an M16A2. But they were answered by fire from unfamiliar weapons.

Hawkins hesitated, watched for Brennan and Bishop, but all he could hear were excited voices coming from where they'd seen the Marder.

"Get ready to move out," he told his two team leaders.

"We're short two men, sir," one of the sergeants said.

Hawkins turned on him. "I *know* that," he said.

He was angry because he knew what he had to do. Hawkins got up, still stooped over so as to make a smaller target, and began to move to the edge of the clearing.

"Over here. Over *here*."

It was Brennan, crouched close on Hawkins's side of the firebreak. Apparently he'd just dashed across the open area.

"Where's Bishop?" Hawkins asked. His voice seemed about to crack.

"He's over there," Brennan said, gesturing across the way.

"What's he doing over there?" Hawkins asked.

Brennan looked at his lieutenant as if the man had just sprouted wings. "You sent him to get us, remember?" he said coolly.

He turned back to look for some sign of Bishop.

"We ran into a patrol after we sent those other two back," Brennan said. "They shot at us just as we were about to cross. I made it."

The yelling off to the right had increased, and Hawkins was frantic to get out of the area. Worse than that, he heard the Marder's engine start up.

"We've got to get out of here," Hawkins said, trying to control his voice. "That Marder will be coming up here looking for us."

Brennan looked up at Hawkins. "Sergeant Bishop is over there," he said. His face was badly swollen, hard to read, but his voice was calm. "I ain't leaving him."

"Is he alive?" Hawkins wanted to know.

"I don't know," Brennan said. "Might be."

They both heard the sound of the Marder breaking brush as it rolled out of its hiding place some two hundred meters away. Hawkins was standing just behind Brennan, looking down on the much smaller man.

"We'll come back for him," the lieutenant offered lamely.

"Maybe he's hit," Brennan said. "He could be bleeding to death."

"I said we're pulling back," Hawkins countered. "We can't afford to get caught here by that Marder."

As Hawkins became more frantic with the sounds of the approaching machine, Brennan seemed to become more calm. The private turned around to face Hawkins. When they were square, he spoke slowly, in an almost conversational tone. "And I say you're a big fucking coward and a blowhard," he said. "And if you don't want to come with me to get Sergeant Bishop, then fuck you, 'cause I'm going."

And with that, he bolted across the clearing.

Hawkins tensed for the firing he expected Brennan's appearance on the trail to elicit, but the Marder gunner must have been too busy to notice the movement.

Hawkins turned toward where his two teams waited in their small perimeter.

Fuck that punk, he told himself as he ran. *I can't jeopardize everyone for his sake.*

But then he reached his men, who waited solidly, expectantly for orders. Part of him wanted to turn away and clear out of the area. He failed to defeat that voice even as he began giving orders.

"We're moving back up the trail. Get the AT-4s up close," he said, pointing at one of the team leaders. "There's at least one Marder headed this way. Set up a flank shot."

His breath came in shallow drafts, so that his head felt light. If he'd had the time, he might have wondered if these breaths were to be his last.

There was no sign of Brennan or Bishop along the trail, but Hawkins could see where the soldiers had entered the trees on the far side. He glanced down the alley of the firebreak, saw the corner of the Marder as it hid in cover along the trail.

They're coming up slowly, he thought. *Afraid of the shot from the woods.*

But even as he congratulated himself for sending the AT-4s to kill the Marder, he remembered that there were GPU foot soldiers on the far side of the clearing, if not on this side. As if to confirm this, he heard his Rangers exchange shots down near where the Marder was trying to hide.

Still no sign of Brennan.

Shit!

If he waited any longer, the Marder might be on top of him. Certainly the foot soldiers he expected to run into must be close.

In an instant he saw the flash of an AT-4 igniting, then another. A second or two later the Marder exploded, sending an orange ball, cut through with black smoke, rolling up the firebreak.

He looked to his right, saw a sudden movement toward him on his left, and tried to bring his weapon around. Something crashed into him, shoving him into punishing brambles. It was Brennan, with Bishop right behind him. Hawkins stood, too startled to speak.

"They're right on our ass, Lieutenant," Bishop said. He didn't appear to be hurt. "Let's get out of here."

Hawkins signaled his patrol, and the two teams hurried away from the trail. Hawkins waited until his men were clear; then, to Bishop and Brennan, he said, "Let's go."

The three men ran from the trail, a reckless, almost frantic romp that sent them colliding into trees, twisting their ankles, scraping themselves on low branches. But they didn't slow down, except to fall.

"You hurt?" Hawkins managed to say in Bishop's direction.

"No," the sergeant answered, panting. "I went down to see what our friends were up to."

He stopped talking, struggled to catch his breath without losing his gait. "I think they're marshaling there at the end of the trail. I saw at least three Marders, besides the one you hit."

Hawkins formed another question: *For an attack? They're marshaling for an attack?* But he couldn't find the wind, and in a moment he realized that the question didn't need to be answered.

Of course for an attack.

Mark Isen and Tommy Chang, the Air Force liaison, knelt side by side in the snow just behind Alpha Company's position. They each held a handset, though they were on different frequencies, and they worked like translators. Isen received the input from his GIs as to where the GPU was marshaling, then showed Chang, on the map and by hand signals, what he wanted. Chang, in turn, translated this into orders for the Air Force planes that were back on call to support the Rangers.

"What's their ETA?" Isen asked, checking his watch. It had been three minutes since he'd gotten the call about the Marders marshaling between the airfield and the town.

"Fast movers in two, two and a half minutes," Chang answered. "Specter will come in behind those guys."

"What good are the fast movers going to do us?" Isen wanted to know. "The targets are too fucking close." He knew he was punishing the messenger, but he was tired of the lack of support and frightened at the prospect of another mounted attack against his beleaguered troops.

Chang had no answer for him, so he turned back to his own command net to try to find out what he could about the GPU. The Charlie Company patrol was already back in—they'd been shot at and had destroyed one Marder and located three more. But now Isen had no one in visual contact with the enemy, and so couldn't tell what they were up to.

"Let's go," he told Chang. The Air Force officer and his RTOs, along with Isen's retinue, all saddled up immediately to follow the battalion commander. "We're going down to get a look at this mess."

The fast movers cracked open the sky before Isen reached his forward-most position. The two flights of three planes each then stood on their wingtips just above the horizon, where Isen could still see, and circled about for another pass.

"They can't acquire the targets," Chang told Isen. "But they're flying over to shake up the bad guys, maybe throw things off if they're preparing an attack."

Isen brought his group to the intersection at the east end of town, where he found cover on the walled-in playground of a school. On the paved road headed east, Bravo Company had set up its ambushes. A narrower road running almost due south was marked with a low, pointed sign: *Flugplatz.* Airfield.

Isen sent a runner to let Colonel Schauffert know where he was, and another to round up Captain Dettering and Lieutenant Hawkins.

"Three minutes until Specter is on station," Chang said.

Isen looked at his watch again. They'd been on the ground four days, and every emergency came down to how things would align themselves over a period of a few minutes. Specter might be a few minutes early or a few minutes late. The Rangers had started their move from the airfield a few minutes after the major GPU ground assault, and that meant that his Charlie Company had lost a platoon's worth of men killed and wounded. It would take a couple of Marders only a few minutes to work their way through his position here, scattering whatever troops it didn't kill. He couldn't get that scenario out of his mind, and the pictures his subconscious drew only served to push him closer to the edge. Four days without being rescued. He felt like killing someone.

"Sir."

It was Dettering, the Charlie Company commander, and Hawkins.

"Lieutenant Hawkins had the patrol that ran into that Marder," Dettering said.

"*That* Marder?" Isen said hopefully. "You mean there was only one?"

"No, sir," Hawkins answered. "We only ran into one. Sergeant Bishop saw at least three more in the woods between here and the airfield. He thought they were moving forward."

Isen studied this junior officer. Hawkins had probably lost ten pounds since they'd jumped in here. These things were always hardest on the big men, Isen knew. The best men for hard soldiering were the wiry little guys with the rubber band muscles who seemed barely big enough to carry everything they had to hump. Those were the ones who surprised, who kept going when other people were dropping out. Hawkins didn't look so good.

"You OK, Hawkins?" Isen asked.

"Fine, sir."

Right, Isen thought. But he didn't have the time to go into it now.

"Specter on target," Chang said. He covered the mouthpiece of the handset with one hand and addressed Hawkins. "How far north of the airfield were those vehicles?"

"Just two, three hundred meters," Hawkins said.

Isen turned away from his subordinates and tried to watch the sky, but the trees here in the town were too tall, and the only patch of blue he saw was directly overhead. But then there was the sound.

"Yes," Dettering said.

Isen felt a sense of relief so palpable that he thought it must have been visible to anyone looking at him. It was as if a big friend had just stepped in between him and the meanest bully on the playground. Since he couldn't see anything above, he watched Chang's face.

"Target identified," Chang said. He was listening to the reports from the Specter's weapons crew.

The great ripping sound was closer than Isen had ever heard it, and he and the others reacted immediately. In an instant, they were all spitting dirt out of their mouths as they lay belly flat in the churned-up mud and melted snow.

It was finally Chang's turn for grandstanding.

"Scratch one Marder," he said.

"I wish we had some way to pick out the other targets," Isen said.

"Shit," Chang said, pressing the handset closer to his ear. "Oh, god-damn."

Isen suddenly felt exposed. He didn't know what was troubling Chang, but he didn't want anything going wrong while the big Air Force weapons platform was pumping out thousands of rounds a minute so close to where his troops lay under flimsy cover.

"What's the matter?" Isen asked.

"Three bogies . . . three bogies up above," Chang answered. He was trying to listen in on the Specter's transmissions and communicate with Isen without missing anything. He breathed out, relaxed his grip on the handset. "They've identified themselves as Luftwaffe."

Now it was Isen's turn to be frightened, remembering what Schauffert had said about being suspicious of anything they got from the regular German forces. He looked up, still couldn't see anything.

"Pass the word along for everyone to get under some overhead cover," Isen told his RTOs.

Chang saw immediately what Isen meant.

"The Germans are friendlies, sir," he said carefully, as if Isen had merely missed his first message.

"What makes you so sure?" Isen said. He was looking about for overhead cover, finally decided to crouch as close as possible to the high brick wall in the corner of the yard.

"The Specter is staying on station."

"So?"

"Well," Chang continued, unsure, a little unnerved. "Someone must have coordinated with the Germans before we took on this mission . . . don't you think?"

"I don't know what the hell to think anymore," Isen said as he tried to make himself as small as possible in the shadow of the wall.

They waited without speaking as the sounds of the approaching jets became apparent. The machines passed directly overhead, shaking everything in the village.

"Specter is leaving station," Chang said after a few more moments of listening.

"That's just fucking great," Isen said.

They could hear the jets pull around again somewhere to the south, but they still couldn't see anything. It was like listening to giants wrestle on the floor above: you knew they were there, but you couldn't tell who was doing what.

"Where's our air cover?" Isen asked. The slow-moving, vulnerable Specter always had some fighters around to protect it.

"Moving into position," Chang said.

Isen thought about the German pilots, the regulars who flew the top caliber jets. Could the GPU have gotten to some of those guys? As he fretted, he stared at a black-edged shell hole on the other side of the schoolyard, the result of one of the mortar rounds the GPU had lobbed into this little town—this little German town. Isen decided he didn't like the answer he came up with about the Luftwaffe.

"Anything?" he asked Chang.

The Air Force captain shook his head. Isen waited another thirty seconds, then stood up.

The *swish boom* of the rockets was obviously pretty far off, but the noise sent Isen to the ground again. He lifted his helmet off the bridge of his nose and raised his head in time to hear several jets kick into full throttle.

"Lost contact with Specter," Chang said. He lowered the handset, which slipped from his grasp so that he held only the coiled wire. He gave Isen a look that read something like, *We're fucked, aren't we?*

Isen wanted to put his head down, wanted to sleep through this next problem and have someone wake him up when it was time to get his men on an aircraft headed west. He lowered his head until the leading edge of his helmet pressed into the muddy snow in front of his face. Then he sucked in a long breath and rolled over, away from the wall and onto his back.

"That certainly does change things," he said to the blue circle of sky above him.

Colonel Schauffert found him like that. Flat out.

"You OK, Mark?"

Isen sat up. "Sounds like some Luftwaffe jets took a shot at Specter, sir," Isen said in reply. "So I guess the answer to your question is no."

Isen felt the anger return; he was holding Schauffert responsible for their being abandoned.

"Sir, what the hell is going on out there? Why doesn't somebody come and get us out of here?"

They'd been over this before, of course, and Isen suspected that he had all the answers he was going to get, perhaps all the answers that Schauffert knew. The United States wanted to give Berlin latitude in handling what was, for the most part, a domestic crisis, no one wanted to react with too much force, blah, blah, blah.

But Isen had had enough.

"What are we supposed to do if those jets come back to start hammering us?" Isen asked, his voice rising, unmistakably, in fear and anger. "When is Washington going to decide that this is serious over here? When I've lost half my command? When we're all dead?"

Isen looked around. Chang was staring at the ground in embarrassment. The radio operators were less circumspect—they were watching to see what would happen as this major, their major, challenged the colonel.

Schauffert turned and walked toward the school building. "Follow me," he said.

When he and Isen turned the corner, they were as alone as they were going to get in the crowded perimeter. Schauffert stepped up to the major, so close that he could see the dirt ground into Isen's face, into the tiny lines engraved beside his eyes, his chapped lips.

"Let me tell you something, Major," Schauffert began. "This situation is going to get worse before it gets better, and I need somebody in command here who is ready to handle that."

Isen didn't flinch. If anything, the physical confrontation of Schauffert's approach fueled his anger. "That's my whole point," he said. "It doesn't have to get worse. You can't stand there and tell me that the Army, the Air Force, somebody, can't come in here and get us out. I'm sick of hearing about limiting the use of force. Do you think those motherfuckers out there limited the use of force when they tried to overrun us down at the airfield? Huh? Ask that kid back in the fucking aid station if the twenty-millimeter round that took off his hand had limited force behind it."

His voice had rolled up some dangerous slope; there was spittle on his lips, and he thought he might be shouting, but the anger filled his head, his hearing, left him with no sensation other than rage and the feeling that he might slug Schauffert.

"You afraid?" Schauffert asked.

Something broke in Isen. He pulled his pistol from its holster, saw Schauffert flinch slightly as he waved it in the air.

"I'm not fucking afraid," he screamed. "You want to go out there? You want to charge the fucking Marders? Come on . . . come on."

Isen could feel the tendons in his neck, the tightness of muscle in his face as he shouted at Schauffert. He stepped toward the road and was ready to run down it at the German positions . . . all just to make a point. "I'm not afraid, Colonel. I'm sick to fucking death about being left out here, about being kept in the dark."

And that was it. The anger rolled off of him, off of his head and shoulders, off of his upraised arm and out of the black pistol that was an extension of his hand. His voice came down to a recognizable pitch. "I'm sick to fucking death of my guys dying when they don't have to . . . that's all."

Isen slumped down in the snow, sitting now, legs curled under him, ankle twisted painfully to one side. If he'd had the energy, he might have wept.

Schauffert walked over to him.

"You want to help your men?" he asked, pausing for one beat, two. "Get up and be the commander they need."

Isen sat, head down, snot and spit running from his nose and mouth. His anger was gone, and he was left empty. Where would he get the strength to fill the void? He listened to Schauffert's receding footsteps.

Maybe the fucker is right. There's nothing to do but go on.

In a moment, he pulled himself up from the ground and walked toward his command.

21
· · · · · · · · · · · ·

NO ONE LOOKED AT MARK ISEN AS HE WALKED UP ON HIS command group, and that confirmed for him that they had all heard his outburst.

"We just got word from EUCOM that those were Luftwaffe jets that shot down that Specter," Chang said when Isen joined the group.

None of them, from the captains to the privates who carried the radios, missed the significance of this pronouncement. They all wore hang-dog looks, they all watched Isen for his reaction.

I guess they think I'm going to freak out again, Isen thought.

John Taylor, Alpha Company's commander, broke the silence.

"Whatever Marders weren't taken out by Specter must have pulled back. We went out and looked; Specter killed one."

Ronny Norden, the operations officer, took a few steps toward Isen, hesitated, stood holding his map before him awkwardly, like a child with a bad test paper. "Sir," he said tentatively.

"What is it, Ron?" Isen said. His voice, at least as far as he could tell, was even again.

"We got more bad news here," he said. "Colonel Schauffert's guys are trying to get an independent confirmation on this message."

Norden placed his map flat on the top of one of the climbing toys that dotted the playground. The large-scale map sheet covered a good portion of northwest Germany; at its center was the city of Hamburg, which lay some eighty kilometers east of Karlshofen. There were two red rectangles marked on the acetate overlay. The center of one bore the simple X that denoted an infantry formation, the other had the oval—mimicking a tank tread—and the single corner-to-corner slash that meant cavalry. The top of each symbol, where the formation size should have been marked, was blank.

"Red?" Isen asked.

"Yessir," Norden said.

Enemy formations.

"I wondered how long it would take them to send reinforcements here," Isen said. "Any idea how big these are?"

"Two or three battalions here," Norden said, pointing to the infantry marker. "Maybe more. We're working off satellite stuff; the air force hasn't done a low-level flyover yet."

"And they might not," Isen interrupted him.

"Sir?"

"Never mind," Isen said. "How long before they reach here?"

"Nightfall," Norden said. "Four hours, five at the outside. Most of them are on foot, but they do have some transport."

"What about this one?" Isen asked, poking the map with his finger on the red cavalry symbol.

The answer came from behind him. "That's the big problem, right there." It was Colonel Schauffert. Isen turned around to see his boss, followed by his radio operators, join the little command group.

"That's a Bundeswehr armor formation . . . er, a reinforced battalion, sent out yesterday from Magdeburg."

"Good guys or bad guys?" Isen asked.

"Nobody seems to know," Schauffert said. "Their marching orders were to get here and pound the GPU. But that was yesterday. Since then, the commander has dropped off the net. He refuses to respond to radio messages from his superiors. As far as Berlin can tell, he isn't talking to the GPU, either; he's not in radio contact with anybody. Complete silence."

"Doesn't sound very friendly to me," Isen said. "Why would he refuse to respond to Berlin if he was a good guy?"

"Remember I told you about their Chief of Staff getting ambushed?" Schauffert said. "Turns out the security leak was in signals, as they suspected. A few of the big communications honchos in Berlin had turned on the government and—apparently—were in on the plot to kill the heads of services who didn't come over to the GPU."

Isen looked up. "I guess the head of the air force is safe for a while."

"We don't know that the whole Luftwaffe has gone bad, Mark," Schauffert said. "The whole problem with this is we don't know how far the fascists have gotten in their attempts to recruit people."

"So we have an infantry formation and an armor formation bearing down on us, and we don't know who's the enemy and who's not?"

"No," Schauffert said. "We do know the infantry units are GPU. We don't know about the armor formation."

"Clever move on their part," Isen said.

"What's that?"

"Well, if the armor commander can keep everybody guessing as to which side he's on, then he's pretty much safe from attack by our Air Force."

"That's one way of looking at it," Schauffert said.

"Is there another way?" Isen asked, trying to keep the sarcasm out of his voice. *Schauffert isn't the enemy*, he told himself again.

"Could be that the armor commander is afraid he'll get bad orders from Berlin. If he comes out here and finds the GPU and they fight, he can't go wrong by far if he takes them on."

Isen was tired of the argument. Finally, there was no answer he could provide. Perhaps someone could force the armor commander to show his hand, but it wouldn't be Mark Isen and his ragged battalion.

"If this infantry formation gets here before dark, they could occupy the drop zones," Isen said.

"I'm sure that's their plan," Schauffert said.

"And there goes Firefall," Isen said.

Schauffert didn't answer.

All of these concerns belonged to the colonel, of course, who was busy planning how to bring all the forces to bear at the critical place. But plans weren't enough. The airborne assault might still go off as planned, but the Rangers would be jumping directly onto the heads of a large formation of combat troops. If the GPU won the race to Karlshofen, chances were good that there would be another delay in the relief.

And that would be a disaster for Isen's men.

"Anything out there that can stop that armored unit?" Isen asked Schauffert.

"There's a U.S. Cav unit coming up by train from the south," Schauffert said. "We might be able to redirect them, have them intercept that column."

"What about stopping this?" Isen asked, pointing to the infantry marker on Norden's map, which was the closest red symbol to the American position.

"We've got nothing else available," Schauffert said. "Our other two battalions of Rangers are on tap for a drop time tonight . . . we can't get here any sooner."

"And the Air Force?" Isen asked.

"They'll be protecting the drop planes," Schauffert said haltingly. "And besides, Berlin is still hollering that they can handle it."

"If Washington listens to that bullshit, after what happened to Specter. . . ." Isen gave up on that tack, turned to study the map. The GPU
troops, if they were fresh, could close in on Karlshofen in a matter of
hours, maybe an hour or so before nightfall. Isen knew, as did all paratroopers, the fear of jumping onto something completely unexpected. It
had happened to the British, in World War II's Operation Market Garden,
just a few hundred kilometers from where Isen stood. A huge airborne
assault had landed right on the heads of a German Panzer division that
just wasn't supposed to be there . . . with predictable results.

When Isen looked up, Schauffert was watching him. The old man was
thinking the same thing Isen was, but was waiting for Isen to say it.

"So it's just us, right?" Isen said.

Schauffert nodded.

"Ron," Isen said to his operations officer. "We've got to come up with
a plan here."

"To defend against that approaching column, sir?" the operations officer asked.

"No," he said, feeling a little light-headed. "We're too weak to defend,
and that's not something we do well anyway." Isen looked up at Norden,
felt Schauffert's measuring eyes on him. "We're going to attack."

Mark Isen lay on his stomach amid the melting snow and the scraps of
pine branches that had been shaken—or shot—loose in Charlie Company's fight in the woods. Isen and the fifteen men from Bravo Company
that made up this combat patrol had moved south from the town, past the
shattered hulk of the Marder destroyed by the Specter, through the scrub
woods north of the airfield that was their original drop zone, to a point
from which Isen and Captain Wisneiwski could observe the administration building at the *flugplatz*.

"You were right, sir," Wisneiwski said. "They're hanging out near that
building."

Isen had guessed, rightly, that at least some of the GPU forces still in
contact would be around the airfield. The Panzergrenadiers wouldn't
want to be separated from their vehicles, Isen reasoned, which was why
there was only a two-man observation post in the woods the Americans
had just passed through. The Bravo Company Rangers had dispatched
the isolated GPU soldiers noiselessly. A patrol Isen had sent east had
found no sign of any mounted GPU troops—Bravo Company had made
that approach too dangerous. Whatever was left of the GPU formations
facing them had disappeared, or at least pulled back quite a distance.

"Are these guys supposed to keep us here?" Wisneiwski asked, sounding somewhat amazed. "They're holed up like they're on the defensive."

"Wouldn't you be if you thought another Specter might show up?

Besides, they're probably just supposed to keep an eye on us until that column gets here," Isen answered.

One of Wisneiwski's NCOs crawled up to the two officers with a report. "We counted eleven guys," he said. "There's the one Marder you can see from here and another one backed into that burned-out building."

"Not very good odds," Wisneiwski said.

"Since when have the odds been on our side?" Isen countered.

He studied his map once again. His patrols reported no activity elsewhere around the village. It looked to him as if the GPU, through bad planning or lack of men, or perhaps because they'd expected the reinforcements earlier, had backed off far enough to give him some room to maneuver, provided that he destroyed this overwatch team first. But that window would close in a few hours. Maybe less. Every moment that Isen used to reach his decision meant that the GPU infantry had moved closer.

"OK, Gene," Isen said. "We're going to go with the plan I talked about earlier. Think you can do it?"

"We got it, sir," Wisneiwski said. He crawled backward a few feet, then raised himself to an awkward crouch as he made his way back to where his NCOs waited. Isen hesitated a few moments longer, then went back to listen to his company commander brief his men.

"You'll be within sixty, sixty-five meters when you set up," Wisneiwski was telling the support team. "Start out with the grenade launchers and machine guns, then mix in some smoke. Keep your eye on the woods to the right. I don't have any pyro, so you'll have to watch us. When we start to move forward, shift fire."

Isen would have liked a third ammunition drop. They needed more pyrotechnic signals, hand grenades, forty-millimeter grenades for the launchers, mortar rounds—just about everything. They weren't so short that they had to lay low and wait for the ax to fall, but they hadn't much of a margin of comfort. He would have preferred to wait until nightfall to try this raid—his men would be rushing across open ground in bright winter sunlight—but that, too, was out of the question. He had made the choice to attack, but nearly everything else was out of his control.

Wisneiwski finished briefing his patrol. Normally, the company commander would not be leading an assault team in a raid, but three of Bravo Company's four lieutenants were wounded, and Wisneiwski had left the fourth back with the majority of the company.

Isen watched the soldiers as they broke off into the support and assault elements and moved into the woods. These were the same men he'd sent to derail that mounted attack on the southeast side of the village, the very men who'd crawled into the hedges and ditches and waited for the oncoming Marders with their little antitank rockets and their faith in their training. They'd done the job then, and he was calling on them once more.

If this first part of Isen's plan didn't come off, there was no way he could stop the GPU from occupying the drop zones and destroying Operation Firefall—and with it, the Rangers' best chance of getting out.

Isen found a spot between the assault and support teams from which he could observe the raid. The hulk of the administration building was directly opposite him, across a few meters of underbrush and about twenty meters of open ground.

The false security provided by the now-dead observation team was obvious here. The crews of the two Marders lounged carelessly about, mostly in the open, walking back and forth between the shallow fighting positions they'd scratched in the open space before the building and the piles of duffel and sleeping bags up against the wall. There was something about these undisciplined troops that almost made Isen feel sorry for them—matched man for man, they wouldn't stand a chance against the Rangers. Even with the huge weapons and tremendous mobility the Germans brought to the fight, Isen's men had managed not only to ward off disaster, but to send the mounted Panzergrenadiers running each time they made an advance.

But the cost had been tremendous. The makeshift aid station was filling with seriously wounded, a number of whom had already died. And the company positions were full of walking wounded—men who were hurt but could still fight. These men, Isen knew, would have to be carried out of the line before they left their comrades. But even in the face of such sacrifice, Isen knew that there were limits to human endurance, and they were being tested. At some point his men would be able to give no more. For all his experience, Isen wasn't sure where that point was.

I need my luck to hold out for just a few more hours, Isen thought. He checked his watch. Wisneiwski had been positioning his men for twenty-five minutes. That was breakneck speed for most operations, but Isen had given him only thirty—every second that ticked by brought the reinforcing column a footstep closer.

The explosions startled him, shook him down his sides and his back as he pulled his head down reflexively. The area in front of the burned building came suddenly alive with the flowering of orange flame. Isen saw two men tossed aside by the impacts, but the rest had managed to take cover. He watched the decks of the Marders to see if anyone would try to climb on board, but none of the GPU soldiers seemed willing to expose himself long enough.

The men on the support line were almost close enough to the GPU fighting positions to throw the hand grenades, but Isen didn't know if they were trying that or not. He hoped the Germans would think they were being mortared, but the orange bursts were rather small.

Now there was smoke rolling over the holes, pushed this way and that by the less frequent explosions of the grenades, and suddenly Isen could distinguish the yammering of the light machine guns and the intermittent popping of rifle fire.

Come on, he thought. *Come on.*

He pulled himself forward on his elbows, moving a few feet toward the clearing.

Where's the assault?

He glanced back at the GPU position. The support fire was waning—they didn't have enough ammo to keep it up for too long—and Isen thought he could see some of the GPU men over there begin to move. A few of the enemy were returning fire now, and Isen knew that the precious seconds of complete surprise and confusion were draining from the moment.

Shit, shit. Let's get going.

"Sir?"

Isen had gotten to his knees, and his RTO wanted him down.

"Hey, stay down, sir."

But Isen was up, sidling off to his right. A few rounds of small arms—most of the shots far too high—streaked through the trees above his head.

Then he saw the assault line—or what might be the assault line. A few Rangers were visible in the trees, but they were unsteady, dividing their attention between the objective in front of them and something else going on along their line. The firing was evenly divided—there was as much coming from the GPU as from the Rangers' position.

This was only the first part of Isen's plan—probably the easiest part—and it had to work or they were dead in the water.

Isen stepped toward the clearing, painfully aware of the bright sunlight that glittered off the churned-up snow and highlighted him. Then he saw the body, and he knew immediately it was Wisneiwski.

The legs were still hidden in the undergrowth, but the big torso lay in plain view, facedown, arms up as if in surprise. Even from this distance, Isen could see the hands were still.

Something plucked at his jacket, surprising him, and then there were hands on him, pulling at his legs, his clothing. Isen fell backward.

"You want to get killed?"

It was Gamble, his RTO. Isen had fallen on top of the big sergeant, but Gamble was still pulling him back even as he scolded. "Stand up there like some damn fool and leave *me* here alone . . . shit."

"OK, OK," Isen said, pulling Gamble's hands off him. "We got a hang fire on the assault line over there. I've got to get over there."

"As long as you don't try to walk across that open area," Gamble said, "I'll be glad to follow you. Looks like you need somebody to keep you straight."

Isen worked his way back from the clearing, then looped around to his right to approach the assault line from the back. The ragged fire from the support position was dying, and Isen knew that the balance would tip in a matter of moments.

"Shit," he said as he crawled. Only now he thought of using a sniper or two to keep the GPU soldiers from climbing back onto their Marders. He hoped the support team leader would think of it.

When he came up behind the assault line, he found two Rangers who'd crawled back from the edge of the woods. One of them had been shot in the hand; the other, unwounded, was treating his buddy.

"Captain Wisneiwski's dead," the healthy soldier said. His hands were shaking as he tried to use the green-backed compress to capture all the wayward pieces of the other soldier's shattered palm. "He just stood up, then, whap, he was down."

Isen crawled past the soldier, who kept repeating the story to himself.

"Just like that. Whap, and he was down."

There were five men in the support team, now trying to stretch their ammunition and keep the GPU tied down, and no doubt wondering what had happened to the assault. That left ten men on this side. Wisneiwski was dead, one Ranger badly wounded and another out of line to tend the hurt man.

Seven men. Isen had no rifle. Gamble and Hatley, Isen's RTOs, had rifles but were weighed down by the radios. He could call for help, he thought, have Charlie Company send up a team and try the whole thing over again, but that would give the enemy more than enough time to react.

"God*damn*," Isen said. He hadn't pressed Wisneiwski to make a contingency plan, something to use in the event this attack fell apart—which was exactly what was happening. He crouched in the spindly branches and mud of the undergrowth so that he could see the GPU position.

One man, cut off from the support team's view by the hull of the armored vehicle, was working his way to the rear of the Marder parked behind the shell of the administration building. In a minute or two, Isen knew, he would hear the whine of the big turret's hydraulics swinging the twenty-millimeter gun into action. And while the Germans were ignoring the assault team at the moment—the GIs to Isen's right and left had stopped firing—that wouldn't last long.

Now.

Thought and movement were one as he pushed into the brightly sunlit space. His feet felt leaden, caught in some child's nightmare of not being able to run fast enough. He heard Gamble yelling somewhere near him, and he remembered to unholster his pistol.

Behind him, men were yelling, "Let's go, let's go." Then there were two or three more voices shouting, and somehow the twenty-meter distance between Isen and the building began to close.

Isen could see one German soldier in profile, the sharp turtle helmet and black outline of his rifle pointed to Isen's left, where a few Rangers on the support team were still firing. Isen brought his pistol up, fired wildly, slowed down enough to steady the weapon and pulled the trigger twice, three times more. He didn't see the results, but the silhouette disappeared.

He ran harder, his equipment pounding his sides, his helmet sliding down on his nose. And then he was at the ragged line of holes. He leaped too soon, caught his foot on the lip of one fighting position and was carried by his momentum face forward to sprawl in the mud. He rolled as he hit and locked eyes with a GPU soldier crouched half in, half out of the charred door frame. Isen's hands and pistol were somewhere beneath him, and for a half-second eternity he pondered the impossibility of bringing his weapon up in time.

Then the German seemed to leap from the door, crashing backward in a tangle of dark clothing. The Ranger who'd shot him passed Isen, took a stutter step back.

"You OK, sir?"

"Uhhh," Isen said, pushing away from the wet ground. The assault team had followed him and was now closing the last few meters. Isen saw two GPU soldiers—men whose holes he'd passed—with their hands in the air. Gamble, who'd kept up with Isen in spite of the big radio, had his weapon trained on another soldier at the open rear door of one of the Marders.

Then he heard the turret.

The gray-black barrel of the second Marder's gun poked through a break in the wall of the burned building, and as Isen turned, it searched for a target.

"*Get down*," he screamed at his men. He dove for the front of the vehicle, wondering how far down the barrel could be depressed. But the realization that they couldn't reach him that close to the vehicle was instantly replaced with the mental image of his being run over. When he was close he brought his legs under him and leaped onto the front of the Marder.

If someone's manning that coax, he thought as he glanced into the maw of the smaller machine gun mounted, coaxially, alongside the big barrel, *I'm gone.*

Now he was on the vehicle, with no clear idea of what he was going to do. He stood, then bent over to keep both hands in contact with the hull as he moved inside the muzzle's reach. The twenty millimeter spewed a two-foot tongue of flame that hammered for a count of five rounds, and Isen felt as if his head would burst from the noise.

He slipped sideways, almost fell off the vehicle, but managed a handhold at the last second. Above him, he could see the partially open commander's hatch. Isen clambered for the turret, groping with one hand for his pistol, which he'd dropped and which he hoped was still attached by its lanyard. The weapon was banging along behind him, and he palmed it before he made his way to the top of the turret. He thrust his hand under the lip of the hatch and had a second to think that when he opened it he might be the one to be surprised.

The rush of sunlight caught the top of a man's head inside the turret, and Isen, primed to kill or be killed, pushed his pistol inside and pulled the trigger.

When they took the corpse from the back of the vehicle, feet first, Isen noticed how normal one side of the head looked: thinning hair and white scalp. But then there was the cruel edge of the wound and the startling exposure of skull and brain, grays and reds. Isen caught his breath, turned to where Gamble stood over the three prisoners—three living prisoners—from the other Marder. He almost succeeded, by concentrating on the image of his being caught on the turret and torn apart by the twenty-millimeter rounds, on keeping at bay the nagging question of whether he might have been able to take the man alive.

The adrenaline rush from the close combat threatened, all during his orders brief, to make Isen vomit all over himself. But he held his own while Norden talked through the plan he and Isen had developed, and by the time the questions started, Isen felt somewhat in control again.

"If we run into them while we're moving, we go right into the attack. That right, sir?" Lieutenant Drake, who had been second in command of Bravo Company, was nervous about filling Gene Wisneiwski's shoes. Isen, who hadn't gone more than few hours at a stretch without thinking about Ray Spano, his dead colonel, understood how the kid felt.

"That's right, Sam," Isen said patiently, although the concept was clear from the order. "We've got to slip out of here first," Isen said, "without alerting whoever is left out in the woods. There's always the possibility we'll run into more of whoever is still around Karlshofen first. Even if we do clear here, we might bump into the GPU relief column. I'm hoping we get to the spot I picked out before we have to start shooting, but I really don't know how much progress they've made, or even if they've switched avenues. So we may be heading out to a meeting engagement."

Isen's daring plan had pleased them, for these were men who loved panache. But now, with the time to execute it at hand, and with their broader understanding of just how far in the dark they were, Isen's subordinates were a bit more subdued. They asked good questions and they did not linger, for they understood that the time for decision was quickly approaching, and opportunity would rush past them.

They would plan as best they could with what little they knew about the enemy and with what little material they had on hand. They would provide for their men and they would not hesitate to expose themselves to the same dangers their soldiers faced. They would take Isen's plan, Isen's idea, and they would bet their lives on it.

This was what constantly surprised Isen about command. The mere fact that he was senior to them—a couple of years older with a few more years in the Army—had placed him in charge when Spano died. And now these men before him, and several hundred others waiting in the woods and houses around them, would place their lives in jeopardy to carry out *his* plan.

The responsibility weighed most heavily on the imaginative; less-confident commanders faltered, sowing doubt among their subordinates; while the foolish and the brash embraced a dangerous inflexibility.

Isen was neither boastful nor timid. He knew that there were hundreds of things that could incite disaster, from the simplest misunderstanding of orders, to the appearance—deus ex machina—of an unexpected and over-whelming enemy force. But he would never grow comfortable, never com-placent, with the knowledge that, when his hand traced lines upon the map, he committed the lives of other men, saving some, dooming others.

After dismissing his officers and NCOs, Isen and his command group, the operations and intelligence officers and their radio operators, moved to one corner of Karlshofen's crossroads intersection. It was after one o'clock in the afternoon, and the winter sun had passed through the peak of its low-slung southern parabola, succeeding in melting only a tiny bit of the ice and snow that clung to everything in messy globs.

Isen pulled a rag from his cargo pocket and wiped down the rifle he'd picked up at the aid station. His experience earlier that day had reminded him why, as a company commander, he had carried a rifle instead of a pistol. Now, with his command whittled down to two-thirds its normal strength—and with some of the able-bodied being left behind here to care for the wounded—he needed every rifle he could get.

"You read German, sir?" Gamble asked.

Isen turned to see Gamble staring up at some tablets embedded in a brick wall, the outside of the nursery school fence where Isen had had his row with Schauffert.

In the center was a light-colored panel inscribed with forty or so names. Atop the center panel sat an enlarged stone version of the Iron Cross with "1914–1918" engraved on it, and a stonework scroll that said *heimatliebe-heimatdanke.*

"Love," Isen said. "With love and thanks of their native village."

There were four other, darker panels that had been added after the Great War. These bore no remarks about the fatherland, about duty or the thanks of a grateful nation. There were nineteen or twenty names on each panel, some surnames repeated, as for brothers, with birth and death dates.

"World War Two," Isen said.

"All these guys?" Gamble asked. "From this little village?"

Isen didn't answer.

"What does *v-e-r-m* mean?" Gamble asked, pointing to the notation beside one name. The letters were repeated for every third or fourth soldier.

"Short for 'missing'," Isen said. Then, remembering his travels about Germany as a lieutenant, "There's one of these monuments in nearly every little town."

And who remembers these men? Isen thought. *Their families? Brothers? Sisters? Sweethearts? Children now grown and with grandchildren of their own? And where are the graves of the* vermisst, *the missing? Scattered from here to Egypt and under the Atlantic?*

"All that," Gamble said, "and they lost the war to boot."

The men around them were moving northeast, the lead elements setting off on what would be, one way or the other, their last mission. Isen shouldered his ruck, cradled his weapon, and watched the lines of soldiers move out. They dragged their feet, some of them, and sported bandages on less serious wounds, but they held their heads up.

Everybody loses, Isen thought. But he kept his observation from Gamble.

22

As HE LAY, BELLY DOWN, ON A SNOW-COVERED RIDGE ABOVE
Highway 71 from Bremervörde, Lieutenant Ken Hawkins had time to
remember how excited he'd been, four days earlier, to be chosen to lead
the battalion's movement from the drop zone to their objective. Now,
centuries later, he wished he was the forgotten junior officer in the trail
platoon in this latest move.

"See anything?" Hawkins asked Sergeant Bishop, whose squad had the
point.

"Nah," Bishop replied. "But I could have sworn I heard something
down there."

The two men were looking out onto a gentle fold in the land that
sheltered a two-lane blacktop running generally north and south. They'd
traveled some six kilometers from Karlshofen, which lay to the southwest, and were still some eighteen kilometers south of Bremervörde,
moving steadily north and northeast. This was the road on which Isen
expected to encounter the column of GPU infantry that was headed toward Karlshofen. Hawkins's ad hoc platoon, made up of the unwounded
soldiers from the other shattered platoons in Charlie Company, had been
given the task of taking the point for the battalion. They were some fifteen
hundred meters ahead of the main body, and their mission was to find
the enemy, report to Isen, and avoid contact long enough for the battalion
to deploy.

Avoid contact, Hawkins remembered from his orders brief. *You got that right. Out here looking for a couple of enemy battalions with one measly platoon.*

"I think we should back off and head up the road a little bit farther," Hawkins said tentatively.

Bishop nodded and immediately began to move. The rest of the platoon moved with him, unbidden, as if they were all attached to the sergeant.

Hawkins bit his tongue at the tone he'd used. He was seeking Bishop's approval, and while there was nothing wrong with that idea in general, Ken Hawkins was realizing that it went further than a lieutenant bouncing ideas off his most trusted NCO.

Ken Hawkins had lost his nerve.

Or, more precisely, he'd lost whatever nerve he'd had. The incident on the trail with Brennan had introduced into his thinking something Ken Hawkins had never had to contend with to any great degree in his life: self-doubt.

Fucking Brennan, he thought, rolling onto his back and looking out over the moving patrol. *Where is that little weasel? I should have punched the little bastard when he mouthed off to me.*

Hawkins had convinced himself, immediately after the incident at the firebreak, that Sergeant Bishop would have made it back without his help. Everything would have been fine. Now Brennan had probably told all his buddies how he'd told the platoon leader to get fucked, how he'd all but called Hawkins yellow.

Hawkins stood, began to walk, and found his position behind the lead wedge of soldiers. He studied Bishop's back—the NCO was directly in front of him, about twenty meters out—and wondered how Bishop made his decisions so confidently. Bishop seemed to Hawkins to be the perfect Ranger leader: self-assured, decisive, wry in the face of danger.

All it takes, Hawkins thought, *is decisiveness. I can't hesitate, I have to act.*

The pace of Ranger operations in peacetime didn't allow much time for introspection. There were plenty of afteraction reviews, but these tended to focus coldly on techniques, tactics. No one talked about the distasteful aspects of leadership: *What if I'm afraid?* This was an environment in which every man expected that he would be the next Audie Murphy. Each man carried a marshall's baton in his knapsack.

As he thought about the last few days, it seemed to him that he'd done nothing but make mistakes: leaving his radio operator, losing control of his platoon during the withdrawal. And every time he had to make a decision, he was wracked by doubt and uncertainty. It wasn't so bad comparing himself to Bishop, who'd been at this longer and who was, by all measure, an outstanding infantryman. But when he compared himself to that weasel Brennan and still came out on the short end, Hawkins began to think that perhaps he didn't have it in him to be a combat leader.

As he mused to himself, Hawkins saw Brennan in the lead wedge, some fifteen meters ahead of him and off to one side. Hawkins turned, as if he were checking the woods on either side. When his rifle was pointed at Brennan, he paused for just a second.

Bang, he thought.

There was still nothing on the highway when they checked several hundred meters farther along, but the left-side security—the side away from the paved road—reported that they were about to reach a wide dirt track that cut across their path ahead of them and probably intersected the highway. Hawkins moved up to see it, taking along Bishop and a couple of riflemen for security. If they were to continue parallel to Highway 71, on their right, they would have to cross this new danger area.

The ground just south of the unpaved road rose a few meters, leading them to a small, wooded hill that looked down on the northeast-southwest road.

"Pretty good size, for a dirt road," Bishop said.

Though marked on the map as unimproved, the road was hard-packed earth, wide enough to accommodate large vehicles.

"I don't see any tracks," Hawkins offered. He was afraid that the GPU would slip past them and surprise the main body. He was about to send a runner back for the platoon when he saw Bishop freeze. He heard nothing but the sound of his own breathing, but Hawkins knew better than to speak.

A few seconds later, it came to him through the whitened woods. Voices.

Hawkins cocked his head, trying to hear better. Somewhere above him, a bird protested their closeness.

"Sie ist nach links abgewichen, wird aber wahrscheinlich dicht an der Strasse bleiben."

"Shit," Bishop said under his breath. "What did they say?"

Hawkins shook his head emphatically. He couldn't speak German, either.

Bishop waved at the riflemen behind them to get down, then he flattened out on his stomach. Hawkins mimicked him.

"There," Bishop breathed.

Hawkins scanned the road, seeing nothing. Bishop pointed a little farther out, and, after a moment, Hawkins was able to make out two men in GPU uniforms moving along the dirt road away from the highway, talking as they walked. As he watched, one of the men pointed to the woods on either side of the road. The other shook his head, gestured back the way they'd come and then pointed forward, southwest toward Karlshofen.

"The relief column?" Hawkins whispered.

"The scouts, at least," Bishop said.

"We can watch them from here," Hawkins said, looking around for the best place to hide. "Bring a recon team up and get a good count."

"Probably no time to bring a team up, Lieutenant," Bishop said. He took his eyes off the men in the road and studied Hawkins.

This isn't how it's supposed to happen, Hawkins thought. He'd brought along a whole platoon so that he could have some backup when he spotted the enemy. Now, because he'd crashed into them unexpectedly, he was out on a proverbial limb. He looked at Bishop, whose patience was draining. Something in Hawkins's brain tripped. *Decide,* it told him.

"So we'll stay here, leave the patrol where it is?" He was aggravated that it still sounded like a question, as if he were asking permission instead of Bishop's opinion.

"We got to send those two back," Bishop said, pointing a thumb at the two soldiers they'd brought along for security. "They can call in a report about what we're doing, in case . . . just in case."

Hawkins didn't like the idea of sending his security back. "Can't we send just one?"

"One guy to move alone when there might be enemy in the woods?" Bishop asked. He didn't wait for an answer.

Hawkins sucked his cheeks in. *I knew that,* he thought. *Why can't I think of all these things?*

It occurred to him that he could send Bishop back, but he doubted the NCO would go. For the smallest part of a second he thought about going himself.

"OK," Hawkins said. "You and I will stay here and see what comes down the road."

"Sounds good, Lieutenant," Bishop said. He moved backward and briefed the two riflemen, who seemed glad to be headed back to the patrol. By the time he crawled forward again, Hawkins had settled in under an evergreen bush.

"You got a combat knife, sir?" Bishop asked, his face inches away from Hawkins's.

"Yeah."

"Better get it out, and keep your bayonet on your rifle," Bishop said. "Anybody comes up here and spots us, we got to kill 'em quietly, or else they're on to the whole patrol."

"Right," Hawkins said. He slipped his hand down to the sheath of his knife, which he always kept sharpened but which, up to this point, had only been used to open plastic meal bags. Hawkins thrust it into the ground directly in front of his hand.

The two men they'd spotted first reappeared and walked casually down the middle of the road, their rifles slung over their shoulders. One of the men was dressed in a camouflage uniform that fit him poorly. The other had on camouflage pattern pants and a solid green shirt. Neither man wore headgear, neither carried anything other than a small canvas bag that might have contained spare magazines for the weapons. One of them had a cigarette dangling from his mouth. They were obviously not expecting to run into the Rangers.

When they had passed, Hawkins couldn't resist making a comment. "Don't look much like soldiers, do they?" he said.

"No," Bishop answered in a fragile whisper. "But that could mean a lot of things." He took his eyes off the trail for a moment. "Maybe the GPU is getting all kinds of volunteers."

"No rucksacks, even," Hawkins offered.

"Maybe they're living off the land," Bishop countered. "Maybe the people around here are supporting them, you know?"

Hawkins quieted, thinking about the last comment.

A few minutes later another squad passed by them, followed by the main body. No one seemed at all concerned about local security—Hawkins guessed that they all assumed someone else was responsible for that. Perhaps they believed the two men strolling ahead of them were enough. Maybe they didn't care.

The infantry marched raggedly in a column of companies. At first, Hawkins busied himself with counting, but as he watched, he became more aware of what he was seeing.

The formations were not in good order, for these were men unused to road marches. They straggled along, holding their weapons haphazardly, dragging their feet, looking at the ground. Like the men who'd gone before, they were poorly dressed and outfitted. Hawkins was reminded of a joke about the Air Force pilots' dress code: any time two of them came out of the Officers Club in the same uniform, one had to go back in and change something.

It took nearly thirty minutes for the whole body of troops to pass by. Behind the formations came a half-dozen or so trucks, at least two of them commandeered, Hawkins thought, from local businesses. Then there were the stragglers, walking in twos and threes, some of them dragging their weapons. They did not seem to be in a great deal of pain. It looked to Hawkins as if they just weren't all that interested in keeping up.

"Let's go," Bishop said.

The two men crawled backward until the lip of the little hill hid them from the road. Then they stood quietly and Bishop began walking while Hawkins checked his compass. The lieutenant, already rattled, wanted to make sure their navigation was dead on when they headed back to where they'd left the patrol. He folded the compass, dropped it in its small case on his pistol belt and took a step forward before looking up.

His first thought was that he'd bumped into Sergeant Bishop, but the figure that came running from the thick evergreens to his left to careen off

Hawkins was too short. He put his hands out before him and suddenly had a handful of child.

Before he could even register surprise or warn her to be quiet, the little girl chomped down on his right hand. Hawkins drew in his breath mightily, trying to suppress a scream. He pulled at his hand, felt the flesh tear—she meant to hold on—and drew back his other hand. He swung, but the little girl ducked and he caught only air. Now she was free and already running toward the road and the GPU formation.

Hawkins ran after her, pressing his bleeding hand up against his side and trying not to drop his rifle. The Germans were on the road, and if she warned them, chances were good that he, Bishop, and the rest of the patrol would be killed or captured, to say nothing of Isen's approaching column.

He ran in agonizing slowness, and although he caught the girl within a few steps, he was terribly aware of how close the road was, how close the enemy was. He drew the wicked combat knife in his bloody hand and reached for the girl's hair with his left. As they drew near the crest of the hill from which he and Bishop had been watching, he could feel the sergeant's eyes on him.

We have to kill anyone who sees us, Bishop had told him.

Decide, Hawkins's brain thundered. *Act. Dozens of men will die if she sounds the alarm.*

He drew back the knife, from the corner of his eye saw it glint red and black.

"I couldn't catch her," Hawkins said. "She got a head start and I had to stop before I ran out on the road."

"Let's get the hell out of here, then," a stunned Bishop said without looking at Hawkins. "She tells them we're here and they'll be on us like stink on shit."

The two men ran, Hawkins moving effortlessly now, his wounded right hand slinging blood onto the snow as he pumped his arms. They would have to collect the patrol, disseminate the information about the enemy column, and move to the linkup point.

In the perimeter, Bishop radioed Isen, then passed the word of what they'd seen. As the NCO readied the patrol for movement, a soldier bandaged Hawkins's hand.

"How'd this happen, Lieutenant?" the soldier asked.

"Just wrap it up, OK?" Hawkins said testily. "You wouldn't believe me if I told you."

I did it again, Hawkins thought. *I hesitated when I should have . . . oh, shit.*

He looked around at the men in his platoon, scanned the woods beyond them for some sign of their pursuers. *I put all these guys in danger.*

They began to move quickly, with Bishop exhorting the men to stay alert, to stay together. Hawkins found that he kept falling behind, and he let his bandaged hand dangle at his side, hoping that the soldiers would think that he was weak from blood loss. As he walked, he wondered if he was just weak.

When word of the GPU column had come in from his advance party, Mark Isen halted his own formation and began preparations for the upcoming fight. They'd slipped out of Karlshofen without attracting any unwanted attention; Isen figured they'd battered the GPU units enough to force them to withdraw. But he was still several kilometers short of the area he'd picked on his map reconnaissance, his latest objective, so the first order of business was to pick the place to attack the approaching column. He ordered his companies into a defensive posture and called for the leaders, whom he would take with him as they searched the ground immediately around them for a suitable spot.

"If they continue southwest from where Hawkins spotted them," Isen said, "they'll be on one of two roads." He used a stick to trace an upside down Y in the snow. Then he poked his finger in between the branches. "We'll position ourselves in between so that we can strike in either direction."

"We'll try over here first," Isen said, looking at his map as his captains and platoon leaders gathered around him. He used his finger to trace a gentle crescent formed by some low-lying hills that skirted the road the enemy column had been on when Hawkins spotted them. The high ground sat above the track on the southeast side like a thick, horseshoe-shaped hill.

"If it turns out there's enough room here," Isen said, "for us to set on this ridge and for them to all fit in the kill zone, this is where we'll do it." He got a couple of nods in response. "Then we'll come up with a contingency in case they should double back and use the other road. Questions?"

As Norden talked them through a few more details, Isen studied the group. More than half of the men around him had what used to be called the "thousand-yard stare," a featureless gaze that was so hollow and vacant as to defy description. Isen had seen photographs of men with such looks, men who'd been in sustained combat, men on the verge of mental and physical collapse.

He felt the need to say something inspirational, as this might be the last time he would get to speak to them in a group. From here, they would move across the hills where Isen hoped to fight, then back to their commands, and off again to their positions. They would be separated, spaced along the hill, and while Isen would visit the individual commands, the men would generally be isolated. And that was the thing that terrified.

Isen, who had been kneeling, stood up. "Come in close, here, and take a knee," he said.

The men moved in: Dettering, Charlie Company's wounded commander, whose arm bore grenade shrapnel he'd taken on the move to Karlshofen; young Sam Drake, who had jumped in as Bravo Company's executive officer and was now the company commander; Master Sergeant Hendricks, the ops NCO, steady as always. A few short months before, Isen had met them as an outsider, the newest man in the battalion and the one with no experience in the Rangers. Now he was about to lead them into a desperate fight against a superior force that meant to crush them.

"I'm not big on speeches," Isen said, "and you have a lot to do and a short time to do it in." His mind was foggy with fatigue and worry, and his words lagged behind his thoughts. "I know that. . . . " He almost said "whatever happens," but caught himself.

"I know that you all will do your best today. I don't have to tell you how important it is that we stop the enemy before he can reach the drop zones around Karlshofen. You know all that. What I do have to tell you is that I'm proud to be associated with you men, proud to serve with you. . . . "

He left the thought, obviously unfinished, but couldn't seem to muster more.

"You forgot the part about 'I wouldn't rather be anywhere else but here,' sir," Master Sergeant Hendricks said.

The soldiers laughed, and Isen was glad for the release of tension. They stood, ready to begin.

A simple comment came unbidden from Isen's memory. Though he couldn't remember where he'd heard it, he thought it appropriate.

"Let's do it," he said.

Mark Isen watched from atop the little ridge as his Rangers found their places for the attack plan he'd worked out. He'd walked the line with his commanders, now it was up to them to get things set up. He could see only a small number of the men—which was good, they were supposed to be hidden. He checked his watch and his map, trying to estimate the arrival of the enemy column.

Turning down the hill behind him, he spoke to Sergeant Gamble. "Any word yet from the scouts?"

"Nothing, sir," Gamble answered. Isen had thrown out a screen made up of his scout platoon. They were on foot—their armed jeeps were supposed to have been on the follow-up aircraft—so they couldn't cover as much ground as he'd have liked them to. But with Hawkins out there, and the scouts. . . . Still, he was afraid of being surprised.

"Did you call the companies and tell them to put out OPs?" Isen asked.

"Observation posts are all out, sir," Gamble said, tolerating the fact Isen had begun to repeat himself.

Isen walked down the hill and looked over the shoulder of his fire support officer for a while. The mortars were set up, but they would have no time to drop the smoke rounds so that the forward observers could accurately fix their targets. The first rounds would be high explosive. On target, Isen hoped.

"Is everything going according to plan, Major Isen?"

Major George Rhone, the Bundeswehr intelligence officer who'd stumbled into their perimeter that first day, sat on the ground next to Sergeant Gamble. Rhone's left arm was in a sling, but otherwise he was fine and seemed happy to be away from the aid station, where he'd worked voluntarily after his own wounding.

Isen had asked Rhone to come along in case he needed an interpreter, or in case he needed Rhone's skills as a negotiator. But Isen had not let him see the overall plan, nor had he allowed Rhone to walk the position with him. Rhone took the snub good-naturedly, remarking how he needed the time to rest.

"Very well, thank you, Herr Major," Isen said. "Good thing, too, since we don't have a lot of time."

"What's your estimate of the enemy's arrival time?"

"Based on the word we got from our advanced element," Isen said, "I'd say an hour, maybe a bit longer."

Isen studied Rhone's reaction. The major's fortunes still rode with the Rangers: if the Americans were defeated, it would probably mean Rhone would die, if not in combat, then as payment for his aiding the GPU's enemies.

"I know that you are just being prudent, in not letting me see your battle plan unfold, Major Isen," Rhone said. "And I suppose I can understand that, although I have done a great deal to help you and your men."

"I appreciate the work you've done in the aid station, Major," Isen said sincerely. "But my orders from Colonel Schauffert are clear."

Rhone stiffened a bit. "If I am to be a prisoner, then you cannot force me, under the Geneva Convention, to do any sort of work for you, including interpreting. If I am to be an ally, then you shouldn't treat me as a pariah."

"Look," Isen said wearily, "I ain't got the time or the energy to get worked up about your complaints. You can certainly refuse to help us."

Isen had Rhone pegged as a brave, if sensitive man. He was in a tough position, no doubt, trying to pass himself off as an ally while all around him, Isen's men were dying because of German duplicity in the GPU schemes. Isen was fed up with the whole scenario, and if he'd thought for a second that Rhone was a serious threat to the security of his command, Isen could probably have shot the man. Still, he might be useful.

"But I could use your help," Isen said honestly.

Rhone gave him a knowing smile.

"Unfortunately, I am not unused to being in such awkward situations, Herr Major."

"How's that?" Isen asked, dropping onto his butt next to Rhone. He uncoiled his legs and pressed his fists onto the knotted muscles of his thighs.

"We Germans have been suspect for a long time."

"Mmm," Isen said.

"When the wall came down between East and West, do you know what our allies in Europe were saying? Our fellow democracies? They were all afraid of a resurgent, militant Germany. And those of us who wanted one country again thought all those Frenchmen and Englishmen and Russians were just being paranoid." He shook his head sadly. "And now it looks as if what they feared is coming to pass. No jackboots on their streets," he allowed. "At least, not yet."

Rhone leaned back against the small rise and folded his hands behind his head.

"How could we not see it?"

Though the question was obviously rhetorical, Isen felt obliged to say something.

"No one saw that it was coming to this," Isen said.

Rhone was suddenly animated. "But we should have seen," he said, stabbing his heel into the earth below his feet. "We were watching the whole time they were beating up immigrants and setting fire to worker housing."

He looked at Isen with what the American took to be desperation, the by-product of frustration.

"Of course, they made it a little harder," Rhone continued. "They don't go around giving the fascist salute to each other. Racism has dressed itself up in a suit, and that, apparently, is all it took to get into the political process . . . again."

Rhone propped his elbows on knees, lowered his face onto his hands. "It isn't easy being German," he said. "This is a country of incredible pain, pain that we keep in, pain that we hide from the rest of the world behind the highest standard of living in Europe. And we hide behind our legendary efficiency that leaves so little room for reflection."

Rhone glanced at Isen, who was listening, then at the radio operators, who were not.

"But our people hurt. In the East, people lose their houses after reunification when westerners, themselves forced out by the Communists, or by Hitler, come back to claim the property. And now suddenly we have homeless people in a nation in which everyone had a place to live. And the eastern workers, old men and women who were raised to think they would always have jobs, are now jobless."

"The easterners must also live with the debris left by the Stasi. They find out that their neighbors informed on them, that their relatives informed on them, their own families sold them out, sold tales—true or false—of illegal or anti-Communist activities, sold tales of their very dreams of freedom. Imagine having a relative tell the state that at night you lie awake and dream of another life. Should that be a crime anywhere?"

Rhone seemed almost overwhelmed, though he kept his eyes fixed on the horizon visible through the trees.

"And now all this. Even if the GPU kills only other Germans, the nation will be set back again, and we will have to atone for the sins of a new generation."

Isen looked about him in the pleasant woods. The snow had started to retreat from the tree bases, and the bark and the wet leaves beneath were richly black and wet. Above him, between the tops of the trees, he could see a few winsome clouds slide through the blue vault.

Rhone was right, of course. Germany's modern history was a sad one. But Mark Isen, whose command had been attacked without warning, whose men had been denied medicine and evacuation, was in no mood for sympathy.

"What about nukes?" Isen asked.

Rhone's eyebrows flicked upward, a tiny gesture of surprise.

"Ah, yes," he said. "The mythical nuclear warheads."

"So, are there any?" Isen pressed.

He'd been briefed by Schauffert on the best guess of the American intelligence community, but he wanted to hear what Rhone had to say. He wasn't sure if he was testing Schauffert or Rhone, and at this point he didn't care. "Does the GPU have nuclear weapons?"

"We don't know for sure," Rhone answered. "There is circumstantial evidence that seems to indicate that it's possible."

"What evidence?"

"We traced GPU money into some odd places. They control a couple of old freighters that sail regularly between the Middle East and the northern European coast. And we heard—though we weren't able to prove—that their payroll includes some scientists from what used to be the Soviet weapons programs."

"I would have thought your intelligence apparatus could have kept track of those guys," Isen said. This got no response from Rhone.

"What about these ships?" Isen said, switching tracks. "What are they carrying?"

"We don't know that they're carrying anything," Rhone said. "We do know that—as everybody feared—the nuclear forces in what used to be the Soviet army lost accountability of the warheads. We know that at least one was tracked to Iran by Israeli agents. They don't think it's left that country."

Rhone paused, frustrated, Isen thought, by how little he did know, by the realization that his government had been poorly prepared for this threat and was now suffering the consequences.

"That leaves two more," Isen said.

"As of the time I came and joined you, we didn't know where the ships were," Rhone admitted. "It's possible that, since then, we got together with your people . . . the Navy and CIA. Maybe together they've tracked it down."

Rhone cradled his arm, pulled at the sling wrapped around his neck. He was winding down. Isen suddenly thought about how frustrated Rhone must be, stuck out here with the Americans—who didn't trust him—when he knew his country was under siege.

"But, if the GPU had them, don't you think they'd threaten to use them?" Isen asked.

"Actually, there's nothing keeping them from making the threat even if they don't have control of the warheads," Rhone answered. "Who knows? Maybe they can't agree on how to play those cards."

Behind them, the radios squawked as the companies called in their reports. Isen turned around and made eye contact with Gamble, who was supposed to let him know if Hawkins or the scouts called in with fresh reports of the GPU column. The sergeant shook his head.

The tendency among strategists, when nuclear arms are involved, was to discount the importance of small actions, like the one in which Isen was about to engage. A few men, struggling with weapons they carried in their hands, couldn't shock the world the way one nuclear warhead could. The question of the missing warheads went a long way toward explaining why Washington and Berlin had been so slow in reacting: this stand in Karlshofen was a sideshow.

Maybe that was why Schauffert had come; he expected that Isen would figure out his relative insignificance and would need some bolstering. Angry as he was about being so isolated, Isen could understand why the policymakers would be more worried about the use of nuclear weapons in the developing civil war than they were about Isen's command.

"But it might not come to that," Isen said.

"Pardon?"

"Oh, I was just thinking out loud," Isen said. "If we can hang on," he continued, "at least long enough to get our other forces on the ground, we have a chance to stop them. The GPU is counting on the people to rise up and support them, right? If they can't beat us, we might just undercut their support, leave the GPU high and dry."

Mark Isen had managed to convince himself that his mission was important, but he was too tired to wonder if he had done so just so he would be able to face the deaths that were sure to come.

As he stood to busy himself, Isen knew he wouldn't shake the image of that ship, appearing and disappearing like an apparition on the icy sea, its cargo hidden, terrible to ponder.

Now it was a footrace, and Hawkins's only hope was that the GPU infantry, moving southwest as he was, would be confident as the hare, and that he and his platoon would be able to bypass them and link up with Isen.

"How far you reckon we are from the road?" Hawkins asked Bishop as they walked. The lieutenant had come up close beside his most trusted NCO and was walking next to him. If Hawkins noticed that he was bothering Sergeant Bishop—with his proximity as much as with his questions—it didn't deter him.

"I figure we're about two hundred meters," Hawkins said before Bishop had a chance to answer. The lieutenant, who was a good eight inches taller than Bishop, looked over the sergeant's head into the woods on their right—the direction of the enemy. "You think we're far enough away? Huh?"

"Yes, Lieutenant, I think we are," Bishop said, at the end of his patience. "Otherwise I'd move farther away, right?"

Bishop sidestepped a few feet, trying to move away from Hawkins. The big man made a handy target in the woods, and besides, he was talking too much.

"Let's spread out a little, OK, Lieutenant?" Bishop said. One of the soldiers on the flank of the lead wedge heard Bishop's request. The man looked over at his leaders, but Bishop glared at him until the soldier turned his attention back out to the threatening woods.

Bishop had naturally assumed control of the platoon when Hawkins began to falter. He just hoped his platoon leader didn't lose control completely before they got back to the rest of the battalion.

Hawkins stayed away for less than a minute. He was looking at his map when he came back over to Bishop. The NCO noticed at least two Rangers watching them, and then he realized that they weren't just curious, they were probably afraid that Hawkins would do something to place them in jeopardy.

"Maybe we should veer off to the left a bit more up here . . . ," Hawkins began.

Bishop held his hand up for a halt. As the men all around them found positions from which they could watch the perimeter, Bishop took Hawkins to what he thought was the center of the formation—as far as possible from any soldier's earshot. They each took a knee.

"Lieutenant," Bishop said. "You OK?"

"Yeah," Hawkins said, blinking rapidly. He looked at Bishop, then down at the map still in his hand. "I just . . . I mean. . . . " He wiped at his mouth with the back of his hand. Even under the layers of dirt and the lines of exhaustion, Bishop could still see why some of the NCOs thought Hawkins looked like a kid.

"I fucked up back there," Hawkins whispered.

"Maybe you did," Bishop said. "Maybe you didn't. We won't know unless that little girl rats us out, and then it really won't matter."

Hawkins lifted his eyes, but he seemed to be looking at something on Bishop's helmet.

"Right now we got to get this platoon back without running into those goons on the road," Bishop said. "I can do it with you, or I can do it without you." A cool pause, nothing personal here. "Your choice."

He was on his feet and moving as quickly as he said it, and the platoon reacted to his movement without hesitation. By the time Hawkins got to his feet the first squad of soldiers had already passed him by. He looked around, considered abandoning the middle of the formation, where the leaders moved, then stuffed his map in the cargo pocket of his trousers and followed the man in front of him.

It occurred to Bishop that, in any other situation, he would have handled Hawkins differently, trying to salvage some of the officer's self-respect, which was clearly at an ebb.

Tough shit, he thought as he watched the men of the lead squad, watched his map, watched the woods, and listened for any sign of the GPU infantry. *I got enough to worry about.*

As if to confirm this impression, two or three of the men in the lead squad held up their hands. While the rest of the platoon halted and passed the signal back, Bishop hurried forward.

"What is it?" he asked the point man.

"Smell that?"

Bishop turned his head into the breeze.

"Something burning," he said. "Smells like rubber, tires maybe."

"Yeah."

"You hear anything?" Bishop asked.

"I . . . I'm not sure. Sounds weird, but maybe somebody crying."

Bishop paused. "Like a kid, maybe?"

"Yeah," the soldier said. "Except what would a kid be doing way the hell out here?"

"That's what I'd like to know," Bishop said.

He conferred with the team leader, sent word along the platoon that they should form a security perimeter, and selected three men to go forward with him to the road.

"It's a car or truck," the lead soldier told him as they closed in on the forest road.

Bishop halted their forward movement when he could see, through the trees, black smoke from a dying fire. He sent a Ranger a few meters off to each flank and moved forward on his belly, bringing one soldier with him.

There was a small truck in the ditch on the far side of the road. The tires and whatever had been in the bed of the vehicle burned slowly, pushing thick, oily smoke into the air.

"Look," the soldier beside Bishop said.

The little girl Bishop had seen only fleetingly sat by the ditch on the near side of the road, off to the soldiers' right. She was about ten, Bishop guessed, with thick, dark hair that hung wildly past her shoulders, dark features. Dark skin. There were two bodies sprawled in the road near her, and at least one more tumbled into the shallow ditch at her feet. She sat with her arms wrapped around her knees, rocking back and forth and sobbing. The bodies in the road had had their throats cut, the black gashes clearly visible.

"Immigrants," Bishop whispered.

"Huh?"

Bishop took his eyes away from the scene on the road, steeling himself for the decision that was coming.

"They're immigrants, foreigners."

"The GPU did this?" the soldier asked.

"Doesn't much matter," Bishop said. "If they take over the country, this is what foreigners have to look forward to." He began to crawl backward. "The GPU hates all foreigners."

The soldier began to understand that Bishop wasn't going to help the little girl.

"Aren't we going to . . . I mean, shouldn't we go out there?"

"What the fuck are we going to do for her?" Bishop said testily. Then, in a quieter tone. "She'd just slow us down."

When they returned to the platoon, Hawkins was standing, carelessly, at the edge of the perimeter. The soldiers around him were clearly nervous about the lieutenant's apparent lack of good sense.

"The GPU caught a truckload of people, immigrants, probably trying to get out of the area," Bishop said to Hawkins as he waved for the platoon to saddle up. "Killed them. Cut their throats. That little kid was with them."

"The little girl?" Hawkins opened his mouth. "Oh. . . ."

"They didn't get her," Bishop said.

He turned away from Hawkins and began to walk, trying not to think about the little girl alone in unspeakable grief, in unimaginable horror.

You'd have been doing her a favor if you'd killed her, Bishop thought.

23

"CRUDE, BUT EFFECTIVE," KILGORE COMMENTED TO HIS ASSEMbled platoon leaders.

The men had gathered on the platform of a small train station on the rail line north of Hannover, some ninety plus kilometers south of Karlshofen. Where the track narrowed to pass between the platform and a stone retaining wall on the opposite side of the tracks, at least a truckload of concrete had been dumped from the roadway above the wall. Haphazard chunks of metal—meant to reinforce the obstacle—stuck out at odd angles from the mess: auto parts, a section of fence, pipes. Kilgore could even make out what looked like the top of a rusted refrigerator.

"Guess they knew all along that we were coming," Second Lieutenant Bonham said, pointing out the obvious.

"Thanks for that observation." Kilgore's XO, a lean first lieutenant named Russell who'd lost all his patience with fools on the mean streets of west Philadelphia, gave the immature Bonham no slack. Bonham failed to notice even the most thinly veiled cuts.

Whoever had staged the bloody attack at the rail yard had passed the word about the American movement. Besides the damage to the track, a few sniper shots from the sides of the right-of-way had sent most of the Germans rail workers scurrying. The GI guards had managed to detain the engineers, who were huddled in the cab.

"Who are those guys?" Bonham asked.

Up ahead on the track, Kilgore noticed some men in camouflage walking toward them. He had a moment of alarm when he realized that they'd posted guards to the right, left, and rear of the stopped train, but had sent no one ahead.

"They're GIs," Russell said, recognizing the distinctive coal bucket shape of the Kevlar helmet. "But not cav guys."

As the men moved closer—Kilgore counted three on the tracks and spotted at least one more up on the street level, covering the movement of his buddies—Kilgore could see that they were infantrymen. The point man waved. Kilgore waved back.

"Go get the squadron commander," Kilgore told one of his officers, who turned and trotted back along the length of the stopped train. Kilgore's boss had, after inspecting the damage, returned to his radios.

"You guys the cavalry?" one of the approaching trio asked cheerfully when he got closer.

"That's right," Kilgore answered.

Bonham piped in with the cavalry motto, "All cav."

Kilgore looked at him from under hooded eyes. "I can handle the talking, Lieutenant," he said. Then he turned back to the approaching men, who had formed a wedge and who, Kilgore noticed, carried their weapons lightly, as if they wouldn't be surprised if they had to shoot the cav troopers.

The speaker was a young man, comfortably in charge, though he wore no insignia of rank.

"When you guys didn't reach us on this line, I thought maybe you got held up by something," he said, pointing to the pile of concrete that blocked the tracks on both sides of the platform. "Clever little bastards, ain't they?"

Kilgore, who still didn't know whom he was talking to, didn't answer.

"My name's Zappasodi," he said. "Tenth Special Forces." He came up to Kilgore and extended his hand. "Call me Zap."

"Glad to see you, Zap," Kilgore said. He looked over his shoulder for Lieutenant Colonel Janisek, his squadron commander. There was no sign of Janisek yet, so Kilgore turned back to the SF soldier. "What the hell are you guys doing way out here?"

"Waiting for you, lately," Zappasodi answered.

The two soldiers with him had moved off some distance to either side, relaxing only slightly.

"We came out here to observe enemy movement, and we got a call this morning to link up with you guys on the railroad." He paused, looked round at the junk sticking out of the dried concrete, and offered, "But this looks like the end of the trip."

Kilgore heard Janisek approaching.

"What's up, Ted?"

"We have some visitors here, sir," Kilgore explained.

Zappasodi squared his shoulders a bit—a mere nod at military formality—introduced himself to the colonel as Captain Zappasodi and produced a large map from his rucksack.

"We were dropped up here," he told the cavalry officers. "Along one of the possible routes for the armored column that's moving toward Karlshofen. We were too far west, but another team picked them up here, northeast of where we are now."

He poked at the map sheet in the center of a triangle formed by some of the major highways leading toward Hamburg.

"And they're racing us?" Kilgore asked.

"Not exactly," Zappasodi answered. "They're not on a train or on flatbeds or anything, so they're moving slower. The commander is taking time to keep his vehicles closed up, pick up broken down tracks, all that."

"Sounds like you know something about armored movement," Kilgore said.

"I know that these machines aren't made for long hauls on the autobahn," Zappasodi answered. "And I know that you have a choice of going balls-to-the-wall or keeping your force intact."

The cavalry officers nodded silent agreement.

"And it looks to me like this guy is more interested in arriving with all his force than he is in getting some part of the force there as soon as possible."

"So the question," Janisek said, "is whether or not we can get in between them and the Rangers."

The colonel squatted beside Zappasodi's map and traced two lines on the sheet, vectors that converged in Karlshofen.

"S3," Janisek called for his operations officer.

"Right here, sir."

"It's pretty obvious that we're not going any farther by train," Janisek said, surveying the damage done by the saboteurs. "How far back do we have to go to find a siding where we can unload these vehicles?"

The S3, who was something of a martinet, in Kilgore's estimation, whipped out his map and answered without missing a beat.

"I had the railmaster mark the sidings on my map before he took off," he said smugly, laying the sheet on the platform next to Zappasodi's.

"Great," Janisek said.

"But that's the good news," the S3 continued. "The bad news is that we'd have to go all the way back to Hannover."

Zappasodi shook his head. "The Rangers will be in a hurt locker by then. Isn't there any way to get the vehicles off the trains? Can't you just drive them off?"

"That's a five- to seven-foot drop," Kilgore said.

Janisek stood and walked to the edge of the platform. He glared at the concrete as if it might melt. "Goddamn motherfuckers."

"Maybe we could blow the wheels off the bottoms of the cars," Bonham offered. "That would bring the beds down far enough."

Russell, Kilgore's XO, looked as if he might choke Bonham, but he was restrained by the colonel's presence. Kilgore reminded himself to leave Bonham with his platoon sergeant the next time they had a conference with the commander.

"Well, we'll have to get back to Hannover and make up the lost time on the road," Janisek said.

While the squadron commander and his operations officer worked on the details and runners went for the other troop commanders, Kilgore and Russell walked back along the platform and the length of the train.

"If we have a bust-ass road race from Hannover to Karlshofen," Russell confided, "we'll lose at least four tanks, maybe four or five CFVs."

Kilgore nodded. Russell's job at XO was to know, inside and out, the maintenance status of the tanks and cavalry fighting vehicles. Russell was not one to panic—his predictions would be accurate.

"Going back to Hannover isn't the solution," Kilgore said.

"Sir?"

Kilgore stared up at the retaining wall. The station platform here was some fifteen feet below street level.

"Well, if everybody and his brother knows where the American convoy is," Kilgore said, "then chances are the skinheads are behind us right now, doing the same thing to the tracks."

"So we're stuck here?" Russell asked.

"Mmmmm, I'm not so sure."

Kilgore looked behind them at the station. The street there was at least twenty feet higher than the tracks. Here, some fifty meters down, the difference was not as dramatic. As he gazed down the tracks, he saw that the wall gradually approached the tracks until, at some point he couldn't see because of a bend, the tracks were at ground level.

"There's your answer," Kilgore said, pointing. He pivoted immediately, leaving Russell staring and wondering what his boss had pointed out to him.

"Damned if I see it," Russell said before turning to follow.

Forty minutes later Lieutenant Russell, enlisted for skills he'd learned as an inner-city teenager, completed hot wiring the ignition to a bulldozer parked in view of the railroad tracks. One of the Abrams drivers moved the dozer behind a pile of construction rubble, which he nudged toward the railroad cut.

"What made you think of this?" Russell asked. He and Kilgore stood on the deck of the car that held Kilgore's tank.

"My grandfather was a combat engineer in World War II," Kilgore answered. "And he used to brag about how a sergeant defeated Germany's west wall with a little bit of NCO common sense. All the engineer officers wanted to blow gaps in the dragon's teeth antitank obstacles, but that would have taken days and thousands of pounds of explosives."

Russell nodded. He had seen some of the dragon's teeth that had been left in place: row after row of little concrete pyramids, ten deep and four to six feet high, too high for the tanks to negotiate.

"This sergeant used a bulldozer to push a bunch of dirt on top of the teeth," Kilgore said. "Just buried them. Then the tanks drove over the top."

Russell smiled and grunted as the bulldozer pushed the first load of rubble down beside the tracks, where it came to rest between the rail car and the retaining wall.

"Should have that filled up in about thirty minutes, wouldn't you say?" Russell asked.

Kilgore nodded. He watched to make sure the rubble wouldn't block the tracks. As long as they could move the train, they could line up each car with the makeshift platform until they'd unloaded all their vehicles.

"What about them?" Russell asked. "Think they'll be a problem?"

Kilgore looked up to where his executive officer pointed. About a block away he could see five or six men—young men—gathered on the corner and in the doorway of a closed and boarded-up shop.

"Skinheads?" Kilgore asked.

"Doesn't make much difference," Russell allowed. "If they get in our way, that is. What's the policy, sir?"

Kilgore knew that Russell was as angry as he was about the official response to Leonard's shooting. The EUCOM commander had told them to "do everything possible to preserve German property and avoid bloodshed."

"I think that until we get away from these buildings we're in danger," Kilgore said. "You know, Molotov cocktails and grenades thrown from the upper stories."

"We could have some of the troopers ride on top of the CFVs to keep an eye out," Russell offered.

"Good idea."

"And . . . uh . . . do we return fire if they shoot at us?"

Kilgore looked down the street at their antagonists. They were a motley crew, some as young as fifteen or sixteen, all of them raggedly dressed in the uniform of the disgruntled: dirty jean jacket, black T-shirt, and filthy work boots. They didn't look as if they would be much of a threat to a troop of armored cavalry. But they'd managed to stop the train. And it would only take one shot, one lucky shot from a darkened window or doorway, to send one of Kilgore's men home in a box.

"We'll follow the commander's guidance and do everything possible to maintain a peaceful relationship with German civilians," Kilgore said. "But if they shoot at one of my troopers, well, it ain't gonna be pretty."

Down the track, the first tank rolled off its flatbed and onto the German streets. As soon as it was clear of the men working the siding, the tank commander rotated the turret out of travel lock, bringing the gun forward, pointing it north toward Karlshofen and whatever lay in between. It was fourteen hundred hours.

24

MARK ISEN KNEW EXACTLY WHAT WAS HAPPENING TO HIM as he lay in the thin wet snow and watched the road and felt the shakiness come up over him, from down in his legs, his testicles, his lungs. He was losing his battle with doubt.

Isen had chosen the spot for this attack on the GPU column from a map reconnaissance. Like many such choices, it looked better on paper than it did out here on the ground. Nevertheless, he had set his men to work in a race against the approaching enemy, and the Rangers were making the best of it.

Isen and Hendricks, his operations NCO, had crawled to the edge of the dirt road to see what the American position would look like to the Germans when the shooting started. And it was down there, looking back up at the lip of the hill through the surprisingly sparse cover offered by the thin trees, that Isen began to worry too much about what might happen.

A little bit of worry was good, of course, because it spawned a healthy caution. But there was such a thing as too much imagination in a commander. Isen had seen it before: a leader could be paralyzed by the staggering array of imagined disasters that faced his command.

And all those demons were here in the woods. What if the GPU force was bigger than Hawkins and Bishop had reported? What if the Germans arrived ready to fight? What if the Rangers lost the element of surprise?

What if this formation proved tougher than the units they'd faced thus far? What if they'd doubled back and were now coming down another dirt road, or even the highway, which would put them behind the Rangers.

"What do you think?" Isen asked Hendricks.

"Not too bad," the NCO responded. "Not too bad."

The older man—eighteen years in the infantry—was not being cagey, he was merely studying the lay of the ground. Isen watched his eyes for some notice of alarm, but Hendricks seemed satisfied.

Still, the major couldn't shake the feelings of disaster that crept down on him.

"I don't like it," Isen allowed.

"What's not to like?" Hendricks asked, as calmly as if they were inspecting a range back at Benning.

"If we catch them unawares," Isen said. "we'll be all right. But if they draw us out on anything approaching even terms, what with their advantage of numbers and all, I'm not sure this area is the best place for us to take them on." The argument sounded coolly logical when he framed it that way, Isen had to allow. He wondered for a moment if this sense of his own panic was some sort of mental hypochondria.

Hendricks looked at his commander for a long moment. He knew that Isen had been shaken by his confrontation with Schauffert. Maybe he'd lost his nerve. Hendricks was walking a difficult line: he had to shore up his commander's self-confidence, and he had to offer the best advice he could. The problem was that the best advice might contradict Isen's plan. Or it might not. And he wouldn't really know until after everything was over. In a close call such as this, it was only possible to judge effectiveness after the fact.

"Of course it's not a good spot," the NCO said, trying not to sound like he was talking to a lieutenant. "There won't be any good spots if we have to get out and maneuver against them. Not unless we knock the hell out of them so bad when we first come down that hill that they don't have a chance to regroup."

He paused, ran a finger under the tight chin strap of his helmet. "I wouldn't be surprised if their leadership just fell apart when the shooting starts."

"The one-punch theory," Isen commented.

"What's that?"

"The one-punch theory," Isen repeated. "Hit them so hard with the first punch that there's no more fight left."

"Something like that," Hendricks allowed. He was becoming more cautious, more aware that Isen was off on some mental trip—maybe thinking through the battle, which was what he got paid to do, or worrying about it too much.

"Just like an ambush, sir," Hendricks offered to buttress his point. "You open up with the biggest casualty producer. *Bam.* Fuck 'em up from the start."

Isen nodded, crawled back up the slope a few feet before he stood. "Let's go up to the lip of the hill," he said.

From the top of the small ridge, they could see no more than a hundred meters of the road, and most of that was at least partially obscured by bare trees. Behind them, men were digging shallow fighting positions, stashing their rucksacks under the sheltering branches of trees, checking their fields of fire. One soldier sat hunched over, sharpening his bayonet on a small whetstone. The blade sang back and forth, back and forth.

Things are in motion, Isen thought. *Set in motion by my command.*

He didn't know how much of this shakiness was within him—caused by his blow-out with Schauffert, and how much came from outside him—from real concerns about the plan. It was tough trying to assess his own ability to make decisions. He'd been awake for days, with no real rest, and had been under a tremendous strain. Was he ready to make decisions such as this one? Could he see the ground as clearly as he needed to, or was he just content to pick a spot for the slugfest and let things unroll as they might, set in motion by the gods of war, by chance or fate or whatever?

Mark Isen couldn't escape the idea that he was in over his head. Here he was, a junior major, trying to take a battalion into combat. And, for the first time, he began to think he had no business being there.

"Shit," he said.

"What's that, sir?" Hendricks asked.

"I . . . I'm not sure," he stuttered. "I'm not sure this is the best way," he said, waving vaguely over the side of the hill.

Isen caught Hendricks's look of mild, but growing, alarm.

"What's wrong with it, sir?"

Isen caught his breath. There was something definitely wrong with this position, but he wasn't sure how to say it, and he couldn't tell where his professional judgment ended and his fears began. All around him, the men were finishing their preparations, walking the line as much as they dared, looking at the road and the kill zone and rehearsing how they would advance. They were settling in for the fight, readying themselves, preparing to kill.

Isen looked again at the ground, at the shallow slope of the hill that fell before them to the neat road down in the woods, at the white stripe of snow that would soon be burned by explosions and stained with blood, if things went as he wanted them to. And quite suddenly Isen knew he had to change the plan, although that made as much sense to him as trying to change your mind about jumping from an aircraft after you'd stepped out the door.

His company commanders would think him a lunatic. The soldiers, knowing how close the enemy was, would be frightened by his seeming lack of resolve, and that was not a feeling he wanted to engender in his troops just before the shooting started.

Everything about Isen's training told him that he should be able to study this tactical problem objectively: there was a list somewhere in his memory, drilled into him in all those hours at the Infantry School and days on field problems, a paradigm that could reduce all the frightening possibilities to something he could measure, check off, weigh. And the result of all that objective thinking would be a decision that was as clear as cool water. But he was fried, his brain fuzzy as it might have been after a serious bout of drinking and eating bad food.

They'll go nuts, he thought, looking over the hill and thinking of his subordinates' reaction. *Maybe they'll get Schauffert to can me.*

But deep down in the pit of his stomach he knew he was right.

Fuck it, he thought.

"This isn't the place," Isen said at last. "This isn't going to work."

He turned his back to the road and headed to the interior of the battalion's crescent-shaped position, his operations NCO following some meters behind.

"Get me the company commanders down here," Isen told his radio operators.

"What's the problem, sir?" Hendricks asked when he caught up with Isen.

"The plan we're working on isn't the best way to go," Isen told him with more confidence than he felt.

"You ain't planning on changing it now, are you?" Hendricks asked. "That column of infantry could be here within the hour."

Isen didn't answer, but instead turned to Gamble, his primary radio operator.

"We got any more word from Lieutenant Hawkins about the location of that column?"

"No, sir, but the patrol should be back soon. Charlie Company is in contact with them."

"We can make a good fight of it from here, sir," Hendricks pressed. "This is a natural defensive position, what with the hill and everything. We could sit up there all day long and shoot them as they tried to come up the hill."

"That's what I'm afraid of," Isen said. "We didn't come out here to go on the defensive. To sit on a hill and have them come at us."

"As long as it keeps them from reaching the drop zones, we're accomplishing the mission," Hendricks countered, his anger showing now.

"Suppose they leave a force here to fix us in place and send a few companies on to Karlshofen," Isen said. "It wouldn't take much to fuck things up on the drop zone."

The company commanders were starting to gather. Dettering, Sam Drake, who'd taken Bravo Company when Wisneiwski was killed, and Taylor, all wearing grim looks. They had a lot to do and a short time to do it in, and though they were disturbed by the interruption, they didn't yet suspect that Isen was going to change the whole game plan on them.

"We don't have the time, sir, to change everything," Hendricks said, *sotto voce*, clearly wanting to keep this away from the commanders.

Isen wondered if the old NCO thought he'd slipped a gear.

"We have to make it work," Isen said. "We can't afford to make a mistake out here, with our asses hanging in the breeze."

Hendricks, who had five or six inches on Isen, drew himself to his full height. "We're making a mistake if we try to change now, with those motherfuckers practically breathing down our necks."

He may be right, Isen thought. Maybe it was idiotic to try to change at this point. He looked at his officers and wondered if they'd have the same reaction that his operations sergeant had.

Do not take counsel of your fears, he told himself. He nodded to Hendricks, just a slight tilt of the head, signaling that the discussion was over.

"I made a mistake in the deployment here," he told his officers, putting the onus squarely on himself. "I'm no longer convinced that my original plan is the best one."

Taylor looked at his watch, no doubt calculating how soon the enemy might be on them. Dettering looked at Isen as if the battalion commander were speaking Urdu. Drake, the least experienced man in the group, looked from face to face, as if the older men might be playing a trick on him and he expected them, at any minute, to own up.

"I know we're pressed for time, and the adjustments I want to make aren't . . . well, we don't have to change everything."

Isen was watching the faces before him, hoping for some acknowledgment of what he'd said. Even a negative reaction was better than nothing and would let him argue his point.

"We don't have time to change, sir," Taylor said evenly. "We'd be crazy to try now, with those guys closing an hour away."

"We have a little more time than that," Dettering interrupted. "Hawkins and his people got back just as I was leaving to come here. They said the GPU column halted. Looked to Sergeant Bishop like they were trying to collect their stragglers."

"What else about the column?" Isen asked, daring to hope that the odds might not be as bad as the first estimate.

"About six or seven companies, we figure, but not all from the same unit." Dettering's voice was slow, thick with fatigue.

"Some of them are pretty raggedy-assed, I guess," Dettering continued. "No uniforms, no march discipline, no security, that kind of stuff."

"What's wrong with the plan we have now?" Taylor wanted to know.

He didn't seem angry, just tired, resigned to being fucked with just one more time.

"We sacrifice too much of the initiative to them," Isen said. "After we hit them, we're up on our little hill and they get to make the moves. We came out here to go on the offensive, and that's what we're going to do."

I sound like a fucking salesman, Isen thought. "Here's what I want."

Isen pulled out his map sheet, but the scale was too small. He knelt down and traced a hasty sketch in the snow.

"I'm going to leave Charlie Company in place here, because this is a natural defensive position," Isen said, using his finger to draw a small crescent facing west. He looked up at Dettering, whose company had been singled out. The man showed no reaction.

"Then I'm going to take the other two companies farther up the road here," he said, pushing his finger along the east side of the road in the direction that Germans were coming from. "When the GPU main body is in this kill zone, Charlie Company will spring an ambush, then fall back to a defensive line. While they're still trying to recover from that, the rest of us are going to come down the road behind them and hit them in the rear."

It looked better to him now that he'd sketched it out. Norden, his operations officer, was comparing the sketch to the map. Lieutenant Drake's eyes were on Isen. Taylor had his eyes closed, and Dettering just looked worried.

"Dividing the force in the face of a numerically superior enemy," Taylor intoned.

"What?" Isen asked.

"We're splitting our force in the face of a numerically superior foe," Taylor said, adding "sir" a second later. "A recipe for disaster."

"Why is that?" Isen asked. He wanted to sound like the solicitous commander, but came off, he thought, as unsure.

"If they react quickly to the Charlie Company attack, they could wipe those guys out before we could bring any firepower to bear," Taylor speculated. "And what if they get wind of us first? Or suppose their first reaction, when Charlie Company opens up, is to try to outflank our guys in the woods. We could run right smack into them. Or they might head away from Alpha and Bravo and get around Dettering's company on the southwest side."

"I don't think they're that good," Isen said. That drew no response, and everyone recognized it for what it was: a guess. It was based on the evidence of the last few days, to be sure, but each formation they'd faced had been different.

"The trick is that we have to do it quickly," Isen said. "We have to get out along that road and smash them from behind before they even have a chance to figure out what size force is opposing them up front."

Taylor looked at the other officers, skipping over Norden, who was a junior captain, and Drake, who was a lieutenant, to address his only real peer in the group.

"Bill?" he said to Dettering.

The Charlie Company commander shrugged. "I don't know," he said. "We don't have a lot of time, you know? No rehearsals, nothing like that. We might be able to get in a leader's recon."

Good, Isen thought. Dettering was on his side. Or at least he didn't seem opposed.

"I don't think it's a good idea, sir," Taylor said flatly. "Seems to me the best thing to do, with the men as exhausted as they are, and with time as short as it is, is to stick with a simple plan. Right now we're ready to spring a big ambush, and chances are good those jokers aren't ready for it. We can do the job without all this fancy stuff."

Isen rolled his shoulders forward, trying to relieve the dull ache that had settled in his back. He needed Taylor, who would be the senior company commander in the important attack along the road.

"We can do it better with the 'fancy stuff,' as you call it," Isen said. The comment had come out with more sarcasm than he'd intended. *God, I'm at the end of my friggin' rope,* he thought.

"We came out here to seize the initiative. All I'm saying is that if we shoot at them from this hill," Isen said, indicating their surroundings with a small sweep of his arm, "we're just going on the defensive. Fighting from a defensive position. Why do that when we can keep on attacking?"

"We should do that—stay on this hill—because our force is too small to maneuver against them," Taylor said, his jaw tightening, "and because we don't have time to get the attack together before they get here."

"Bill?" Isen asked Dettering's opinion.

"I have to agree with John," Dettering said. "I don't think we ought to be moving around when these guys are almost on top of us." He looked squarely at Isen as he spoke, and there was no trace of nervousness in his eyes.

Isen's two senior company commanders—Taylor would take the battalion if anything happened to Isen—were against him. He looked at Norden and Drake, the two most junior officers in the conclave.

"I think we should just stay put," Norden said. "Like John says, too little time to get things going."

Isen didn't even ask Drake, but the lieutenant offered his opinion anyway. "We have to go with the best plan available. If that means changing it," he said, "then we have to change it."

The little sucker has balls, Isen thought.

The other officers didn't look at the lieutenant, as if his opinion didn't even merit comment. But Drake, who felt his new responsibility heavy on his shoulders, wasn't letting it go.

"It's like if you move into a line and tell the machine gunners to dig their position a certain way. Later on, if you figure out that you made a mistake and the machine gun should be somewhere else or oriented a different way, you tell them to change it. They'll be pissed off—they've done all that work—but you have to keep the best interests of the unit and the mission in mind." He paused for a minute, looked up at the captains around him, the cast of worried machine gunners.

"Looks like we have a consensus here, sir," Taylor said.

Isen looked up at the company commander. Taylor was bold in combat, had been encouraged to be bold during his whole career as an infantryman. And he was being bold now, the bold paratrooper.

Isen was acutely aware of the fact that every decision rested on his shoulders. He would bear the consequences, it was his responsibility to make the call. If he disagreed with the majority after weighing what they had to say, he had to have the guts to override them. It could be that Taylor was right. It was entirely possible that Isen had lost his sense of perspective, that he was about to screw the pooch in a big way. He thought about it, waited for a few seconds, as if the answer might come to him in some divine voice, as if Mars might whisper in his ear. But it wasn't about to happen. He was all alone here. He had made his decision and would live by it. Or die by it.

"We're not taking a vote," Isen said.

That was it, of course; it was Isen's call. But there was something righteous boiling up in Taylor, and Isen knew he should let the other man vent his frustrations, even if he, as the commander, had already made up his mind.

"Go ahead, John," Isen said.

"It's a fucked-up idea to change things now, sir," Taylor insisted. His voice rose, but he fought for control. Isen had a second to be amazed at the way they held on to the old habits of military courtesy, even in the face of exhaustion, *in extremis*. Maybe this was the way to hang on to sanity.

"I understand your concerns, John, I really do. We're short of time," Isen said. "And we're opting for a more complicated scheme." He paused to let that sink in, but he knew that Taylor knew, and that Dettering and Norden knew, that he was about to override them.

Taylor looked around at the faces in the small circle, weighing something. "You're under a lot of pressure here, sir," Taylor said. "What with Colonel Schauffert and all. Are you sure. . . ." He stumbled. "Are you sure. . . ."

"Am I sure I haven't lost my mind?" Isen said.

Keep control, he warned himself. *If you blow up, that'll be the evidence they need that you've lost it.* He breathed in, let it out.

"No. It's just that I think this plan is better. So much so that I'm willing to take the chance and change things."

I'm willing to take the chance.

That's the heart of this thing, Isen thought. *I take personal responsibility for the choice. But the results will not be borne by me personally. If things turn out badly, we all share in the disaster.*

That's what made command decisions so difficult. He was deciding on behalf of several hundred men, few of whom had any say in things, and none of whom had the authority to contradict him. This sort of power intoxicated some men, Isen knew, but not in this situation. Not in combat.

He looked at his captains, the men who had to make the plan work, who had to convince the hundreds of others that they were doing things the right way. He could hardly call them enthusiastic, but they no longer challenged him.

As he knelt again by his crude drawing in the snow and prepared to talk more about their responsibilities, Isen said a simple prayer.

Dear Lord, please don't let me fuck up.

"Can you believe this shit?"

Brennan knew that soldiers were supposed to bitch, but he wasn't sure when he should cut off the chatter and make them concentrate.

"We get all set, and the bad guys are just up the road a piece, and suddenly we're changing the whole fucking game plan?"

The speaker was a private named Akers, a Georgia farm boy who rolled out his complaints on a carpet of heavy drawl that gave them a sonorous weight all out of proportion to his diminutive size and his lowly place on the totem pole.

"I had me the best position," Akers continued, badgering his squad-mates. "You just couldn't even believe it."

"That's enough, Akers," Brennan said. "We've heard it all. Now it's time to get to work."

"Hey, Sarge," one of the other men said to Brennan. "Maybe we can just put Akers out on the road and he can whine the fucking GPUs to death. Huh?"

Brennan chuckled with the rest, and even Akers managed to laugh at his own expense.

Brennan wasn't a sergeant, of course. He was still wearing the specialist insignia he'd had on for ten months now. But he'd been moved up to team leader by Sergeant Bishop as the men who outranked him were killed or wounded. Bishop hadn't hesitated when given the chance to use Brennan as a leader, but Brennan had resisted.

"Not me," he'd told Bishop flatly.

"Who else am I gonna put in charge?" Bishop had asked, bypassing all of Brennan's arguments.

"But I screwed up, got Charis shot. . . . "

Bishop had cut him off. "Just stop right there with that bullshit. That wasn't your fault. It just *was*."

"I don't want the responsibility," Brennan had said.

"Well, I need you," Bishop had answered with an unmistakable finality. "So the job is yours. Do your best, and more of these guys will make it through than if you lay down on us."

Brennan knew that Bishop was right: there was no one else left. By the time Bishop took over as platoon sergeant, there were only six men in the squad, all of them less experienced than Brennan. They had jumped in with eleven—two five-man teams and the squad leader. Bishop put all the men in Brennan's team, which made him—as a result of there being no other team—the de facto squad leader, responsible for accomplishing his part of the mission and preserving the lives of his men. He was twenty years old.

"How far away are the other companies?" Akers asked, suddenly serious as he peered into the woods off their right flank. Brennan's group was the right-most end of the defensive line—the side closest to the advancing GPU.

"Less than a klick, probably six, seven hundred meters," Brennan said. The truth was that he didn't know with any certainty; he was guessing. But he didn't think it was such a great idea to talk about how exposed they were out here.

"You've got the most important part of the line," Captain Dettering had told him. "When they counterattack—and they will—you'll get hit first, and you have to stay put."

Brennan wasn't rattled at this. He had welcomed Isen's change of heart, mostly because Brennan tended to agree that it would be better to attack than to sit on the hill and wait for the GPU. The problem was that Charlie Company's part, and thus Brennan's, was to launch the ambush and pull back, sit until the other companies attacked the rear of the GPU formation. The battalion was on the offensive, but Brennan's little group had much the same mission as before, had, actually, a more dangerous mission, since Charlie Company would be alone.

"You're the end of the line here, Brennan," Dettering had told him. "You fold and we'll all get rolled up and stuffed if the bad guys come up the hill. You have to hold this position no matter what. Kind of like Chamberlain at Gettysburg."

Brennan had met that comment with a blank look.

"I'll tell you about him sometime," Dettering finished.

That was an hour ago. In the meantime he and his men had prepared as best they could for the upcoming fight.

"Get in your positions."

It was Sergeant Bishop, walking the line. Leadership by walking around, the NCO called it facetiously.

"We get word from the OP?" Brennan asked. The platoon had an observation post several hundred meters down the road to warn about the approaching GPU.

"Yeah," Bishop said. He wasn't looking at Brennan, but was inspecting the fighting positions, looking for the kind of correctable mistakes that might save a man's life. His eyes darted back and forth, back and forth. Everything was hurried and Bishop, no more than Brennan, was on the lookout for the kind of deadly mistakes caused by haste.

"You got that status?" Bishop asked.

Brennan flipped open his pocket notebook and tore out a sheet that noted how much ammo his squad had on hand.

"It would have been nice to be able to spend a little more time getting ready," Brennan said.

Bishop grunted as he read.

"You know that you have to hold here, right?" Bishop said, looking up. Then, more slowly, "You absolutely have to hold here."

Brennan nodded, not trusting himself to answer. There was something in Bishop's eyes that startled Brennan, some pointed shadow of alarm.

Does he think we aren't going to make it through this? Brennan wondered.

Bishop took one last look at the scene, then stuck out his hand to Brennan. "Good luck."

"Thanks," Brennan said, taking the offered hand.

His men were already in their positions: shallow two-man holes partway down the slope, one on each side of Brennan's own two-man position. The idea was that they'd open fire on the GPU column from this position close to the road, inflicting as many casualties as they could in the first minute, using hand grenades, antipersonnel mines, machine guns, and automatic weapons. Then they'd withdraw uphill, their movement partially concealed by the trees and undergrowth, to the line of prepared positions on the low ridge.

The tricky part would be disengaging once they traded shots with the enemy—unless the GPU formation just fell apart. Brennan didn't like this part of the plan—there was always the chance that they'd be pinned down, thus giving up the advantage the ridge held for them. But it was dictated by the lay of the ground. The road was too far away from the hilltop, too obscured by trees to let them get in a good first lick, so they had to get close. But getting close meant occupying low ground, almost as low as the road, and fighting from there.

Brennan had picked Akers as his partner because he wanted the youngster close enough to make him keep his mouth shut. Akers was stretched out prone in the shallow hole, with freshly cut pine branches resting on the barrel of his squad automatic weapon. He had plastic drums of spare ammunition next to him, and two hand grenades, their pins straightened for easy pulling, at hand.

"How you doing?" Brennan asked as he lay down in his side of the hole.

There was no answer, and Brennan glanced to his side to see that Akers was asleep over the stock of his weapon. The men were that tired. With a large enemy force expected at any moment, with the prospect of having to leave this position under fire and make it to the top of the rise, with all that on his mind, Akers was asleep.

Brennan raised himself to a crouch, satisfied himself that at least one man in each of the other two positions was awake, then settled in to watch the road. He let Akers sleep. In a moment, the deep, rhythmic breathing of the other soldier had calmed Brennan somewhat. He concentrated on the white strip of road before him. Shadows slipped across the snow as the sun swung round the southern sky, and all around him the woods grew silent, save for the wind brushing the treetops. But Timothy Brennan heard only the steady, worrisome thumping of his own heart as he gulped back his fears and watched the ribbon of virgin snow that was the kill zone.

When the word came in from the Alpha Company observation post that the GPU column was approaching, Mark Isen left Alpha and Bravo in their positions just off the road and made his way southwest back to Charlie Company. He had earlier picked out a spot just behind the rightmost platoon, Hawkins's platoon, from which he thought he'd be able to see everything, or at least enough to know what was going on.

His plan was to stay with this force until they had pulled back up on their tight little hill. When Charlie Company was dug in, he would move back over to Alpha and Bravo so that he could be with the main effort. Even if Isen didn't show up in the attack position, Taylor would drive the attack into the rear of the GPU column. The captain had resisted the plan, but once Isen had decided, he would carry it out as best he could, putting his own life on the line unhesitatingly.

Isen felt someone tug at his leg. It was Gamble, who was lying on his stomach behind Isen.

"Linebacker, sir," Gamble said.

That code word, called in from Taylor, meant that the OP had come in and the GPU column was passing by the two companies that would crash down on its rear. Isen nodded, and Gamble passed the word to Charlie Company.

Isen wondered what Taylor was thinking as he watched the Germans march by him down the road, wondered how much of the enemy formation the other officer could see. Isen checked his watch. It had been only a minute since he received the password, but it probably took a couple of minutes, maybe three or four, for the message to get to Isen. He strained to see the road, resisting the temptation to raise himself on his hands and knees for a better look. Just a few meters below him, the Rangers of Charlie Company waited in their holes.

They came up quickly, four men out in front like skirmishers. The way they appeared suddenly on the road made Isen think that there must be a curve, or perhaps a small rise not too far from the Charlie Company position that might shield part of the GPU column once the shooting started. Dettering's plan covered that problem—the Charlie Company commander would be talking to men out beyond either end of his line and would have a fix on the head and tail of the enemy column before he gave the word to fire.

As the GPU soldiers moved, they came more and more into Isen's view. Two of the men had helmets, the third a wool field cap pulled down over his ears, the last was bareheaded. The two with helmets carried their weapons at the ready, moving the muzzles back and forth as they scanned the sides of the road. The other two—Isen was getting the distinct impression that he was looking at men from two different units—walked with their weapons down at arm's length across their thighs.

Isen thought that these were the lucky ones, the ones who would pass through the kill zone and be on the other side when the shooting began.

The main body wasn't far behind the skirmishers. Two files—one on each side of the road—moving just as Americans did on a tactical road march: three or four meters between each man, somewhat staggered on either side of the road so that no one was walking directly across from a comrade on the other side. If there were six or seven companies, as Bishop reported, the column would stretch for a kilometer or more. Although his other two companies were positioned back far enough so as to be behind the tail, Isen was suddenly concerned that Charlie Company would not be able to catch enough of the enemy in the first assault.

He watched carefully, salty sweat running into his eyes.

Brennan watched, fascinated, as the GPU soldiers moved along the road just a short distance away from him. He had already nudged Akers awake, and the gunner had his cheek pressed against the stock of his weapon, the muzzle trained on the road. His line of fire was close to the axis of the road, so that the gunner could hit, with enfilading fire, many targets by moving the gun only slightly, walking it up and down the enemy column.

Brennan tensed, waiting for the shooting to start. Captain Dettering had several antitank rockets he was planning to fire, an unmistakable signal to begin the shooting. Brennan knew that it was against the Geneva

Convention to use such munitions on troops, but the argument seemed pointless out here. Instead of using rockets, this nineteen-year-old farm boy next to him was about to use a machine gun to kill as many men as he could. Finally, it came down to a few brutal, simple facts: if they didn't kill enough of the enemy to break up the advance, the men on the road would kill them. All the rest—rockets, machine guns, ambushes—all the rest was technique.

Brennan concentrated on what was about to happen. Everything else was like scenery on a distant stage. Beside him, Akers's face was an impassive mask just above the black stock of his weapon.

Akers picked out one man who was just coming around the corner of the road, rested the sights squarely on the dark torso, and wondered, for the briefest moment, who this man might be, and what had brought him to this exact point in the road, in Akers's sights.

25

TIM BRENNAN SAW THE CHANGE GO THROUGH THE GPU FILES like a gentle ripple. One man, thirty meters away and slightly below Brennan's position, looked up into the woods, then down at his feet, then quickly back up. The sudden motion caught the attention of a few men around him, who looked into the woods as if to see what had caught their comrade's attention.

Brennan shifted his point of aim to the man who'd looked up first. The soldier did a sort of shuffle, hesitating, his face still turned upward. Brennan felt a sickening lurch. Could the German have seen them, or spotted one of the antipersonnel mines beside the road? In the agony of seconds while he wondered if Dettering would give the signal to open up, Brennan had to decide whether or not to fire, knowing that he could screw the whole thing up if he misjudged. But all that quickly fell away as the German Brennan was watching stepped to the side of the road, fell to his knees, raised his weapon and fired directly at the Ranger position to Brennan's right.

The explosion of fire that was supposed to roll down from the hill never materialized. What they got instead was an almost accidental flare-up as men on both sides began popping off rounds. The Rangers, who were at least behind their weapons and aware of the enemy's presence, were faster, but the Germans were responding.

Brennan pulled the trigger on his rifle, then heard the hammering of

Akers's SAW. Below him, GPU soldiers were breaking for the side of the road nearest the Americans, and still there was no sign of Dettering's signal. Brennan knew that the Americans were losing control of the first few crucial seconds of the fight, when the advantage of surprise should have worked in their favor.

Somewhere behind Brennan, Sergeant Bishop screamed at the platoon. *"Open fire, open fire!"*

There was a splintery *crunch crunch* as squad leaders along the line blew the claymore mines, spraying the road with thousands of steel balls. Some of the Germans had taken refuge right next to the mines, and these men were killed by the explosions. But many of the intended victims had moved out of the kill zone of the mines simply by stepping off the road, and these men were now shooting back.

The crescendo of fire wasn't building fast enough on the Rangers' side, Brennan thought, and the competing sounds of firing from the bottom of the hill seemed to be closing the gap. Brennan looked left and right—his own men were shooting. He chanced a look back along the platoon line. Every man he could see was firing, but it still didn't seem enough. He popped the empty magazine out of his rifle and inserted another.

After the days spent moving around and being hunted, after the pressures of changing the plans and tightening the position, after the realization that his company was alone here, and that his squad was on the edge, the firing was a tremendous, almost sexual release.

"Choose your targets," he shouted at his men, afraid that they would fire all their ammunition in the same orgiastic release of fear and tension.

He looked down the hill and saw that the Germans were trying to maneuver against him by sidestepping off to the American right. Two figures made a rush up the slope, and Brennan brought his rifle around in time to catch a third. He pulled the trigger, lost the sight picture when the muzzle jumped, looked for another target.

"They're trying to get around us," he yelled to the men on his right.

"I see 'em," one of the soldiers said. The men in the next hole heaved two grenades down the slope, but the brushy *crump* of their reports seemed small in comparison to the ripping sounds of gunfire rolling back and forth all along the road.

Brennan turned his back to the fight, looking for Bishop, "They're trying to get around us," he yelled in the direction of the platoon sergeant's hole.

"There sure are a lot of the motherfuckers," Akers said as he worked his weapon along the depression on the near side of the road. The GPU soldiers had naturally gravitated toward the bottom of the hill and the tiny depression that shielded some of them, left some of them exposed. Brennan pulled the pins from Akers's two grenades and tossed them down, aiming for the ditch and the men cowering there. He saw two more men break away from the false security of the road to begin the uphill climb.

And the thought struck him cleanly. *They're moving under control now,* Brennan thought. *No panic, not even just reacting. They're maneuvering against us.*

Down below he could hear the voices—he assumed they were NCOs—giving orders. He rested his weapon on the front edge of the hole and shot at the men who were now among the trees, above the road but still below the Rangers.

"Fuck," he said. "*Fuck.*" The Rangers' mistake, Brennan knew, had been in expecting the GPU to crumble, to cower by the road as soon as they were hit, to fall apart as the poorly led mechanized unit had done.

Below him, the voices of command gained against the screams of the wounded and the sound of chaos. The GPU was struggling to gain control of the fight, and they were succeeding.

Brennan looked back for Bishop, afraid he'd miss the signal to move back up the hill.

Now the Germans were shooting at them from the front and the side, and were no doubt trying to move up the hill to get behind them as well. Brennan thought he could stay put a few more minutes, at the most, before his men were outflanked. But he could not move his squad back without the platoon, and the platoon could not move back until the company was ready. The company was not a solid mass, but a string of individual positions, each depending on the others, and the whole could come unraveled if one gave way. Everyone depended on everyone else, and at the far right end, the critical point for the attackers, the spot they'd aim for, sat Brennan's understrength squad.

You absolutely have to hold here.

Something kicked him in the back of the head, and his upper body shot forward, tearing muscles in his neck. He raised his hand to his helmet and fingered a hot gash there. He'd been shot in the head, saved only by his helmet. Brennan pivoted on his knees and yelled for the men in the adjacent positions.

"You guys still OK?"

"Yeah," came the answer from his right, the last hole in the line. "But the fuckers are getting around us. When do we pull out of here?"

Brennan turned back.

"Sergeant Bishop," he screamed. But men were screaming all around him. Hand grenades sailed down the slope—and a few came up—to bounce in the thin snow and explode in great orange bursts that wiped out everything but what one could see and hear within a circle of a few feet. There seemed no way Bishop would hear him.

"Akers," Brennan said. "I'm going over to Bishop's position to tell him we're getting flanked. OK?"

Akers, bent over the barrel of his smoking gun, diligently searched for targets and fired a perfect staccato of five- to six-round bursts. He nodded. "I'm OK."

Brennan looked back to his right. Whatever GPU soldiers were over there, trying to get up the slope, hid themselves well. If they kept going uphill they would soon be behind Charlie Company, might even occupy the positions up the hill. It was time to do something, and as frightened as he was, with bullets sailing by in every direction, Brennan was completely focused on just one thing: *Don't fuck up.* This, finally, is what drove him from the relative safety of his hole in the ground, this little depression where incoming rounds couldn't reach him. He grabbed a sharp breath and pushed off to his left, hunched over, scuttling as fast as he could toward Bishop, sliding in like a runner intent on stealing a base.

"They're getting around us on the right," Brennan said before he even stopped moving. He fell into the hole right on top of Bishop and Hawkins. The lieutenant was firing his weapon down the slope, grunting, cursing. He didn't look around.

"How many?" Bishop asked.

Brennan was unprepared for that question. "I don't know . . . maybe four or five. They're getting up behind us," he said again, as if Bishop might have missed the point.

"I heard you," Bishop said, pulling the radio handset up to his ear. He made his report to Dettering. When he finished with the radio, he checked his watch.

"We move in five minutes," he said to Brennan. "Check your watch."

Brennan dutifully noted the exact time. "We going straight back up the hill, right?"

"Bound back within your squad," Bishop told him. "Don't leave anybody hanging their asses out on the line."

"Right," Brennan said, already too terrified to consider the difficulty of moving men under fire. He looked again at Hawkins, who was consumed with his own weapon, his own fight, and who didn't seem to notice that the rest of the platoon was all around him.

Brennan made it back to his position, crawling the last twenty meters as the incoming rounds sang by somewhere above him.

"How many more got by?" he asked when he reached his positions.

"A couple," Akers answered. "We moving?"

"Yeah."

Brennan divided his men up into two three-man teams. Bishop had told him to bound up the hill—that meant that one team fired as the other moved back, and the teams switched roles as they progressed.

The men were calm enough, firing steadily, looking for their targets, spotting for one another, answering Brennan when he questioned them. No panic. That was good.

Brennan looked at his watch, and suddenly, in his frantic state, couldn't remember the time he was supposed to move. It was five minutes from . . . from when?

"Jesus," he said. Then, "Let's go."

Three of his men clambered out of their holes as the other three picked up their rate of fire to cover the move. The men began to run, and Brennan watched them over his shoulder. When they stopped to fire down the hill, Brennan and the last two soldiers prepared to move.

"C'm'on, c'm'on," he said. He popped some smoke, tossing the canisters out to cover their move.

He saw the grenade coming at them, small and black, floating against the backdrop of the trees and ground. He let his legs go out from under him so that he fell back in the hole. He yelled at the other two, screaming mightily and trying to pull them back to him. Akers had a good lead, but the grenade went off right behind the other Ranger.

Brennan felt the heat of the flash and the sudden, sickening impact on his own skin of flesh atomized and sprayed about. The grenade had exploded directly under the feet of the Ranger. Brennan stood, saw the twitching legless torso, already dead. Only the popping of small arms fire behind him got him moving again, and he lifted first one leg, then the other, and forced himself to run past the corpse.

Akers was down, sprawled over his SAW, his legs peppered with red and bleeding from a dozen places. Brennan reached him just as one of the men came running down the hill.

Brennan grabbed Akers's arm and leg and hoisted him in a fireman's carry.

"Get the SAW," Brennan told the other soldier. "And my rifle."

He stumbled forward under his load—the wounded soldier outweighed him by fifteen or twenty pounds—heard Akers moaning somewhere off in his left ear, churned his legs furiously against the pull of gravity and the slippery face of the hill. In front of him, small geysers of dirt and snow leapt upward. The GPU was firing at him, *at him.*

Brennan felt a great coiling within him as every part of him—muscle, will, blood, anger—worked against the hill and Akers's weight. His foot slipped, and there was one icy cold instant when he thought he was going to fall over backward, but the soldier behind him shoved, and Brennan ran up the hill, carrying his wounded Ranger on his shoulders.

He ran past the men firing down the hill and kept going, lifting his eyes up to the top of the ridge some seventy meters away. The Rangers behind him fell back, covering him, shooting, moving, watching the flanks. They were magnificent.

Brennan collapsed on the hill, his legs buckling under the strain of Akers's weight and the climb. He was sweating in torrents, gasping like a landed fish. He broke Akers's fall with his own chest, arms, face, the wounded man on top of him.

Akers barked in terrible pain from somewhere out at the edge of consciousness. Brennan struggled from under the soldier, pushing, legs and arms fiery with exhaustion. When the other Rangers reached him, one bent down and grabbed a handful of Akers's jacket, tugging uphill. Brennan fought his way upright, grabbed Akers, and began to pull.

The wounded man slid slowly at first, but then the two of them lifted him under the armpits, caught each other's rhythm and began to make headway. Now the edge of the hill was a few meters away. Brennan's breath came in wet, jagged bursts. His legs were granite, his knees shattered glass. He was out way beyond the end of his physical endurance, his body long past quitting. Only his brain, his instinct for survival, drove him upward.

A few more steps, just a few more.

He felt the rounds bump through Akers's body, the sudden shocks transmitted through flesh and bone to Brennan's hand, up to his brain. He looked down, incredulous, and saw the soldier's back torn, shredded, black with blood. Akers was dead. Ten feet from the top of the hill.

He stopped, arched his back, lifted a hollow mouth and screamed his insane protest to an uncaring sky.

One of his soldiers came and shoved Brennan the last few feet up the hill, so that he tumbled over himself and fell, face-first, into one of the scratched-out positions they had prepared. Brennan rolled, lost his helmet, grabbed his rifle in a perfect ecstasy of rage.

"You motherfuckers," he screamed as he sought targets on the slope below him. *"You motherfucking motherfuckers!"*

The move up the hill had gained them some advantage, in that their position there was stronger. But it had gained them no reprieve, no time. The GPU soldiers had reacted with uncharacteristic aggression and had pursued the Americans step for step up to the last covered positions below the top of the hill. They reached for the Rangers with a nightmarish persistence that threatened to engulf the GIs. The Rangers sensed that they were in a bad way, a bad position. Now, instead of just being outnumbered and besieged, as they were at the bottom of the hill, they were outnumbered, besieged, and exhausted

So much of the Charlie Company's lower line was wreathed in smoke—green, yellow, purple, red—that Mark Isen, who should have been able to see quite a bit from his perch on the hill, lost sight of nearly everything.

"Looks like it's time to move," Sergeant Gamble said. He had a way of nudging his commander with such comments, reminding Isen that every time he took an unnecessary risk, his RTOs took it too.

Isen turned, motioned for Gamble and Hatley to move.

"Anything from Taylor yet?" Isen asked. He had left the timing of the flank attack to Taylor, but had stressed to him that it must all move very quickly.

"Nothing," Gamble said, leaning into the hill.

Isen looked off to the right of Charlie Company's line as he climbed. He could just make out, like shadows appearing and disappearing in the smoke, several figures running there. Behind him, however, the center of the line had not yet begun to move. He turned downhill, paused, looking for some sign that the rest of the positions were about to begin their bounds upward.

"Get me Dettering," Isen said.

Gamble tried to raise the Charlie Company commander, but there was no response. "Nothing, sir."

Dettering's position was below Isen and to his left as he faced the road below. The ragged beginning of the ambush had shaken Isen's confidence. Did Dettering know that his right flank was moving back? That it was time to move the whole line? He thought about running down the hill, but the last thing Dettering needed was to have his commander around when he was trying to run a fight.

"Hatley," Isen said.

"Yessir."

"Go back down the hill, over that way," Isen said, pointing, "and find Captain Dettering. Tell him that his rightmost positions are moving back."

"That's it, sir?"

Isen thought about telling Dettering to move the middle of the line. "Yeah," he said after a moment's pause. "He'll know what to do."

Hatley took off down the hill, and Isen and Gamble turned back to the climb.

True to his instincts as a combat veteran, Isen fell to the ground when he heard, close at hand, the distinct *thump thump* of rounds hitting something solid.

By the time he yelled "Get down," Gamble was already falling forward. Isen crawled up beside his radio operator.

"You OK?"

"I'm fine," Gamble answered. "Did you hear something?"

"Yeah." Isen slid back and checked Gamble's rucksack. There were two large tears in the green nylon, less than three inches behind Gamble's back.

"Radio work?" Isen asked.

Gamble keyed the handset, which he held close to his ear. "No. They get it?"

Isen's first reaction was relief that Gamble wasn't hit. But a second later he realized that, with Hatley gone as a runner, he was out of radio contact with his command.

"Shit!" Isen said, punching the ground in front of him. "Why the hell didn't I take Hatley's radio?"

"Look," Gamble said.

Off to the right side of the American line, the smoke was drifting away. Isen could see men running uphill, too far off the flank to be within the Rangers' position. That meant that they were getting flanked. "Let's get up there," he said.

Isen and Gamble made it to the top of the hill, where they dropped into the hasty positions prepared by Charlie Company. Below them, the center of the American line was still in place down by the road. Isen couldn't see enough to tell if they were pinned down, unable to move, or if they just hadn't started yet. And since he had no radio, he had no way to contact Dettering to find out. And no way to call Taylor to see if the attack—the one that would relieve the pressure on Charlie Company—had started yet.

Off to his right, some of Dettering's men were engaged in a firefight. Isen crawled off in that direction and found four Rangers firing at the GPU soldiers who were pressing the attack from the side, from a point along the same ridge. The kid named Brennan was in charge. He was missing his helmet, and his back was bloodstained, though Isen could see no wounds.

"Where's your platoon?" Isen asked.

Brennan didn't miss a beat, but continued firing. "They told me five minutes . . . pull back in five minutes. I waited, then started up. I don't know where the hell they are, sir."

"I'm going down to get you help," Isen said, trying to make his voice calm. "You hold on here." He ducked, leaning left as something whistled by his right ear. "If those fucking goons get in here, the rest of the company will be caught down below."

"I know," Brennan said. "I know."

Isen turned back to the center of the position, still manned only by Gamble.

"Hey, sir," Brennan called. Isen looked back.

"I didn't bug out of there," he said. "I didn't run."

"It'll be OK," Isen answered.

Back at the center of the position, Gamble had the radio out of his rucksack. There were two small holes, like puncture wounds, where the bullets had entered the aluminum casing, and two fist-sized tears where the tumbling rounds had exited.

"We ain't talking to nobody on this thing," Gamble said.

Isen heard shouting below him and looked down to see some Rangers running uphill. They were not bounding, moving and covering each other's moves; they were just running.

Isen drew in a sharp breath, afraid of what might be happening down there. He had no reserves at this point; if Charlie Company faltered, the whole unit might be overrun. They might buy enough time for Taylor to get started and finish the fight, but there wouldn't be many pieces of Dettering's unit left to pick up.

Below him, men emerged from the smoke in twos and threes, some of them pausing to fire back in the direction of the road, some of them helping wounded buddies. They reached the top exhausted, a ragged procession, the officers conspicuously absent.

"Where's the CO?" Isen asked as the men came pouring in. "Where's Captain Dettering?"

Some of the men ignored him, too out of breath to even answer. A few shrugged. Finally, a buck sergeant Isen didn't recognize told him.

"They took a grenade in the command post," he said. "I don't know if the CO made it or not. Your radio man was in there, too."

With that, the sergeant turned and began to gather his soldiers for the difficult stand on the hill—the hill Isen had chosen for their solitary fight.

Isen looked off to the right, trying to hear something of Taylor's battle on the road, the attack on the GPU rear.

Brennan's platoon came up last, and were the least ready when the GPU soldiers, pressing close behind, began to assault the Americans isolated on top of the hill.

Brennan crawled out to the very end of the line, the right-most point, where he had positioned two men manning Akers's SAW.

"They're gonna try to get us first, right here," Brennan yelled over the sound of the light machine gun. The barrel of the weapon was beginning to glow red from the continuous firing.

"You keep feeding us ammo," the gunner said, "and we'll be OK."

Brennan looked up over the small berm, and, for his efforts, was nearly shot in the face. He pushed his nose to the ground as several rounds zipped by. He wanted to stay that way, for only a moment, and have the battle just pass by. He looked up, blew dirt out of his mouth, came back to the business at hand.

"You guys got grenades?"

"None."

"I'll see if I can get some." He pushed with his hands and slithered backward a few feet until the gentle bowl of the hilltop, which was flat here, hollow in places, sheltered him from the incoming fire. Here he had the luxury of being able to crawl on his hands and knees instead of having to scrape along on his belly.

There were men on the position now, some firing, some tending their own or others' wounds, some simply collapsed in formless, still-breathing heaps. Brennan looked for Sergeant Bishop.

"Where's Bishop? Anbody seen Sergeant Bishop?"

There was no one standing, no one giving direction, no one in charge, and this frightened Brennan in a way that he couldn't name. They were supposed to be a fighting unit, but here, for these few seconds, at least, they had become an exhausted mob—not panicked—but without direction.

One of the men near him rolled over. It was Lieutenant Hawkins.

Brennan wanted to shout at him to take charge, to do something to ready the platoon for the impact of the GPU attack. Instead, he simply asked, "Where's Sergeant Bishop?"

Hawkins looked at him blankly, as if he didn't recognize Brennan. The soldier repeated the question.

Hawkins inclined his head toward the slope. "Down there," he said.

Brennan didn't even want to ask if that meant that Bishop was dead. He looked left and right, where no more than a handful of soldiers were doing anything to return the GPU fire. He couldn't tell, from his position, how much incoming fire there was—most of the enemy rounds sailed by overhead, thanks to the angle of the hill—but he knew they were being pressed, that they would be attacked.

"We've got to get the line together here, Lieutenant," Brennan said. "They're not going to give us much time."

Hawkins stared, slack-mouthed, his shallow breathing forcing his cheeks in and out in wet bursts.

The gunfire rose suddenly off on his left, toward the center of the platoon, like some giant crackling fire. Brennan looked over in time to see a Ranger, followed closely by two GPU soldiers, come running up and over the lip of the hill. The Germans got into one of the shallow holes and held out there for a few panicked, heart-pounding seconds, trading frenzied automatic fire at close range with a half-dozen GIs. But these Germans were unsupported, and were silenced when a Ranger exposed himself long enough to toss a grenade into their hole.

The attack galvanized a few of the Americans, who suddenly realized that there would be no respite on the hilltop.

"Lieutenant," Brennan tried again.

No response.

If Hawkins didn't take charge, someone else would have to—he would have to. And that possibility frightened him more than anything that had gone before.

"Hey," Brennan shouted, grabbing Hawkins by the front of his field jacket, "if we don't get things organized up here we're fucking going to get overrun. *You hear me?"*

Hawkins pushed him away, sending the much smaller man backward over his heels. Brennan was like that, almost on his back, his rifle at his feet, when the GPU made the first big push.

They led with grenades, five or six air-splitting concussions that forced the Americans to the ground. Before the Rangers could recover, the GPU soldiers were shouting and moving. Now they were among the GIs. Brennan saw a Ranger off to his right go down as a German opened fire at point blank range. The American tumbled backward, squeezing the trigger of his weapon as he fell, spraying the ground at his feet with ineffective shots.

Brennan fumbled for his rifle, found it just as he saw something appear above him. He looked up at the belt buckle of a GPU soldier who was no more than three feet away. Brennan lowered his shoulder and drove into the man, both of them tumbling down the face of the hill.

Now he was on the wrong side of the fight, vaguely aware of at least a half dozen forms around him, all of them running uphill. There were a few long, twisted seconds without sound, with nothing there but a certainty that he must act or be killed. The German had found his way to his knees and was struggling to bring his weapon up. Brennan lunged forward, leading with the butt of his rifle, catching the GPU soldier full in the face.

Brennan felt the heat from the muzzle of the man's weapon as the German fired, falling backward. Something plucked at his sleeve, but he managed to point and shoot before the German could react again.

The fight had moved past him, up over the edge of the hill that was supposed to be Charlie Company's holdout. He glanced toward the center of his company's line. The attack wasn't pressing the whole company, but that would make little difference if the Germans crushed the flank. If the GPU gained a foothold here, the rest of the line would be untenable. All this came clearly to Brennan, not as a sequence of thoughts, but as a fully realized picture, a portent of disaster. He scrambled to his feet, dodging this way and that up the hill.

The American position was covered with a thick pall of smoke. Here and there, smoke grenades hissed and sputtered and filled the air with choking, colorful clouds. Brennan could see, shifting in and out of the haze, quick flashes of the struggle: a man swinging a rifle like a club, two men scuffling on the ground, another—an American, he thought—walking steadily forward, shooting from the hip. There was no way to tell which way the fight was going. There was no advantage here—no one could see in the smoke, no one could hear clearly the commands being shouted amid the close sounds of gunfire.

Brennan paused, knowing that wading into the haze would do no good, would merely add another lost figure to the single combat going on there. He turned right, toward the rest of the company, dropped down on the inside edge—the American side—of the hill, and began to make his way to the adjacent platoon to get help. Then, in an instant, the smoke cleared, and Brennan saw something completely unexpected. There were Rangers running off the back side of the hill, away from the fight.

"Stop," Brennan shrieked, incredulous. "Come back here, you moth-erfuckers!"

He turned, chased after the men—there were only a few—screaming at them as he ran. A figure materialized from the dense smoke—red here—and crashed into Brennan.

It was Lieutenant Hawkins.

Hawkins was wide-eyed, a textbook picture of panic. Brennan knew, in an instant, what was happening, but played it as if Hawkins were not yet lost.

"We've got to get those men back," Brennan screamed in the lieuten-ant's face. "The whole line will collapse."

Hawkins stared dumbly, moved as if to run again. Brennan seized him, yanking on the big man's arm, all but panicked himself now.

"We can hold it together, we can. . . . "

But Hawkins pulled free, flipping Brennan's arm away as easily as he might avoid a child's grasp. He turned suddenly, pivoting—quickly, for such a big man—and swinging a roundhouse from somewhere way down at his knees.

Brennan ducked, and the blow glanced off the top of his head. He was bent over at the waist, and he pushed Hawkins, hard, two hands at the big man's hips. But the lieutenant didn't even stumble, didn't come after Brennan. He turned and disappeared into the smoke on the back of the hill.

Brennan ran back into the chaos, off in the direction of the rest of the company. Just out of the fog he came across six or seven men from the second platoon. They were on the ground, prone behind their weapons and facing, not downhill, but toward the sounds that came pouring out of the smoke where first platoon had disappeared. There was a buck ser-geant in the group, no other leaders.

It was a time for action, one of those crystal moments that men who live through them remember all the rest of their days—the sounds, the smells, the sharp taste of fear. Brennan, out beyond thought and planning, acted.

"Fix bayonets," he told them.

The Rangers did as they were told, then looked up. Unflinching, steady.

"Follow me," Brennan said, turning back into the red smoke that writhed through the trees and curled up from the scarred earth.

*   *   *

Mark Isen was afraid that he had let it go too far.

Everything now hinged on whether Taylor, leading Alpha and Bravo Companies, pressed his attack against the rear of the GPU column in time to save Charlie Company. But as he looked around him at the unsteady line the Rangers manned on the crest of the hill he'd put them on—*he'd* put them on—he thought that things might be too far gone.

"I have to see what's going on with Alpha and Bravo," he told Gamble.

The RTO, perhaps better than any other soldier, knew how crucial it was for Isen to be able to talk to his subordinates. Without that ability to influence things, Isen was as useless as if he'd stayed back in Karlshofen.

"We gonna head down there?" Gamble asked, referring to the jump-off point for the attack.

Isen looked around him, chewing his lip. There was no sure way to tell how the battle was going even here, within a few meters of his position. Would he be able to change things down at the road if he found, as he thought he might, that the attack had fallen apart?

He stood, began to move toward the right of Charlie Company's position, for it was here that the GIs were having the most trouble. This was the *schwerpunkt*, the critical point the GPU would concentrate on to break the American lock on the hill. Take this section, and the whole thing would crumble.

They had gone only ten or fifteen meters when they saw two Rangers running down the back side of the hill. Isen trotted a few meters down the slope.

"Where are you men going?" Isen yelled at them, straining to be heard above the gunfire so close by. "Who told you to withdraw?"

He ran after them a bit more, could not catch them, wanted to see what was back on top of the hill. "Who told you to pull back?" he screamed after them.

Isen turned back uphill. Gamble, straining under the weight of the dead radio he refused to abandon, was right there behind him.

"They're running, sir," he said.

Isen looked at his radio operator as if the man had just suggested that they fly over the battlefield.

Another figure passed them in the smoke that drifted off the back of the hill. The man came toward them, then turned back to the anonymity of the covering haze.

And Isen knew it was true.

He raised his weapon and fired into the air above the running soldiers. They were beyond the range of his voice.

"Let's go up here," he said to Gamble, heading for the back of Charlie Company's position.

At the top of the hill, amid the swirling smoke, he saw unnerving snapshots of hand-to-hand fighting.

He knew, with lightning celerity, that it would be decided in the next few minutes. Charlie Company would be overrun, or the GPU would be forced to withdraw by the pressure of Taylor's attack.

If the position was lost, his place was here, and he could give no more thought of leaving than the captain of a sinking ship could imagine abandoning his crew. Noble as that might be, it was the way to defeat. But if the Charlie Company leaders could do their jobs, hold their men and the hill, Isen could apply himself to the critical point. If the battle still hung in the balance—and he had no way of knowing, since he couldn't talk to anyone—his duty was clear: he would have to run to the Alpha and Bravo positions and do his best to push that attack forward successfully.

The unit needed leadership at both places, on the hill and in the attack; and finally it came down to the fact that Isen could be in one place only.

He stepped back off the hill, turned halfway around, ready to begin his run to the rear.

To the rear.

Now there were Rangers pushed back as far as where Isen stood. They knew he was there.

Beside him, two soldiers knelt side by side, firing calmly, steadily, at the GPU soldiers who stepped clear of the smoke or were exposed when the choking coils shifted. There was no "line," of course, nothing that constituted a barrier. The only thing left here of the American effort was a few pockets of determined Rangers, and all that separated these men, who stayed, from the men who had run, was the fact that these few hadn't yet accepted that their position was hopeless.

Isen turned to Gamble, who had knelt and was also searching for targets.

"I'm going down to find out what happened to the attack," he said as evenly as he could. "Do you understand?"

"You want me to go with you?" Gamble asked.

He looked up when Isen didn't answer, but the commander was gone.

"Looks like even the old man beat feet," one of the Rangers next to Gamble said.

The RTO went back to firing. All around him and his few companions the line shook and wavered, like a leaf in a stiff breeze.

Brennan and the seven men from the adjacent platoon formed a tight wedge and trotted into the smoky gloom. Brennan picked up the pace, then had a second to worry about running across his own men, other Americans, and in the heat of the moment shooting friendlies, or being shot by friendlies. He had no running password, nothing to identify him to the men of his platoon. Thinking of Charis, he began a long yell, *"Ranger!"*

The man behind him picked it up, then another and another. Some said it quickly, over and over, some of them dragged it out. Brennan saw the result on the first two GPU soldiers he encountered: the two men had stopped their advance and turned to the eerie sounds. It worked as the Rebel yell was purported to have worked on federal soldiers during the Civil War. The enemy hesitated—and that was all it took.

Brennan, at the point of the wedge, ran into a little eddy of nearly clear air and spotted two GPU soldiers on the opposite side. He lengthened his stride, firing from the hip. One of the Germans went down, falling backward, as if pushed. The other swung his rifle at Brennan, then saw the other Rangers following and tried to decide which one to shoot first. Brennan reached him in that second of hesitation, thrusting forward, feeling the blade of his bayonet slide into the soft midsection of the man before him.

Before he could free his blade, there was firing, incredibly close, the bright tongues of muzzle flash seemingly right at hand, piercing the smoke. Brennan heard a grunt beside him and one of the Rangers pitched forward. The other men slowed. Their reaction—drilled into them in a hundred field exercises—told them to go to ground, to avoid the incoming fire and maneuver against the enemy.

But something in Brennan knew this wouldn't work, at least not here. Because of the smoke and the confusion, he felt they had to keep on moving, pushing the GPU off the hill—physically pushing them or killing them—until the hill had been swept.

"C'm'on, c'm'on," he screamed. "Keep coming."

Two or three of the men had gone to their knees, then to the prone. They pushed themselves up, uncertain, but apparently willing to obey this little madman who'd appeared in smoke and fire.

Brennan moved forward again, taking the men parallel to the edge of the hill and what should have been his platoon's front. The firing picked up in front of him—the GPU knew there was a counterattack in progress. A light machine gun opened up off to his left, from the lip of the hill, he thought. He slouched forward, as if in a rainstorm, then heard the rounds sing by several feet above his head. They were shooting high. *They can't see us,* Brennan thought.

But the sound of the gun, so close to them, sent the Rangers behind him to the dirt. They returned fire, shooting at where the machine gun's signature gave away its position, but they were not advancing.

That's not enough, Brennan thought.

"Keep moving," he yelled. "Get up and keep moving. They're firing high."

As if to prove him wrong, a half dozen rounds smashed into the tree trunk behind him, spraying his back and legs with shattered wood and bark. Brennan dove for cover, rolling himself into a tiny depression.

"Shit," he said, raising his eyes carefully to look for the chattering gun.

They had stopped him. He'd been on his way to turning the whole thing around—or at least he'd allowed himself to think that—when they were stopped by one determined crew who sat no more than forty feet away and who couldn't, he was sure, see him and the other Rangers clearly.

"Shit, shit, *fuck*," he said, pounding the earth with his fist.

He checked his equipment for a grenade, then looked around frantically for the closest Ranger. They were all hugging the ground, and it was a good thing. Brennan could see chips of wood break off the surrounding trees, smaller plants get cut down, all at a height of two or three feet. Perfect grazing fire. The gun crew had adjusted its aim and was determined to keep the Americans down.

"Hey," Brennan called in between bursts of fire. "Somebody gimme a grenade. Who's got one?"

There was no answer, but a few seconds later two grenades came at him, tossed from behind, their pins still in place.

"Can you hear me?" Brennan called, wondering how many of the remaining six men he could control. He got five short yells back in ragged acknowledgment. That was a start, anyway.

"I'm going to take out that gun," Brennan said. He didn't yell it, but it was necessary to be loud so his own men could hear him. "You guys be ready to follow. I want you to push through the whole platoon area. Sweep the whole thing."

He wished he knew who the next ranking man was. He should give specific instructions—in the event that he was killed in the next minute. The realization that he was preparing to die did not hit him particularly hard—he was too tired, too drained, too focused to think of anything else but lifting that machine gun fire.

He braced himself for it, pulled the pin on one grenade and, drawing a deep breath, raised himself on an elbow. He could see the edge of the hill, but no gun. He lowered himself, imagined that he felt the tide shifting to the GPU. He had been away from his own squad only seven minutes, but they could have been completely overrun by now.

He pushed himself up again, felt the air near him shake as the gun sought him out. He raised one arm and pitched the grenade like a baseball, straight at the stabbing light that pierced the smoke.

He reached down and put his hands on the ground. At the instant that the first grenade went off, he shoved against the earth and rose, the second grenade in his hand. The gun spoke again, and before Brennan could lift the second grenade to throw—the angle was much better like this—he fell to his right, away from the searching spray of lead. He landed on his side, jamming his rifle painfully up into his ribs. He still had the second grenade in his hand, and he could feel the thumping sounds and see the geysers of dirt and snow that the rounds raised as the gunner tried to find him.

For an instant, everything hung on a knife-edged fulcrum, then Brennan found his feet once again, rushed forward, hurled the ball-like grenade before him and followed it into the maw of the gun chattering there at the edge of the hill. There would be no more indecision—something was going to give now.

The picture of the gunners flashed on his consciousness: a man with a helmet was feeding a gleaming band of ammunition into the weapon, while the gunner, hatless, his face grimed and glistening sweat, hugged the stock of the gun, his cheek jumping with the methodical shaking. The assistant gunner saw Brennan's approach, pushed the gunner's shoulder toward the figure coming at them from the smoke.

Brennan fumbled with his rifle, then was knocked flat by the grenade's explosion. The first *crunch* was followed closely by one, two more—someone else was attacking—and the concussions rolled over him in a bright wave that pressed his breath out of him like a giant hand.

He was unable to move, could not feel his weapon. Gravity pulled him off his side onto his back, and he spied the sky through the trees and the curling ends of smoke. Something big fell beside him, landing with such force—like dead weight—that Brennan was sure it was a corpse. He looked over quickly, right into Lieutenant Hawkins's face.

Hawkins didn't speak, but simply nodded, as if his appearance had been choreographed before and was completely expected.

"You ready?" Hawkins asked.

Brennan was incredulous. He was also hurt badly. There were hot spots on his right leg—shrapnel—but he was afraid to look. He tried to answer Hawkins, but nothing came out.

"The one who keeps pressing when he's tired is gonna win," Hawkins said. He looked out at where the GPU was still struggling to push the Rangers off the hilltop. "They're tired, too," he said.

Brennan rolled over, his ribs stabbing him where he'd landed on his rifle. "I'm OK," he rasped. He tried to say more, but all that would come out was, "OK. OK."

Hawkins looked over his shoulder, waved his big arm in the air, signaling the men behind to get ready, once again, to move forward.

"I didn't run, you know," Hawkins said to Brennan.

The younger soldier didn't comment but whistled pain through his teeth as he held a hand to his side.

"I got those guys to come back," Hawkins said again.

Brennan looked at him squarely. "Maybe you did, maybe you didn't," he said through clenched teeth. "Doesn't much matter right now, does it?"

Hawkins looked back into the thick smoke. "Well," he said. "I still didn't run."

With that he pushed his big frame up and plunged forward. Brennan tried to stand, stumbled on weakened legs, and fell on all fours. He lifted his head in time to see three or four other Rangers pass him, their rifles at high port, their bayonets glinting dull and deadly in the smoke-filtered light.

26

. . . .

MARK ISEN WASN'T PREPARED FOR WHAT HE FOUND AT THE bottom of the hill, the jump-off point for the attack by Alpha and Bravo companies. He thought he might find the attack in progress, but behind schedule; or that, for some reason, the companies might not have started yet, in which case he would send them forward, into the rear of the GPU column, to relieve the pressure on Charlie Company.

He stumbled on two dead Rangers sprawled in gruesome poses around a scorched circle of earth, a small crater probably made by a grenade. A little farther on, he passed several more GIs sitting in the woods amid the trees. One or two men, not so badly wounded as the others, were trying to make the wounded comfortable.

"Where's your company?" Isen asked the first man he saw.

"Up on the road, I guess, sir," the Ranger answered. "We got out there and got pushed back." The soldier worked his jaw, seemed about to say something more, then just shook his head.

"Captain Taylor?" Isen asked.

"Don't know," the man answered.

Isen did a quick count; there were at least seven wounded men here, and he'd seen two dead. The soldier had told him they'd been pushed back. If that were true, then the GPU was reacting well at both points of the American attack.

Isen checked his rifle, pulling back the charging handle to reveal the round seated in the chamber. Then he trotted toward the road.

Here the road ran a bit higher than the surrounding ground. He would not be able to see anyone on the other side of the track, which was also low ground, without crossing through the open area. He kept the road on his right as he moved toward the sounds of the firing, and he soon came upon Sam Drake, the lieutenant who'd taken over Bravo Company. Drake, huddled at the base of a tree that offered him little real protection, was shouting into his radio. Isen came up beside him and knelt down. Drake's right leg was a tangle of shredded cloth and dark blood. Someone had applied a tourniquet, using the long ends of a battle dressing.

"Can you walk?" Isen asked.

Drake shook his head.

"What happened? What's going on now?"

"They stopped us," Drake said, his voice cracking. "We got out behind them and started moving, but the road here is higher. See?" He pointed to the roadway, and Isen began to see what had happened. The Americans, straddling and moving along the track, had been split in two by the open space, and the separation became more dramatic as they advanced. Now the two wings of the attacking force were out of contact.

"We got pushed back, and Captain Taylor was trying to get us all on one side, you know, so we could make a push." Drake had both hands on his wounded leg now, squeezing it just below the dressing. The harder he pressed, the more his voice cracked.

"He was running back and forth. . . ." The lieutenant paused, drew a sharp breath. "But he got hit out there," he said, pointing to the road.

Isen looked out to the road, but there was nothing out there. He moved toward Drake, touched the man's shoulder, then moved past him to where the Rangers were trading small arms fire with the GPU.

Some fifty meters farther out, Isen found one of Drake's NCOs directing his platoon. The man had been shot in the foot, and he was crawling, his foot a bloody stump of bandage, and encouraging his men to hold their position. Isen had moved forward to make an assessment—he had no plan formed in his head. He crawled up next to the sergeant, who was leaving a bloody trail in the churned-up snow. Before Isen could even speak, the Ranger asked, "We going forward, sir?"

Isen looked at the soldier, who was wounded, but far from beaten.

"What kind of shape is the enemy in?" Isen asked.

"They ran at first," the man answered. "Then we ran into trouble with this here road, and they got a little backbone. But I think we could move 'em back if we pushed."

"You know how far up the Alpha Company element is on the other side of the road?" Isen asked.

"No, sir," the NCO said. "I was trying to see for myself a little while ago, and I got this for my efforts." He patted his leg.

"Can your men move forward?" Isen asked.

"I reckon we got to, sir," the man said. "We got no place to fall back to, and if we stay put they're gonna get us eventually. Can't fall back, can't stay still. Only one thing left."

Isen thought about the GPU response he'd seen up on the hill. This formation wasn't like the others he'd faced over the past days. Somebody on the other side was in charge and was capable of holding things together. But this NCO was right, if the Rangers didn't advance, they lost. The critical thing was to advance before the GPU got organized for a counterattack.

"Tell your men to be ready to move out. We have to break them here," Isen said. "I'm going over to Alpha Company."

"They got that road zeroed in, sir."

But there was no time to back up and cross someplace safer. By the time he went around, the day might be lost. Isen secured the flap on his holster and moved closer to the road. As he got into a sprinter's stance, it occurred to him that Alpha Company might be far behind this Bravo Company element, that he might be running into a GPU element on the other side.

"Wish me luck," he said.

He sprang out into the road, out into the surprising sunlight, one step, two steps, three to the middle of the track, where he began to think that perhaps they wouldn't see him.

Then he heard the snapping sound of rounds leaving a muzzle—a sound that is entirely different from what the shooter hears behind a weapon. The air about his head sizzled, and he felt something smack his left hand as he dove for the other side of the road. He smashed his shoulder into a tree, stunning his arm and his side, but managed to continue the roll down the small slope. He flipped over once, landing in a sitting position.

There were three Rangers within ten feet of him.

"Hey, sir," one of them said.

Isen's right shoulder felt as if someone had hit him with a pole, and his left hand was on fire.

"Who's in charge here?" he asked. His voice sounded strange.

"The first sergeant is right up there," one of the men answered. All three of them were staring at him.

"Take me up there," Isen said, trying to stand. A tremendous bolt of white hot pain greeted his effort to move, and he fell back.

"Give me a hand," he commanded.

The soldiers moved, lifting him gingerly.

"I should dress your hand, sir," one of them said.

Isen looked at the Ranger, then down at his hand. Most of his ring finger had been shot off, down to the second knuckle.

The soldier already had Isen's compress out of its case on his suspenders, so he let the man wrap his finger. He wouldn't do anybody any good if he passed out from blood loss.

The little group only had to move a dozen meters to hear Alpha Company's First Sergeant Perreira, a fiery Puerto Rican from New York City, running from position to position, exhorting his own soldiers in English and cursing the enemy in Spanish. Isen sent a soldier after him.

"Can you move forward?" Isen asked.

Perreira looked at Isen's hand, as if for some clue to what was coming. Perreira had been Taylor's first sergeant and, like Taylor, had opposed Isen's change of plan.

"Captain Taylor is dead," Perreira said. "He was going to get the Bravo Company element to back us up over here. Did you bring them over?"

Even through the thick fog of pain, Isen could see that Perreira meant to resist him.

"No time for that," Isen said curtly. "The GPU is reacting quickly. We're going to push up both sides of the road before they can counter-attack."

Perreira shook his head. "Can't do it," he said.

Isen blinked against the pain, afraid he might throw up. They were all watching him, waiting for him to pass out, and thus to hand over command.

"What did you say?"

"My men can't do it," Perreira said. "Not unsupported. We have to have Bravo Company over here to back us up."

Isen studied the man's face, which, in Isen's pained sight, had split into two images that swam before him. He looked beyond Perreira to where one of the platoon sergeants, a hard charger named Thompson, had come back, helmetless, bleeding from a gash on his jaw, to see what was going on.

"All the lieutenants are down, wounded," Perreira said, as if that closed the question.

"First Sergeant Perreira," Isen said as calmly and evenly as he could manage, "I'm ordering you to move your company forward to destroy whatever elements of the enemy are in front of you alongside this road." Isen was swaying, but he could still see that Perreira knew what was going on here. He pulled himself up as straight as he could, lest the soldiers watching think he was too weakened to command. He had to make this work. All he had to do was get this one man, this good soldier, to do as he was ordered.

"No," Perreira said. "No, sir."

Isen didn't hesitate. "You're relieved. Consider yourself under arrest."

Isen looked past Perreira to where Sergeant First Class Thompson stood, open-mouthed.

"Sergeant Thompson," Isen said, fighting back another wave of nausea and the urge to sit down. "You're in charge of this company now, and I want you to attack along this road."

Suddenly, Perreira was beside him, his hands on Isen's arm. "You can't do that," he said.

"I just did it," Isen said, forcing himself to focus through his pain. Perreira didn't back down.

"I won't let you get more of my men killed," Perreira said, turning as if to speak to Thompson.

He sounded, Isen thought, remarkably sure of himself, and it was that note of calm self-assurance, that arrogance, that brought the rage up like a dark sea. Isen tried to move his right arm, but it was still stunned from the blow to the shoulder. He reached around to his right side with his left hand, now missing a finger, drew his pistol, and poked Perreira in the back with the weapon.

"If you get in my way," he managed, the words coming low and threatening through clenched teeth, "I'll shoot you myself."

Perreira turned, looked down at the pistol, and backed off. Isen felt a ripple through the men around him. He was still in command.

"Thompson, I want you moving in five minutes," Isen said, finding his voice again. "Push them until they break." He turned to the soldiers he'd first encountered. "You," he said, pointing to one of them. "I want you to cross the road and tell Bravo to move forward in five minutes. You other two stand by, cover him going across."

Sergeant Thompson nodded and turned away, and the three Rangers Isen had chosen to carry the message jogged off toward the road. First Sergeant Perreira hadn't moved, hadn't changed his expression from the look of incredulity that had come over him when he saw Isen's pistol and knew that it was over for him. In a similarly tough situation, Colonel Schauffert had given Isen a second chance, had not relieved him of command. Isen pushed the thought away.

"Get a weapon," he told Perreira. "You can fight as a rifleman."

The NCO did as he was told.

27

WHILE THE RANGERS FOUGHT THEIR DESPERATE BATTLE WITH the GPU near Karlshofen, the Marine contingent of the relief force was coming ashore at Bremerhaven, some fifty kilometers away.

"Move, move, move," Staff Sergeant Bobby Pascal shouted at his men as they hurried from their helicopter and out into the bright winter sunlight. The flyboys had done a great job, putting them down on some high ground where two highways climbed out of the southeast side of Bremerhaven. The autobahn ran north and south, and would be the road used by any GPU reinforcements coming north from Bremen. The other, smaller road, Highway 71, ran east from this point in the general direction of where the besieged Rangers were holding out. The Marine armor scheduled to come ashore later would use Highway 71 to approach Karlshofen.

Pascal's role was to take his squad to the edge of the roadway, where they would be part of a blocking position to hold off any GPU forces that tried to interfere with the landing of Marine vehicles. As he moved his men into position amid the cover provided by some trees planted along the highway, Pascal looked back over his shoulder to see another flight of helicopters bringing in the vehicle-mounted TOW antitank missiles that would provide the firepower for their roadblock—should they need it.

The day was crystal clear here, with no trace of the cold, wet haze that had been skipping across the water when they took off from the *Wasp*. Yet even though he had confidence that things were going according to plan,

Pascal had a strange sense that something was out of joint. He and his Marines, indeed, the whole of the assault force, had left their ships ready for battle. There were Super Cobra gunships circling overhead, ready to pounce on anything that resisted the landings. The infantrymen all around him were heavily armed, and ships just offshore stood ready to answer calls for supporting fires in case the GPU tried to push the Marines back off the beach.

But the scene below this sunny hill was tranquil. There was no shooting, and just a short distance from where he stood, people went about their business as usual: delivery trucks, buses, and private autos drove by, some of the drivers not even noticing the combat troops on the side of the hill above the road. Pascal felt as if he were on a field exercise stateside, except that training in the United States never took place this close to civilians.

"Looks kind of quiet," Pascal said out loud as he looked over the southern end of Bremerhaven.

"Maybe we got all dressed up for nothing," one of his men said.

"Don't worry about that," Pascal answered, "we'll be plenty busy soon enough."

But they didn't move right away.

Pascal had anticipated moving out as soon as his and the other rifle companies had all their men and their antitank weapons on the ground. That point came and went with no word other than "Stand by."

He could see activity in the town below, which he took to mean that the Marines were unloading the rest of their LAVs, or light armored vehicles. There was still no sound of resistance, and still no order to move. Pascal got out his map and looked again at the distance to Karlshofen, wondering if perhaps the Rangers didn't need them anymore. Maybe the GPU had fallen apart. Maybe the Rangers had been whipped.

Pascal's platoon leader, Lieutenant Gunnison, walked down the hill three times in their first hour and half on the ground: once to check Pascal's position, once to tell him that the Marines' light armor had come ashore in Bremerhaven with no problem. The third time, Pascal figured the lieutenant was getting bored.

"This turned out to be pretty easy, wouldn't you say?" Gunnison remarked by way of making conversation. The word from the company was still the same: stand by for further instructions.

"It ain't over yet, sir," Pascal allowed.

"Maybe it is over for those Rangers. The old man said we might not go down to that town—what's it called, Karlshofen?—right away. We might stay here in Bremerhaven and conduct some searches."

"Searches for what?" Pascal wanted to know.

"Not sure. Weapons and stuff, I guess. Some of the guys who work around battalion staff said everyone up there is running around nuts over changes," Gunnison replied. "This *invasion* could turn out to be a waste of time."

"Better than having to fly in here and duke it out with a bunch of those fanatics," Pascal said.

"Oh, sure, sure," Gunnison admitted. He paused, studied the squad leader for a few seconds. "But aren't you kind of disappointed that, after all that build up, we didn't mix it up even a little bit?"

Pascal thought about that. Smart money said that no shooting was a good deal. No casualties, no Marines wounded or killed, no bodies wrapped in plastic and headed for the refrigerators on the *Wasp*.

But there was something of a letdown, too. Even so, Pascal had trouble saying it out loud.

"Weren't you on the float off of Kuwait?" Gunnison asked.

Pascal nodded. He'd been a private when, as part of a Marine amphibious force, he'd taken part in the biggest deception operation since World War II. Thousands of Marines, kept in a flotilla off Kuwait City, forced the Iraqis to keep tens of thousands of their own troops deep in Kuwait to counter the expected invasion. The plan worked: the Iraqis, far from their escape routes, were cut off by the army offensive. Most of the Marines didn't leave the ships until the shooting was over. Though they'd served their purpose, a lot of the men were unhappy that they hadn't been called on to fight. Pascal still wasn't sure, years later, how he felt about it.

"We don't have to kill people to do a good job here, Lieutenant," he said, sounding a bit more fatherly than he'd intended.

"Yeah, I know," Gunnison said, unconvinced. "But I'd sure like to fuck up those guys who've got the Rangers surrounded."

"Uh-huh."

Gunnison's radio operator was only a few feet away, and Pascal clearly heard the call for the platoon leader.

"Maybe something's happening," Gunnison said as he took the handset. Pascal watched him nod his head as he listened. The lieutenant pulled out his map, checked it against the highway below them. But he was looking back toward Bremerhaven.

"Saddle up," Gunnison said as he gave the radio handset to his RTO. "We're going that way." He pointed toward the city below them.

"What for?" Pascal asked. "Are we pulling out?"

Before Gunnison could answer, Pascal had signaled his Marines, and the team leaders were getting the men moving.

"Don't know for sure," Gunnison said. "I'm gonna run over to where the CO is and get some more instructions. Maybe it has something to do with the rumor about looking for weapons caches or something. Move your men along the edge of the road toward those vehicles and I'll get back to you as soon as I know something." His troops were excited to be moving, but Pascal knew he'd take the wind out of their sails when he told them they were going into Bremerhaven, probably to look for weapons.

They moved a hundred meters or so to the roadblock, staying undercover in the woods off the road. Pascal walked out into the open to talk to the Marines manning the antitank missiles mounted on humvees.

"You hear what's going on?" an NCO asked Pascal as he approached.

"Not really," Pascal said. "Just some rumors about going in to Bremerhaven to look for weapons and stuff."

"Shit," one of the other men said. "I did that in friggin' Somalia. Great combination of boring and dangerous."

"Company coming."

Pascal looked up to where one of the Marines had spotted a large truck approaching from the direction of Bremerhaven. It was about the size of a USMC five-ton truck, with green canvas covering its cargo area.

"Keep under cover," Pascal called to his men, but they were already dispersed and alert.

Pascal tried to radio Gunnison, but the platoon sergeant said that the lieutenant was talking to the company commander.

"There's a truck coming, over," Pascal reported.

"So?" the platoon sergeant said. "Just stay under cover, over."

"Three-one," Pascal continued, identifying Gunnison by his radio call sign, "said we might be searching for weapons. Should I stop this truck?"

"I'll get back to you when I know something, out."

Pascal watched it approach. He had no business stopping it, especially since they weren't at all clear on their mission, and he could even get into trouble for being too aggressive. He was about to walk back to his squad in the woods when the Marine in charge of the two-vehicle antitank section said, "Should we stop this thing?"

Pascal hesitated only a second. "Yeah."

The truck was about two hundred meters away when the driver saw the American humvees pull into the road, the big maws of the TOW missile launchers pointed at the oncoming vehicle. The truck pulled off the shoulder of the road and into the mud.

Four or five people—a couple of them women, Pascal saw—climbed out of the back of the truck. They talked among themselves for a minute while Pascal approached, and then two of them unloaded a silver container.

"Maybe they brought us some coffee," one of the Marines shouted from behind Pascal as the sergeant walked toward the civilians.

"Hear that?" Pascal said to his radio operator, who was a step behind him. "Marines who ride are soft. Call the lieutenant, tell him what's going on here."

The guess about the coffee turned out to be correct. The little group of civilians carried a large insulated container—the Marines called the big steel bottles "silver bullets"—toward the American vehicles, which were only thirty meters or so in front of the truck.

"We have some hot coffee for you, Lieutenant," one of the men said in clear English.

"It's sergeant," Pascal said. He was close now, and caught the smell—it was indeed coffee, and it gave off that delicious aroma that was two parts warmth, one part taste. There looked to be enough for his squad and the antitank section. He studied the visitors. Not one of them was younger than forty, Pascal guessed. They were completely harmless looking and reminded him of nothing more than a church group from back home.

"I appreciate your generosity," Pascal continued. "I'll have to speak with my platoon commander."

The man who spoke English handed a paper cup to Pascal. Several of the Marines in the missile section had climbed out of their vehicles and were approaching. Pascal turned to say something to the section chief about security when he saw the truck begin to move.

"Where's he going?" Pascal asked. Even as he said it, he expected the German to say the driver was just turning the truck around for the return trip, or something like that. But the man hesitated, stuttered.

Pascal dropped his cup of coffee and began to run toward the truck. One of the Germans shouted something to the driver, who was already nosing past the first unmanned humvee. The truck's back wheels spun in the mud just off the road's shoulder.

"HALT," Pascal yelled. He saw the driver glance at him, then turn away to concentrate on getting the truck past the roadblock.

Pascal thought about shooting, then dismissed that as overreacting. This was too easy for such a drastic measure. The truck was only a few meters away, and, like an athlete who sees the play unfolding, Pascal knew he could get to it before the man could get the vehicle clear of the mud. He leapt for the running board, feeling a bit melodramatic—this was the coffee truck, after all—and grabbed hold of the side mirror.

"Stop this truck," he shouted, wondering if the man could understand him.

Then he saw the pistol.

It was beside the driver on the seat, and it was sliding away from him and toward Pascal as the truck began to turn. Pascal found the handle and yanked the door open, almost losing his balance. He reached inside and snatched the weapon off the seat. He had no idea if it was loaded or cocked, but he pointed it at the driver's head and shouted, "Halt."

The driver slapped at the seat, looking for the pistol. When he saw what was happening, he applied the brakes and began a litany of fearful explanations in German, none of which Pascal could understand.

"Just shut up, pal," Pascal said. He waved the muzzle of the pistol until the driver understood he was to get down. In a few minutes the Marines had taken their guests prisoner, and Pascal was rooting around in the back of the truck. There was a big pile of tarpaulins, some loose paper cups, a couple of wooden pallets. Then Pascal found something large under the mass of green canvas.

"What's in there?"

It was Lieutenant Gunnison, looking over the tailgate at Pascal.

"Don't know," the sergeant replied, pulling the covers back. Underneath was a large steel locker, such as might be used to ship a tank engine or some other large, fragile item.

Pascal tried the latches, but they were locked. He looked out of the back of the truck to where he could see the leader of the group framed by the canvas.

"Hey, Fritz," he called. "What's in here?"

The German looked up, and something vital seemed to drain from his face, as if he'd just learned of the death of a friend. He lowered his head and muttered something indistinct.

"What'd he say?" Pascal yelled down to the Marines guarding the man.

"He said it's a bomb."

28

HE'D PUSHED THEM TOO QUICKLY.

That was the assessment Isen made within a few minutes of his driving the remnants of Alpha Company forward on the west side of the road. Thompson and his men were moving forward in starts, but there was no matching sound of an attack from the Bravo Company side.

"Goddamn," Isen said to himself. "God . . . *damn* . . . it." He crawled up the little slope that led to the level of the road, but couldn't get close enough—without exposing himself—to see what, if anything, was going on over there. He turned back when he heard men rushing past, moving toward the fight.

Bent over, they dashed from cover to cover, their faces indistinct. Isen shouted at them, "Who are you?"

"Second platoon," the answer came back. "Alpha Company."

One of the shapes steered away from the movement and came at him. When the figure broke through the trees—still running—Isen recognized the soldier he'd sent to Bravo Company with the message to attack.

"Did you get to Bravo?" Isen asked.

"Uh-huh," the youngster answered, kneeling, gulping air. "Yessir, I found 'em."

Isen was impatient, forced himself to wait as the soldier spoke in rushing breaths.

"They're in . . . a bad way . . . said they didn't know . . . how soon they could start. . . . I . . . lots of wounded over there, sir," he managed. "Lots of Rangers down."

"Are they attacking?" Isen demanded.

"Not when I left."

This was it, then. It was all coming to a point, all of it—his life, the lives of these men—had come down to whatever might happen in the next few moments. It wouldn't matter what was going on elsewhere, wouldn't matter if the GPU was stopped by Firefall or some other intervention—none of it would matter to him or these Rangers if they couldn't hold out for a few more minutes. A great balance swayed above him, and he didn't think he could tilt it.

"Might as well join the fight," Isen said, standing and gingerly shouldering his weapon.

"Right, sir," the Ranger answered, finding his feet.

Isen moved toward the sound of the guns, watching the road off to his left as he did so. He stumbled on some men lying prone, waiting to move forward. The woods were full of men, unmoving, all of them waiting. It took all of his control to keep from screaming at them to get up and run forward. His instinct told him to trust the leaders—but encroaching panic pushed against his control.

"What's going on?" he asked.

An answer came up from the ground. "We pushed them back a few yards, then got slowed down."

Isen peered down. The voice belonged to First Sergeant Perreira.

"Anything on the other side?" Perreira asked.

Isen shook his head. If the Bravo Company attack failed to materialize, the American companies would be defeated in detail, one company at a time, just as the NCO had predicted.

Suddenly men were up again, moving toward the crackle of small arms fire in the woods before them. Isen followed, pushing against black branches, rifle slung over his useless right shoulder, his left hand swathed in a bulky bandage. The fight was close now, and a man off to his right grunted, went down. Isen stepped that way to help, couldn't find the soldier in the undergrowth.

He looked up, dizzy with the loss of blood, wondering if he was seeing things clearly enough to command. Some men were moving forward, others had halted. The firing was haphazard; it defined no clear lines. In the close quarters the sounds of the American and German weapons were indistinguishable. Nothing made sense to him; woolly with fatigue and pain, he couldn't see where to begin to sort things out. This was infantry combat—confusion and terror—and the seconds were slipping away from him.

The popping of small arms spread, so that the woods in a broad arc in front of Isen seemed aflame.

"Major Isen."

Isen looked up, toward the road. "Here," he said, turning to the sound of the voice.

"Come here."

It was Perreira, still close by, and for a brief instant Isen wondered if the NCO might, in all the chaos, shoot him.

"Take a look."

Isen found him crouched at the edge of a little open space that paralleled the road.

"They're coming across," Perreira said.

It took a moment for this to register, but as he sighted along Perreira's outstretched arm, Isen saw what was happening. GPU soldiers were crossing the road about a hundred and fifty meters down, coming over to the near side in quick rushes of three or four men at a time—controlled, relentless.

Isen looked down at Perreira, then into the trees just behind them, hoping to see some matching movement on the American side. There was no momentum to Alpha Company's advance; the men here were not moving forward in any great number. The advantage belonged to the Germans. He looked down again at Perreira, and he began to think about defeat.

"They stopped us," Isen began. "We have to pull back—"

"No," Perreira interrupted. He pulled Isen down. The major fell on his side, grunting with the pain in his arm.

"All we have to do is hold," Perreira said when the two men lay side by side. "Hold here, and get Bravo Company moving on the other side."

Isen stared at Perreira's face, which was only inches away.

"See?" the NCO went on. "They think this is the only attack we got going. If they put everything over here, then Bravo Company can advance on that side of the road—" he gestured sharply with one hand— "and roll 'em up."

"Bravo Company isn't moving," Isen said, fighting sluggishness. He felt as if he was functioning underwater.

"Not yet, they ain't," Perreira said. "Here's what we'll do." He rolled back on his stomach, looking out on the road as he plotted with Isen. "You go up to Thompson and tell him to hold what he's got," Perreira said, nodding as he spoke to encourage a response from Isen. "And I'll get over there and get Bravo Company moving."

"Right," Isen said, comprehension coming like a slow dawn. "Right. You gonna go around?" Isen asked.

"Shit, no," Perreira said. "I'm crossing right here." He pulled his helmet low on his forehead and gathered himself up for a rush. "No time to go around." He was on his hands and knees now, coiled and ready to strike.

"You ready to do your part, right, sir?" Perreira asked.

"I'm ready," Isen said.

Perreira was up like a shot, across the road before anyone even noticed the movement. Isen dragged himself away from the road, then lurched forward through the woods to find Thompson. He hadn't gone far when someone grabbed his leg and pulled him down.

"Shit, sir," the soldier said. "Sorry, but this is all there is."

The Ranger indicated the woods in front of them. A short distance away, Isen could see vague movement. GPU.

"They'd have been happy to have you, Major," the soldier said, nodding at the Germans. "But I reckon you should stick with us."

"Where's Sergeant Thompson?" Isen asked.

"Over here."

The voice had come from over his right shoulder, so Isen pushed back and crawled toward the platoon sergeant who was leading what was left of Alpha Company.

"Looks like they're getting ready to come again," Thompson said as Isen drew close.

"They're sending reinforcements from the other side."

Thompson's face sagged. He was bleeding from a long, deep gash that started beside his eye and disappeared into his collar. His speech was slurred with exhaustion; he was holding on, Isen knew, out of habit.

"We're strung out already," Thompson continued. "I don't even know how many men I've got up here."

Isen took a moment to gather his thoughts, concentrating on retying the bandage around his hand to stop the bleeding.

"Consolidate here," Isen said. "Stand your ground. Bravo Company will hit them on the other side in a few minutes."

"They were supposed to start their attack at the same time we did," Thompson said. "What happened?"

"I don't know," Isen said, hesitating. "But they're going to get moving. All you have to do is hold on for a while longer. OK?"

Thompson nodded.

"Good. You go this way," Isen said, pointing away from the road, "and I'll go this way. Just get the men into some sort of defensive posture. Tell them help is on the way."

Thompson drew a ragged breath, then crawled off without saying another word. Isen angled back toward the road, looking for other Rangers to bring up on line. As he crawled, he wondered if he'd lied to Thompson about a Bravo Company attack.

The German fire built sharply, like the drop of a violent thunderstorm. There were three explosions, one right after another, before Isen, his face in the wet earth, realized that they were grenades and not mortar or artillery fire. By the time the fifth and sixth concussions rolled over his back, he knew that they were behind him, over by where he'd sent Thompson. The Germans were coming in another push.

Isen moved by short rushes through the woods, cementing a haphazard line with whatever Rangers he found along his way. The NCOs came forward, working with him, moving among their men, steeling themselves for the attack that had already begun to hammer the American position.

Isen felt as if he were trying to outrun a forest fire, and the hot sounds of the firefight chased him through the woods. The attack reached him before he could cover the whole of the narrow front, forcing him to the ground some seventy-five to a hundred meters from the road. He shouted to the rear of Alpha Company, where some of the men, he suspected, hadn't moved all the way up onto the line he wanted them to man.

"Move up here," he screamed. *"MOVE UP!"*

Wet wood sprayed the side of his face as a half dozen rounds tore into a tree next to him. He dropped flat and rolled over to face the enemy. Down here, on the forest floor, visibility was cut to a few meters. The Germans knew that, of course, and were keeping the Rangers low by walking the fire of their machine guns over the area at a height of about three feet.

Isen looked to his left, toward a gap in the line—between him and the road—that the Germans might find and exploit. He made a move out from behind the doubtful shelter of the tree base, but jumped back when a burst of automatic fire churned up the wet ground beside him.

Pressing his face to the mud, he chanced a look forward, where he saw something dart across his front. He yanked his rifle up, but the numbness in his shoulder still wouldn't allow him to hold the weapon properly. He pointed the muzzle out at the woods, set the butt of the weapon against his chest, and squeezed off a few rounds. The movement had stopped, at least within the small circle he could see. He tried to pull himself out from behind the tree again, but this time the rounds struck even closer.

He was in someone's sights.

The Germans were moving steadily, in a disciplined advance that was, Isen was now sure, aimed at the gap by the road. Out beyond what he could see, there were voices giving commands, pushing, prodding, moving. One rush here and Alpha Company would be broken.

Two Rangers crawled up behind Isen, a corporal and a private from one of Alpha Company's platoons.

"They gonna rush us, sir?" the corporal asked.

"Looks like it," Isen said.

The three men lay close together, breathing heavily but otherwise quiet while a few meters away, the Germans marshaled for what Isen expected would be the crucial drive.

"They make it past us along the road," the private observed, "we're kinda fucked."

"We've got a SAW here," the corporal said to Isen, indicating the squad automatic weapon the private carried. "And a few hundred rounds. Might be able to stop them with that."

Isen looked around at the two men, his mind registering *fat chance.* "We sure will," he said.

The three men put all their grenades on the ground and set up the automatic rifle so that it would cut diagonally across the space between them and the road—any Germans trying that route would have to cross through its fire. But, in the dense undergrowth, the targets would be next to invisible. And the few hundred rounds of ammo wouldn't go far. Mark Isen watched for the enemy as from a doubtful citadel defined only by the stubborn presence of three men who hadn't yet admitted defeat.

"Here they come," the corporal said. As if on this cue, two GPU soldiers stumbled into view just a few meters away. Before Isen could swing his own weapon to bear, the corporal beside him had squeezed off four rounds, sending the two Germans stumbling back into the dark brush.

"More over here," the private barked as he hunched over his weapon and began to walk the rounds through the undergrowth, holding his fire close to the ground. "I can't see shit," he said.

But they could hear the Germans, who were yelling now as they rushed the gap between Isen and the road. The enemy smelled blood, sensed a victory close at hand.

The corporal got up on one knee and tossed a grenade, then a second into the gap. Isen picked up another grenade with the bloody stump of his bandaged left hand and held it out to the soldier, but the Ranger fell over on top of him, shot through the throat.

Isen, fumbling with his handicaps, grabbed at the man's combat dressing, trying at once to get the bandage unwrapped and pull the man's scarves off. He couldn't move fast enough, and all he could see was the blood, thick red and steaming in the cold air, running across the soldier's dirty jacket.

The bandage free at last, Isen found the wound and pressed the dressing home.

"No arteries," he said to the man, who was on his back, his eyes wide with terror. "You'll be OK," Isen shouted.

Now the other private was on his own. If Isen let go, the wounded Ranger might bleed to death.

The SAW gunner rose in a low crouch, leaning on a thin tree. "I can't see the motherfuckers," he said. Isen knew that the man couldn't last long exposed like that, but they couldn't let the GPU tide wash past them.

Then the SAW stopped firing.

"Ahh . . . ," the soldier moaned, dropping the muzzle of the weapon to work on a jammed cartridge.

That was the only lull the attackers needed. Two men came rushing out of the bushes ten meters away. One of them took but a few steps, shouldered his rifle and fired, sending the GI above Isen sprawling backward.

Isen let go of the wounded man below him and found his own weapon, rolling off to one side. The Germans hadn't seen him at first, and one of them ran up to the wounded gunner, his weapon pointed down. Isen lunged into the clear, shooting the first GPU soldier through the back of his black field jacket. Isen, on his knees now, looked about frantically for the second soldier, expecting to die at any second. He pulled himself up from the tangled mess of the forest floor, and only then did he spot the boots, jutting out from beneath some low-hanging branches where the Germans had emerged from cover.

"You OK?"

Isen wheeled, almost firing, before his brain sent the message that this was a GI speaking.

First Sergeant Perreira wasn't looking at Isen; he kept his rifle on his shoulder and trained on the GPU bodies as he closed in and kicked away the weapons.

"Where'd you come from?" Isen managed.

"You didn't think I'd stay over there with those stupid Bravo Company motherfuckers, did you?"

Kilgore had the fever again, and he fought to keep from swaying as the hot waves came and went. He leaned against the cold hull of a tank and blinked his eyes, trying to clear his head so that he could check the positions of his troop's vehicles and weapons.

The U.S. Cavalry that had rushed north to relieve the pressure on the Rangers in the little town of Karlshofen had been diverted, and all that firepower now sat on a hill just east of the town of Zeven, some sixty kilometers southeast of Karlshofen and the Rangers' fight. They were waiting to intercept a column of German armor that had started out as a Bundeswehr relief force—sent out to crush the GPU—but which had now, for some reason Kilgore didn't fully understand, become suspect. Their orders were to be prepared to stop the German advance.

As his lieutenants reported to him beside his vehicle, Kilgore plotted their positions on his map of the area. When he had heard from all the platoons, he would check the area personally, ensuring that the weapons were laid in correctly and sighted on the highway the Germans were supposedly using in their efforts to get to Karlshofen.

Kilgore saw Colonel Janisek's vehicle drive up, and the captain moved in that direction.

"How you doing over here?" Janisek asked.

Kilgore attempted to answer, but the sudden movement and the smell of diesel from Janisek's vehicle made him nauseous again. He took a step to the side, leaned over, and vomited on his boots.

"Oh, you're doing great," Janisek said.

Kilgore spit on the ground, washed his mouth with a swallow of water from his canteen, and tried to stand up straight.

"We're about set up here, Colonel," Kilgore managed. "I was just about to check the area again. Want to come along?"

"In a minute," Janisek said. Then, lowering his voice, "We got some more bad news. I just got word from this Ranger colonel—Schauffert—that the GPU may have tactical nukes."

"Shit," Kilgore said. "Where would they get 'em?"

"He didn't say," Janisek said. "But I'm guessing that only the Bundeswehr has access to that kind of stuff."

Kilgore wiped the back of his hand across his mouth. "So you think the regular army has come in on the side of the GPU," he said.

"That would explain why this colonel wants us to be ready to engage this column of Bundeswehr armor. He must think there's a good chance that they've sided with the bad guys."

"The regular army?" Kilgore wasn't quite ready to buy it. "I don't know. We hear anything from those recon guys?"

Several companies of U.S. Special Forces soldiers had dropped, in team-size units, across the band of highways in front of the advancing German armor. These teams, serving as pickets, pinpointed the Bundeswehr column and conveyed this information to the U.S. Cavalry. But there was nothing the Green Berets could say about the intentions of the approaching force.

"If the regular German armed forces have gone bad, then the Luftwaffe will try to find us," Janisek added as a soldier brought a map board from Janisek's vehicle. When the man withdrew, Janisek continued. "If that happens, we're in deep shit."

"Wouldn't they have attacked by now?" Kilgore asked. The colonel unfolded the map board and leaned it against a tree.

"The word from on high is that the German Air Force has managed to contain the few renegades from its own ranks, and up to now our guys have accepted that and submitted to Berlin's prohibition on U.S. Air Force flights."

Kilgore shook his head. Those assurances might disappear in an instant, leaving his men wide open if the Luftwaffe attacked. So Kilgore fretted about the approaching armor and the phantom aircraft and the possibility that they might witness the first ever use of nuclear weapons on the European landmass, and the worries—which Janisek told him and the other troop commanders to keep to themselves—swirled around in his already fevered brain until he was nearly overwhelmed.

"You trust this Schauffert guy, Colonel?" Kilgore asked. "I mean, we're dealing with the same people who didn't see this thing coming."

"What choice do I have?" Janisek asked.

Kilgore gave him a sideways look. "I don't buy that crap about the Bundeswehr," he said.

"You think he's making this shit up?" Janisek asked. "Why the hell would he do that?"

"I don't know, but . . . Jesus Christ, we landed smack in the middle of a civil war here, and we only find out that there's trouble *after* the shooting starts. I don't know about you, but as far as I'm concerned, that doesn't inspire much confidence in the boys upstairs."

Kilgore's head was swimming; the fever had come back with a vengeance. He tried to remember the last time he'd eaten.

"Look, Ted," Janisek said. "I don't like this either. I've been over here for a couple of tours, and I like the Germans . . . well, maybe not the civilians, but the army guys, at least. But the situation is too complicated for us to be calling the shots from down here. The President is involved in this thing, for chrissakes. Decisions are coming from way up the chain of command."

"You're telling me the President wants us to fire up this column?" Kilgore demanded.

"I'm telling you that we're taking orders from Colonel Schauffert, who's controlling this whole relief effort. And if he says shoot. . . . "

"We shoot," Kilgore said.

Janisek nodded, no happier than Kilgore at the prospect.

But Kilgore couldn't stop. "What if we're wrong?"

"Then we're wrong," Janisek said. "If these guys aren't GPU, I hope to hell they come down that road with the stars and stripes flying."

Tim Brennan was afraid of losing consciousness. He felt some tempting darkness pulling at him, promising him rest and relief from the hurt in his legs, his neck, his face.

Brennan forced his eyes open but was only able to see the mud he was lying in. Still, the effort to focus made him aware of sound. He heard footsteps nearby, and shouted commands too indistinct for him to make out. He struggled to piece together what was going on, and in this desire he managed to push himself toward the lip of the hill. After a few painful meters, he could see down onto the front slope, where the GPU had pursued the Rangers and almost won control of the hill. There were bodies visible among the trees. He looked to his right, where his own platoon had been decimated, and he suddenly remembered Lieutenant

Hawkins rushing off to regain control of that side of the company position. There was still firing there, but because it was some distance away—at least a hundred and fifty or two hundred meters beyond the original end of the Rangers line—he could only figure that Hawkins had been successful. It sounded as if the Americans had driven the Germans off the hill.

Brennan heard footsteps behind him, but before he could turn around, another soldier was at his side.

"You gonna be OK?" the Ranger asked, helping Brennan to a sitting position. Brennan recognized the man, a soldier named Globinsky, from another platoon. Globinsky was favoring a bandaged arm.

"Yeah, I'll make it. Where's the company?"

"Over there," the Ranger said, pointing out to the east with his good arm. Brennan's assessment had been right.

"They pushed the GPU off this hill?"

"Sure did. I'm gonna try to catch up, soon as I get my wind."

Brennan stared past his feet, which were stretched out in front of him and pointed downhill. "I need your help, man," he said.

"Well, I can't carry you, but I reckon I can drag you," Globinsky said.

"No, I want to go down there," Brennan said, pointing to the bottom of the hill.

Globinsky nodded, understanding without asking. "Could be a little tricky," he said. "I don't know how many of those GPU fuckers might be roaming around down there."

When Brennan didn't respond, Globinsky pressed his lips together, nodded his head. "OK."

He dragged himself and Brennan upright.

"Who is it we're looking for?" Globinsky wanted to know.

"Guy named Bishop," Brennan said.

"Tango one five, this is Charlie three six, over."

Kilgore snapped out of his daze and picked up the handset to answer his platoon leader. The woods around him and the east-west road before him were quiet.

"Tango one five," he said.

"This is three six. We got a chopper approaching. Sounds pretty low, over."

Kilgore tugged his crew helmet away from his ears. Off to the east, he heard the sharp beating of a rotor.

"See anything on the ground, three six? Over."

"Not yet . . . wait."

There was a break in the signal, then three six came up again.

"Roger, the chopper is past me and I have the target in sight. Lead element is three wheeled scout vehicles and two Leopards, over."

That was it, then. The German armored column had appeared right where the Special Forces teams had said they would appear, right on time and with air cover.

Kilgore acknowledged the report and relayed it to Janisek, his commander, as he watched the sky. They were in thick woods here, well camouflaged. But without their own air cover to chase it away, the German scout helicopter could get close, call in fire, maybe even guide in some tank-killing choppers.

Janisek came up on the net. "Mike four zero says to engage the column, over," he said.

"Shit," Kilgore said. He had been hoping for a reprieve, some way to determine if the German column was hostile. He had lost confidence in the higher command's picture of what was going on.

"They haven't done anything, over," Kilgore said, abandoning procedure.

There was a pause at the other end, presumably Janisek was talking to mike four zero, the Ranger Commander who was, to the cavalrymen, just a voice on the radio. In a moment, Janisek came back on to relay the order again. "Four zero says to open fire."

Kilgore pushed the top of his helmet back on his head. He was sweating heavily, though he could no longer tell if it was the fever or the anticipation of what was to come. He had set his troop in well; they would have enfilading fire on a good portion of the German column, and would succeed in giving them a bloody nose, and forcing them to deploy into a combat formation. The fight here would mean the Germans wouldn't get to the Rangers before the airborne operation commenced.

Kilgore listened distractedly to the reports coming in from his platoons. The Germans were moving into the kill zones, and soon his troop's weapons would all be bearing on the unsuspecting armor.

"This is X ray one five," Janisek called again. "Did you read my message? Fire when ready, over."

Kilgore looked up at the helicopter, which was appearing and disappearing among the trees. No sign that it had spotted the Americans yet.

"Tango one five, this is charlie three six, over."

One of his platoons.

Kilgore answered. "This is one five, over."

"Do we engage? The lead elements will be out of the kill zone soon, over."

Before Kilgore could respond, another platoon broke in. "I think the chopper has us, over."

Kilgore looked up, saw the dark bulb of the scout helicopter's nose dip down at them, the way a dog might turn its head to the side at a curious—but not frightening—noise. Down on the road, he could hear the treads of the lead German tanks.

"Tango one five, why haven't you engaged, over?"

Kilgore heard the frustration in Janisek's voice, knew the old man would be ready to commit murder if he didn't hear some shooting soon. Below him, the armor was moving through the kill zone.

But what if we're wrong?

A strange voice came over Kilgore's headset.

"Tango one five, this is mike four zero. Do you have visual on the German armor? Over."

It was Schauffert.

"Roger, four zero," Kilgore answered.

"Then open fire, one five. Acknowledge. Over."

On his troop internal net, his platoon leaders were also worried; the Germans were past the point when the cav should have begun shooting. Kilgore turned the volume knob down.

"Lester," he called down to his gunner. "Hand me that bag."

Kilgore kept an American flag on board, stuffed in an old canvas map case. He had, on occasion, flown it from the radio antennae—a bit of cavalry panache. He took the flag and two handheld flares from the bag.

I may just be out of my fucking mind, he thought as he crawled out of his hatch.

"If I get killed, call the platoons and tell them to open fire," he told his crew. As he stuck his head out into the air, he could hear Schauffert's voice, tiny on the headset, shouting at him to shoot.

Kilgore jumped from the back deck of the track and ran toward a small clearing they'd driven through, some sixty meters or so behind his vehicle. He could hear the slapping of the helicopter blades somewhere over his shoulder. He began to think about the consequences of what he was about to do. If he was wrong, he'd be killed. If he was wrong and survived, Schauffert might shoot him.

I sure as shit hope I'm right.

When he reached the clearing, he uncapped one of the flares and slapped it on the bottom of the tube, sending a bright red streak up into the patch of sky overhead. He waited, listening for some change in the timbre of the chopper sounds.

What if the pilots are looking the other way?

There were a lot of things he hadn't considered, and he began to worry. He calculated his chances of getting back to his vehicle in time to salvage the ambush. He figured them at about zero.

He sent the second flare skyward. Waited.

Then the helicopter sounds grew louder, and he wondered if the scout had anything on board to shoot him with.

The aircraft appeared over the open space. Kilgore held the flag over his head. He couldn't see the chopper because of the flag. He lowered it after a few seconds, gritting his teeth as he looked up.

The man in the copilot's seat had opened the door and was waving at him. The chopper came lower. Now the man was nodding head. Smiling.

The Bravo Company attack that Perreira set in motion was uncoordinated, with no indirect fire support, and without the normal control measures that define the job to be done.

It was also unexpected.

The GPU soldiers down along the east side of the road, where what was left of B Company made their push, weren't ready for another American effort. The best GPU troops had been in the front of the column, and their commander's decision to put them there was vindicated when those lead companies counterattacked the Rangers who ambushed the column. The less effective companies had been in the rear in the order of movement, and these formations absorbed the surprise attack. Worn out by their long march and caught in attacks from several directions, these less-disciplined soldiers had nevertheless beat back the first American attack, which had faltered because of the accident of terrain—the road split the American effort.

But the same road that had caused the American attack to falter now plagued the GPU, and the latest Ranger effort caught the GPU straddling the road. Bravo Company Rangers rushed forward into the flanks of small groups of German soldiers bunched together in shallow depressions beside the road, waiting to cross to the west side. These GPU soldiers, who were expecting to be the attackers, panicked when they became the targets.

Mark Isen saw signs of this panic from his position behind Alpha Company.

"They're running," he said to Perreira, who had stayed beside him.

Perreira crawled forward. He and Isen were now only about a meter off the west side of the road. Across from them and down about sixty meters, they could see the spotty movement of Rangers pressing the attack, moving forward in short rushes. Some distance beyond the Rangers, the road curved to the right, and Isen and Perreira could see GPU soldiers running away. There was nothing controlling their movement—their backs were to the Rangers.

"Now's the time to make a push here," Isen said. "Help me get the word around to Alpha Company, let them know what's happening on the other side."

"Got it, sir," Perreira said. He was functioning again with the same sort of confidence that had served him so well as First Sergeant; he was holding nothing back.

"Once the Germans on this side see that their buddies are making a break for it and leaving them . . . that could be the end."

The two men dragged themselves back away from the open area, then began to move southwest, paralleling the road and looking for the Alpha Company elements who were attacking.

Isen found Sergeant First Class Thompson, who'd been shot in the hand.

"They've broken on the other side of the road," Isen said.

"That explains why they're melting away here, then," Thompson said. He was holding his hand up in the air to help stop the bleeding, and he looked to Isen, as if he was waiting for the teacher to call on him.

"We can really roll 'em up now," Thompson said.

"You've got to be careful," Isen cautioned. "Go too fast and you'll lose control of your men. And watch out for a trap."

"I don't think they've got anything left, sir," Thompson said. "But I hear what you're saying." He paused, and it occurred to Isen that Thompson had deliberately avoided looking at Perreira.

"There's one more thing, Major," Thompson said.

"What's that?"

"I took some shrapnel in the leg, too." He turned on his side so that Isen could see the bloody holes on the back of his right thigh.

Hand grenade, Isen thought.

"Can't move much, not fast anyway," Thompson said. He still hadn't looked at Perreira.

Isen turned to the first sergeant, who had done everything possible, and more, to make the attack work.

"I'm going to have Bravo Company consolidate," Isen said to Perreira, flipping out his map and pointing to a prominent bend in the road, "right here. Mind what I said about not losing control of your platoons. When we get a feel for what's left in front of us, we can move the two companies forward at the same time, one on each side of the road."

If it struck Perreira that this was the plan he wanted in the first place, the one that had gotten him into the argument with Isen, he didn't let on.

"Yes, sir," the first sergeant said. Then, to Thompson's radio operator, "Stick with me."

Brennan and Globinsky reached the bottom of the hill just as the first panicked GPU soldiers began to run past them, away from the renewed attacks and through the kill zone of the original Charlie Company ambush site. The two Rangers dropped into a shallow depression just off the road.

"Look," Brennan said, peering through the thin underbrush to the road. There was little cover, and if the Germans hadn't been so intent on escape, the Rangers would have been discovered.

"Look," Brennan said again.

Globinsky had his head down, so Brennan tapped him on the back of his helmet.

"They dropped their weapons."

"I'll be damned," Globinsky said.

The sounds of the Alpha and Bravo Companies' assaults were close.

"Sounds like Alpha and Bravo pushed them back," Brennan said. He looked back over his shoulder, up the hill for some sign of his own company. "Charlie Company must be up on that ridge, still."

"Maybe they're in on this attack, too," Globinsky offered.

"We could take these guys prisoner," Brennan said.

Globinsky turned his head slowly, as if he was suddenly surprised to see Brennan next to him.

"Have you lost your fucking mind?" Globinsky asked, incredulous. "Do you see how many of them there are? Do you see that there's only two of us?"

"There's only two of us right here," Brennan said. "But there's bound to be more coming down this way. These guys are running from *somebody.*"

Two more stragglers came down the road, one of them stopping to help a wounded GPU soldier who called from the opposite side of the road. The other unwounded man didn't even hesitate, but kept right on running.

"They might regroup down the road," Brennan said. But Globinsky was watching the top of the hill behind them.

"You thinking of crawling back up there?" Brennan asked.

"To tell you the truth, I was. But now I think I see some of our guys up there."

Brennan looked up to where Globinsky pointed. Some men were moving along the crest of the hill above and behind them.

"They must be getting ready to come down this way," Brennan said. "See, we aren't alone."

While Globinsky was still watching for movement at the top of the hill, Brennan rolled over into the prone firing position, with the muzzle of his rifle just above the surface of the road. The German who'd been enough of a comrade to stop to help the wounded man was almost directly across the road from him, less than fifteen meters away.

"HALT!" Brennan called

The first prisoners to come back were disorganized, ones and twos, trying to run with their hands over their heads as Rangers shouted and prodded them along. Then there was a group of ten, moving in a file, under guard.

"You're not going to believe where these guys came from, sir," one of the guards said as Isen approached.

"Where?"

"Two guys from Charlie Company, who were so messed up they could barely stand, had all these guys lying down on the road up there a little ways. Said once they got the first two on the ground, spread-eagled, the rest of them who came running along just joined in, practically fell down almost without being asked."

"Where are they . . . the Charlie Company guys?" Isen asked.

The soldier dropped his voice. "Down there by the side of the road, wrapping bodies. A bunch of other guys from Charlie Company are down there, too, doing the same thing."

Isen saw that the Germans did not look as bad off as the Rangers guarding them. The GPU soldiers were ragged and unmilitary, certainly, but they were also clean, fed, and relatively rested. The Rangers were tense, having found a target for their anger at all that had happened over the past days. The young Germans, though certainly afraid, mostly looked relieved to be out of the fight.

29

THE AIR FORCE CAME IN FIRST, FAST MOVERS CUTTING ACROSS the falling darkness with nothing to shoot at, but making a terrible racket for all that. The army aviators came next, big Apache gunships just visible against the night sky, tracing a frenzied geometry as they searched the ground for targets. But the area around the battered little town of Karlshofen already belonged to Mark Isen's men: the weary, the wounded, the dead.

The drop planes came in low, just as the planes carrying Isen's battalion had over the same field. By the time the aircraft were making their second pass, the men just landing had determined that the message they'd received was true: the fighting around Karlshofen was over. While the lead companies sent out platoons to secure the area against any GPU units that might be intact and waiting to give the Rangers more trouble, the medics of the first and second battalions went to work on the wounded.

Isen's exhausted Rangers handed over their prisoners and moved to assembly areas in the town for a roll call while patrols from the follow-on battalions began to comb the area for wounded. With the cordon of fresh troops around him and the Air Force finally in the sky above, Isen let his men build fires to warm themselves and the rations that the newly arrived soldiers gave freely to their comrades.

*   *   *

When Tim Brennan wandered into the aid station, the first medic he encountered took one look at his face and sat him down under an electric lantern.

"You got a little beat up there, pal," the soldier said as he cut away the compress Brennan had tied above his eye. "What'd you walk into?:"

"A big boot, I think," Brennan said. "Look, I really came here to look for my partner."

"Hang on a sec," the soldier said as he held a penlight close to Brennan's wounds. "OK. You'll be good as new once we clean that up. You hit anywhere else?"

"Some shrapnel in my legs, I think. Can you look for him?"

"Who?"

"My partner," Brennan said, sitting back against the wall behind him. He was suddenly without strength, tired as the dead. "His name's Charis."

The medic disappeared for a few minutes; when he came back, Brennan was alseep. He woke to the stinging of something dabbing at his face.

"This is just some antiseptic," the medic said. "We gotta start cleaning all these cuts."

Brennan opened his eyes wide to make sure it was the same medic he'd asked to look for Charis. It was, and the soldier worked silently.

Mark Isen was sitting with Major Rhone on the curb beneath the town's war memorial when Colonel Schauffert found him. Rhone stood as the American colonel approached.

"Mark," Schauffert said, "I heard you got your goddamned finger shot off." He was in the paratrooper mode, Isen noticed, his radio operators and staff officers hovering close as pigeons, his voice booming in the still dark street.

"Yessir," Isen said. He was inside a circle of light from a gas lantern, leaning against a rucksack he'd found. He had no idea where his own equipment was.

"You're divorced, ain't you?" Schauffert said, holding up the ring finger on his own left hand—most of which Isen was missing.

Isen let the joke fall flat.

"One of your lieutenants did a hell of a job up there holding Charlie Company together. Fellow by the name of Hawkins," Schauffert said.

"I hadn't heard," Isen said.

"Word among the troops is that he led a charge—a friggin' bayonet charge—that pushed the bad guys off the top of Charlie Company's hill," Schauffert said. "I'm putting him in for the Silver Star."

"I haven't seen him, sir," Isen said.

"Oh." A dark look passed over Schauffert. "He didn't make it," he said. "The award will be posthumous."

Isen wondered how long that list would be.

"We really kicked some Kraut ass here, Mark," Schauffert said. He seemed to notice Rhone for the first time. "No offense."

Rhone nodded.

One of the radio operators came up, tapped Schauffert on the shoulder, gave him a handset. When the old man was on the radio, Rhone dropped again next to Isen. The two men sat quietly for two or three minutes.

"There was a report circulating in intelligence," Rhone said, "about infighting in the GPU."

"Oh?" Isen said. He wasn't sure if he had the energy to be curious.

"I didn't put much stock in it myself," Rhone said. "The intelligence has been, well, unreliable."

Isen snorted in agreement.

"Anyway, there was a faction in the GPU that argued strongly against any violence." He turned to look at Isen. "On the premise that the United States would use any opportunity to move a large force back into Europe. Supposedly there was—is—a faction in the U.S. military that thinks it's time for a new American imperialism, an imperialism of the one remaining superpower."

Isen was pretty certain that Rhone understood Schauffert's position: that this was an opportunity to get back into Europe.

"Pretty farfetched," Isen said.

Rhone shrugged. "As I said, it was just a theory."

Schauffert was back, still beaming. "The Marines at Bremerhaven found both of those missing nukes—one was on a truck trying to get out of town. Some people are saying the GPU didn't have the know-how to make them work, anyway. Still, we shut 'em down. Yessir, we really kicked ass here. The Chief is pleased, very pleased."

The "we" grated. Isen thought about the bodies wrapped up, very much individually, in the street behind him.

"Some of us got our asses—our individual asses—kicked," Isen said.

Schauffert looked down, as if noticing for the first time that Isen wasn't standing.

"Yeah, well, some people will say we responded too slowly over here. Others will say we were too fast, too quick to use force."

Before he could check himself, Isen gave voice to what he happened to be thinking. "I guess if we had troops over here all the time, we could really lay down the law. Then they wouldn't be able to say anything, right, Colonel?"

Schauffert stared at some point behind Isen's head.

"You can never control what people are going to say, Major," Schauffert said. "For instance, there are a couple of soldiers around, I hear, who are saying that you ran away from the fight."

He let that hang for a moment.

"And while I'm sure it isn't true, it is being *said*, you understand. Idle gossip like that can ruin a man." Schauffert turned on his heel and walked down through the half-lit street.

"Real prick, isn't he?" Rhone said.

"He's a piece of work," Isen answered. He was about to say something to Rhone, explain that he was moving from the Charlie Company position to the attack position when those soldiers saw him running. Then he recalled half a line from somewhere, something about protesting too much.

"He's enough to make you believe in conspiracy theories," Rhone said. Then, when Isen didn't meet his eyes, "If you're inclined to that sort of thing."

Isen was immensely tired, more tired than he had ever been. "Right now I'm just inclined to get these men back home."

Out beyond him in the dark, soldiers moved toward the airfield, carrying the bodies of the killed under flimsy poncho shrouds that swayed with the uneven gait. All around him the flashlights of the medics twinkled like grave stars.